*fleur-de-lis*

# OTHER BOOKS AND AUDIOBOOKS
## BY SARAH M. EDEN

## CHRONOLOGICAL ORDER OF ALL RELATED
## SARAH M. EDEN GEORGIAN- & REGENCY-ERA BOOKS

# Fleur-de-lis

*A rejection he'll never forget*
*An adoration she doesn't remember*
*A second chance at a first chance for love*

# SARAH M. EDEN

Covenant Communications, Inc.

Cover image: Lee Avison © Arcangel

Cover design by Hannah Bischoff, copyright © 2023 by Covenant Communications, Inc.

Published by Covenant Communications, Inc.
American Fork, Utah

Library of Congress Cataloging-in-Publication Data

Name: Sarah M. Eden
Title: Fleur-de-Lis / Sarah M. Eden
Description: American Fork, UT : Covenant Communications, Inc. [2023]
Identifiers: Library of Congress Control Number 2022944933 | ISBN: 978-1-52442-316-2
LC record available at https://lccn.loc.gov/2022944933

Printed in the United States of America
First Printing: June 2023


32 31 30 29 28 27 26 25 24 23     10 9 8 7 6 5 4 3 2 1

# Praise for The Gents

"What a treat! Old friends and new ones abound in this delightful series."

—Esther Hatch, award-winning author of The Proper Scandal series

"Great start to a new series! I'm already looking forward to reading about the other Gents."

—Tiffany Odekirk, author of *Summerhaven*

"The Gents have already stolen my heart! In this first book of Eden's new series, readers will laugh and root for this unique cohort of men and the women in their lives. Block your schedule—this series will keep you reading 'just one more chapter.'"

—Rachel Fordham, author of *Where the Road Bends*

"The plot of this book is one that may have been seen before, but the way Sarah M. Eden writes the characters brings it to an entirely new level."

—*InD'Tale* Magazine

"Beautifully written and highly entertaining, this book is one for the keeper shelf. I'm anxiously awaiting more stories about the Gents. It's such fun to see the characters reappear in each book and find out what they've been up to. I would recommend this to those who enjoy clean and wholesome historical fiction."

—Winnie Thomas, Inkwell Inspirations

"A fun group of Gents!"

—Chalon Linton, author of *Chiara's Choice*

"Sarah's books always exceed my expectations, but this one was a whole new level!"

—Karen Thornell, author of *Edward and Amelia*

"I have plenty of practice happily rereading Eden's past books, so there's no doubt in my mind this one is destined for my reread pile too. Highly recommended!"

—Melissa Tagg, *USA Today* bestseller, Christy and Carol award-winning author

"Heartfelt, amusing, and, oh, so romantic, this exciting series is one you don't want to miss."

—Regina Jennings, National Readers Choice award winner, author of The Joplin Chronicles series

"This is Eden at her best—witty one moment and heartbreaking the next."

—M.A. Nichols, author of the Generations of Love series

"Luminous historical details as well as a romance that sighs between two deliciously complex characters, *Forget Me Not* is more proof that Sarah Eden excels at any period, including the sumptuous Georgian period."

—Rachel McMillian, author of *The Mozart Code*

"So much to love about this book. The cover. The time period. The Gents themselves (and, yes, I am looking forward to reading each of their stories). This book is like a Sunday afternoon drive. It may take a while to get to the destination, but it's all about the journey anyway."

—Sarah Monzon, author of *Kiss Me on Christmas*

"I am a big Sarah Eden fan, and I am thrilled that she is doing a story on the Jonquil parents. And *Forget Me Not* knocked it out of the park!"

—Julie Coulter Bellon, author of *The Viscount's Vow*

"I have enjoyed this unique series about a group of young men bound together in life's experiences, determined to see each other through the ups and downs of life's drama. Have you ever noticed how best friends can be so very different, yet they mesh well—perfectly, it seems—when times get tough. Thank you, Sarah Eden, for a remarkable read that focuses on inner values. I look forward to the next Gent's story."

—Marguerite Gray, author of the Revolutionary Faith and Gardens in Time series

"Fans of Eden's Jonquil and Lancaster series are in for an absolute treat with Eden's The Gents series. Transporting us back to the Georgian era, this new group of friends will quickly feel like family; after just one book, I am already in love with the lot of them and utterly thrilled for each of their stories!

"Eden has a way of creating deep and meaningful characters and storylines that simultaneously make you laugh and touch your heart, leaving you ridiculously satisfied. The Gents shine, and this series should not be missed."

—Probably Bookin It

"*Forget Me Not* is a beautifully romantic tale that showcases Sarah Eden's masterful storytelling abilities."

—Marilee Loves to Read

"I love a good series. And I'm really loving this one by Sarah M Eden."

—My Book a Day

# Chapter One

*Cambridge University, 1774*

THE BRITISH WERE A DECIDEDLY odd people. Henri Fortier had lived among them for months now, but he understood them less every day. The only aspect of his interactions with them that made any sense was that in which his fellow Cambridge students mocked, ridiculed, and otherwise browbeat him. He had spent his life in a family in which they had learned cruelty early on. His father had made absolutely certain of that.

Henri walked with his copy of *Poems* by the Earl of Carlisle out toward a field not far from Cambridge. The volume had been published the year before and had subsequently become his very first purchase of an English-language collection of poems. He was seldom without a volume or two, which he borrowed from the Cambridge Library. His income would not allow for the *purchase* of terribly many, but the university's collection was extensive. He meant to study English poetry during his years at university, though his father had insisted his chosen field of study was worthless and emasculating. He had called Henri all sorts of a fool. Father called him a great many things; none in memory had been complimentary.

"The Fortiers are French. We belong in and to France." Those had been nearly the entirety of Father's words of farewell when Henri had departed for Cambridge. He'd added only one comment more. "You are still a sniveling infant."

*A sniveling infant.* Father had no qualms about delineating the many ways in which Henri was unworthy, disappointing, and incompetent.

Henri had remained at Cambridge through the Christmas holidays. He'd not felt confident in his ability to disobey again when his father would inevitably demand that Henri not leave France. The fortitude he had summoned to leave initially had drained him, but it had also gained him freedom from his father's cruel grasp. He didn't mean to give that up.

A stone bench sat near a footpath at the edge of the field where students often gathered to enjoy a bit of sport: cricket and football, skittles and foot races. Henri never participated. He was never asked to and didn't know the rules of most of the games anyway. But he found he liked the spot for reading and listening to the conversations of people who passed. He thought himself rather proficient in the English language but knew his pronunciation was atrocious; Father had forbidden the speaking of English at home, so Henri had had few opportunities for practicing. An entire term of eavesdropping on English speakers had helped. A little.

Poetry though. Poetry had taught him to understand the language's nuance. Poetry had made English feel familiar and comforting.

He sat on his favorite bench and opened the book of Lord Carlisle's poetry. English was his language of rebellion—a language his father didn't share, with words his father couldn't steal from him.

Henri had marked the book with notes in the margins, helping him dissect the language he was determined to master.

What avails the Poet's art?
What avails his magic hand?
Can he arrest Death's pointed dart,
Or charm to sleep his murderous band?

The stanza began with cheerful imagery but ended with death and murder. He needed to study more closely if he had any hope of making sense of the contradiction.

"Well, look there. Harry Castle himself."

Henri didn't have to look up to know who was speaking. Timothy Baker was a nuisance of the highest order, and he thought himself terribly clever. During Henri's first weeks at Cambridge, Baker had taken to calling him Henry, an anglicized version of his name. Henry had transformed into Harry. And since *fortier* was derived from the French word for "fortress," he had then become Harry Fortress. That had eventually become Harry Castle.

Clearly, Henri was not the only one without a truly intellectual mastery of the English language.

"*Timothée Boulanger*," Henri responded, gallicizing his heckler's name. "*C'est dommage que vous ne puissiez pas rester bavarder.*"

Most every student at Cambridge had some understanding of French. Henri's ability to speak it quickly and heavily accented had proven a challenge to Baker and his ilk.

Henri allowed the briefest of glances, counting three of his tormentors hovering nearby. He had acquired dozens during his brief time in England, all on account of being very French and not having claim on so much as a single friend. Those who were different and those who were lonely often found themselves targets of the unkind and unfeeling. All three gentlemen who stood near carried the various accoutrements necessary for playing cricket. With a bit of luck, they would be on their way, their thoughts shifting to sport.

"Harry Castle could be speaking English, for all we know," Baker said to the others. "Poor simpleton can't make himself understood in any language."

There was little point in defending himself. Not only did he know his English was not always easy to decipher, but he also knew arguing with those who disliked him didn't do any good. It had never swayed his father.

"Pull your nose out of your books for a bit, Harry Castle," Baker said, a sneer evident in his words. "There's to be an informal match on the pitch. You might learn a thing or two about how to stop being such a milksop."

*Milksop.* Henri didn't know that word. He suspected it wasn't a compliment.

The others laughed and congratulated Baker on his wit, which Henri thought overly generous of them.

With his head cast downward toward his book, he watched them out of the corner of his eyes and said a touch dryly, "Milksop? That is what you add to tea after it has been in the Boston harbor?"

Baker and his disciples looked back, grimacing as they pieced together what he'd said.

With a snort, Baker said, "Hardly surprising you would take the part of those uncouth colonists. Disgusting foreigner."

One of Baker's friends threw a cricket ball directly at Henri's head. Though he might very well have been a "milksop," Henri wasn't entirely useless. He caught the ball easily and, in one singular flow of movement, threw it high over his tormentors' heads and far out into the field. Then, without comment or reaction, he turned the page of his book and set his focus there.

Or wrapt in solemn thought, and pleasing woe,
O'er each low tomb he breath'd his pious strain,
A lesson to the village swain,
And taught the tear of rustic grief to flow!

*Village swain.* He didn't think *swain* was the same as *swine.* There was something satisfying in the idea of teaching a lesson to the village pigs. The *Cambridge* pigs had shown themselves in sore need of an education in decorum.

Someone sat on the bench beside him. *Ça m'énerve!* Could not those who disliked him leave him be?

"Baker is a particularly horrid variety of vermin."

Henri looked up in shock, not because of what was said but because it was said *in French.* Few people even attempted to speak to him in his native tongue, unless it was to mock him. Stanley Cummings—he was the one who'd sat beside him—had just spoken without a hint of disdain and with a rather atrocious accent. Somehow, the inexpertness of his effort made it feel more sincere.

A quick look told Henri the man they were discussing had continued his walk toward the field where that day's cricket was to be undertaken.

"He must be an unhappy person to bathe himself so thoroughly in his bitterness," Henri said. "I feel pity for him more than anger."

Stanley's friends had gathered around as well. Lord Jonquil, Lord Aldric Benick, and Digby Layton were, along with Stanley, known to all as "the Gents." No group of friends were as close as they. And unlike Baker and his band, they were not scoundrels, neither had Henri seen any evidence that they were cruel. Admission into their very exclusive brotherhood was widely and deeply coveted.

"Would you consider abandoning your book and, instead, join us in a *somewhat* friendly cricket match?" Stanley asked.

"Join you? This means you wish me to . . . participate . . . *with* you?"

"We are hopeful you will participate in the match as part of our team," Lord Aldric explained in utterly perfect French.

"I have watched cricket these months," Henri said. "I do not understand it. The rules elude me."

Stanley shook his head. "Rules can be taught. But throwing as expertly as you just did . . . that is a gift from heaven itself."

He'd not realized there'd been witnesses to his bit of petulance. To his relief, Stanley and his friends didn't seem to disapprove. "Even being able to throw a cricket ball, my inexperience might still prove a detriment. You may not win the match if you have me on your team."

"Winning is not always the goal," Lord Jonquil said. "This match is against Baker and his collection of rats. The very best part will be the commentary."

*Commentary?* "You will be saying things they do not wish to hear?"

Mischief touched all their faces. These were gentlemen with a plan.

Rising very solemnly, Henri said, "They do not care for discussions of tea. I will make certain to mention that often."

Stanley grinned. "I suspect this will prove the beginning of an exceptional friendship, Henri Fortier."

Friendship. Henri hadn't a single friend in all of England. But looking around at the Gents as he walked with them toward the cricket pitch, "friendship" suddenly began to feel within his grasp.

*Derbyshire, 1787 (thirteen years later)*

Once every year, the Gents gathered for a house party, two to three weeks of time spent together, enjoying old memories and creating new ones. This group of friends—as loyal and close-knit as ever they were—numbered seven. They always included Stanley in their count, though they'd lost him to war. Kester Barrington had been one of their number when Henri had been brought in, though he'd still been at Eton. And Niles Greenberry had found himself part of their brotherhood not long after Henri. Seven of the very best gentlemen Henri could ever imagine knowing and they thoroughly enjoyed themselves whenever and wherever they were together.

For this year's gathering, Aldric had secured the use of one of his father's holdings, Norwood Manor in Derbyshire. Neither he nor Henri had ever been the host of a Gents house party, as they were both without a home of their own. The plan was to share the duty this time.

"I am still in shock that your father agreed to this," Henri said, closing his book of poetry as their traveling carriage approached Norwood. He'd been slowly adding to his collection of books since his Cambridge years, but his meager funds were well spent on his subscriptions to lending libraries now that he hadn't the university collection to borrow from.

"For my part," Aldric answered, "I am holding my breath for the inevitable discovery of what unforeseen 'cost' the duke means to attach to this bit of benevolence." In recent months, Aldric had referred to his father as "Father" less and less often.

"Perhaps he will require you to empty all the chamber pots." With a smile Henri knew was more teasing than Aldric was likely currently in the mood for but that he still needed, he added, "Or trim the back lawn with a dull scythe."

"He would likely make me do it with my teeth." It was an exaggeration but likely didn't feel like much of one.

The Duke of Hartley's cruelty to Aldric generally came in the form of slights and dismissals. Henri's father's cruelty had been cutting words and demeaning evaluations. Both approaches were miserable.

"What did His Grace require of you after allowing us the use of his boat for our journey to Portugal?"

"My mother left me a ring, nothing overly valuable but meaningful to me. The duke wished it to be given to Roderick."

"A five-year-old boy?"

"A future duke, I was reminded," Aldric muttered. "At least it wasn't given to Mowbary."

Lord Mowbary was Aldric's older brother and one of the more unpleasant people Henri knew. Roderick was Mowbary's son and was rather angelic, really. That wasn't likely to last long under the influence of his parents and grandfather.

Henri and Aldric alighted when the carriage stopped in front of the grand house, one smaller than the principal estates belonging to their respective families but certainly large enough for the house party they were planning. Aldric had confided in Henri that he hoped to one day convince his father to allow him to assume the reins of this minor estate in the Duke of Hartley's holdings. Unfortunately, the duke was likely to refuse simply as a means of keeping his younger son crushed under the ducal thumb.

"A shame your father never had a chance to meet mine," Henri said. "They could have consulted on methods of torturing their children and become even more adept at it."

"A shame?" Aldric shook his head. "Their failure to meet, Henri, was an answer to my fervent prayers. The very last thing either of us needed was a father who was *better* at being a source of misery."

Henri slapped a hand on Aldric's shoulder. "If it is of any consolation to you, my father is still managing to cause misery even from beyond the grave."

Aldric gave him a look of drawn-brow confusion. "Why would that be a consolation?"

"Misery enjoying company?" Henri suggested with a shrug. "Perhaps the utter delight of knowing we are unlikely to be permitted to forget after death those whom we do not enjoy during life."

A silent laugh broke the sternness of Aldric's expression. "The other Gents would be shocked to know how often the one we call Archbishop makes irreverent comments about the afterlife."

"Stanley wouldn't have been."

Aldric turned his gaze to the house once more and, with a sigh, said, "Few things escaped Stanley's notice."

"Shall we go discover what penance you are to pay for this admittedly minor bit of benevolence on your father's part?"

The Norwood butler was standing in the doorway, having sent a footman to assist with the luggage being removed from the traveling carriage. The man had the expected demeanor of austerity for the highest-ranking servant in a fine house. Henri hoped the butler was equal to the disruption that would soon descend. The Gents were not known for their serenity.

"Lowe," Aldric acknowledged the butler as they reached the door.

"Welcome back to Norwood Manor, Lord Aldric." He bowed, as was expected.

"This is Mr. Fortier, the first of the guests to arrive for the house party."

The butler offered another bow.

"Have you been provided with sufficient information to make preparations?" Aldric asked Lowe.

"I believe so, my lord."

They stepped into the small but relatively grand entryway. Henri was on the hunt for just such a place to live, one he could afford despite his diminishing income. If he could find one near Norwood, and if Aldric could lay claim to this estate, they'd be near enough to visit each other often.

Stapleton Grange, a property nearby, had recently become available on terms Henri could afford despite his brother's having reduced his income once again. He hoped fate meant to offer him a spot of uncharacteristic good fortune.

"I would like to speak with Mrs. Lowe," Aldric said as he was divested of his outer coat. "My mind would be more at ease if I knew she was in possession of all the information she needs to accommodate the guests due to arrive."

"That has all been seen to, my lord," Mr. Lowe said.

A maid took Henri's coat, hat, and gloves in the same moment another left with Aldric's.

"I am certain the duke did his best to relay an accurate report," Aldric said, "but I do not wish for your good wife to be surprised or caught unprepared."

The butler shook his head. "Our directions did not come from His Grace."

Aldric's expression turned as confused as Henri's must have been. In near perfect unison, they both asked, "Then from whom?"

"Lord Mowbary." Lowe clearly thought they ought to have known that. But why, in heaven's name, had Aldric's brother been involved at all?

"Why would he involve himself?" Aldric posed the question, but to whom was unclear. It might very well have been rhetorical.

It was answered just the same. By the very person being spoken *of.* "Because I am to be the host of this gathering."

Standing in the doorway of an adjacent room was Lord Mowbary himself, heir to the Duke of Hartley, older brother of Lord Aldric, and an expert at being an unmitigated irritant. That was something else Aldric and Henri had in common: they both possessed brothers who took delight in making their younger brothers suffer.

"What has this house party to do with you, Mowbary?" Aldric asked.

"Father felt it best that *I* act as host. Failure here would reflect poorly on him."

"Of course," Aldric muttered under his breath.

"Makes a fellow wish he were trimming the back lawn with his teeth," Henri said.

A flit of a smile touched Aldric's face, and Henri felt better seeing it. Spending time with his father never failed to dampen Aldric's spirits, but time spent with his brother made him a bit stormy.

"I cannot imagine this house party will hold any appeal for you," Henri said to Mowbary, giving Aldric a chance to regain his equilibrium.

"You underestimate the significance of your family, Henri. Connections in France would do my wife a great deal of good. After all, someday, she will be the mistress of the family estate in Normandy."

"My sister will be pleased to make Lady Mowbary's acquaintance, I am sure." Poor Céleste. Henri would have to warn her upon arrival. He'd been so looking forward to seeing her again, and now a bit of a dark cloud hung over the reunion.

With a look of smug satisfaction, Mowbary said, "I took the liberty of inviting the entirety of the Fortier family."

"All of my family?" Henri didn't bother hiding his shock or dismay. His sister-in-law was endurable in small doses. His little niece was an angel, or had been as an infant, when he had last seen her. His brother was best avoided, something he'd thought he'd managed in making arrangements for his sister to journey to England *without* their sibling. "I was not told of this change of plans."

Mowbary lifted an eyebrow, an expression clearly meant to give the impression of great importance and authority but which somehow only looked laughably pretentious. "*You* did not invite them, and this is not *your* home. Father reminded me that guests of standing are important for a future duke. That only a portion of your family was making the journey was a waste."

His sister was *not* a waste in any sense. *J'en ai marre*, there were times when Henri wished he had a cricket ball handy. A cricket bat would do in a pinch. Arrogance like Mowbary's faded quickly when one was nursing a bloody nose.

If the Gents would have been shocked to hear Henri make light of the after-life, they'd have likely toppled over in a stupor to know how often his thoughts were less than charitable. They had nicknamed him Archbishop. In his mind, the moniker often felt more ironic than fitting. Father would have insisted on Sniveling Infant or Worthless Child or Pitiful Imbecile.

"Dare I ask what other changes have been made to the arrangements I initially made?" Aldric asked, sounding more weary with every word.

"There is but one more."

"Heaven help us," Henri muttered.

"Father issued an invitation of his own to a family in Paris who is of tremendously important standing and with whom he feels it best Theodora and I forge a bond. They will be arriving with the Fortiers, having readily accepted the invitation."

Aldric looked to Henri, but he hadn't the first idea to whom the invitation had been extended. Paris boasted a great many families who matched that description.

"Whatever you do, Aldric," Mowbary said, "do not ruin this opportunity for us. These connections will benefit the family. They will benefit my Roderick when he is older. The last thing any of us needs is for you to ruin it all."

"I am not in the habit of ruining things."

Mowbary's nostrils flared. He didn't verbally respond; he didn't really need to. These brothers simply didn't bother to hide how poorly they got along.

Feeling it best to disrupt any argument before it grew too pointed, Henri intervened. "We'd best settle in. Point us to the bedchambers we are to use, and we will do so."

"One of the servants can direct you." Mowbary's tone would not have been much different if he had been directing a stablehand to address a mess left behind by one of the horses. "I have pressing matters to see to."

Henri whispered to Aldric, "He is likely late for his lessons in being an utter slubber."

How well he knew the look that crossed Aldric's face when he was holding back a laugh. Seeing it in that moment lessened Henri's worries a little. Mowbary's being present would make the coming weeks a misery for Aldric, which was more than a shame. It was a tragedy. The Gents house parties were the highlights of every year. For this one to be ruined before it had even begun felt terribly unfair.

Aldric hailed a passing maid and requested they be shown to the rooms assigned to them.

As they made their way up the grand staircase, Mowbary called up to them from the ground floor. "Are you not even curious who our French visitors will be? I daresay you will be impressed."

"I daresay I won't be," Aldric muttered.

"The Beaulieus," Mowbary declared.

Henri stopped with his feet split between steps. His mind halted midthought. *The Beaulieus.*

He knew them well. Too well.

Sébastien and Gaëtane were the *crème de la crème* of Paris society. Dared he hope they were coming alone? Dared he comfort himself by insisting Sébastien's sister, Nicolette, was not making the journey as well? That seemed unlikely. She and Céleste were the very best of friends.

*Nicolette Beaulieu.*

Henri had avoided Paris for three years on account of her—the lady who'd first claimed, then shattered his heart.

# Chapter Two

*Paris*

NICOLETTE HAD OFTEN HEARD THE grand drawing rooms of Paris described as glittering. She, however, found far too many of them gaudy. The opulence was loud and demanding, leaving her tired after hours spent within. Perhaps she'd simply grown a bit cynical. When she'd first begun mingling in these circles at the tender age of seventeen, the experience had filled her with excitement. She'd imagined with anticipatory delight taking her place in this lustrous world: hostess, arbiter of fashion, leader of discussions, and receptor of the envy of all.

The seven years that had followed had taught her the emptiness of that dream. Pierre Léandre had taught her even more painfully than had the passage of time. He'd flitted into this world of glittering gatherings, seemingly exactly what she'd hoped for in a husband. Acquaintance had led to courtship, which had led to engagement, which had led to . . . abandonment. He'd left her to pick up the pieces of a broken engagement.

Most young ladies would have sunk socially under the weight of that. She nearly had. But the last two years of working tirelessly to maintain her standing had proven successful. She had reached heights in French society that even her brother, who valued such things more than most, found both shocking and gratifying.

Her social position pleased her family. But it benefited *her* in ways they would never guess.

One of the gentlemen hovering about her at this particular gathering leaned a touch closer while still maintaining a very proper distance. "Do you mean to take a turn about the room with any of us, Mademoiselle Beaulieu? You must know we are desperate to be shown such a kindness from one as lovely as you."

She gave him the smile that had become her signature expression. It was enigmatic and impossible to find offensive, but it was also entirely noncommittal. She had been declared utterly unreadable, and the gentlemen of Paris were clamoring to become literate. "How very unkind I would be to focus my attention on one of you when there are so very many deserving of conversation," she answered.

Every last one of them puffed up, clearly thinking she was paying them an individual and pointed compliment. She managed to keep the annoyance from her expression, something she had practiced for long hours in front of her mirror upon returning to society after her engagement had come to an abrupt and humiliating end. A large portion of Paris society had begun calling her *La Dame de Glace*, the Ice Lady, because they found her socially sanctioned iciness intriguing. Others finding her intimidating or unreachable styled her *La Reine des Ours*, Queen of Bears. There was safety in both impressions.

She swept her eyes over the gathering without being obvious about it. Her family would be departing for England the very next day. She had not originally meant to accompany her brother and sister-in-law to that night's soiree, but she had a very important rendezvous arranged for that evening that she simply could not miss. However, she'd not yet spotted the person she needed to find.

"Promise to dance with me at the de Golier's ball next week," another of the would-be suitors requested.

"Ah, but I will not be in attendance," she said. "You must content yourself with other partners."

Expressions of dismay escaped nearly every masculine lip in the gathered circle of competitors. With hardly a pause, the gentlemen resumed their futile and, at times, irritating attempts at flirtation. She managed the coy and elusive responses expected of her.

She was beyond the age when an unwed lady was generally declared past her prime. She had one broken engagement and gave no one the slightest bit of encouragement. If not for her dizzying standing, her family's fortune, their generations-old importance in Paris, and her carefully executed return to these circles, not one of these gentlemen would be paying her the least heed. If they knew how she spent her time when not spinning her way through the social whirl, they'd denounce her entirely.

Society was fickle, but that served her purposes rather well.

Sébastien and Gaëtane, her brother and sister-in-law, stepped up beside her. They were, as always, the very picture of French fashion and grandeur.

"You will excuse us, gentlemen," Sébastien said dismissively to the gathered would-be suitors.

With bows of regretful farewell and promises to return to Nicolette's side before the evening concluded, they dispersed.

"Do you not mean to entertain any of the gentlemen's attempts to court you?" Gaëtane asked.

"It is tremendously difficult to entertain anything at all when one's brother continually sends the would-be suitors running." She skewered her brother with an accusatory but friendly glare. She did not always see eye to eye with him, but he was not a bad person. And she didn't at all dislike him. He was, in fact, generally quite easy to spend time with and enjoyable to tease.

"They were all pups," Sébastien said. "I cannot imagine you giving a second glance to anyone so unsophisticated and immature."

"Is this why you are dragging me to England?" she asked. "Because *that* country has such an abundance of mature and sophisticated gentlemen?"

The tiniest moment passed. Then, in perfect unison, they all laughed.

"The house party is being held at a holding of a duke," Sébastien said. "Such a connection is well worth forging, especially as I understand the family also has a holding or two in France."

"If nothing else," Gaëtane said, "the Fortiers will be present. Their company is always delightful."

Céleste Fortier was Nicolette's dearest friend in all the world. That she was making the journey had convinced Nicolette not to object to the request that she take part as well. Her friend's oldest brother was sometimes difficult to spend time with, but the brother just younger than he had shown himself pleasant and companionable during his brief visit to Paris three years earlier. Time spent with Céleste's siblings was rather a neutral prospect taken as a whole.

In almost the instant Sébastien and Gaëtane abandoned Nicolette upon seeing friends in the crowd, Céleste stepped up to Nicolette's side and brought her back to the present. Soirees were always like this. So very many people and so few places to hide. Under ordinary circumstances, Nicolette would not have minded at all having her dear friend's company, but her contact at that evening's gathering would appear at any moment, and she could not— *would* not—fail to meet her obligation on that front.

"I daresay we will all sleep for the entirety of the first day of our coming journey with how late we are likely to be here tonight." Céleste exuded French fashion sense, managing the thing in a way that was pleasing without being arrogant.

"Will the journey to England be worth making, even if you arrive exhausted?" Nicolette asked as they cut a circuit of the room, nodding to people they knew. Nicolette, for her part, kept watch for the one person she awaited. He had not yet arrived.

"I would travel halfway around the world without sleeping if it meant seeing Henri again," Céleste said. "He is the very best of brothers."

"My friend, you have *two* brothers."

Céleste tipped her chin at a firm angle. "I know."

There was tension in the Fortier family. It seemed there was tension in most every family. They'd completed a full circuit of the large, very crowded room when Nicolette's gaze settled on the one person she had been watching for all evening: the Marquis de Lafayette.

She didn't give any indication that she saw him approaching, and she took extra pains not to draw attention when he stopped directly in front of her and Céleste. He offered a very aristocratic bow. They returned it with deep curtsies in deference to his rank and his importance.

"Mlle Beaulieu," he said, lowering his head in her direction. "Mlle Fortier." He offered the same to Céleste. No one would ever guess that the marquis had not stumbled upon them by accident. "I had not thought to see your families here this evening, knowing you are bound for foreign shores soon."

Céleste smiled quite prettily, the expression free of flirtation but eye-catchingly lovely just the same. "We depart in the morning. While I will enjoy seeing my brother Henri again, I will be very pleased when I find myself back in France once more."

"As one who has been separated from France on more than one occasion," the marquis said, "I understand your sentiment perfectly."

Fate was smiling upon them: Céleste was called aside by her sister-in-law a moment later, leaving Nicolette in the exclusive company of the very person she had come to see.

He motioned for her to walk with him. "The weather in England is likely to be quite wet this time of year," he observed.

"From what I have heard," she replied, "the weather in England is likely to be wet at any time of year."

He acknowledged the quip with little more than a twinkle of amusement in his eyes. The marquis was not unfriendly nor impersonable. Nicolette had come to like him a lot as she'd become better acquainted with him the past two years.

He was only six years her senior, but he seemed older than that. Not in appearance or in lack of vitality. Indeed, he was quite handsome and very full of life. But he had lived so much more life than she, so much more than most anyone their age. He had played a prominent role in the war between the American colonies and the British, and he had held positions of influence in France as well as abroad. He was well-known and generally well respected.

He was also involved in far more than most people realized.

So was she.

He had created a network of individuals with whom he worked in secret for the benefit of the French people, a group who referred to themselves as *La Tapisserie*. Nearly two years earlier, as she had been reemerging in Society after the ending of her betrothal, the recently returned Lafayette had made her acquaintance and had applauded her resiliency and courage in surviving and thriving in circumstances that would sink so many others. To her shock, he had asked her to join the efforts of *La Tapisserie*, and when she had accepted, he had seen to it she was trained in gathering information without drawing attention and in being a reliable and skilled spy. Now she was one of his most trusted contacts and one of the most senior members of the organization.

She'd allowed herself to be duped by a gentleman who'd very nearly destroyed her. All she had imagined she would be had proven little more than a distracting fog. Life had crumbled, and she'd not had the first idea how to build a sure foundation for herself. But she'd found strength in herself and an ability she'd never guessed at in her work with *La Tapisserie*. She'd found purpose. And she was both grateful and gratified by all she'd accomplished.

Their circuit of the drawing room brought them to the large french doors, which they stepped through. Many people passed in and out, the terrace serving as an extension of the gathering space, but there was a bit more privacy outside without the isolation that would cause whispers.

"I understand you are bound for Derbyshire," Lafayette said. "The area in and around Swarkestone."

It was a safe topic to fill the time until she could make the report she'd come to deliver. "That is my understanding as well."

He made a picture of perfect casualness, though he was undoubtedly aware of every movement, every sound. She had learned to be as well.

"There is a couple living in that area, M. and Mme Beaumont." He spoke quietly but not in a whisper; whispers in what was meant to be a casual public conversation would draw attention rather than deflect it. "M. Beaumont's parents were French, and she herself is a Parisian."

"You weave a very French tapestry." Nicolette offered her customary enig-matic smile so as to not do anything out of the ordinary.

"A very French tapestry, indeed."

The Beaumonts, then, were part of *La Tapisserie.*

"Would you consider delivering to them a letter from me?" the marquis asked. "We would all be indebted to you for such a kindness."

"It would be my pleasure." Anyone who happened to overhear would think it was a simple act of kindness between friends.

In the ballroom, another set began. The only other occupants of the ter-race slipped back inside to join in the dancing, affording Nicolette and the marquis a brief moment of as much privacy as possible.

"Make your report as quickly as you can," Lafayette said. "I've an addi-tional matter to discuss with you before we lose this moment of privacy."

"Mme Ponteleaux let slip that her redecorating efforts at her country chateaux have grown ever more elaborate as a result of a financial windfall. I managed to get her to admit without her realizing she had that her husband has joined a group of investors who are buying textiles in Cholet at painfully low prices, which they insist are made necessary by the Eden agreement and the high price of French goods in England. The people of Cholet have little choice but to accept the price insisted upon. She didn't know how her husband and his associates are making such a profit, considering all the tariffs in place."

"That is a riddle worth pursuing further," Lafayette said.

"I'll see if I can ascertain whom M. Ponteleaux is working with."

"Fèvre can dig further into that. I need you to take on a more delicate matter."

"A matter related to the letter you wish me to deliver, perchance?"

Lafayette nodded. "There is danger in the undercurrent of France. I have seen revolution. I have heard of all that led to it. We are on that path, and whether we will veer from it has yet to be seen. There are important mecha-nisms we need to have in place for smuggling endangered people out of the country should widespread violence take hold in France, and we need to do so without anyone realizing what we're doing."

"Why such secrecy?" Nicolette asked. "Once in England, the poor souls would be safe from the dangers in France."

"Those 'poor souls' must first reach England. There is every chance those being smuggled from our shores will be pursued, hunted. If their destination is known, their departure location can likely be ascertained. If those in England who help facilitate these escapes are identified, their counterparts in France will be easier to identify. If those who are already mumbling about uprising and revolution and blood spilled in the streets have not yet thought about exacting very focused vengeance on those whom they see as the cause of their suffering, knowing provisions are being made to guard against that—"

"Might plant the idea in their minds," Nicolette finished the thought in unison with him.

"It is my fervent hope that I am wrong about the future that awaits this country," the marquis said. "I would far rather make difficult and complicated arrangements that prove unnecessary than to wait too long and see lives unnecessarily lost."

The musicians inside brought the current tune to a stop. Nicolette and Lafayette would not be alone much longer. "We haven't time for more details. Can you give me instructions before I leave in the morning?"

He pulled two folded bits of parchment from inside his silk jacket. "The top letter is for the Beaumonts in Derbyshire. The bottom is for you, all the information you need to complete this assignment, in coded language of course."

"Of course."

He once more assumed his very casual demeanor, though his voice remained earnest. "Letters take time to pass between these countries, making it nearly impossible for correspondence swift enough for answering questions with any degree of haste. You will be acting alone."

"I have undertaken assignments under similar conditions before."

"And did so expertly," he acknowledged. "We need you to do so again. A great many lives may soon depend on your success."

# Chapter Three

STAPLETON GRANGE WAS LARGER THAN Henri had been led to expect. And the rent was steeper. Every property he'd looked at for months had proven beyond his means. That those means continued to shrink was certainly not helping the situation.

He set his gaze on the view beyond the windows of the traveling carriage. Derbyshire was lovely. He could have so happily lived in this area of England. For thirteen years, he'd simultaneously felt like a stranger in his adopted homeland and like he'd finally found a place where he belonged.

*Pitiful imbecile.* Father had often described Henri that way. He'd have most certainly done so again if he had been present to hear Henri so much as mention his struggle to define the place where he'd made his home.

His brother had echoed their father's descriptors of Henri in the years before and immediately following their father's passing. The last time Henri had seen Jean-François, his brother hadn't flung any of those cruel words in his direction. Henri had told himself the change had been an indication that his brother didn't fully agree with their father's assessments, which gave Henri some hope that Father had been wrong to some degree.

But Jean-François *hadn't* abandoned their father's desire to punish Henri for abandoning France.

At first, Henri had been proud of himself for having made his departure from France to create a life for himself in England. He'd felt himself quite the brave and daring young gentleman, defying his father and making his life what he chose. Father had referred to it as running away, a pitiful tantrum enacted by a petulant child. Jean-François now called Henri's continued insistence on remaining in England a matter of "infantile stubbornness." Henri did his best to avoid the topic whenever possible.

Soon enough, he would need to decide whether he meant to broach the topic of his withheld income with his brother or if he meant to keep the peace. He couldn't do both. He hadn't been able to before Father's death either. Peace *or* fair treatment. He'd always had to choose, and he had almost always chosen peace.

He opened the small book of poetry he'd brought with him on this house-seeing excursion. He meant to do a thorough search of the Norwood Manor book room for any poetry that might be hidden there to supplement the very few volumes he'd brought with him to Derbyshire.

The Gents likely ought to have called him the Librarian.

This offering, *An Ode on the Peace,* was written by an author whose work he had read before, one identified, as so many were, as simply "A Young Lady." He had not disliked her earlier publication, but he had seen more potential than polish in her efforts. Those thoughts had made him feel terribly judgmental, but he was certainly well able to dissect and evaluate this area of literature after his Cambridge days. But even those poems he found not to his liking were a credit to those who'd written them and, further still, published them.

Poetry was his escape, and in addition to his reading it, he wrote his own—a lot of it. And anonymously publishing a portion of it was providing him a small bit of desperately needed income. His father had forbidden him to pursue publication, insisting that such a "common" and "mercenary" vocation would be a stain upon the Fortier name. Publishing in *English* only added to the dishonor of it, he'd felt. That insistence had been backed by quite effective threats, and Jean-François had, during Henri's last visit home, repeated those threats almost verbatim, something he'd not done before. What hope Henri had had of publicly claiming his poems had disappeared.

He turned to the first page of his book, seeking refuge in poetry in this very moment.

As wand'ring late on Albion's shore
That chains the rude tempestuous deep,
I heard the hollow surges roar
Whose tears her rocky bosom steep;
Loud on the storm's wild pinion flow
The sullen sounds of mingled woe,
And softly vibrate on the trembling Lyre,
That wakes to sorrow's moan each sad responsive wire.

An evocative beginning. If this were any indication, the author had improved upon her previous talent. Henri had always appreciated seeing a poet grow. There was hope in that discovery, a promise that what one had been did not define the entirety of what one could become. He had rested on that promise for years.

"And what is it you have been, Henri Fortier? Other than a sniveling infant?" He disliked how often his father's words slipped from his own lips. "I'll prove I'm more than that," he said, as much to his blessedly absent father as to himself.

The carriage arrived at Norwood before Henri had read so much as one additional stanza. His mind had been wandering too far afield. But upon spying another traveling carriage entering the coach house, all thoughts of poetry and pondering fled.

Who had arrived? One of the Gents? Henri's family?

The Beaulieus?

He could, he supposed, simply refuse to leave the carriage, request a blanket, and make his home there until Nicolette returned to Paris. If he asked nicely, Aldric would likely bring him a few books to help pass the hours. Julia, wife of Lucas, could be counted on to make certain Henri didn't starve.

Henri hadn't Aldric's flare for strategy, but he thought his plan an excellent one . . . perhaps not truly excellent. But acceptable. A valiant attempt, at least.

A *pitiful* attempt.

Over the years, he'd managed to convince himself of the lie inherent in most of his father's insults. But that one word, he could not seem to dismiss. So much about his life felt entirely pitiful.

He pushed out a breath. There was little point in putting off the inevitable. Nicolette would arrive at Norwood if she hadn't already. He would have to face her, no matter how many carriages he wanted to hide in. He refused to be a coward.

Feeling quite brave while at the same time entirely ridiculous, he made his way inside. He was quickly divested of his hat and gloves—far too quickly for his peace of mind. Voices echoed into the entryway from the nearby drawing room, which meant several people had to be in the room.

"Any chance the carriage might be called back?" Henri muttered, but no one was near enough to hear.

Screwing his courage to the sticking place, as it were, he stepped through the drawing room doorway. It was not his family nor the Beaulieus who stood inside. Lucas and Julia had arrived. The Gents had been reunited.

Lucas spotted him as he stepped inside. No matter the circumstances, there always seemed to be mischief lurking in Lucas's eyes. He and Stanley had been the inventors and instigators of most of the trouble the Gents had fallen into over the years. Henri could only imagine how much more mischief they'd have caused had Stanley remained with them.

"Aldric said you were off looking at a property," Lucas said. "Did it prove promising?"

"It proved beyond my reach, I fear."

Lucas appeared genuinely disappointed for him. If asked, most people would describe the future Earl of Lampton as energetic and good-humored. Those who were fortunate enough to call him friend knew he was also deeply compassionate and driven to help whenever and wherever he was needed. Henri had been the recipient of that compassion more times than he could recall.

Not particularly wanting to dwell on past miseries, Henri turned his attention to Julia. "*Notre* Julia." *Our Julia.* It was what the Gents all called her. Her entrance into their group had been a difficult one, as the first few months of her and Lucas's marriage had been a struggle for them both, but the Gents had all come to love her as a sister and an indispensable part of their circle of friends.

"*Mon cher, Henri. Tu m'as tellement manquée.*"

All of the Gents spoke French, and all of them had taken pains to improve their grasp of the language in the years Henri had been among them. Julia had needed no instruction. Her French was impeccable. As was her Italian. She also spoke Latin remarkably well. And she willingly and eagerly spent time studying theoretical mathematics. She was quite possibly the most intelligent person Henri knew.

"Aldric was only just telling us that we are expecting additions to the house party," Julia said. "Beyond your sister, whom we all were anticipating."

Quick as that, they landed on yet another topic with a miserable flavor. "My brother and sister-in-law are joining Céleste, along with their three-year-old daughter. The Beaulieus are expected as well, a married couple and his younger sister, who is a very close friend of my sister's."

He'd not told any of the Gents what had transpired in Paris three years earlier with Nicolette Beaulieu, and he didn't intend to make the admission now. A fellow was entitled to a few secrets, and no one was required to undermine his peace.

"We hadn't heard about the Beaulieus yet," Lucas said. "We'd only just been informed that Lord and Lady Mowbary and little Lord Draycott are in residence."

"More than in residence," Julia said. "It sounded as though Lord Mowbary is *in charge.*"

Across the way, Aldric looked as quietly annoyed as he ever did when the matter of his brother was discussed.

"His Grace made that arrangement," Henri said. "He thought Mowbary would be a good host."

"A host who does not greet his guests upon their arrival is hardly worthy of praise," Julia said.

"He didn't greet you?" Henri would not have expected so significant a breach of etiquette.

"I daresay he will greet our French arrivals," Aldric said. "Their inclusion is about all he has spoken of since Henri and I arrived."

Fate had seemed determined to make certain Henri had to work particularly hard to keep his hopes up for this gathering. "I believe all the Gents are arrived now, are we not?"

Aldric indicated that was true. "Niles and Digby should return momentarily from a walk around the grounds. Kes and Violet are in the book room and likely didn't hear the arrival of your carriage."

Everyone *was* there. Everyone but Stanley.

"And did you bring your little Philip with you?" Henri asked.

Lucas nodded, the very picture of a proud father. "He and his nurse are settling into the nursery." Lucas and Julia's son was not yet a year old, but all the Gents adored him.

"You will no doubt think me unforgivably rude," Julia said, "but I mean to go directly to the book room. I've not seen Violet in ages, it seems."

"I, for one, intend to discover if Violet's little cousin has made good on her plans to return to the seaside and live there as a very dramatic recluse," Lucas said with a grin. Few people enjoyed the antics of children as much as he did. If ever a man was born to be a father, it was Lucas Jonquil.

"Stapleton was supposed to be within your reach," Aldric said after Lucas and Julia had left. "Were the terms of the lease changed?"

Henri nodded. "Not by much, but enough. And upon seeing the house and grounds, I think the adjustment is warranted. What I was originally told the owner was asking was far less than he ought to have been."

Aldric laughed quietly. "And people wonder why we call you Archbishop. Only a saintly gentleman would applaud a lost opportunity because he felt the one snatching it away was doing well for himself."

"At the risk of losing my saintly status, I am strongly considering sitting in a silent huff during mass on Sunday just to make certain the heavens know how displeased I am at the lack of domicile-related miracles in my life."

Aldric smiled a little, as he often did when Henri was being a little ridiculous.

"I had hoped Stapleton would end my search." He returned to a more somber tone. "I would have a home at last, and you and I could have lived near each other."

"I suspect we wouldn't have been near even if you'd secured Stapleton," Aldric said. "The duke installing Mowbary during this house party is a rather telling indication that he does not mean to allow me any opportunity to prove I am capable of overseeing an estate."

"That he thinks Mowbary *is* capable doesn't speak well for the duke's judgment," Henri said.

"He is shockingly proud of his judgment. 'My investments are returning beyond what anyone else is seeing.' 'I have championed causes in the House of Lords that have met with universal approval.' 'Many are mimicking *my* social calendar, knowing I attend only the best of balls and fetes.'" Aldric could hardly have looked more annoyed as he'd repeated his father's words.

"Perhaps your father ought to be asked how to increase my income enough for me to afford a home somewhere." Henri offered a shrug. "He *is* very wise, he will have you know."

Aldric laughed but without much sound and with no show of true humor.

"If Jean-François had not reduced my income, I might have managed a humble residence somewhere. It feels unfair."

"It feels unfair because it is. And he is obligated to honor your father's instructions on this matter. Have you any recourse in the law?"

"*Oui.* Pursuing that course would require being in France for a long stretch of time, which I don't particularly want to do. It would also require money, which Jean-François knows I do not have. I would likely end up penniless, still without a home, and unable to return to England where I wish to be. Though it is uncharitable of me, I struggle not to suspect that forcing my hand in this way and requiring me to make my home permanently in France is my brother's aim."

Aldric set a hand on his shoulder. "You are forever apologizing for what you see as uncharitable thoughts. It has been my observation that your 'uncharitable thoughts' are simply statements of what is true."

"I don't care to speak ill of people if I can avoid it."

With a joking bow, Aldric said, "Archbishop. A saint among Gents."

"A saint who has proven he can blacken your eye," Henri tossed back.

Aldric's smile grew. "I deserved it."

"Yes, you did." That long-ago scrape had been one of many among the Gents. They were more like brothers than mere friends, and sometimes that meant they tore into each other a little. Skirmishes had been far fewer and much farther between in recent years.

Beyond the drawing room door, Mowbary could be heard snapping out instructions to the staff. "Make a good showing for yourselves. You are representing a nation." Hurried footsteps and muddled voices echoed from the corridor.

Henri shot Aldric a look. "Representing a nation?" he repeated dryly.

His friend, with an expression of resignation, said, "I would wager our French visitors have arrived. Mowbary means to bow and scrape his way into their good graces."

*Our French visitors.* A mishmash of emotions flooded over Henri. He would see his sister again, a reunion his heart had desperately longed for. He would also see his brother again, something he generally went to great lengths to avoid. His little niece, now three years old, was likely with them. He longed to see her again as well. He wanted to discover for himself if she was as quiet as Céleste's letters had repeatedly said she was. His sister hadn't relayed that bit of information with words of concern, but Henri had felt anxious on the matter just the same.

Nicolette Beaulieu had made the journey to England, and that knowledge filled him with more than mere dread. Every wave of embarrassment he had endured three years earlier returned on a tide of nervousness. Would she laugh when she saw him? Recount to everyone what had transpired between them? Point out what a fool he'd made of himself? How pitiful it had all been?

He pasted on a benign and quietly pleased expression. Céleste had never mentioned his ill-fated declaration of love, which he hoped meant that Nicolette hadn't told her of it. If that were the case, there was a good chance she wouldn't mention it to anyone now.

There was also, he supposed, a chance the ceiling would simply collapse and save him the embarrassment that awaited him. Either way, he'd be appreciative.

Mowbary continued issuing orders in a voice more shrill than was generally heard among the *ton*. Aldric would have managed the expected calm and decorum. In every conceivable way, the Duke of Hartley was utterly wrong about *both* his sons. Henri knew that experience all too well. While Henri's father's mistreatment had sent Henri fleeing to another country, it had slowly turned Jean-François into an echo of the man they'd both detested.

In the midst of the commotion beyond, the drawing room began to fill. Digby and Niles entered, Niles looking a bit windswept and red-cheeked from their walk, while Digby, as always, looked immaculately put together. Lucas and Julia returned, and Kes and Violet arrived with them.

"Our French visitors are to receive a greeting fit for royalty," Lucas said. "Didn't know ol' Mowbary had it in him."

Their host hadn't overly bothered with his brother's guests. Had he been less of a coxcomb, his opinion of them all might have mattered. As it was, his bumbling attempts at being impressive would likely become conversational fodder among the Gents and a point of laughter for years to come. Aldric might even reach the point, eventually, when he could laugh about it.

"I know the Fortiers will appreciate the regal reception," Digby said. "But will the Beaulieus?"

"They likely will," Henri said.

"A bit high in the instep, are they?" Lucas asked.

Henri didn't want to think of Nicolette that way. She had rejected him, embarrassed him, and broken his heart, but she was not actually a cruel person. He knew the difference. Heavens, he knew the difference. "They are French," Henri said with a shrug. "The English often misinterpret Frenchness as haughtiness."

"You have insulted my English discernment," Digby said dramatically. "I believe I ought to be offended."

"Another misinterpretation." Henri raised an eyebrow and pursed his lips, re-creating an expression he'd seen countless times in his homeland.

The Gents all laughed.

Carriage wheels crunched on the gravel outside, and a hush fell over the room.

Niles, standing near the window, offered them all a description of what was occurring outside. "The carriage has stopped. The staff is pouring out onto the drive. Hmm. Did you know the household has only three male servants?"

"We do not need a head count, Puppy," Kes said. "Has Mowbary fallen on his face yet? That is what we are all hoping for."

Aldric smiled a bit. It was good to see.

"Mowbary and Lady Mowbary have stepped out onto the drive," Niles continued his commentary. "Tiny Lord Draycott looks annoyed with the whole thing."

"Most intelligent member of that family," Lucas muttered, pulling more of a smile from Aldric.

Julia stepped over to where Henri stood. "I'm looking forward to meeting your family," she said quietly. "Especially your sister. You have spoken of her often."

"Céleste is a delight," he said. "My sister-in-law is—" He wasn't entirely certain how to finish his evaluation. Marguerite was not unpleasant or unkind.

She also was not overly welcoming or warm. "Lately, my brother—" None of the characteristics he could think of were appropriate to be uttered by one nicknamed Archbishop, and certainly not in the presence of a lady.

"Families are a complicated thing," she said generously. "I will not press you to simplify your connection with yours."

He offered his gratitude.

"Besides," she continued, "I find myself more intrigued by the arrival of the Beaulieus."

Henri kept his expression unchanged. "Why is that?"

"They are well-regarded in French society. Lord Mowbary looks upon the promise of their presence with an odd mixture of awe and pride."

Henri nodded.

"And when you spoke of *Mlle* Beaulieu"—Julia eyed him with that intelligent and too-seeing gaze of hers—"you blushed."

He was not afforded an opportunity for response as the entire group watched the drawing room doors open. Julia stepped back to where Lucas stood.

Mowbary preceded the new arrivals, scraping and bowing to them repeatedly.

Jean-François and Marguerite were precisely as elegant and sophisticated as they had always been. No one could mistake them for anything but people of birth who knew their importance.

Walking alongside them were Sébastien and Gaëtane Beaulieu, older brother and sister-in-law of Nicolette. Where Henri's brother and sister-in-law made a person feel a bit nervous and a little inferior, the Beaulieus left an impression of almost unfathomable grace. One felt honored to be in their presence, as if not a soul could actually be worthy but everyone wished to be.

Céleste, his darling, delightful sister, stepped in next, holding the hand of little Adèle. His heart soared at the sight of them both. The Gents teased him about not being able to withstand the pull of France. But it was his sister whom he longed for more than his homeland. And now that his tiny niece had joined the family, she added to that longing.

But he wasn't afforded more than an instant's pleasure at seeing his two beloveds arrive, for Nicolette herself entered the room.

There was no mistaking her. Her dark hair was perhaps not as ornately coiffed as it had been during their acquaintance three years earlier, but it was as elegant as ever. And she did not powder her hair as heavily as she had then, as fashion no longer dictated a lady do so. No one would describe her as tall, but neither was she shockingly short, and he suspected there were few ladies in Paris who did not envy her softly curved figure and exquisitely dark blue eyes.

She still wore the elegant gold cross with emerald inlay that she had worn then. It was small but elaborate, managing to be opulent without being gaudy. He'd always thought it a perfect reflection of herself.

She was still the most beautiful woman he'd ever seen. It was little wonder he'd made such a fool of himself over her.

Bows and curtsies were exchanged, and Fate, being the fickle mistress she was, placed Nicolette nearer to him than anyone else. To refuse to offer a personal word of greeting would have been rude, and he suspected his heart, foolish organ that it was, would never forgive him for so quickly erecting a barrier between them.

"Mlle Beaulieu," he said. "*C'est un plaisir de vous revoir.*"

"M. Fortier," she returned. "*Combien de temps s'est-il écoulé depuis notre dernière rencontre?*"

Did she not actually remember how long it had been since they'd last been in company?

He continued on in French. "Three years now, I believe."

She nodded. "Your sister, as you can imagine, has been most anxious to see you again."

The comment was made with an air of friendliness, precisely the way one conversed with an acquaintance with whom one had a perfectly unexceptional connection. Was she a remarkable actress, or had she genuinely forgotten all that had transpired between them? Perhaps she remembered and simply didn't care. He'd been shaken upon realizing he would be seeing her, fearful of the inevitable discomfort. He'd thought she might laugh or look on him with pity or think him as pitiful as his father always had. Instead, she seemed to only vaguely recall him.

He hadn't the first idea how to feel about that.

# Chapter Four

NINE GENTLEMEN, SEVEN LADIES, AND two children. Nicolette took note of each one. That was a great many eyes potentially seeing and ears potentially overhearing things she needed to make absolutely certain they didn't. She'd faced worse odds before and managed to complete the mission she'd been given.

"The mask a spy wears is most convincing when it fits the one wearing it," the Marquis de Lafayette had told her before her first assignment two years ago. "Choose a facade you can maintain and that will not entirely contradict the person you are."

And so she'd allowed herself to continue being unabashedly curious and observant while leaning into her reputation for occasional iciness and intimidating self-possession.

To begin this current assignment, she meant to keep her expression vaguely pleased and her demeanor that of one completely satisfied with her situation until she could gather enough information about the other guests to know how best to proceed.

Céleste hooked her arm through Henri's, looking utterly pleased to be with him once more. Nicolette had met him briefly in Paris three years earlier. He had been rather quiet and had very kindly listened when she'd spoken her mind more freely than she likely ought to have. Her memories of him were vague, but she remembered that about him. He'd listened.

His visit to Paris had occurred nearly a year before she'd met Pierre Léandre, who'd seldom listened to her. Even after they'd become engaged, Pierre hadn't been overly interested in her thoughts. And after their engagement had ended in disaster, she'd kept her most personal thoughts entirely to herself.

"I have not ever before visited this country," Nicolette said to him. "Am I likely to find it drastically different from France?"

He shook his head. "The weather is wetter. The people are as varied as in our home country."

"There is quite an assortment here." She looked over the gathering once more. "Are they all friends of yours?"

"Most of them, yes."

"Henri's friends are known as the Gents," Céleste said. "They are quite sought after when in London."

Nicolette didn't remember Henri being the sort to draw that much notice, nor to welcome it. Pierre had been exactly the opposite. She glanced around the room at the others gathered there. "Does all of English Society call you and your friends 'the Gents,' or is that a name you use only amongst yourselves?"

"The name is widely used." Henri was very obviously uncomfortable around her. She didn't remember that being the case during his time in Paris.

Either not noticing her brother's discomfort or not being particularly bothered by it, Céleste said, "They all have sobriquets within the group as well. Henri has told me his name among them is Archbishop."

"Is there a reason they call you that?" Nicolette asked.

He didn't quite look at her as he responded. "They like to tease me."

A pointedly incomplete answer. Intriguing.

Nicolette looked over the gathering again. With such a sensitive and difficult task ahead of her, she needed a better understanding of those she would be surrounded by. Navigating a maze filled with people was challenging. With *strangers*, it would be particularly difficult.

"I would guess that Lord Aldric is one of your number but not Lord Mowbary."

"Yes." The answer was a little terse.

"And Lady Jonquil and Mrs. Barrington appear to be good friends." Though Nicolette suspected they'd not known each other overly long.

"They are." Another short answer. Was Henri upset with her? That hardly seemed likely. She had only just arrived and had been perfectly pleasant.

She'd spent the past two years constantly evaluating her behavior, her every expression, each word she spoke. She told herself it was a matter of protecting her work with *La Tapisserie*, but she knew that was not at all her most significant reason for the constant vigilance. It was the legacy of her time with Pierre. The unexplained, sudden, and public defection of a man who had once insisted she was someone worthwhile enough to marry had shaken her. Even the passage of two years hadn't entirely freed her of the lingering doubts that experience had etched into her view of herself.

With a quick curtsy, she slipped away. Her primary goal for this house party was to accomplish her mission and establish the network the marquis felt would one day be necessary. She would do well to focus on her purpose when her thoughts filled with painful memories and regrets.

As she wandered past her brother, deep in conversation with Lord and Lady Mowbary and Lord Aldric, he motioned for her to stop and join them.

"This is a lovely home," Sébastien said with obvious satisfaction to their host. "And what a warm welcome we have received." He'd spoken entirely in French.

Lord and Lady Mowbary appeared neither surprised nor confused. Lord Aldric looked to be following the conversation easily as well.

So Nicolette responded in French. "Perfectly lovely. And our welcome was everything we could have hoped it would be."

"I trust His Grace is in good health," Gaëtane said to their host with the expected show of concern and deference.

"Always," Lord Mowbary answered.

Lord Aldric stood very quietly, his expression entirely impassive, yet Nicolette felt certain she saw annoyance flash through his eyes. This was a gentleman who seemed to intentionally make himself difficult to analyze.

A bit of a bump from Gaëtane, one so minor it might very well have been an accident, shifted Nicolette closer to their host's younger brother. He didn't adjust his position, didn't even seem to notice.

"Lord Aldric," Gaëtane said, "do you speak French as well as your brother does?"

"I daresay I speak it better."

His brother did not appear to appreciate that answer, and Lord Aldric did not appear to regret it.

"Have you been to France?" Gaëtane asked Lord Aldric.

He gave a small nod. "His Grace has an estate in Normandy, part of my late mother's dowry."

Gaëtane turned a pointed gaze and an overly large smile on Nicolette. "The family of an English duke with such strong ties to France. How remarkable."

A quick glance at Sébastien combined with the look Nicolette was receiving from Gaëtane explained their enthusiasm. They were plotting. More than plotting, they were matchmaking. *Sérieux?* She would appreciate a bit of a bolster to her self-confidence after yet another reminder of Pierre, but this was not at all the way to accomplish it.

Céleste was brought over by her brother and sister-in-law in the next moment.

"Lord Aldric," M. Fortier said, "I believe you have met my sister."

"Yes, though many years ago."

"She has grown into a beautiful lady since then," Mme Fortier was quick to add.

"She has." His tone was kind but impartial.

The conversation had not shifted from French. One might almost have believed they were still in Paris.

"How fortunate that we will have so much time to all become reacquainted," Mme Fortier said.

Nicolette met Céleste's eye. They were dear enough friends that no words were needed. The barely concealed smile in her friend's eyes was, without question, echoed in Nicolette's own. Not only were their brothers and sisters-in-law matchmaking, but they had also taken aim in the exact same direction.

What an utterly ridiculous turn of events. Once back in France, she and Céleste would laugh about it for years to come. Provided things didn't go too terribly, they might manage to laugh about it while it was happening.

Nicolette turned to Lady Mowbary. "I am not familiar with this area. Are there a great many local families of significance?"

"The Marquess of Grenton and his family live at Tafford, which is a lovely estate nearby. The Haddingtons are in the area as well. They are not titled, but are a family of standing. The Saunders are the same."

Nicolette nodded and smiled as if quite pleased. None of those families were her aim.

"The Beaumonts are newer to the area. He is a younger son of a respected French family with impressive holdings. His wife is, herself, from France. They are already extremely well thought of by the local families." Lady Mowbary seemed to quite suddenly realize how significant that might be. "Perhaps you know her. Her name is"—she had to think a moment—"Modestine, I believe."

"Unless you know her maiden name, I am unlikely to place her." Nicolette did her best to appear as if the Beaumonts were nothing at all to her. She had not actually met them, but she knew precisely who they were.

"I do not know anything about her beyond her current name and former home." Lady Mowbary looked a little perplexed. "The duke gave us a list of the names of local people whom he deemed worthy of notice. That is the extent of my acquaintance with the area."

"Perhaps, if there is to be a gathering of the local families, I might have the opportunity to discover if she is known to me." Nicolette offered the vaguely worded hope while watching their hostess closely.

Lady Mowbary grew increasingly eager as the conversation went forward. "We intend to make certain all at the house party have the opportunity for mingling with the neighbors. If we were in London, you would have your pick of the very best of Society. I do wish we could have hosted you *there*."

"Having only just left Paris, I find myself entirely pleased with the prospect of time spent in the countryside."

That seemed to placate Lady Mowbary.

There would be an opportunity to meet the Beaumonts. How easily she could arrange a private discussion with them remained to be seen, but she wasn't discouraged. Yes, she sometimes doubted herself, but her own history with *La Tapisserie* told her she was more likely to manage what was asked of her than not.

As if to undermine that moment of self-directed reassurance, Nicolette felt the hairs on the back of her neck stand on end. Someone was watching her.

She looked around only to find Henri Fortier's gaze on her. More than a casual happenstance, he appeared to have been watching her quite closely and without any indication of pleasure. His gaze shifted almost immediately but not before she saw the crease of a frown tug at his features.

What could she possibly have done to earn this unexpected disapproval? They hardly knew each other. Perhaps she'd do best to keep it that way.

## Chapter Five

THE NORWOOD BOOK ROOM WAS quiet the next morning, which worked to Henri's advantage. He was swiftly approaching the time when he needed to have his poems ready to send to the publisher, which had expressed interest in a second volume of his work. There was, as he'd discovered these past years, no guarantee that they would proceed with the offer they'd made once they received his submission. But since his last publication had both been accepted and known some success, he felt himself on firmer ground than he might have been otherwise.

Disinterest, however, was not his greatest obstacle.

This publication was meant to include three poems, and he'd written only two. He was no mathematician, but he suspected one and one did not, in fact, make three.

The first two poems, he had easily completed shortly after the previous Gents gathering. But the third was still eluding him. He'd done as he often had when the words refused to flow through his pen: read. He'd been filling his soul with the words of other poets, making mental notes of those aspects of the poems that spoke to him and those that were not in the style he would prefer. He spent time walking about in nature, reflecting upon the people and places he knew, searching for that evasive whisper of inspiration.

As he'd eaten his breakfast, an idea had formed in his mind. Perhaps he might write descriptive poetry reflecting on the many estates he had visited in the hope of temporarily calling one of them his own. There were lovely aspects to all of them that could easily inspire a very evocative poem.

He'd been recording a few lines and phrases here and there all morning, snippets of descriptive language that he hoped would grow into something larger. Though he was still struggling, he knew that did not necessarily mean the idea was a bad one. He often struggled in the earliest stages of a new composition.

How confident he'd been whilst studying at Cambridge that he had found his calling, his sense of purpose, his claim to freedom. He had gained a grasp of the language and learned a great deal about himself. In poetry, especially poems *he* composed, he'd felt himself grow more independent and confident, more able to express what he felt and what he needed. He'd found himself increasingly brave enough to do what he wished to do regardless of his father's feelings on the matter. For a time, he'd found reason to begin disbelieving that man's evaluation of him. But it hadn't lasted.

He'd dreamed during those long-ago Cambridge days of publishing his works and having his words known and praised. He would finally *know* his father was wrong. He'd depended on it. But his poems hadn't met with the acclaim some writers' had, and his name was not attached to them in any way. As far as anyone knew, his time at Cambridge had been a waste, just as his father had insisted it would be. Henri couldn't shake from his shoulders the weight of failure despite having inarguably accomplished some of what he'd set out to do.

"You will think me mercenary," Nicolette's voice echoed to him from across the passage of years, "but I find it terribly unfair that a lady is so quickly dismissed as coldhearted for searching out a suitor who has the means of keeping the both of them out of poverty."

That ought to have been his first warning three years earlier that his imagined life of bliss with her was destined not to become reality. But he'd reasoned with himself that he was not *entirely* without money. He was not wealthy, but at that time, he'd had a higher income than now and had been fully confident he could obtain a small home and live a comfortable life.

A bit of ink dropped from his quill, held still above his paper of jotted phrases and fleeting ideas. The past was distracting him, as it so often did. Was it any wonder he struggled to complete his work?

"Your criteria for marriage seems to place younger sons and poor gentlemen at a disadvantage," he'd said to Nicolette in Paris, hoping to hear her contradict what he'd begun to suspect.

"Is not marriage a matter of overcoming disadvantages, of building upon what one has in an effort to obtain that which one has not?"

How he wished he could look back and congratulate himself on having skirted the disaster of losing his heart to a lady who saw things so differently than he. But all it seemed he could do was sit in silent reflection and feel rather foolish. She truly had been a lovely person, and though she'd taken a very logical approach to the question of marriage, she'd not been unfeeling. And when she had smiled at him in that way that others had declared inscrutable but that had spoken to him from the first moment of their acquaintance . . .

He sighed at the memory. He had well and truly loved her. But who was to say, even if his circumstances had been different, if there would have been a happy outcome for the two of them when his heart was set on a home and family built on love and her mind was in search of a match society would approve of?

He shook off the memories, quite literally. Physical movement often brought his mind back to the current moment.

Concentrating once more, he bent over his parchment, dotted by stray drops of ink. A poem about the places he'd seen. He needed to focus on that. He jotted down a few phrases that flitted through his mind.

*Verdant glades of emerald hue.*
*Soaring arches of almond stone.*

Perhaps a bit affected, but something he could adjust and build on. If he scratched out a few more phrases, he might find something worth keeping.

*Locks of deep, chestnut brown.*
*Eyes like pools of cerulean water.*

Henri groaned silently. Not only was it a dismal bit of pretentiousness, but the words weren't even describing a place; they were describing a person. And not just any person but the very lady he was attempting *not* to think about.

An unfamiliar, very English voice spoke from the direction of the doorway. "Begging your pardon, Mr. Fortier."

He looked up and over to see a girl of likely sixteen, whom he thought he remembered was one of the nursemaids, standing just inside the room, holding the hand of his niece, Adèle. "Mrs. Fortier said she thought you ought to have a bit of time with your niece, sir. Said as how you would enjoy it."

The girl obviously thought he would be upset to have been given the task of looking after the child without having first been consulted by the one requesting he do so. In his experience, the French were more imperious with their servants than the English. It was, of course, not universally true. But his sister-in-law could be even more dictatorial than most. The poor nursemaid was likely more afraid of Marguerite's displeasure than Henri's.

"I would be delighted to spend time with her," he assured the maid. Dropping his gaze to the little girl, he motioned her over. "*Viens ici, ma choupette.*"

She came over. Her expression was wary, and she moved with noticeable hesitation. He was pleased to see that she didn't seem truly afraid of him, simply a bit unsure.

"I can stay in here if you'd like, sir," the maid said.

"That will not be necessary, but thank you," he responded. "Is Miss Fortier meant to return to the nursery at any specific time?"

The maid shook her head.

"Then I shall keep her with me until she is called back."

The maid dipped a curtsy and slipped out once more.

Henri smiled at Adèle, hoping to offer her some reassurance. He suspected the girl did not understand any language other than French—her instruction in English would come later—so he kept to his native tongue. "Do you know who I am, little one?"

"No." She studied him.

He had not seen her since shortly after her birth, when he had visited the family estate with the express purpose of meeting her.

"I am your *tonton* Henri," he told her.

Her gaze narrowed, so focused for a three-year-old child. "*Tonton* Henri?"

He nodded. "Your father is my brother."

Her smile was fleeting. She really was quiet, but Henri was more than willing to give her time to warm to him.

Adèle stretched her neck a bit, eying the papers on the desk in front of him.

"Would you like to see what I'm working on?" he asked.

"Yes, please." The little one didn't actually seem truly bashful, but her voice *was* quiet and she gave the very real impression that she never was one for stringing together more than two or three words at a time. He wished he knew her better.

Henri inched his way over a bit, then offered Adèle his hand to help her climb onto the chair he sat on. She managed with a degree of elegance that felt a bit out of place for a three-year-old but that somehow suited her. She knelt on the chair next to him, leaning forward to look at his papers. Henri set an arm around her to keep her steady and safe.

"I have been visiting houses and am writing down what I remember about them."

She nodded solemnly as she examined the paper in front of them. He was certain she didn't yet read French, let alone English.

"I need to think of a lot of colors," he said. "How many do you know?"

Adèle listed several, warming to the topic. Something about hearing such simple words uttered in a tiny French voice left Henri a little homesick. Sharing a little of his poetic efforts with her made him wish all the more that she wasn't growing up so far away from him.

Being at odds with Jean-François meant Henri wasn't certain how often he would see his niece in the years to come. That broke his heart.

"How do you like England?" he asked Adèle. "If I asked you, would you visit me here?"

She looked away from the paper and directly at him. "You live here, *Tonton* Henri?"

"Not in this house, but in this country."

She moved around, shifting so she was facing him rather than the desk. There was a look of expectation in her eyes.

"Have your nursemaids taught you any games yet?" he asked her. "Your *tante* Céleste was wonderfully fun to play games with when she was little." There were enough years between him and his sister that he vividly remembered those parts of her childhood he had been present for. "And I used to call her *abeille* because she flitted around like a little bee."

"*Tante* Céleste isn't a bee." The smallest hint of a laugh lay in the simple declaration. She was warming to him.

Oh, how he would miss her when she returned to France. Her wispy curls would change from the thin strands of babyhood to the thicker curls of childhood. He and Céleste had kept their golden hair, the shade only growing a bit darker as they'd grown older. Jean-François's hair had darkened to brown. Adèle's likely would as well.

"What shall I call you, Adèle?" he asked. "Do you flit about? Hop like a grasshopper, perhaps?"

"I can hop." That hint of a laugh emerged as almost a giggle. It gave him hope in his efforts to claim even a tiny place in the life of this little girl he loved so dearly.

"*Sauterelle,*" he said. "That will be my name for you. My grasshopper. My lovely, little bouncing girl."

In the next moment, Nicolette stepped into the bookroom. In a flash so quick and so instantaneous he wasn't certain which thought occurred to him first, he remembered the need for gentlemen to stand upon the entrance of a lady, realized he likely looked shocked enough to give offense, and remembered that his poetic attempts were still on the desk and fully in view, including the two bits *about her*. He managed to jump to his feet and set an arm around

Adèle so as not to accidentally knock her off the chair, all while hastily stuffing his sheets of parchment into his traveling desk. He snapped the lid closed.

"Mlle Beaulieu." He bowed. His arm around Adèle rendered the movement less elegant than he would have preferred.

"M. Fortier." She curtsied, as was expected. When she looked up at him once more, it was with confusion and a little bit of concern. "Am I interrupting? You do not seem overly pleased at my arrival."

He apparently hadn't hidden his shock well. "I am not displeased, I assure you."

Disbelief remained in her expression. "You also seemed less than pleased by my arrival yesterday."

One thing had certainly not changed about Nicolette Beaulieu: she was remarkably observant and often very direct.

"On the contrary," he said. "I had assumed you would not be overly comfortable at a house party at which *I* was present."

As forthright as she could be in her words, her face could be even more expressive no matter that others insisted she was unreadable. In that moment, she looked genuinely baffled. "Why would I be displeased for you to be here?"

He'd had his suspicions during their brief interaction the afternoon before and upon watching her during supper last night that she didn't recall the entirety of their interactions years earlier. He, on the other hand, would never forget them.

Henri didn't know whether to feel relieved at discovering his embarrassment had been forgotten and his unrequited affection had not caused her lasting distress or if he ought to feel offended that his genuine love for her had meant so little. A gentleman didn't like being shown that he was an utterly forgettable sort of person with no ability whatsoever to make an impression. It was little wonder his father had deemed him pitiful.

"I suspect my sister told you I would be here," Henri said.

"According to your sister, you being here is the very reason for the visit."

Surprising. "*Her* reason for visiting, or *my entire family's* reason?" His brother and sister-in-law, after all, had not chosen to visit until they were invited to do so by someone other than him.

"Your brother and sister-in-law did express some gratification at seeing you again," she said. "Céleste, however, could speak of little else beyond her excitement that you were awaiting her arrival and she would be granted your company during this house party."

That did his heart good, but it also brought to mind concerns he had long held.

"Do you speak English, Mlle Beaulieu?" he asked, having spoken in French up to this point.

"I speak six languages, M. Fortier, and English is most certainly among them."

The declaration momentarily distracted him from his purpose. "Lady Jonquil, she's the lady with the reddish-brown hair, and her husband is—"

"The one the Gents call the Jester," Nicolette finished for him.

He nodded. "She is also a polyglot. If you have not yet made her closer acquaintance, you should. I suspect you would find you have a lot in common."

"I look forward to knowing her better," Nicolette said.

It was the expected polite reply, but Henri could not mistake the sincerity with which she uttered it. It was one thing he had deeply liked about her when they'd interacted in Paris: she was generous with her time and showed people true kindness. He was pleased to see that had not changed.

"I only ask after your proficiency in English, because this little one"—he squeezed Adèle's shoulders—"only speaks French, and there is something I wish to ask you."

Nicolette smiled fondly at the little girl. "She is only three years old. There is a chance she would not understand even if you spoke in French."

He didn't dare risk it. In English, he continued. "As the question involves both her parents, I would prefer to make absolutely certain she cannot understand."

Nicolette nodded. "That is both sensible and wise. Please, ask your question."

She sat on the nearby sofa. Henri retook his seat at the desk but turned to face her. To his delight, Adèle remained at his side, leaning a little against him.

"Is my sister happy?" he asked Nicolette. "Is she treated well by Jean-François and Marguerite?"

"Do you have reason to believe she might not be?" Nicolette tipped her head a bit, her stunning blue eyes holding his gaze.

"I love Céleste," he said. "But I'm so far away. And I am painfully aware that life amongst my family can be terribly unpleasant."

She nodded. "Céleste does not speak overly much of her life at home with your brother, but what she has said leads me to believe the situation is not ideal. Not entirely miserable or truly abusive, but not always happy."

"That is what I have been worried about," Henri said.

"But she has forged a place for herself in Paris. She is beloved and sought after. All of my observations tell me she's delighted with that aspect of her life. I have the very real impression that your brother and sister-in-law wish she would make a match, likely because in the eyes of many, she is growing old."

Nicolette gave him a dry look that brought a smile to his face. She and Céleste were very nearly the same age. "Céleste seems perfectly content to be taking her time on that matter. I suspect she wishes to make certain whatever match she enters into is one she can be pleased with."

"Is there someone she has in mind?" he asked. "Someone she is waiting on?"

Nicolette didn't offer any spoken response. Her expression held intrigue and amusement, teasing and secrecy. She had been a delightful puzzle to sort when he'd known her in Paris. His heart whispered that he would enjoy that aspect of her company once more.

"You must realize my curiosity will not be satisfied with that answer," he said with a smile.

Adèle reached toward Nicolette, clearly wishing to be transferred into the lady's arms. Nicolette reached toward her. Henri lifted his *petite sauterelle* from the chair and set her on the sofa beside the lady she knew much better than she knew him. He wanted Adèle to have pleasant memories of the time she spent with him, even if the entirety of that time was not spent *exclusively* with him.

"And what if, Henri Fortier, the answer I have given you regarding your sister's potential romantic interests is the only answer I am willing to give you?" She had not lost the thread of their conversation, neither had she lost the coy sense of humor he was enjoying seeing once more.

"I suspect I should warn you that I am perfectly willing to pester you over this."

She tipped a slim eyebrow upward. "And *I* should warn *you* that I'm rather exceptionally good at dealing with pests."

He didn't often laugh out loud, but he did then. Nicolette joined him in the very next instant. It was a familiar sound. He'd often laughed with her in Paris. He'd loved her smile in all its incarnations, but his heart had been particularly partial to the smile that emerged when she laughed. Seeing it again . . . He inwardly sighed. Even with the passage of years and the pain of rejection, that smile wrapped itself around his still-partial heart.

"Only because your sister would not approve of me torturing you," she said, "I will tell you that, to my knowledge, Céleste's heart is wholly her own. Her resistance to being wooed most likely arises from her decision to be very particular, which I applaud. A poor choice of husband leads to a lifetime of misery."

He had been firmly in her "poor choice" category three years earlier. He hoped she didn't discover how much truer that was now. He didn't mean to press his suit or anything humiliating like that, but he still didn't wish for her to realize how . . . pitiful his situation had become.

"When last I was in France," he said, "you and Céleste were considered quite the diamonds of Paris society. I suspect that has not changed for either of you."

His compliment appeared to miss the mark a little. Her gaze narrowed almost imperceptibly. "How much has Céleste told you of the last two years?"

Why did she seem concerned by the possibility? "She writes to me about Adèle and sometimes a little about our brother and sister-in-law," he said. "Her letters also touch on the balls and soirees she attends and what she sees at the theater, but there aren't a great many specifics."

Relief flickered through her expression. Something had happened in the years since he'd seen Nicolette, something she was grateful he didn't know about. That was decidedly intriguing.

"You likely think me the most meddlesome of brothers," he said, "but living as far away as I do and seeing her so seldom, I often feel helpless to know if there is something I might do for Céleste or encouragement I might offer that she particularly needs."

A soft smile played on Nicolette's lips. "You may think you are meddling overly much, but she recently declared you the very best of brothers, and I assure you she was sincere."

That touched him, warmed his heart. He'd been away so long that he'd missed a great deal of Céleste's life. Yet, she loved him still. Had he not kept his poetic efforts a secret, his father would have made good on his threat to cut off all contact between Henri and Céleste, a punishment he knew with certainty Jean-François would inflict on him in their father's stead. Losing his connection to his sister would irrevocably shatter him.

If he could increase his income through his writing and continue to keep the secret of it, he might eventually have the funds to see her more often. If he could convince Jean-François to give him the funds he was owed, he might at last secure a home where she could visit him, perhaps even come to stay.

"I find myself, as a loyal and good friend, needing to add one thing more," Nicolette said.

He indicated she should feel free to do so. They were still speaking in English, which meant Adèle would still have no idea what was being discussed. She was watching them as they conversed and didn't seem displeased to be left out of the conversation. Céleste's reports that their niece was very quiet were proving true.

"It has become abundantly clear in the brief time we have been here," Nicolette said, "that your brother and sister-in-law have arrived with their minds set on the possibility of securing a match for your sister. I do not yet know your friends, and I am not the least acquainted with any of the neighboring families, but if you love your sister, and I know you do, stand her champion, offer her a bit of respite from the scheming. She is strong-willed enough to resist their efforts, but I do think she deserves to enjoy this house party, something that will be difficult if she is constantly defending herself against unwanted matchmaking."

"You have my sincerest gratitude for the warning," Henri said. "My friends will not impose on her, I can assure you. And I will do what I can to see that the local families treat her as she deserves."

Nicolette dipped her head. "You are indeed the very best of brothers."

Adèle slid off the sofa and walked to where Henri sat.

"May I look at the books?" she asked in French. It was the most she'd yet said to him at once.

"You certainly may, *ma petite sauterelle.*"

She took his hand and tugged him to his feet. He had to lean a bit to walk beside her with their hands entwined, but he couldn't imagine being happier with the arrangement. Adèle led him to the nearest bookshelves, pointing to various books and asking him what they were.

Nicolette rose as well but wandered toward a shelf away from where he and Adèle stood and began perusing the titles, no doubt looking for something to read. He had expected their first true conversation to be painfully awkward. It had proven rather pleasant.

The weeks they were to be in company might be enjoyable after all.

Nicolette stood facing a row of books but not truly seeing them. As she had stepped into the book room, Henri had frantically and immediately tucked out of sight whatever it was he had been writing. There was no point denying it: Henri Fortier was hiding something.

*Chapter Six*

AFTER A QUIET DAY TO allow the weary travelers rest, the house party began in earnest with an afternoon spent on the expansive back lawn of Norwood Manor. The weather was fine, and the grounds were gorgeous. Nicolette found herself perfectly pleased with the day's plans.

Until *other* plans almost immediately interfered.

"Nicolette." Sébastien set a hand on her back the moment she arrived among the gathered chairs and merry makers. "There are to be lawn games, and I have it on good authority that Lord Aldric is hopeful you will be his partner for the afternoon."

She hadn't any confidence in the "authority" Sébastien referenced. It was far more likely that his information arose from his own wishful thinking.

"I would prefer to sit and watch," she said. But he was already pushing her toward the area of the lawn where the Gents had gathered, along with Lady Jonquil, holding her little boy in her arms.

"Look who I have found, Lord Aldric," Sébastien said. "An excellent partner for your game of—" He looked around, likely trying to find some clue as to what the gentlemen were about to undertake.

"Bowls," Lord Aldric supplied.

"Excellent." Sébastien nudged Nicolette closer to her would-be partner.

"It would be even more excellent if *you* were designated the . . . bowler." She hadn't the first idea how to refer to the game she'd never even heard of.

Sébastien shrugged and laughed a bit. "Bowl your best bowls, Nicolette." At least he was allowing a bit of teasing into their interactions. She'd missed that in the short time since her brother had realized an unmarried gentleman of rank and fortune would be within throwing distance of a hastily tossed cupid's arrow.

"I will have my revenge, dearest brother," she warned in an aside.

He did not seem at all concerned but simply beat a hasty retreat.

All the Gents were watching her with varying expressions ranging from surprise to amusement. A person didn't have to be a trained spy to recognize her family's painfully obvious scheming.

"I haven't the first idea how to play bowls," she admitted.

"Aldric, we have found you a partner," Lord Jonquil declared. "We will finally best you."

Nicolette assumed an overly dramatic expression of offense. "And how do you know I won't prove a very quick study and an excellent bowls player?"

"Because *he*"—Lord Jonquil pointed at Lord Aldric—"is not that lucky."

"I think the real question, Lord Jonquil," Nicolette said, "is, Are *you* that lucky?"

"No," the others answered in near unison.

Laughter rumbled through the group. Even Lord Aldric, who had not thus far seemed the sort to laugh easily, joined in, though in a subdued way. But it was Henri who caught Nicolette's attention. He was laughing with the others, smiling easily. She had not sorted out the mystery he presented, and her mind could not entirely move on from the memory of him hastily tucking papers out of her view.

"At the risk of sounding contrary," Lady Jonquil said, "I am of the decided opinion that Lucas"—she looked to her husband—"is, in fact, exceptionally lucky."

"Oh, I am." Lord Jonquil slipped his arms around his wife, in essence holding his entire family in an embrace. "Lucky." He kissed his wife's cheek. "Blessed." He kissed the tip of her nose. "Joyous." He kissed her lips.

"Nauseating," Mr. Barrington tossed out, setting the Gents laughing once more.

The Gents called Mr. Barrington "Grumpy Uncle," but Nicolette hadn't seen anything truly grumpy in his behavior or demeanor. His was a very dry and intellectual sense of humor.

Lord Jonquil kept one arm around his wife, clearly not the least offended by the teasing he was receiving. "I am claiming Julia for my team. She is brilliant at bowls."

"Not fair," the usually very quiet Mr. Greenberry said. "You will have three on your team."

Lady Jonquil glanced at her baby with a smile. "Philip here will be assuming an advisory role only."

"An advantage still," Mr. Layton said with every indication of sincerity. "If the infant has even half the intelligence of his mother, he can outthink all of us already." While the remark was an exaggeration, it was not the first time Nicolette had heard Lady Jonquil's intelligence praised by these gentlemen. *La Tapisserie* valued intelligence in women, but it seemed so few others did.

A quick glance at Lord Jonquil revealed him beaming with pride as he looked at his wife. Nicolette vividly remembered various expressions Pierre had worn during their brief courtship and disastrous engagement. While there had sometimes been pride in his expression, it had always indicated pride in himself.

When her family had first begun considering the possibility of Pierre courting her, she had found his approval of her appearance, however shallow, to be perfectly acceptable. It was what she had been led to expect from a suitor. Only when it was too late and the engagement was official had she realized how little comfort such a thing actually offered and how little approval *of her* it conveyed.

"If we are to form teams, I mean to see if Violet will join in," Mr. Barrington said, stepping away in search, no doubt, of his wife.

Mr. Layton managed to look both shockingly handsome and thoroughly annoyed at the same time, and something in the combination made Nicolette want to laugh. "'*If* we are to form teams'?" he repeated in a tone of doubt. "*If*? We always play bowls in teams. There is no 'if' about it. I fear our Grumpy Uncle is losing his faculties." He tapped at his temple.

"Your numbers are uneven so long as I am in the count," Nicolette said. "I'm happy to relinquish my brother's claim on Lord Aldric. Or better yet, go fetch Sébastien, and he can join in since he is so apparently fond of the idea of causing you difficulties in the forming of your teams."

She earned smiles of amusement from Mr. Layton and Mr. Greenberry. Lord Aldric maintained his neutral expression, something she was quickly deciding was rather a permanent thing.

Henri watched her with that same narrow-eyed look of evaluation she had seen on his face so frequently since her arrival two days earlier. Of all the Gents, he was the only one who actually knew her and, thus, the one she had assumed would be most comfortable with her. But he wasn't, and for reasons she could not fathom. She'd been drastically wrong about Pierre. But he and Henri were so different from each other. To discover she had also been mistaken in Henri's character would deal her confidence yet another blow.

"I believe our numbers are about to even up, after all." Henri, still speaking to all of them, motioned subtly a bit away from them. Everyone turned in time to see Marguerite Fortier accompanying a very annoyed Céleste to where they all stood.

"M. Beaulieu indicated this was to be a game in which teams were formed," Marguerite said without preamble. Her eyes found and remained on Lord Aldric. "Céleste would make an excellent partner for you." She emphasized the declaration far more than was warranted.

The only person who looked more annoyed with the situation than Céleste was Lord Aldric himself, though the indications of vexation were well enough tucked away that one had to look very closely to see them.

Marguerite offered Céleste the same unwelcome nudge that Nicolette had received from her brother moments earlier and abandoned her with the same alacrity.

"Our numbers may be more even," Mr. Layton said, "but there seem to be too many for a single game of bowls. Niles and I will join Kester and Violet and undertake a very dignified game of shuttlecock and battledore." His words and expression turned a bit dry as he added, "The rest of you can attempt to sort out exactly what game it is that's being played here."

Mr. Layton went to great lengths to appear frivolous, Nicolette had noticed. But she'd also seen indications that he was keenly observant and very intelligent. Why did he hide that about himself?

Under her breath, Céleste said to Nicolette, "I do not know if I can endure weeks of our families' attempts at matchmaking."

"By the end, they will either be desperate or you will be engaged. It must be one or the other."

"Why Céleste and not you?" Henri apparently had overheard.

There had been some indications during their brief conversation in the book room the day before that Henri had not heard of Nicolette's ill-fated engagement. For reasons she chose not to explore, she was grateful for that. It was hardly her fault that Pierre had proven to be absolutely dreadful. She'd weathered that storm at great cost, something she was oddly reluctant to have Henri know.

"I suspect your brother and sister-in-law are more obstinate than mine," she said.

"*Malheureusement*," Céleste said. "I would say it is *your* obstinance, Nicolette, that is the more significant element here."

Rather than argue that she wasn't stubborn, which she knew she was, Nicolette simply offered a minute curtsy of agreement.

Lord and Lady Jonquil smiled. Even tiny Philip—who must have had a title of his own—made little cooing sounds as if equally entertained by it all.

Lord Aldric looked wearily annoyed with the situation. Henri was still studying Nicolette. It seemed nearly all he did when they were together.

"I will hold to my determination to be partnered with my wife in the coming competition." Lord Jonquil eyed his friends. "Which means you have to decide whether it is safer to antagonize M. and Mme Beaulieu or M. and Mme Fortier."

Without hesitating, Nicolette, Céleste, and Henri all answered, "Beaulieu."

The three of them exchanged glances that were, at first, startled but quickly shifted to the knowing look one offers to people who have a misery in common. Nicolette's family could be imperious and, at times, difficult, but though Jean-François did not often inflict sorrows on his sister, Nicolette knew he was capable of it.

Lord Aldric's expression softened a little, something she suspected he didn't allow often. "I'll make a team with Mlle Fortier if it'll save us all a headache."

"*Quelle galanterie,*" Céleste muttered.

While the offer had, perhaps, been ungallantly worded, Nicolette thought her friend was being a bit ungenerous. It was clear Lord Aldric wanted nothing to do with either of their family's matchmaking schemes. Having been the focus of such efforts herself on many occasions, Nicolette could appreciate his frustration.

She stepped over to where Henri stood since the two of them had yet to find a partner. "I feel it my duty to declare once again," she said to him, "I haven't the first idea how to play this game."

"It matters little, as Lucas will probably cheat." The shrug he offered her was so very French. It identified the land of his birth and upbringing as surely as any document ever could.

His comment earned him a scoff from Lord Jonquil, but one offered good-naturedly.

Nicolette was beginning to understand these friends. They enjoyed ruffling each other's feathers. More than that, they thoroughly liked each other. If not for Céleste, Nicolette wouldn't have the first idea what having a true friend was like. Far too many of the people she interacted with in Paris hid themselves behind facades. Prestige held greater importance than sincere connection in the social marketplace of France.

She hadn't realized until now that she had always expected something of that to drop away as she and Pierre had come to know each other better. Instead, she'd discovered there had been nothing else to him, that he had never intended for *their* connection to be any more genuine and authentic than the ones she now spent every minute of every social soiree discouraging.

That she couldn't imagine Pierre participating in a lighthearted game of lawn bowls made her even more determined to learn to play and enjoy the undertaking as much as possible.

She turned to Henri once more. "How do I play?"

He quickly explained the game to her in French, for which she was grateful. She likely could have comprehended had instructions been offered in English, Italian, Spanish, Portuguese, or German, but receiving the explanation in French made the game that much easier and quicker to grasp.

More than that, there was something surprisingly comforting in the sound of his voice speaking French. She'd felt it the day before in the book room during the portion of their conversation that had occurred in French. She'd felt it in the drawing room upon first arriving at Norwood Manor.

He'd been kind to her in Paris three years earlier, listening to her as she'd spoken of the things she had been thinking about and pondering on. Her memories of those few weeks were vague, but *that* she remembered. He had listened to her and shown her compassion. And he had never mocked or belittled her. It was likely why hearing his voice now was so comforting despite his suspicious behavior.

The game of bowls began casually enough, with each team taking their turns.

Lord and Lady Jonquil passed their infant son between themselves while they made their throws. Nicolette found them distracting. Her parents had not been truly unhappy in their marriage, and she didn't think Sébastien and Gaëtane were unhappy either. But never before had she seen a marriage like these two had, where the couple seemed to genuinely, deeply, and fully love each other. They clearly took delight in simply being together. What would that be like?

Pierre had all but laughed at her when she'd expressed frustration over his seeming indifference to her. "Indifference is better than what most have," he had said.

Indifference *was* better than hatred, she supposed. But it was still far from ideal. That had been one of many conversations that had made her question what she had done in accepting his proposal. On the surface, he'd seemed the perfect choice for a husband. He'd met every requirement a lady was meant to search out, and yet, by the time he had run off, she'd known that he was quite possibly the last person on earth with whom she could ever build a happy life.

"Hold off our opponents a moment, Julia," Lord Jonquil declared. "I see two additional players I wish to have join our team." And then he ran off.

"Four against two would be unfair," Lord Aldric called after him.

Henri met Nicolette's eyes. With a humorous raise of his brow, he said, "I told you he would cheat."

"At this point, he has to," she answered. "We are winning."

A smile spread across Henri's features. It was a nice change from the suspicious frown he usually wore. Besides, he had a very nice smile.

Lord Jonquil returned a moment later with Adèle held on his hip and his free hand holding Lord Draycott's, Lord and Lady Mowbary's five-year-old son. Lord Jonquil was grinning as if he had secured the participation of the world's finest bowls players. Lady Jonquil watched her husband's approach with equal parts amusement and adoration.

Nicolette turned to Henri. "Do you suppose he truly means to invite the children to play on his and Lady Jonquil's team?"

"I haven't the least doubt," Henri said. "Lucas has a tender place in his heart for children. He and Julia both lost all their siblings at far too young an age. I think it has made them ever more aware of the needs of lonely children and children who are longing to feel included."

She'd known a few people like that in Paris. "Is this a common thing in England, children joining in activities with the adults?"

The smile he'd worn a moment earlier slipped into a look of disapproving evaluation. "Do you dislike that they are being included?"

"Of course not." She could feel her hackles rising. "I have never before visited this country, and I do not know what is common and what is exceptional. If I had realized you would assume I had unkind intentions, I would have kept the question to myself." The retort emerged more stinging than she'd intended. With a twinge of regret, she could see that it had hit its mark.

"Forgive me," he said quietly. "I don't always know what to—You aren't—" He took a quick, and from the sound of it, frustrated breath. "Forgive me. I was wrong to assume you had a less-than-kind motive."

"And I was uncharitable in my swift accusation," she said. "I apologize."

Some of the displeasure in his expression eased. "How fortunate for us that we are both so remarkably humble and forgiving. Less perfect people would likely struggle to resume their game of bowls after a misunderstanding."

Had he been this amusing before? She didn't remember that about him, but she was pleased to see it now. She gladly joined in. "Is it your perfect humility that gained you your saintly sobriquet?"

"Naturally," he said with a courtly bow.

She laughed and was gifted another glimpse of his lovely smile. "I truly am sorry I assumed the worst in your question."

The friendliness in his eyes remained. "And I in yours."

Pierre had never apologized for anything. She was well rid of him; she had no doubts on that score. But he'd dealt such a blow to her faith in her own judgment that even *La Tapisserie's* confidence in her hadn't proven enough to truly overcome that.

The game of bowls resumed. Lord and Lady Jonquil were thoroughly diverting themselves with the undertaking. And due to that couple's joyful attention, Adèle and Lord Draycott were gleefully participating. Even little Philip, though far too young to understand what was happening, giggled and cooed and flailed his arms in response to his father's enthusiasm. Nicolette found herself thoroughly enjoying the afternoon. Henri was kind and fun. He participated in the game with real pleasure and gave every indication of being pleased with her company. For the first time in two years, she lowered her guard a little.

# Chapter Seven

OVER THE PAST TWO YEARS, Nicolette had developed an impressive ability to get in and out of places quickly, often in possession of things no one knew she had obtained, sometimes physical and sometimes informational. The skill was serving her well that evening. The ladies had gathered in the drawing room while the gentlemen were having their after-dinner port. This was Nicolette's best opportunity to sneak into the book room to pursue the mystery weighing on her almost as much as her as-yet-unseen-to *La Tapisserie* mission.

It was in this room that Henri had been working on whatever he had been so desperate to hide from her. The hastily tucked away parchment had clearly been written on, though she'd not been able to make out what the words were. She had little confidence his traveling desk, into which he had secreted the papers, would still be in the book room, but she thought it worth searching for.

For Céleste's sake, she hoped to discover the papers in question were nothing more than a list of items Henri's valet needed to obtain from the various shops in the nearby village. Why Henri would be so determined to keep her from seeing such an innocuous thing, she didn't know. Perhaps they were items of a more personal nature, smallclothes or instructions for the local apothecary on a tonic to address intestinal distress, or something equally embarrassing. The Henri she'd known in Paris had been quiet and rather private, enough that a list of underthings in full display of a lady would prove rather mortifying.

*Oh, please, let it be something like that.*

She made a quick search of the desk where Henri had been sitting. The traveling desk was not atop it as it had been. She made a circuit of the book room, her eyes flitting over shelf after shelf in search of a gap in the books or a spot where a portable writing desk might be tucked away. The bottom half of the shelving on the wall opposite the book room door was drawers. She pulled open each one and combed through it. Nothing helpful.

"*Qu'est-ce que tu cherches?*"

She spun about at the unexpected voice asking her what she was looking for.

Henri himself stood in the doorway. His expression was not accusatory. In fact, if she weren't already a bit suspicious of him, she would have fully believed he was asking because he wished to be of assistance. That was the sort of gentleman he'd seemed to be in Paris. But she'd been wrong about people before.

"I am unfamiliar with the area," she said. "I thought perhaps there was a map or atlas detailing this part of the country."

"Are you planning a journey?"

She couldn't tell if he was teasing, asking sincerely, or digging for information. Nicolette held a position of importance and trust in *La Tapisserie*. She worked very hard to show herself worthy of that faith. In this moment, doing so meant redirecting any suspicions he might have.

"I like maps. They are an interesting way of learning about a place." It was entirely true. She'd always had an interest in maps.

Henri stepped into the book room fully. "I have made a search of these shelves, but as I was not in search of an atlas, I cannot say with any certainty if there is one or not." His eyes began scanning the shelves again. It seemed he was simply hoping to help.

"If you weren't looking for an atlas during your earlier perusal, what was it you were searching the shelves for?" she asked.

"Nothing that would interest you, I suspect."

"I have a wide range of interests," she said.

He looked at her again, brow drawn, eyes searching. "I remember that yours was a very curious mind, always sorting out questions, eager to learn and discover new things." He seemed to remember her better than she remembered him.

"You were kind to me," she acknowledged. "I appreciated that, as I have sometimes struggled to make friends."

His eyes met hers once more. "You did seem a little lonely."

That very simple observation, spoken as it was with compassion but not pity, sent a pinprick of warmth to her heart. She'd not felt anything like that in years. She had guarded herself so wholly for so long that she'd almost forgotten how it felt to be seen. Toward the end with Pierre she'd been desperate not to draw notice. Now, as part of *La Tapisserie*, her safety often depended on disappearing into the crowd. Being noticed, and noticed kindly, was . . . nice.

"I don't imagine you are often lonely," she said, looking over another shelf of books. "Not with friends like the Gents. I found myself today wondering what it would be like to have friends like them."

"You and Céleste are friends," he said.

"Yes, and that means the very world to me. But I can with both honesty and a touch of humiliation admit that she's the first friend I've had since I was a child." Why in the world was she admitting so much to him, who she knew was keeping a secret of some sort? Perhaps because she kept secrets more significant than most anyone would guess, and she knew that things were not always as they seemed.

"When I arrived in England, I knew no one here." His face took on a look of remembered sadness. "I could read English quite easily, but I didn't speak the language overly well. My father had a severe dislike of his family speaking English, and I'd had very little practice. I felt certain I would never make friends, as the attempts I did make to speak to the people here in their own language were often met with ridicule. Many people whom I knew spoke French refused to speak with me."

She leaned against the bookcase, turning to face him. "Why did you stay in such a hostile place?"

"Because the hostilities amongst strangers in my new home were far more endurable than the hostilities amongst my family in my homeland." Henri stepped a bit away, searching the next set of shelves. "Were he still among the living, my father would have a great deal to say about me no longer thinking of France as home. My home*land*, yes. The place of my birth, the place where I knew my mother, the place that holds my sister and my niece and the memory of better times with my brother. But England has felt like home from the moment the Gents embraced me as one of their own. Someday, I'll claim my own corner of it. A home of my own. Here."

A Frenchman whose loyalties had shifted. Considering they were facing a future likely to be touched by revolution, that was not an insignificant discovery.

"I can look for an atlas another day," she said, pushing away from the shelves and stepping toward the door. "I suspect Lord and Lady Mowbary will be particularly difficult if we are late for the night's activities."

"That is actually why I came looking for you," Henri said.

He had her attention.

"We are to undertake vignettes tonight, and I suspect that your brother and sister-in-law and my brother and sister-in-law are determined to see to it that you and Céleste are both required to participate with—"

"Lord Aldric?" Nicolette made her guess with a generous degree of dryness.

Henri smiled a bit. "He will circumvent their efforts as much as possible, but he is also too well-mannered to cause embarrassment to guests of his family. I felt I ought to warn you of the schemes in the drawing room this evening so you don't arrive there unawares."

This gentleman was so difficult to fully evaluate. Secrets and shifted loyalties but also consideration and thoughtfulness. Who was he truly?

She forced herself to continue on with the topic he was discussing. She managed most of her information gathering through repeated observation. She'd not be permitted the chance if she made herself disagreeable.

"Sébastien and Gaëtane have wanted to see me engaged again these past two years. They seem to be trying to manage the thing here. They may very well be insufferable about it, but they will not be successful. We would do well to focus *our* efforts on Céleste. She is stubborn and strong-willed and knows precisely what Jean-François and Marguerite are attempting to do, but your family can be more . . ." She searched for the right word. He would agree with her assessment, but she still did not wish to speak overly harsh of his family.

"More *coercive* than yours?" Henri supplied a much more charitable description than Céleste likely would have.

Nicolette nodded. "While I don't think they will push Céleste into a match in the end, I do think Jean-François and Marguerite are capable of causing misery in their attempts to sway her."

"That is one of the reasons I invited her to visit me without them. Both of us would appreciate time together away from—" His eyes closed for the briefest of moments as he took a quick breath. "I shouldn't speak ill of people."

He didn't sound like a gentleman undertaking suspicious activities. And yet, she'd seen him behave in undeniably suspicious ways.

"Perhaps between the two of us, we can make certain one or the other of us is with Céleste at nearly all times," she suggested. "That would prevent some of the scheming." Though it would make Nicolette's *La Tapisserie* assignment more difficult to complete.

Henri shook his head slightly. "I don't know that it would stop their attempts, but it might reduce the impression of success."

Nicolette disliked feeling helpless to prevent misery. She'd known enough of her own. "We might have an easier time thwarting our families' schemes if we were countering only one instead of two."

"And while it would be easier if it were *your* family we were countering," Henri said, "I suspect, of the two, the Fortiers are the ones least likely to give up the chase."

There was inarguable truth in that, and it gave her a thread to tug at. "If my family thought I had inclinations elsewhere, they might suspend their efforts in order to see if anything came of my own."

"Do you mean to pretend an interest in one of the Gents?" Henri sorted her meaning quickly. "Or perhaps Lord Grenton's heir? He is a little younger than you are but of an eligible age."

That strategy could work. "I can't make a show of pretended interest in someone I haven't met yet."

"I wouldn't suggest asking Niles, the one we call Puppy, to be your focus on this. He's not a weak person by any means, but I think your family might view him that way and would decide to simply push you in another direction. And while Digby would likely enjoy this endlessly, he has a tendency to take dramatization to ridiculous heights, and your family might very well see through it."

"A shame, that," Nicolette said. "He strikes me as being rather exceptionally intelligent and one who never fails to notice a detail little or great."

"Most people don't notice anything about him other than his shockingly handsome face and unparalleled fashion sense."

"His goal, no doubt." She knew an intentionally emphasized façade when she saw one. "If not Mr. Greenberry or Mr. Layton, then what other options do we have?"

"Pretending an interest in Lord Aldric wouldn't accomplish your aim at all," Henri said. "Kester and Lucas are both married, so unless your strategy is to create a scandal, feigning an interest in either of them is not likely to be fruitful." He began pacing a bit, thinking out loud. She needed to add "logical" and "thorough" to her growing list of his character traits. "The Haddingtons have a son about the same age as Lord Yesley—Grenton's heir—but again, we have the difficulty of your not having met him yet."

An idea flashed through her mind, one that was just ridiculous enough to be perfect. One that would allow her to avoid her family's schemes while learning more about any possible ones Henri was undertaking, while also helping Céleste escape her family's efforts. "What if you and I began spending time together?" she suggested. "Not enough that anyone would assume we had come to an understanding but just enough for my family to take a step back in case something came of it? It might even confuse your family enough that they would be distracted from their schemes for Céleste. And with us already spending time together, it would be easy to join forces on Céleste's behalf."

She would not have been the least surprised if he'd hemmed and hawed or looked a bit thunderous. Most gentlemen didn't hesitate to express displeasure at being asked to undertake something not of their proposing. But he did none of those things. Instead, he blushed. Deeply.

"Your brother is unlikely to be pleased with the possibility that you had an interest in me," Henri said. "He might simply redouble his efforts in Aldric's direction."

Sébastien had been quite pleased when Pierre had courted her, and Henri and the Fortier family had far higher standing in French society than the Léandres ever would. "I believe you underestimate yourself, M. Fortier."

He shook his head. "I believe you *over*estimate my suitability, Mlle Beaulieu."

"Nonsense. What we need is a distraction, not an actual commitment. We can feign interest, however vague, for the weeks we will both be at this house party, can we not?"

Embarrassment flitted over his face, but she also saw determination.

"If doing so will help Céleste, I will do my very best," he said.

As quickly as that, she had a means of spying on a gentleman who might not need to be spied on and thwarting her family, who very much needed to be thwarted, and she had added to her mission a complication she had not foreseen.

# Chapter Eight

Engaged again.

*Again.*

Nicolette had said her family was anxious to see her engaged *again.* Henri remembered with clarity that when he had met her in Paris three years earlier, she and Céleste had both indicated that Nicolette had never been engaged, nor come close to it, despite having had many gentlemen clamoring for her attention. Céleste hadn't mentioned in any of her letters since then that Nicolette was engaged or had been. And yet, Nicolette had made the declaration so casually and with such ease that Henri didn't for a moment think she had been jesting or overstating the situation.

A broken engagement was a rare thing. In both France and England, engagements were socially significant and, to an extent, legally binding. There were ramifications for ending one. It was *possible* for a couple to end a betrothal, but it hardly ever happened.

Had her fiancé died, perhaps? Had the engagement been secret and upon learning of it, one or both of their families had objected enough to bring it to an end?

Upon realizing that Nicolette did not remember Henri's tendre for her nor his declaration of love, he had assumed that would be the most significant mystery attached to her. But she was proving an endless mystery.

She had an engagement no one spoke of. She watched everyone very closely, as if searching out what secrets they might be harboring. And despite her insistence that she had simply been on the hunt for an atlas, he knew that was not the whole truth. A lady with her social prowess and understanding of convention was unlikely to step away from the ladies in the drawing room in the midst of an evening's activities in pursuit of a casually wished-for map. And the way she had been searching through papers told him a book was not at all what she'd hoped to find.

Henri did not like to think himself a suspicious-minded person, but Nicolette Beaulieu was being less than forthright, and that worried him. She was important to Céleste. If Nicolette was untrustworthy . . .

But he shook his head even as the thought flitted through his mind. He didn't actually think she was duplicitous. Perhaps he was being misled by the pull he still felt for her. Perhaps this was simply more of his disinclination to think ill of people.

They arrived in the drawing room. Though their entrance was not made loudly or with any degree of theatrics, it did catch the notice of both their families. They weren't going to have much difficulty setting into motion the plan they had concocted. He wanted to be confident the scheme would prove successful enough to outweigh the discomfort he anticipated. His sister needed him. He would not abandon her again.

He and Nicolette stopped where Céleste stood, and Céleste hooked her arms through each of theirs. "Excellent timing. We are to begin vignettes at any moment."

"Has our hostess predetermined who will comprise the various teams?" Nicolette asked.

Céleste shook her head. "I suspect she has realized that two of her distinguished families have schemes in which she does not wish to interfere or choose sides."

Henri offered her an apologetic look. "I do wish Jean-François and Marguerite hadn't been added to the guest list. We would have had such a lovely time here, just the two of us."

"But then Adèle wouldn't be here," Céleste said. "I suspect Lord and Lady Jonquil aren't the only ones who would be sad not to have her company."

Henri's heart dropped a little at the thought. "I do adore that child, and she is only just beginning to come to know her *tonton* Henri."

"Does she talk to you much?" Céleste asked.

"A little."

She squeezed his arm with hers. "That she is speaking to you at all on such short acquaintance is a remarkable thing. She is very, very quiet."

"And I am very, very patient."

Nicolette leaned forward enough to address him from Céleste's other side. "At the moment, you are also being very, very disruptive."

"Our apologies," Céleste whispered with a poorly hidden grin.

Lady Mowbary was in the midst of offering instructions to the people in the room on how to undertake the game. Henri thought that a bit unnecessary, as the parlor game was commonly played in England and in France. A subject matter would be chosen for each team, who would then spend time deciding how they meant to portray it. These were not theatricals, where they would act out the clues they had been given. Rather, the teams were meant to create an arrangement of people in whatever pose they chose that would put the onlookers in mind of the thing they were meant to guess.

No sooner had Lady Mowbary finished her explanation than Sébastien Beaulieu and Jean-François quite loudly and in near unison, though using slightly different wording, firmly *suggested* Lord Aldric join the grouping already forming around Céleste and Nicolette, a group that thus far consisted of the two ladies and Henri. There was no doubt the two brothers' enthusiasm had absolutely nothing to do with a desire to allow Henri to play alongside one of his closest friends.

While the grouping would serve to add a bit of weight to the budding interest all were meant to see between Nicolette and Henri, it would also tend to add weight to any arguments that might be made regarding Aldric's interest in Céleste and vice versa.

Time for a bit of strategy, something that was generally Aldric's forte.

"Puppy." Henri motioned Niles over to where they stood, having spoken loudly enough for him to hear but not so loud as to be overheard by the entire gathering. "Would you be willing to endure a bit of misery for the benefit of one of the Gents?"

"Far be it from me to refuse a request from our Archbishop." Niles was what Stanley had always termed a "bene cove," a good-natured sort, up for a lark, a great addition to any bit of mischief.

"Mlle Beaulieu and my sister are finding themselves the unwitting targets of our families' matrimonial aims, with Aldric being the unwitting victim. Would you join our group for the vignettes? The uneven numbers will help, I think."

Niles nodded without hesitation. A *bene cove*, indeed.

Henri turned to Aldric. "Niles will make five in our group. I think that an excellent number."

Aldric didn't need the reasoning explained. With his voice firm and author-itative enough to get the message across to all who were present, he told Lady Mowbary, "The five of us will make a group. Let us know what it is we are to portray, and we will see to it."

He managed just enough enthusiasm, whether feigned or not, to avoid insulting his hostess. There was no reference to the group as a whole that might allow the schemers any chance to interfere in the arrangements. And his voice contained enough of a businesslike manner to cure anyone of any thought they might have that he was so enamored of the opportunity to spend time with either of the young ladies that he wished to prolong the activity.

Aldric was the master strategist.

Around the room, other groups formed, and Lord Mowbary handed them slips of paper containing their assignments for the evening. Upon reaching their group, Mowbary hesitated. Aldric had his hand extended to receive the assignment, but Mowbary wouldn't offer even this minimal bit of deference to his younger brother.

Henri didn't move to accept the paper. Niles folded his arms across his chest, watching Mowbary with silent determination. Mowbary at last gave Aldric the paper with no effort to disguise his annoyance.

Without acknowledging the unspoken insult, Aldric turned to the group, unfolded the parchment, and read what was written there. "'The Franklin's Tale,' from Chaucer's *The Canterbury Tales*."

"I do not know what this is," Nicolette said. That she immediately looked to Henri for explanation sped his heart up a bit until he remembered that her reasons were likely not the least bit a reflection on him personally. She was better acquainted with him than the other two gentlemen. Their assigned topic was an English reference, and of Henri and Céleste, he was most likely to know what was being referred to. And she was meant to pretend as though she had a preference for him.

It was a lowering realization, but between tiptoeing around his father's disapproval and, in happier times, undertaking mischievous larks with the Gents, he had become something of an adept actor.

"'The Franklin's Tale' involves two lovers whose romance is sent into upheaval by the interference of another. It is relatively well-known amongst the English."

"And Henri is even more familiar with it than the rest of us," Lord Aldric said. "His specialty is poetry, but he is well-read in other areas of literature as well."

Nicolette looked to Henri once more, the confusion that remained in her expression taking on an edge of surprise as well. "Are you a poet?"

He didn't think they'd discussed this in Paris. Which, when he thought back on it, was a bit odd. He had fully imagined building a life with a young lady he hadn't even told about this significant bit of who he was.

"Poetry was the focus of my study at Cambridge University," he told her.

"I did not realize there were courses in French poetry at English universities."

Ice shot through his lungs. His mind filled with the memory of his father's voice, the anger and disdain with which he'd spat back "*English* poetry?" He'd disapproved of poetry as a course of study, but pursuing it in a language his father had forbidden to be spoken at home had been reason for absolute disgust. "While they do offer some courses in French literature, my studies focused on English poetry," Henri said quietly.

"I would wager you were the only Frenchman with that focus."

"You would win that wager," Lord Aldric said.

Nicolette was studying him. Hers was not an air of disapproval, which was surprising.

"I think our wisest course of action for this evening's undertaking is to choose a moment in the tale that will be familiar even to those with a more casual knowledge of it." Henri looked to Niles and Aldric. "You both are somewhat familiar with 'The Franklin's Tale.' What is the moment you think of when your mind turns to the story?"

Niles proved the first to answer, which was uncommon for him. "The disappearing rocks."

Aldric nodded his agreement.

"It sounds as though that ought to be the scene we depict," Nicolette said.

Céleste was not truly a quiet person, but she wasn't saying much. Henri studied her as they began plotting how to create their scene. She looked utterly annoyed.

He pulled her a bit aside whilst Niles and Nicolette were obtaining items to complete their scene. "You're upset."

"I'm frustrated with our brother. I can excuse Marguerite; she has not known me as long. But"—she lowered her voice—"Jean-François is growing increasingly like our father. I held out some hope that he would prove more similar to our mother. She was far from perfect, but she . . . She didn't make me wish I weren't part of this family."

Henri put his arm around Céleste's shoulders, giving her a brotherly hug. He wouldn't offer any empty platitudes, as there was no way of knowing if everything would in fact turn out for the best or any of the other things people tend to say to those who are struggling. "Nicolette and I have hatched a scheme of our own." He kept his voice to a whisper and spoke to her in English, knowing Jean-François, Marguerite, and even Sébastien and Gaëtane weren't as proficient in the language as he and Céleste were. "We think with a bit of playacting, we can redirect the Beaulieu's focus away from their ideas about Nicolette and Aldric, and we can offer *you* a bit of a buffer from Jean-François and Marguerite's efforts."

"Could you not simply toss Lord Aldric into a traveling carriage and leave him somewhere in—" Her brow drew. "What is the remotest part of this kingdom you can think of?"

Henri laughed silently. "I will not send my dearest friend off into oblivion, *Abeille*, even for you."

"Perhaps by the end of his house party, you will change your mind. He, after all, could put an end to this misery with a single sentence. I think it terribly ungallant of him that he is leaving Nicolette and I to attempt to dance around it."

Aldric, who was not standing terribly far distant, met Henri's eye. He had most certainly overheard Céleste's complaints. Henri hated feeling as though he were in the middle of a battle, but that felt like precisely what was about to descend upon him. Aldric knew perfectly well the misery that awaited him if he antagonized his brother and, therefore, would go to great lengths to be as neutral as possible in anything involving the guests his brother valued.

Céleste, knowing the amount of effort she would have to expend to thwart Jean-François, would be understandably frustrated with Aldric for not helping more directly in her time of distress.

Henri lowered his voice to little more than a whisper. "Aldric is in an impossible situation. His father is about as kind and loving as ours was. And his relationship with his brother is not terribly unlike ours with Jean-François. Worse in some ways. Keeping the peace with his family while also avoiding an unwanted match is a balancing act I don't think most people could manage."

"You are acknowledging that he is not bothering to hide his annoyance while simultaneously asking me to hide mine?" Enough humor sparkled in her eyes to reassure Henri that his sister wasn't entirely unwilling to give Aldric some benefit of the doubt.

"I'm saying that everyone enduring this is a little miserable, so maybe we can all try to be patient."

She reached up and patted his cheek. Their mother used to do that. Henri missed it. "Oh, *mon frère*. You make me realize what I ought to have done."

"And what is that?"

"Kidnapped Adèle and come here without the rest of them."

His darling Céleste was good for his heart. As difficult as it had been to keep his poetic efforts a secret, doing so had kept his sister in his life. And it was now also allowing him to be part of Adèle's life. How could he have chosen any different? The vignette planning continued. It was determined in the Franklin's Tale group that it was best if Aldric did not portray Arveragus, the romantic hero of the piece, as their choices to play Dorigen, the heroine, were both ladies whom they were attempting to prevent anyone in the gathering from assuming Aldric took an interest in. When Henri suggested that Niles might play the role, he colored up so deeply and so quickly that no one had the heart to continue on with that, despite the fact that it would have been vastly entertaining. That left only Henri. But should Céleste portray the love interest, those who were looking on would assume the connection between the characters they were meant to portray was that of brother and sister.

The result was that Henri and Nicolette were cast in the roles of the much beleaguered lovers. It played into the scheme they had concocted. It also created a great deal of discomfort for him, bringing firmly to mind the dream he'd once had of love between himself and Nicolette. Still, for the sake of both the game and his sister's ability to be a little less miserable during this gathering, he agreed.

After over an hour committed to the planning and practicing of their vignettes, all the houseguests returned to the drawing room, ready to see what each group had concocted. One team undertook *Romeo and Juliet*, featuring Lucas's Romeo trying very hard not to laugh as he struck a loving pose beneath the balcony where Julia's Juliet stood, tears rolling from her eyes as she, too, attempted not to dissolve into laughter. They were the happiest couple Henri had ever met, a fact made even more amazing when one understood how difficult the beginning of their marriage had been.

Another team featured Lady Mowbary as Grendel's mother and Jean-François as a very annoyed Beowulf. Whether the displeasure came from the game or the very English nature of the work they were portraying, Henri couldn't say. His father's disapproval of English literature and the English language was not *entirely* embraced by his brother. Henri wished their father's disapproval of *him* was embraced a little less by Jean-François.

Following portrayals of *Candide* and then Daphne and Apollo of Greek myth, Henri's group was called forward to present their vignette.

They assumed positions previously determined, the items gathered and bits of costume utilized in precisely the way that had been decided upon. Céleste and Niles were charged with being the disappearing rocks, a comical task when all they'd managed to find to assist their portrayal were small pebbles from the drive held in each hand. Céleste could sometimes grow embarrassed when she felt people would see her as foolish, but Niles's lighthearted enthusiasm and easy and friendly nature brought a feeling of camaraderie to the ridiculous moment. Céleste played her role with every indication of amusement and no signs of true embarrassment.

Henri hoped the silliness of the moment would prove enjoyable for Nicolette as well. The two of them were required to embrace and gaze deeply into each other's eyes. Three years earlier, Henri would have been delighted. Though he hadn't realized it at the time, Nicolette would have been oblivious to his enjoyment of the arrangement. He had no idea how she would respond now.

They took their place in front of the other guests, and Niles and Céleste held aloft their "disappearing rocks." Henri set his arms around Nicolette, loosely enough for her to assume her hand-to-forehead pose of theatrical suffering but tightly enough to keep her steady on her feet and to give the needed impression of devotion and love.

Guesses flew from the gathering. Henri met Nicolette's eyes. He had described them in his brief distraction the day before as pools of cerulean water. While they were indeed beautifully blue, standing as close to her as he was then, he could see they were darker than cerulean with flecks of green around the edges of her irises.

She still wore the same perfume she had in Paris, the same subtle but rich scent of jasmine. For three years, encountering that scent even for the briefest of moments had transported him back to his happier moments with her, the days when he'd believed *they* were falling in love. Over time, the experience had grown less painful and more nostalgic. Experiencing it now was pleasant again, warming, enjoyable.

Their gazes locked in the midst of the called-out guesses, and she smiled at him. His heart entirely ignored the fact that this was a game, their arrangement was an act, and their supposed connection was a scheme. That traitorous organ pounded in his chest, tapping out a delighted rhythm.

But there was something else in her eyes beyond the echo of her light smile. Her eyes spoke of loneliness. How well he knew how that felt. He'd spent so much of his life feeling alone.

"I think we are acting well our parts," he whispered.

"In the vignette?" She spoke as quietly as he had. "Or in our scheme?"

"Both."

Her smile grew. "We are proving a good team."

Henri struggled not to feel pitiful a good deal of the time. He seemed to have done something right. He'd lightened her mind a little.

This game they were playing, the one that stretched far beyond an evening's vignettes, might offer Céleste some respite from their brother's schemes, but he suspected he had set his feet on a path he knew all too well, one at the end of which his heart might very well be broken all over again.

# Chapter Nine

Henri discovered that little Adèle was very fond of flowers. He spent a good portion of the next morning walking with her through a meadow adjoining the Norwood Manor grounds, along the banks of the river Trent. Wildflowers had popped up with abandon, and she stopped and looked at every single one. She talked about them and asked him questions. The topic of flowers had opened a door to his very quiet little niece.

If only they'd held this gathering at Brier Hill, Lucas's estate in the north of England. He had a beautiful walled garden filled to overflowing with flowers in every imaginable variety, including the fleur-de-lis. There was debate in France as to which was the *exact* flower that had inspired the iconic symbol of France, but Lucas had in that garden a particular variety of iris that matched the shape precisely.

When visiting Brier Hill, Henri had often found himself in that garden, his gaze on those irises, his mind floating back to his homeland. He had told Nicolette rightly that he didn't truly think of France as his home any longer, but that did not mean he didn't still love the home of his birth or that he wasn't proud of his heritage. And seeing the symbol of France so beautifully represented in nature often made his heart long to return for a time. Did all who emigrated from home feel this same dual pull?

In a particularly lovely clearing within sight of the river Trent, Henri flicked open the blanket he had been carrying under one arm and sat on it with Adèle at his side. He'd also brought a small basket with a few things to eat, intending to treat his dear little *sauterelle* to a picnic. The day was fine, and the clouds provided relief from the sun without dropping the temperature too drastically. While Adèle nibbled at a small hand pie, he very carefully tied a ribbon around the haphazard bunch of wildflowers they had gathered during their walk.

"I like the blue ribbon on the flowers," Adèle said in French, pointing to the blooms he held.

"Beautiful flowers for my beautiful girl." Henri held them out to her, and she accepted them in the hand not holding her midday meal.

Adèle ate her hand pie without taking her eyes off the flowers she held. It was a refreshing thing, spending time with children: they took delight in simple things, reminding one of joys too often missed. Between bites, she told him what she liked about the flowers, smiling proudly when *Tonton* Henri agreed with her assessment. It was easy to feel like a hero when interacting with such a genuinely loving child.

But he was far from it in reality. He hadn't been present to ease the trials of home life for Jean-François and Céleste, which wasn't exactly the act of a heroic brother or an honorable gentleman.

Archbishop, saint among Gents. How wrong they all were about him.

He quickly glanced at Adèle, wanting to make certain his suddenly dampened spirits hadn't had the same effect on hers.

The little girl's hand had grown limp, her flowers threatening to slip free at any moment. Her eyelids were heavy, barely held open. She'd not entirely finished her meat pie, and it was on the verge of toppling from her hand as well. Poor dear was falling asleep.

"Lie down, *sauterelle*," he gently instructed.

"My flowers," she objected sleepily.

"They will be safe lying down as well." He set her bouquet on the blanket directly beside her, well within her sight. She let her little eyes close. She would be asleep soon enough.

He reached past her to take up the edge of the blanket and pulled it over her little frame, tucking her in comfortably. Then he pressed a little kiss to her soft cheek. "I love you, my little *sauterelle*."

By the time he'd repositioned himself, having slipped the remainder of her meat pie back into the small basket in which he had brought it, she was breathing heavily and slowly, her limbs relaxing entirely.

They were under the shade of a tree, and there was no reason to fear she would grow overly warm in the summer sun. He was grateful he thought to slip the blanket over her, as sometimes the shade could grow chill. Nearby, the river babbled. Wind-rustled leaves chattered in the trees. It was a tranquil scene.

Unfortunately, his mind was not so peaceful.

He pulled from his pocket two letters he had received earlier that day but had not yet had time to read. With Adèle sleeping soundly, this seemed a good moment to discover what had been sent to him.

The first was from his publisher.

*Mr. Fortier*

*We have, with pleasure, read the two poems you submitted and find them suitable for publication.*

Henri had noticed during his earliest correspondence with Mr. Murray that his communication was not effusive with praise, and Henri had, as a result, interpreted that as proof that his work was barely passable. The small success he'd known never stopped feeling like a delay of the inevitable and unavoidable failure. Lessons learned in childhood were often difficult to unlearn.

*As this volume is to include a third poem, I anxiously await the submission of your final offering. Upon receiving it, I will evaluate the viability of this project as a whole.*
*I anticipate hearing from you and do now remain*

*Ever,*
*Yours, etc.,*
*JM*

There was an undercurrent of frustration in the letter. The date by which Mr. Murray had indicated in his previous correspondence that the third poem needed to be submitted was only a month away. But Henri strongly suspected Mr. Murray hoped to receive it sooner and wasn't confident enough in him to be at ease on the matter until he had seen for himself what Henri had produced.

"And well he might be nervous," Henri muttered.

Henri's poetical attempts at describing the various properties he'd surveyed throughout the kingdom had proven shockingly uninteresting. And while he had momentarily let his mind wander toward the idea of a poem about Nicolette, he'd abandoned that rather quickly. He was not ready to explore the emotions tied to that confusing part of his life.

Their embrace the night before had been a bit of playacting, a representation of the characters in "The Franklin's Tale." But the way she'd smiled hadn't felt feigned. She had seemed comfortable, even pleased by their nearness. He wanted to believe the look in her eyes hadn't been part of the farse they were enacting to distract her family and that she truly was pleased to be partnered with him in this odd endeavor. But he'd been so painfully wrong about their connection three years ago. He no longer trusted his heart in the matter of Nicolette Beaulieu.

He returned his publisher's letter to his pocket once more and set his attention on the other missive he had received. Upon unfolding the parchment, he discovered it was a correspondence from a land agent he'd interacted with in London who knew he was on the search for a humble but comfortable home. Henri was under no delusions about his inability to *purchase* a house, but he hadn't yet abandoned hope that his income, reduced though it was, could allow him to *lease* a property.

> *Mr. Fortier,*
>
> *My attention has been drawn to a property in Cornwall that might be of interest to you. It is small and, unfortunately, not conveniently near a village, but the house is in good repair, and the lands include a home farm for your benefit.*

Céleste had declared in her frustration the night before that she wished Aldric would disappear to the far reaches of the kingdom. Cornwall was located at one of those far ends. It was also where Niles's family hailed from. Such a distant location would make traveling to Town or to the various Gents gatherings difficult. Niles managed it, but Niles hadn't Henri's financial limitations.

> *The terms of the lease are at the upper limit of what you indicated your income could sustain. I wish I could say that I have found a great many properties that were comfortably within your income, but I have not.*
> *Please advise as to your interest,*
>
> *Yours, etc.,*
> *R Castleton*

Jean-François had cut his income further since Henri's conversation with Mr. Castleton. If this property barely fit in the previous range, then Henri could not afford it now.

He folded the parchment and returned it to his pocket. Two letters. Two sources of worry. Was it any wonder he was struggling so much to write a poem? Poetry ought to convey feelings and experiences and emotion, but his life was in such turmoil, he hadn't the energy to toss himself into evaluating and experiencing even more.

He closed his eyes and simply breathed for a moment. He would find an answer. He promised himself he would. Father had called him a fool, a simpleton. Henri had taught himself not to believe that, not to carry that dagger in his heart. That, he had decided, was the closest thing to forgiveness he was likely to ever feel where his father was concerned.

"We too often wrongly think forgiveness looks like absolution," Stanley had once said. "But I think forgiveness is becoming the person the one who hurt us would have prevented us from being. Forgiveness is never about the one who inflicted the pain but rather is the gift we give ourselves: permission not to be the proof of their hateful prophecies."

Henri was working hard not to be the proof of his father's prophecies.

He opened his eyes once more, determined not to sink under the weight of these latest setbacks. Adèle was still sleeping. When she awoke, she would see the flowers tucked neatly beside her. He had sorted out how to give her that bit of happiness.

*You see, Father. I'm not useless. You were wrong about that.*

Into the quiet stillness of the moment came the sound of approaching footsteps. An approaching couple dressed as one would expect people of means and standing to attire themselves when out for a walk were following a small riverside path that would lead them very near where he sat. He didn't recognize them but guessed they were one of the significant local families.

He made a quick check that both his letters were tucked firmly out of sight before scrambling to his feet.

Once they were near enough for conversation, the gentleman dipped his head in acknowledgment. "Forgive us. We do not intend to disrupt your solitude. The river is a beautiful place to spend a bit of time."

"I could not agree more," Henri said. "My *petite nièce* is sleeping through the entire experience, *le doux enfant*."

The lady's eyes pulled wide with what looked like excitement. "*Monsieur, vous êtes français!*"

"I *am* French," he replied in his first tongue. "Either your instruction in French was excellent, or you are French as well."

"I grew up in Paris," she said, walking with her husband to where Henri stood.

"Then I would wager you are M. and Mme Beaumont," Henri said.

They indicated they were.

"We do not every day meet people in the neighborhood who are French," M. Beaumont said. "My parents were French, and taught me to love the land of my ancestors."

"Then we are doubly well met," Henri said. "For it is my great pleasure to inform you that there are, at this very moment, two families at Norwood Manor who have only just arrived from France."

Mme Beaumont smiled broadly. "We have heard from others in the neighborhood that Norwood Manor has a great many guests at the moment, but we have received no invitation to call, and neither has Lord Mowbary called on us. We have found ourselves uncertain how to proceed."

Once again, Mowbary had proven that the Duke of Hartley was horrendously misguided in thinking his eldest son was a more adept host than his younger son would be. Calling on the neighboring families was one of the most basic duties of a host, and Mowbary had neglected even that.

"If you have no objections or other obligations," Henri said, "I would be happy to walk with you to Norwood Manor so you might make the acquaintance of the guests there. M. and Mme Fortier and Mlle Fortier are in residence, as are M. and Mme Beaulieu and Mlle Beaulieu."

"The Paris Beaulieus?" Mme Beaumont pressed, eyes pulling wide. "Sébastien and Gaëtane, and Mlle Nicolette?"

"The very same," Henri said.

He had known when first hearing that his sister had made the acquaintance of Nicolette Beaulieu that the connection was a significant one. In Paris, he had discovered just how important Nicolette's family truly was. That Mme Beaumont, who had grown up in Paris but had not lived there in a few years, stood in such immediate awe at the mere mention of that family only reaffirmed how much standing the Beaulieus truly had.

*And I genuinely thought she would think me an acceptable choice for a suitor.*

"You will likely think me vain," Mme Beaumont said, "but if I am to make the acquaintance of the Beaulieus and the Fortiers, I should very much like to look as though I did not arrive from Paris on a farm wagon."

Henri smiled. "You look nothing of the sort, madame. But neither will I deny that there is something to be said for feeling one's best when making new friends."

"Do you suspect the Beaulieus and Fortiers would wish to be friends with us?" M. Beaumont seemed to doubt it.

"While I cannot speak for the entirety of both families, I can tell you that at least one member of the Fortier family finds himself deeply inclined to think very highly of you."

His meaning struck them quickly.

"You are M. Fortier?" Mme Beaumont asked, breathless.

"I am M. *Henri* Fortier, the younger son of the family. My older brother is here as well, with his wife." Henri motioned to the sleeping little girl. "This is their daughter, my niece."

Mme Beaumont grew flustered. "We have made such casual introductions. What you must think of us!"

"Allow me to offer some reassurance. I do know how very rigid we French can be about these things, but I've lived in England for thirteen years, amongst a group of well-respected gentlemen whom I have found to be far more graceful, forgiving, and openhearted than I would have expected. From them, I have learned that staid first impressions are not always the best ones."

M. Beaumont squeezed his wife's hand, raising it to his lips and pressing a quick kiss to her fingers. "You see, dearest. All will be well. Being in England, I know, is not your first choice, but the longer you are here, the more it will feel like home and the more you will meet people who are as kind and accepting as M. Henri Fortier has shown himself to be."

She did look a little relieved but still seemed embarrassed.

"In addition to the French families visiting Norwood Manor, Lord Aldric Benick, younger son of the Duke of Hartley, is in residence. Lord and Lady Jonquil and their son, Lord Fallowgill, are here. Mr. and Mrs. Barrington, whom you might not have met yet but who are people of very good standing in the *ton*, are also here. And Mr. Digby Layton is amongst the visitors as well."

A bit of color touched Mme Beaumont's face, a sure indication that she had seen Digby and was as impressed by his handsomeness as everyone was.

"Mr. Niles Greenberry, whom you also might not have met but who I assure you is as good a person as you are likely to ever meet, will also be most pleased to make your acquaintance."

"Wouldn't it be terribly presumptuous of us to visit when we've not actually been invited to do so and Lord Mowbary has not called on my husband?" Mme Beaumont asked.

"I am inviting you to call on *me*," Henri said. "We are acquainted, and we needn't explain precisely how we became so. I will happily undertake your introductions, so you needn't feel the least hesitation. Simply tell me what day and about what time is most convenient for you, and I will see to everything."

Mme Beaumont overflowed with gratitude at the invitation. Henri suspected she was lonely for her homeland.

It was decided that the Beaumonts would call the next day in the midafternoon. Henri assured them multiple times that all would be well, that they would be welcomed and accepted. They parted on good terms, and he suspected they were as excited to meet again the following day as he was. Céleste would enjoy knowing them, and they would offer his family and the Beaulieus a bit of a distraction from their schemes. And it would force Lord Mowbary, who viewed himself in terms of infallibility as host of the house party, to be introduced to an important neighbor by one of his guests because he had failed at such a rudimentary task.

As the Beaumonts resumed their walk along the Trent, Henri sat back down on the blanket. Adèle still slept soundly.

Perhaps in time he might find a bit of property in this area, near enough to the Beaumonts that he would have a pleasant reminder of France, and they would have someone with whom they could converse in French. But the thought was immediately subdued by the intrusion of reality.

He couldn't imagine spending the rest of his life wandering, with no place to truly call his home, but what hope was there of his path changing now?

Proof of his father's prophecies.

Heaven help him.

# Chapter Ten

U PON RECEIVING AN INTRIGUINGLY WORDED summons from a servant she suspected was a valet to one of the Gents, Nicolette made her way to the drawing room. The morning had been a quiet one, with most everyone choosing to spend time on their own. Henri had disappeared for several hours, which had at first raised her suspicions, but she had later learned that he'd taken his niece for a walk.

The drawing room was busy when Nicolette arrived there. All of the Gents were present, as were Lady Jonquil and Mrs. Barrington. Céleste had been summoned as well.

Though Nicolette did not know Lady Jonquil well yet, she felt she was not being overly forward in addressing her directly. "Have you any idea why we have been called here?"

Amusement flitted through the lady's eyes. "My husband has concocted an afternoon's diversion. Once the idea lodged itself in his mind, he could think of little else."

"Is this typical for him?"

Lady Jonquil smiled, building on the more subtle enjoyment that had been in her expression a moment earlier. "That mind of his seems to be thinking of dozens upon dozens of things at once. But when one of those ideas strikes him as particularly enjoyable or helpful, he moves heaven and earth to see it happen."

He would be an interesting person to know better. "I am excitedly anxious to discover what he has moved heaven and earth for this time."

Lady Jonquil's smile grew to a grin of absolute adoration. "As am I."

Lord Jonquil stood in front of the group. "Now that we are all gathered, I can tell you the brilliant idea I've had."

"Nothing strikes greater fear into the heart than Lucas declaring he's had a brilliant idea," Mr. Layton said.

Nicolette glanced at Lady Jonquil.

"There is truth to that," the lady said. "Some of his ideas have involved stealing horses and breaking into the homes of influential people in London." The declaration might have been horrifying if not for the laugh underneath it.

"Do all the Gents participate in these schemes?"

"From what I understand, they do."

"Even M. Fortier?" She glanced at him, standing among friends. He did not appear the least concerned about what might be proposed. The man was such a contradiction. Her work with *La Tapisserie* told her not to ignore her suspicions.

"Even him. I suspect he keeps the Gents' questionably brilliant ideas from becoming too ridiculous. They call him Archbishop because he's kind and giving, but they will readily admit that while he is a deeply good man, he is also not exactly a saint."

*Not exactly a saint.* Which reminded her rather forcefully that she still didn't know what he had hidden from her in the book room shortly after her arrival at Norwood nor know why he sometimes watched her more closely than seemed warranted.

An interruption arrived in the form of Lord Mowbary, and he did not look best pleased. Though it was obvious to anyone at even a glance that Lord Jonquil was the one leading whatever this expedition was about to become, Lord Mowbary made directly for his brother. "And what precisely is the meaning of this, Aldric?" He motioned subtly at the group. "You know that *I* am the host of this house party, not *you*. Activities involving the guests should be, if not decided by me, at least approved of by me."

Lord Aldric stood stern, stony, and silent, his eyes not leaving his brother, but nothing in his posture indicated he was the least cowed by him.

It was Lord Jonquil who answered Lord Mowbary's complaint. "Lord Aldric is not the organizer of this afternoon's gathering; I am. When playing host, do you always insult your guests by demanding they do nothing without your approval, or is this a new approach you are trying?"

Lord Mowbary sputtered a bit—not in a theatrical way but in what appeared to be a very real struggle to think of a response.

He need not have bothered; Lord Jonquil continued on. "I have thought of something the young people at this gathering would enjoy. And as I have often heard it said that the Duke of Hartley is quite particular about the happiness of guests hosted at any of his estates, I did not for even a moment suspect that you would storm in here and demand that we cease enjoying ourselves." Lord Jonquil looked out over the group. With overdone sadness, he said, "My deepest apologies to you all. Lord Mowbary has declared that pleasant pastimes will not be permitted so long as he is the host of this gathering."

"That was not at all what I said," Lord Mowbary blustered, clearly trying to disavow his objections despite the abundance of witnesses.

"Then what is it you *are* saying?" Céleste, of all people, asked. "You have cast into doubt my understanding of English, for I thought Lord Jonquil's recounting of all you declared quite accurate."

For the first time, Lord Mowbary truly looked at them all. He must have realized his guests did not view him favorably. His expression turned softer, and when he spoke again, his tone was more conciliatory. "I, of course, did not wish to keep you from enjoying yourselves. Not all the guests seem to have realized that something is planned for this afternoon."

"Everyone I invited to participate is here," Lord Jonquil said.

"Plus one extra," Mr. Layton added dryly.

Lord Mowbary looked around for an ally. If he thought he would find one in his brother, anyone watching that gentleman's expression could have disabused him of the notion.

He caught the eye of Lady Jonquil. "You feel the activity being planned is an appropriate one, my lady?"

"I have never known my husband to undertake anything at a house party at which ladies were present that would not meet with the approval of anyone in possession of a reasonable and discerning evaluative ability."

Nicolette couldn't help but be impressed. This group knew precisely how to put their host in his place without offering direct insults.

Violet Barrington moved to stand beside Lady Jonquil and addressed Lord Mowbary with an innocent expression. "Surely you do not think a future earl would propose a scandalous activity at a gathering with such fine and respected people."

Assuming a look of innocent inquiry to match those of Lady Jonquil and Mrs. Barrington, Nicolette set her eyes on Lord Mowbary as well.

In what she suspected was a rare thing, Lord Mowbary relented without further argument and left them in peace.

"I don't know how you managed that, Lucas," Mr. Greenberry said. "He is not merely stubborn, but he also outranks you *and* is the host of this gathering."

"I simply put into practice what I learned from a very effective duke." Lord Jonquil met Lady Jonquil's eye, and they both grinned quite conspiratorially.

"Perhaps Lord Aldric might take a lesson from this duke," Céleste said. "He, after all, has to regularly interact with Lord Mowbary."

"I do not need tutoring from a child," Lord Aldric said.

"I am not a child," Céleste tossed back.

With exceptional patience, Lord Aldric answered, "The Duke of Kielder is approximately nine years old. Able to deliver a stinging set down and already rather daunting, but by every calculation, he *is* a child."

Nicolette looked to Lady Jonquil, who, upon noticing her gaze, nodded in confirmation. "I love that little duke, but even I must admit he is fearsome in a way that belies his tender years."

"Was Lord Aldric also a fearsome child?" Nicolette asked, motioning subtly toward Céleste's verbal sparring partner. "There is something daunting about him as well."

Lady Jonquil shrugged but in an English way. "I did not know him as a child. I didn't know any of the Gents as children other than Lucas."

"Then you likely do not know why it is Mr. Layton pretends to be less intelligent than he is or why Mr. Newberry carries himself as if he were inept yet showed himself to be rather agile during the lawn games."

She shook her head. "These friends are an endless puzzle."

"Now that we have rid ourselves of Mowbary"—Lord Jonquil's words carried over the low din of voices—"it is time for a bit of fun. We are undertaking a quest."

Everyone looked as intrigued as Nicolette felt.

"Five quests, to be precise." Lord Jonquil watched them all with a smile as wide as the Channel and eyes dancing with excitement. He pulled from his pocket five sealed notes. "I have enlisted my valet and Digby's to fashion five lists of four items apiece. We will divide into teams of two and part company in search of these items. There are two prizes at stake in addition to the enviable ability to crow about one's victory." He pulled from his other pocket two paper-tied bundles, small and oddly lumpy. "Swarkestone has a confectionery shop where I have obtained a few peppermint sweets and a bundle of anise sweets. The first team to return here to the drawing room in possession of all four items on their list will be declared one winner. The other victory will be granted to the team deemed to have met the demands of their list in the most innovative or creative way."

"As determined by whom?" Mr. Layton asked.

"By all of us," Lord Jonquil said. "And in the event that we cannot come to a consensus, we will enlist the aid of a neutral party, assuming we can find one."

As this was clearly meant to be a bit of a lark with so insignificant a prize to be won, Nicolette doubted there would be any difficulty on that score.

"And how are the teams to be determined?" Céleste asked. "Are we to draw lots, or are we meant to select our partners?"

Lord Jonquil offered a small dip of his head. "I believe we ought to allow the ladies to select their partners, and those gentlemen still needing a teammate can settle the rest among themselves." He looked to Nicolette. "Mlle Beaulieu, would you care to make the first selection?"

While neither her family nor Céleste's were participating in the "quest," Nicolette thought it best not to pair herself with Lord Aldric, as word of that arrangement would certainly reach their ears. That, however, was the exact reason why she knew whom she needed to choose. "M. Fortier, *s'il vous plaît.*"

Henri looked pleasantly surprised. He crossed to where she stood and offered a bow of acceptance.

Céleste was permitted to choose next, and she selected Lady Jonquil. Mrs. Barrington chose to be teamed with her husband. The remaining gentlemen paired off, Lord Jonquil with Mr. Layton, and Lord Aldric with Mr. Greenberry.

The questing lists were distributed at random, with Lord Jonquil assuring them all that he had not been made privy to the contents of any of them.

"Shall we see what our list contains?" Nicolette suggested.

Henri broke the wax seal and unfolded the parchment. Tipping it so she could see it as well, he read it quietly aloud.

"Something moving.
Something brown.
Something fleeting.
Something from Town."

It was both a simple list and a strange one. Something fleeting? Nicolette felt she had a good understanding of English, but she was still a little confused. To be fleeting meant to not last long or to be less than permanent. How did one fulfill that request? And "something moving"? Would not that thing be likely to utilize its mobility to render any efforts to bring it to the drawing room particularly difficult?

Henri appeared to be pondering but didn't seem truly concerned about the possibility of their success or failure. Nicolette liked seeing that. She didn't consider herself an overly competitive person, though she wasn't particularly fond of losing. Being teamed with someone who wouldn't grow angry or frustrated if victory was not within his grasp would make for a much more enjoyable afternoon than the alternative.

"At the moment," she said, "my mind is most confused by the first item. Were we to fetch one of the barn cats or a butterfly or something similar, keeping it with us until the time entries are to be shared would prove difficult."

He nodded. "We could approach it as something 'movable' rather than 'moving.' That would allow us to choose an inanimate object."

Around them, the other teams were rushing off in search of their items.

"It seems our best chance for winning one of Lord Jonquil's prizes is by being the most creative questers since we are already not proving the fastest."

Henri glanced at the emptying room but didn't seem the least upset. It was confirmation of what she had seen before, and she was glad of it.

"I have no objections to taking a more creative approach to this," he said. "I'm not certain which of the sweets we would win for being creative."

She shook her head. "As I've not eaten either one, I do not have a preference."

He studied her a moment, but not as if he considered her some abnormality or oddity. His look was one of genuine surprise softened by a friendliness that she greatly appreciated. "You've never had peppermint or anise sweets?"

"I have not, but I suspect you have."

"Peppermint sweets are Lucas's favorite, so all the Gents have it regularly when we're with him. Anise sweets were a favorite of Stanley's, and we indulge in it fairly often in memory of him."

She remembered him speaking of Stanley, the soldier who had died in the war with the American colonies fighting on the opposite side of that conflict from France.

"You must miss him terribly," she said.

Sadness flitted through his eyes, not the sort that overwhelmed but the sort defined by its familiarity. The war had ended nearly four years earlier. His loss was not as fresh as it had once been, but it was nevertheless still real.

She set her hand on his arm, hoping to offer a little comfort. "It is a fine thing that the Gents still choose to honor and remember him. And that they don't seem to hold his loss against *you* despite the fact that your countrymen fought in opposition to his."

He nodded. "The Gents are the very best sort of people. They try very hard to be fair-minded. And they are deeply loyal. And they have good hearts."

Fair-minded, loyal, admirable. Some of that she'd already known about Henri, remembering it in vague snatches from the time he'd spent in Paris.

Even only a handful of days into this house party, her good opinion of him was solidifying. But then, she had been wrong before.

"If we are to take a more creative approach," Henri said, his eyes on their list once more, "we ought to consider the more symbolic meaning of the term 'moving.'"

"I'm not aware of this other meaning."

Far from mocking her for this gap in her knowledge of a language he had studied so closely at university, he simply smiled in that soft way of his and explained. "Describing something as 'moving' could also mean that the thing stirs the emotions or changes one's viewpoint. It refers to moving the soul."

It was her turn to nod, this time with understanding. "'Moving to the soul.' It must also be easy to retrieve and not overly complicated to carry with us as we search out the other three things."

"For myself," he said, "my thoughts and emotions are stirred the easiest by poetry."

She ought to have guessed that about him, knowing his course of study at Cambridge. "I cannot say whether the book room boasts any poetry."

"I have a couple books of poetry in my bedchamber," Henri said.

"Then that, it seems, is where we ought to begin."

He quickly folded the parchment and put it in his coat pocket. Quite as naturally as if they did so all the time, he took her hand in his, and they rushed from the room in the direction of the grand staircase and up toward the wing of the house that contained the guest bedchambers. Not since she was a little girl had Nicolette run through a house, holding another person's hand. She found herself sorely tempted to giggle, something she never did.

They reached the door to his bedchamber. Feeling particularly ridiculous in the very best sort of way, she solemnly suggested, "I will stand guard at the door while you retrieve our treasure."

Oh, how she enjoyed the sound of his laughter. Perhaps it was that she so seldom inspired such authentic laughter in others. In the grand drawing rooms and parlors of Paris, she'd encountered a few gentlemen who had gone to great lengths to make ladies think they were quite wonderfully amusing, laughing at quips not nearly as funny as the response would make them seem. Henri's laughter came from true enjoyment. Perhaps that was why she was finding herself liking him as much as she was: he wasn't insincere like so many people were.

Henri had only been inside his bedchamber for a matter of moments when Lord Jonquil and Mr. Layton came hurrying down the corridor. She stepped out in front of them and held her hand out, palm facing them, and declared, "*Arrêtez!*"

Both clearly understood French, as they halted immediately and looked at her with both surprise and barely concealed laughter.

"Are you interfering in our quest?" Lord Jonquil asked in theatrically imperious tones.

"Are *you* interfering in *ours?*" She did her best impression of a very priggish butler demanding to know why two of the footmen were shirking their duties.

Again, she was treated to the sound of sincere laughter. What was the magic this place was working? She was encountering here so much of what she hadn't even realized she was longing for when spending time with those she knew in Paris who chose to be insincere. She'd found that treasured sincerity in Céleste, as well as the marquis and the other members of *La Tapisserie*. Sébastien and Gaëtane were genuine and kind.

She sometimes forgot that not all of Paris, not all of society, was as untrustworthy as Pierre had proven to be. Who would have thought she would be granted such a potent reminder so far from home and during such a mirthfilled game?

"Are you spies?" Nicolette demanded, knowing perfectly well the absurdity of *her* posing that question.

Joining in the jest quite easily and naturally, Lord Jonquil squared his shoulders and looked at her with a stern expression he had likely never practiced in the mirror, as his inherent joviality undermined it from the beginning. "I will never tell!"

"Very well. But know this, Lord Jonquil and Mr. Layton—"

"*And* Mr. Layton?" that gentleman responded with a scoff. "I have been perfectly well-behaved. Your ire should be directed in its entirety at Lord Jonquil."

In an aside clearly meant to be overheard, Lord Jonquil declared, "Digby, you traitorous coward, selling me to the enemy in this way."

Pretending to be speaking privately, Mr. Layton said, "I intend to undertake a bit of duplicity in order to earn the trust of our enemy, naturally." He pressed his hand to his heart, looking wounded. "How dare you accuse me of betraying you. I never would!" Quick as anything, Mr. Layton looked to Nicolette once more. "I will absolutely betray him. You need only ask."

"Digby, you traitorous coward!"

From within the room, Henri called out. "You've already done that bit, Lucas."

"Have I forsworn his friendship forever?" Lord Jonquil tossed back.

"Not yet," Henri answered from within.

"Don't skip over that part," Mr. Layton said. "It's my favorite."

Were all gentlemen as entertaining as these were when away from the constraints of formal society gatherings? Nothing in their behavior was uncouth or inappropriate. They were simply so wonderfully themselves, so sincerely happy, and such easy and natural friends. She'd not known the gentlemen of Paris to be so unaffected, but neither had she spent time with them away from the elegant balls and soirees of society.

Henri emerged before the performance could continue. She was certain he had retrieved the book of poetry. It wasn't in his hands, so he must have hidden it somewhere.

He eyed his friends with a look of disdain. "No doubt these two have come to prevent us from claiming the sweet treasure that awaits our inevitable victory."

"I am absolutely certain that is their aim," she said, "and I have thwarted them."

"Excellent work *Capitaine* Beaulieu," he said.

Nicolette suspected this group of friends had long engaged in ridiculousness like this. It was refreshingly delightful to be included in it.

With an overdone show of pride, Mr. Layton looked at them all and declared, "As Lucas has not yet forsworn my friendship, I feel it my duty to tell you, *Capitaine* Beaulieu and Archbishop, that we now consider you our sworn enemies and mean to dedicate ourselves entirely to defeating you in this battle of quests." He straightened the lace at his cuffs. "Provided doing so does not muss my hair nor rumple my clothing. Even heroes have their dignity."

In the short time she'd known him, Nicolette had seen how constantly Mr. Layton embraced his persona of a frivolous, fashion-minded, and appearance-obsessed gentleman. He was hiding behind it; she knew that for certain. An endless puzzle, Lady Jonquil had called the Gents. Nicolette agreed wholeheartedly.

The two gentlemen hurried from the corridor. Nicolette was both sorry to see them go and excited to continue her quest with Henri. She looked at him, knowing she was grinning but unable to change it. "I have the most splendid idea for the next item on our list."

"I am most anxious to hear it," he replied.

"The assignment is 'something brown.' Surely you must know something that belongs to either of those two gentlemen that is brown, something we can secretly take from their bedchambers and present to the group in the drawing room without them realizing we have it until *after* it is revealed. Something that is so obviously his that he will know it in a moment. Even if we don't win, it will be well worth the effort to see them shocked."

Henri agreed without the slightest hesitation. "And they will, of all the people in this competition, be the most amused to see us take that approach."

"I believe now is our best opportunity, as neither of them is in this wing and won't catch us."

"We'll have to watch for Julia," Henri warned. "It's possible she will arrive in the midst of our mischief."

"We will be vigilant to the end," Nicolette said, committing herself to the strangest, most amusing prospect for spending a frivolously fun afternoon that she had perhaps ever encountered in her adult life.

# Chapter Eleven

HENRI WAS TRYING VERY HARD to prevent his heart from being inexcusably foolish. Undertaking this questing game with Nicolette was proving delightful. She was a charmingly whimsical partner in this bit of silliness, and he liked her all the more for it. Joining her in the absurdity was lightening his mind and heart as few things had these past years.

They'd slipped into Julia and Lucas's bedchamber. The door had been open wide—and still was—indicating no one was within and they would not be intruding on anyone.

"What shall we take with us?" Nicolette held her clasped hands against her clavicle as she glanced around the room. "Nothing of actual value, in case something accidentally happened to it, and nothing that would truly embarrass them." She sent Henri a pleading look.

He set his hand lightly on her arm. "The name they have fashioned for me was given humorously, but there is also sincerity behind it. When any of the Gents indulge in a bit of teasing that edges beyond what it ought, I am known among them for reminding them to consider their actions with some degree of care. I don't mean to neglect that care in this quest of ours."

"You must not be insufferable about it, or they wouldn't keep you among them." She made the observation with a twinkle in her eyes.

"I simply wax eloquent about the miseries that would await them in jail, and that is enough to give them sufficient pause."

"I hope you do so in stanza form. A poetical warning is bound to have a greater impact."

Hoping his nervousness didn't show, he asked, "Do you not think it beneath a gentleman to compose poetry?"

"A great many people of standing and significance in society have been writers over the centuries, be it prose or poetry or grand tales."

"You truly think such a thing could be acceptable?" He did not keep his shock hidden.

"Did you expect me to think otherwise?" she asked.

He released the breath he didn't realize he had been holding. "My father held decided opinions on the topic, and Jean-François has adopted many of them."

"Likely with as much fervor as my brother holds to his opinions on ladies of twenty-four years not being wed or, at the very least, betrothed. He loves me and is not eager to be rid of me; he simply wishes my situation were different."

She had said she'd been engaged. To now hear that her brother was displeased that she was no longer betrothed was an interesting additional insight. There was history there.

"That is Lord Jonquil's walking stick, is it not?" Nicolette motioned to a walking stick of walnut wood resting against the armoire.

Henri recognized it and knew all the Gents would as well. Lucas had obtained it in Germany during his and Kes's grand tour of the Continent. "Perfect." He snatched it up. "I can't put it in my pocket as I did the book of poetry, but it shouldn't be too cumbersome to carry about."

He pulled their bit of parchment from his pocket and handed it to her, his hands full of their findings. "What is our next task?"

She unfolded the paper, and her sapphire-blue eyes scanned the page. "'Something fleeting' and 'something from Town.'" She shook her head. "It seems unfair that we are required to make the journey to the village, unless all of the teams are."

"When *Town* is capitalized, as it is here, that denotes London."

She turned a confused gaze on him. "Is not London as large as Paris?"

"London is, from what I understand, nearly *twice* as large as Paris," he said.

She shook her head. "But doesn't the word *town* mean a place somewhat larger than a village but not so large as a city?"

"Generally, yes. But London seems to be the exception."

She shook her head. "Do you ever wonder if the English language is made overly complicated on purpose?"

He laughed. "Whether they do so on purpose or not, I still think we should hold it against them."

"I agree wholeheartedly." Nicolette folded the parchment once more and tucked it into the cuff of her sleeve. "So, which is it to be? Do we first search out something fleeting or something from London?"

"As I doubt there is anything in Digby's wardrobe or accoutrements that did not originate in London, unless, of course, it came from Paris, I suspect we can fulfill that bit by searching *his* room."

Nicolette set her free hand in his empty one, just as he had done when they had begun this search. And just as it had done then, the simple touch sent a shiver of awareness through him. She likely had no idea how the hint of jasmine in her perfume and the sparkle of amusement in her eyes set his pulse racing. He was trying very hard to keep his head, and he wasn't certain he was doing a very good job of it. What his heart allowed itself to imagine was beginning to take up residence in what ought to be the more logical recesses of his mind.

They moved swiftly but quietly, glancing up and down the corridor in anticipation of their efforts being discovered, but the other teams must have had lists that took them elsewhere. No one appeared. No one interrupted, and they were soon in Digby's bedchamber, where the door was open, as it had been in the other rooms they had searched.

"As we are not limited by color, our options are many." Henri motioned to the room in general. "Digby is known to be quite fashionable. Everything from his shoes to his hat, his writing paper to his pocket watch are all obtained from the most fashionable and sought after places."

"But how are we to know which things originated in London and which in Paris?" she asked. "It is possible we would be mistaken in the origins of a given item."

A realization struck him. "I happen to know that directly before coming here for this house party, Digby was in London and obtained from the most fashionable hatters in the kingdom a new hat of which he is particularly proud."

"Perfect. If you are aware of the hat and where he obtained it, the other Gents likely are as well and will applaud the choice when it is revealed."

It proved easy to locate. It was in a hatbox on the uppermost shelf inside the armoire. Henri was tall, so he very easily slid the hatbox from its shelf and handed it to Nicolette, then carefully closed the doors of the armoire, leaving no indication they had ever been open. As quickly and quietly as they'd left Lucas and Julia's room, they left Digby's, depositing themselves in the corridor. Henri had a book of his poetry in his pocket and Lucas's walking stick in one hand, and Nicolette held the hatbox.

"All that remains now is 'something fleeting.'" Nicolette shook her head. "I haven't the first idea how to fulfill that request. Most things that are fleeting cannot be captured. How are we to present something that cannot be held or kept?"

It was a quandary. "Among those things I can think of that would be described as fleeting are spring flowers, beautiful sunsets, youth, special moments in life."

"Youth," Nicolette repeated with eyes wide. "Do you suppose we can convince the nursemaids to allow us to borrow one of their charges?"

"Excellent idea," he said as her idea became clear to him. "Childhood is fleeting. I'm certain Adèle would be permitted to come with me, as she has spent time with me at the bequest of her parents."

"Although, if we are to stay with our strategy of choosing items that are of particular significance to our 'sworn enemies,' the child we ought to bring with us is Lord Fallowgill."

How easily he could picture the look on Lucas's and Julia's faces when little Philip was presented. Neither would be upset. They would likely be delighted. "I believe including her little one in the game would win us Julia's vote. And Lucas is such a proud father that he would find himself forced to vote for us even if he were put out over the matter of his walking stick."

"There can be no harm in asking the nursemaid. If she proves reluctant, we needn't press the matter."

"I suspect, Mlle Nicolette Beaulieu, that you are more of a risk taker than many people realize."

"I've learned to be these past two years. Fate and happenstance ought not dictate one's future without one making some effort to direct it."

And once again, he felt certain he was seeing an insight into what had occurred in her life in the years since he had last seen her. She'd not been cowering or fainthearted by any stretch of the imagination, but she *had* leaned toward conforming with what French society had deemed appropriate and desirable even when she'd not seemed entirely convinced. That she had since adopted a stance of choosing her future and her path gave him a moment's hope. He still did not fit what she had been taught to look for in a gentleman, but perhaps that wasn't the insurmountable obstacle it had once been.

"Shall we go attempt to borrow a child?" she asked with a grin.

Pulling himself back into the moment, he nodded, and they made their way directly to the nursery. The three children were not nearly close enough in age to be particularly boon companions to one another, and yet, the nursery was peaceful. The children seemed happy.

Henri approached the nurse he knew Lucas and Julia employed. She was a kindhearted woman, protective of her charge but exuding love rather than the authoritarianism some nurses did. It was to their advantage that she knew Philip had been entrusted to Henri's care in the past.

"We have come to ask a favor," Henri said, "but will bow to your decision on the matter. We are, at the moment, engaged in an afternoon's diversion with Lord Fallowgill's parents. We suspect they would be delighted to see their son take part, and that delight would be heightened if his participation were a surprise. If you consider it appropriate and it will not cause you too much inconvenience, we should very much like to take him with us to the drawing room, where the afternoon's activities will be concluding soon. His parents will be there."

The nurse did not seem entirely convinced, but neither did she appear to disapprove.

Nicolette took up the discussion. "If one of the nursemaids could be spared, we would not object to being accompanied back to the drawing room. We will take whatever approach is least inconvenient and worrying for you." Henri had interacted with a few too many in the *ton* and in French society who would have addressed the nurse with a degree of unfortunate condescension. He was pleased to discover Nicolette was not among their number.

"I don't think it'd be a terrible thing for the little one to have a bit of additional time with his parents." The nurse motioned to one of the young nursemaids. "Janey can sit in the corridor outside the drawing room should the little one grow fussy or his parents wish to see him returned to the nursery."

"We thank you most sincerely," Nicolette said.

Philip, who was nodding off already, was wrapped in a blanket and placed in Nicolette's arms, Henri having taken possession of the hat box. The nursemaid laid a thick cloth against Nicolette's shoulder and the top of her dress to prevent any damage, and then she rested the infant against that shoulder.

Janey, the young nursemaid who was to accompany them, made a suggestion in a quietly conspiratorial voice. "If we was to lay a light blanket over the baby and over your shoulder, the little one's parents'd not know what you had under there. I remember as you said you wanted his being there to be a surprise to them."

"Excellent suggestion," Nicolette said.

With everything arranged, they slowly and carefully made their way toward the drawing room. Janey followed at a distance, saying she didn't want to give the game away.

Nicolette continually smiled at Henri. Such a mixture of emotions filled her expression: delight, contentment, amusement. Had she enjoyed this game as much as he had? He both hoped so and was anxious that she had not. And through it all, he continually reminded himself that his heart had proven itself pitifully foolish in the past and he would do best to keep it as quiet as he could.

He hid the items he carried behind his back as they stepped into the drawing room. All the teams had returned, meaning they were absolutely not the first team to finish their quest. Carefully, he tucked those items he was unable to keep in a pocket out of sight so he could reveal them when the time came. Philip had fallen fully asleep. It was unlikely anyone would guess what the blanket was hiding.

"Now that we have all returned," Lucas said, "including the team that was by far the slowest"—he shot an overly dramatic look of disapproval at Henri and Nicolette—"it is time for us to discover what everyone obtained and what their quest was so that we can determine who our winners will be."

Aldric and Niles had been the first to return. As was expected, especially from Aldric, their approach to their list had been very literal and consisted entirely of items that could easily be obtained in short distance from the drawing room. The General's flare for strategy had served him well in this game.

Julia and Céleste had returned next, and they, too, had approached their quest from a very literal mindset.

For Kes and Violet, the fulfillment of their list included some more creative items.

Despite having made quite a fuss about how long Henri and Nicolette had taken, Lucas and Digby, it was revealed, had returned only a few moments before they had. As expected, their items were creative. The final item on their list was "something bright," which Lucas argued was already fulfilled by Julia's presence in the room, a declaration that won them applause from the gathering and very obvious approval from that lady in particular.

"You will have a very difficult time winning the prize after that," Julia warned Henri and Nicolette, their turn having at last arrived.

"Oh," Nicolette said softly, no doubt on account of the sleeping child she was hiding, "I do believe we can best them."

Laughing exclamations of enjoyment answered that bit of friendly taunting. How easily Henri could picture her taking part in many of the Gents' adventures.

"Our list," Henri said, "was 'Something moving. Something brown. Something fleeting. Something from Town.' Our first: something moving." Henri reached into his pocket. "Few things are as moving to those of discerning taste"—he tossed Lucas and Digby a look of doubt, which earned him grins from that quarter—"as poetry." He held up the volume. "And I find this collection particularly moving." He hoped they would not ask why. On reflection, he was shocked that he'd chosen his own poetry. The author was identified as "a gentleman," but drawing attention to it might lead to conjecture he was not ready or able to satisfy. He set the book on a nearby table.

"Our next," Nicolette said, "is 'something brown.' We found a brown item that will perhaps seem a bit dull and uninteresting, nevertheless it fulfills the request."

Henri bit back a laugh. He stepped over to where he had tucked the walking stick beside the tallboy and, with a flourish, produced it. "Behold Lord Jonquil's very plain, very uninteresting *brown* walking stick."

The room erupted in laughter.

In the midst of it, Lucas called out, "That was in my bedchamber, you thieves."

Nicolette was softly bouncing, something not everyone likely noticed, but which probably meant her secret bundle had been awakened a bit by the sound. Still, Henri felt certain that needed to be the final revelation they made.

"I next will reveal to you the item which is from Town, the word being capitalized and, thus, denoting London." He pulled from its hiding place the hat box and set it on the table beside his book of poetry. "This item, none of us can have any doubt, was obtained in London."

Digby rose slowly and with great dignity. "That is *my* hat box." Henri knew his friend well enough to be certain Digby was not actually offended.

Henri grinned before he lifted the lid and pulled out a thin-brimmed, tall hat of black linen and set it atop his own head. "It is the very latest fashion, I'm told, and soon enough, everyone will be wearing ones just like it, provided they obtain their hats from Lock & Co.—"

"London's *premier* hatter," the other Gents finished with him in perfect unison.

The room was in fits of laughter, equally congratulating Henri and Nicolette on their questionably obtained items and teasing Lucas and Digby at having been duped by them.

"Before we reveal our last," Nicolette said, "which we think will solidify our claim to the title of the team who fulfilled their quest with the greatest creativity but also the greatest accuracy, I believe you all should know that we were, early in our adventures, unjustly harangued in the corridor by those two." She turned her gaze dramatically to Lucas and Digby, a smile tugging at her lips, undoing the bit of theatrical seriousness she was clearly attempting. "While we have, I feel, already quite adequately repaid their mischief with a bit of our own, we have not let off our efforts there. We have fulfilled this last request—something fleeting—in a way that will fully and completely best them." She looked to Henri. "Would you do the honors, M. Fortier?"

"With pleasure, Mlle Beaulieu."

Henri took hold of the very top of the blanket that covered little Philip. "Behold, the most wonderfully delightful and creative fulfillment of a quest request." He flicked the blanket away, revealing Philip, who was not, in fact, sleeping but bright-eyed and smiling.

Nicolette turned him around enough to look out at the gathering, who all applauded and cheered. The baby cooed in delight.

"That child is a performer already, Lucas," Kes said. "You will have your hands full as he grows."

"I am looking forward to it." Lucas tapped his tiny boy on the nose, earning a giggle of delight. "We are going to have so many adventures, Philip."

Henri slipped over to the doorway of the drawing room, where Janey was waiting. "Our plan was perfect. Thank you, Janey."

"Do you think Lord and Lady Jonquil will wish for Lord Fallowgill to stay with them?" she asked.

Henri glanced back to where the doting parents stood beside Nicolette, all surrounded by the other questers, with little Philip looking pleased as could be. "I believe they will. He has become the very center of attention."

Janey went on her way back to the nursery. Henri hovered in the doorway, watching the scene play out. Everyone's attention was on Philip, but Henri's gaze returned to Nicolette.

The time he'd spent with her that afternoon had been an utter delight, as joyous as any he could remember since that last time they'd been together. *More* delightful in many ways. She'd been more comfortable, more lighthearted. More enchanting.

Nicolette set her precious bundle in Lucas's arms and glided gracefully toward Henri. His heart needed to be far more sensible about all this than it was currently: pounding in his neck, attempting to convince his mind to entertain any number of outlandish things.

"I believe we have emerged entirely victorious, Henri," she said, her smile as beguiling as ever.

He told himself he enjoyed the sound of his name on her lips only because it had been so long since a French voice had spoken it. But he knew that was not true. His brother, sister-in-law, sister, and niece had all spoken it, and there was no denying that they had *very* French voices.

"We are a formidable team, Nicolette, a fact I do not imagine Lucas and Digby will soon forget."

She laughed with him. "Promise me when you next visit Paris we can indulge in another ridiculous quest."

She wanted to see him again. That was promising.

"Do you have acquaintances in that city who would undertake such a thing?" he asked.

Her expression fell a little. "I'm not certain. The functions at which Paris society gathers don't allow for quests and silliness. I don't know who amongst my acquaintances there would even consider such a thing."

Seizing on a bit of courage that might very well prove folly in the end, he said, "Then you will simply have to return to England so you and I can best the Gents repeatedly."

Nicolette met his eyes, and the tiniest hint of color touched her cheeks. "Would you like me to visit again?"

"I would like that very much." So much for keeping his foolish heart in check.

She appeared on the verge of saying something more, but Céleste called her over. As Nicolette stepped away, a bit of Henri's heart went with her, joining the bit that had been hers for three years. Was she as unaware of his affection in this moment as she had been then?

She might very well forget about this idyllic day as easily and completely as she had before. How would his heart ever recover if she did?

# Chapter Twelve

THUS FAR, HENRI'S GREATEST OBSTACLE in completing his third poem had been finding a topic. Second only to that was the need to claim time on his own in which to work on it. The next morning, however, he awoke with an idea freshly formed in his mind. Difficult experience had taught him to strike while the iron was hot. Thus, he rushed through his breakfast and made his way directly to the book room. It was empty, just as he'd hoped it would be.

The time he'd spent the day before running about the grounds and generally enjoying himself with Nicolette had driven home once more the contradictions that he lived. He did not wish to return to France, yet he felt pulled to it. Nicolette represented in so many ways the life he had left behind when he'd defied his father's edicts.

The ground beneath him often felt unsteady. His future felt utterly uncertain. In that realization, he found what his poetic efforts had lacked thus far: intensity of feeling.

He opened his traveling desk, pulled out a piece of parchment, and set his ink bottle in position. At last, he could complete this final piece of his next published work. It was another rebellious step toward independence.

"A blight on the Fortier name." Father's sneering words struck him without warning, something they too often did. "No pride of birth, no sense of duty. Pitiful, Henri. Utterly, utterly pitiful."

His grip on the quill turned white-knuckle. He breathed through the crash of those words. He knew he did not truly deserve to be denounced as a blight or accused of being without a sense of duty and pride. But he felt pitiful. He felt it with alarming regularity.

"I can't say I understand how it feels to have a father who treats me as yours does," Stanley had said during one of their many fire-side conversations during Stanley's last year at Cambridge. "But I can tell you this: anyone who thinks you feebleminded or infantile or lacking in soul-deep goodness is not someone whose wisdom I would put any store by."

"He knows me better than you do," Henri had objected. "He's known me all my life. There's not much a son can hide from his father."

With his characteristic mischievous smile, Stanley said, "Oh, I've hidden a few things from mine."

"But not the crux of your character. Fathers see the weaknesses that can be hidden from others."

Stanley had leaned closer, holding Henri's gaze. He'd been quick with a quip and always eager for a lark, but there'd been moments, like that one, when the depth of his soul had been on full display. "Let me tell you what I see, Henri. I see a gentleman who made a life for himself far from home, far from the comfort he might have known resting upon the privileges of rank and wealth in his homeland. That is not a tale of weakness, my friend. And if you ask me, your father doesn't see weakness either. I think he sees that you are stronger and braver than he will ever be, and that terrifies him."

*Stronger and braver.* How often Henri had repeated that to himself while attempting to keep his head above water. Father's words tore him down, the waves crashing relentlessly over him. Stanley's words calmed the storm. Though Henri often felt pitiful, Stanley had thought him strong and brave.

"I am stronger and braver than these doubts," he silently assured himself. "And I have managed to survive the injustices I've endured. That is not pitiful."

But it was not his doubts nor his father's remembered words that prevented him in the next moment from uncorking his ink bottle and setting to work. It was yet another interruption.

Aldric skulked in, looking annoyed and exhausted. There was one thing that brought that particular mixture of emotions to his expression.

"Mowbary?" Henri asked, though he knew the answer.

"Always," Aldric said. "I sometimes wonder how in the world my brother and I can possibly be related."

"A sentiment I find myself feeling with increasing frequency where *my* brother is concerned," Henri said. "For a time before and following my father's passing, I felt some degree of kinship with Jean-François. That is disappearing more every day."

Aldric nodded. "I'm far happier with my brothers by choice than with the brother who is mine by blood."

The Gents had long referred to themselves that way: brothers by choice. Not all of them had strained relationships with their families, but none was entirely without difficulties of one variety or another.

"Do you mind if I hide in here for a time?" Aldric dropped onto a sofa near the fireplace. "Retreat seems my best strategy at the moment."

Henri did mind a little, but he could see that his friend was in some degree of misery. Henri never had been one to ignore the needs of others. "Mowbary might find you in here," he warned. He knew perfectly well how often people wandered into the book room.

"At least I'll have a respite while he's looking," Aldric said. "And with a spot of luck, *your* brother won't look for me in here either."

"Is Jean-François making a nuisance of himself?"

"Naturally," Aldric grumbled. A conciliatory and apologetic expression crossed his features. "I shouldn't speak ill of your family."

Henri did try to avoid that himself, but he could hardly blame his friend. "I wish my brother did not deserve to be spoken ill of as often as he does."

"You'll forgive me for this," Aldric said, "but it is your sister who has me nettled at the moment. I'm certain she is a fine person, but it is swiftly becoming my goal for the remainder of this house party to avoid her at all costs."

Henri both laughed and winced at the declaration. "While I understand," Henri said, "the one whose ambitions ought to concern you most isn't Céleste or even my brother."

Aldric studied him a moment. "If you mean M. and Mme Beaulieu, I assure you they are as aware as the rest of us how much time *you* have been spending with Mlle Beaulieu."

"Yesterday's activities required us to spend the afternoon together." Henri hadn't apprised any of the Gents of his and Nicolette's plan to distract her family from their matrimonial aims. "She wished to emerge victorious and, thus, chose the partner she felt most clever," he preened a bit.

"I still can hardly believe the two of you pilfered things from Lucas's and Digby's rooms. And to convince the nursery staff to let you abscond with Philip . . ." Aldric smiled as he shook his head. "I've not seen you undertake something like that in a long time without the Gents goading you into it. Was it your idea or Mlle Beaulieu's?"

"We hatched the scheme together. It was an opportunity we could not ignore."

Something like approval and even relief entered Aldric's expression. "It was good seeing you having such a lark. Back at Cambridge and during the first couple of years afterward, you were a little better behaved than the rest of us but just as deep in mischief. I've missed that side of you."

Henri dropped his gaze, fidgeting a bit. "I do try not to be too infantile."

"Those are your father's words," Aldric said firmly. "He's been gone for years; he shouldn't be permitted to keep tormenting you from beyond the grave."

"Not all of his criticisms were entirely unfounded." That had always bothered Henri. "I can dismiss many of them. Most of them. I'm not entirely the failure he predicted I would be. I'm happy with that, at least."

Aldric could sometimes be impatient with people who allowed emotion to get the better of their intellect. But he also had a good and compassionate heart. He didn't scold Henri for his struggle or his painstakingly slow crawl toward healing from the wounds his father had inflicted. In that moment, Aldric very generously allowed a change of topic. "Who was it you were saying I ought to be concerned with in the matter of unwanted matchmaking, if not your family?"

"Your father," Henri answered.

Aldric's expression turned immediately somber.

Henri pressed on. "If he decides his younger son ought to make a match with the daughter of an important French family, there might be very little you can do to avoid it."

Aldric muttered something he would not have if a "daughter of an important French family" had been present.

"I think your most important goal needs to be not giving Mowbary any reason to write to the duke and suggest a Fortier might make a good addition to the family."

"Lud," Aldric muttered. "Lucas managed to salvage his arranged marriage. Now that he is thirty years old, Niles will have to bow to his family's plans for him. I'd rather not fall into that trap myself, especially seeing as I've used up what are likely to be my only paternal favors in adulthood when I was granted use of the boat to go to Portugal and then secured this estate for our gathering."

"If those do prove to be the only considerations His Grace shows you moving forward, will they have been worth asking for?" Henri asked.

"For Stanley's sake, we needed to go to Portugal." Aldric nodded. "I'm glad we did."

"So am I."

"But 'borrowing' Norwood Manor was supposed to have allowed the two of us to at last be host of a Gents gathering, and that didn't happen in the end. Feels rather like a waste of a kindness, especially when such considerations are growing rarer."

Sébastien Beaulieu stepped into the book room looking none too pleased about anything. He tucked a letter into his coat pocket as his eyes found Henri.

"May I have a private word with you, M. Fortier?" he asked in French.

Aldric was as fluent in that language as any native speaker. He rose, offered a bow of farewell, and left.

"What was it you needed to discuss?" Henri asked M. Beaulieu.

"It has not escaped my notice that you and my sister are fond of each other."

"I knew your sister before your arrival at Norwood," Henri said. "She is a dear friend of my sister's."

"If you have anything in mind beyond her being 'a friend of your sister's,' I am here to thoroughly disabuse you of it. I know you have not the income nor the prospects to allow you to be at all an acceptable suitor for Nicolette Beaulieu."

This was not a discussion Henri had been expecting.

"And in case you have any ideas about marrying her *because* she has a fortune," Sébastien continued, "let me tell you this: very little of her wealth is hers to control."

Sébastien stopped to take a breath, so Henri jumped in. "There is no understanding between your sister and me." He was impressed at how calm his voice was and how little he allowed the pain of Sébastien's declaration to show in his expression.

His gaze narrowing, Sébastien said, "It is crucial that you understand there never can be."

Most people who knew Henri would not describe him as bold, but he certainly could be when need be. He'd gained that skill in the years he had been refusing to bow to his father's edicts. "My understanding of my circumstances, Society's expectations, and her situation are more than sufficient to render this conversation utterly unnecessary."

Sébastien straightened to his full height, clearly attempting to look down his nose at Henri despite the fact that Henri was taller. "It is entirely necessary. Her situation is not what you imagine. The troubles we have suffered after her engagement—" His Adam's apple bobbed even as the rest of him grew very still. "There is a chance to put things right." He thrust his chin sharply. "Do not interfere."

That sounded like a threat. But coming so quickly on the heels of obvious anxiety made Henri suspect something more was going on than the man's disapproval of a possible suitor. "What is it you think I am interfering in?"

Without a word of explanation, Sébastien turned and left the room.

Henri didn't like the way that conversation had gone. Nicolette had been scheming to find a way of helping distract Céleste's would-be matchmakers, assuming the difficulties from her own family were small. But having seen the look of mingled desperation and determination in Sébastien's eyes, Henri began to suspect Nicolette had seriously underestimated the peril *she* was in.

No matter that his poem still needed to be written, Henri had a more imminently pressing matter to see to: dropping a word of warning in Nicolette's ear.

"'A chance to put things right?'" Nicolette shook her head as she repeated what he'd told her of his conversation with Sébastien. "And this he said after mentioning my engagement?" Embarrassment colored her cheeks.

Henri nodded. He'd run her to ground in the formal garden behind the house.

"You don't have to discuss it if you'd rather not," he assured her. "I searched you out to offer a warning, not to pry."

Nicolette's blush remained. "I imagine Céleste has told you some of that history."

"She has not." Henri set his hand high on her back and led her around a dip in the paving stones.

After a quick breath, Nicolette took up the tale. "M. Pierre Léandre and I were introduced a little over two years ago, a year after your visit to Paris. Our families were in favor of a match. He met every requirement a lady is supposed to have for a husband."

*Every requirement a lady is supposed to have.* How well he remembered her list of requirements: birth, standing, wealth, influence, property. He'd had a firm claim on the first two. The Fortiers were esteemed above even some titled French families. Henri's extended absence from France undermined a little his claim to that standing. He hadn't money or property, and he could not honestly say he had true influence in French society.

"We were destined to be a prominent couple in Paris, everything most in our circles would aspire to claim." She slipped her arm through Henri's, walking at his side. "And yet, the end of our betrothal is something I look back on as a fortunate escape. I dare not admit that to most people."

"Why is that?"

"Most of society would think me a fool." Her smile was weary and sorrowful. "Pierre was the perfect match by everyone's estimation, and . . . I was miserable."

"I am sorry to hear that."

Nicolette's shoulders rose and fell with a deep breath. "Other than Céleste, you are the only person who has expressed sorrow that I was unhappy. Pierre was certainly not overly bothered."

"He sounds delightful," Henri drawled, earning him a laugh.

"I consider myself well rid of him, though it did make the last two years difficult to navigate. Broken engagements don't reflect well on the persons in question."

"Especially, I have found, on the lady."

She nodded. "Salvaging my standing was not an easy feat."

His heart ached for her. "You were mistreated?"

"Not for long." Her shoulders squared. "Most wouldn't dare."

"How did you manage that?" He'd spent most of his life attempting to discover the secret of that.

"I learned to either keep people at a distance or intimidate them." She looked somehow both proud and disappointed. "The glittering circles of Paris call me alternately *La Dame de Glace* and *La Reine des Ours*. I've earned both monikers. The Ice Lady is untouchable," she said, "but the Queen of Bears is terrifying."

He set his hand on hers, telling himself it was a gesture of support. "I don't find you terrifying."

Her smile was delightfully pleased. "It seems to me the Gents ought to call you the Archbishop of Bravery."

"Stanley did once tell me I was braver than I was given credit for."

She held a bit tighter to his hand. "Do they not acknowledge the person you are?"

"They do." The Gents were the very best of friends, and their encouragement had kept him afloat the past thirteen years. "I don't always believe them though."

"You should, Henri. You truly should."

He suspected he would never grow weary of hearing her say his name. She spoke it as if she liked it . . . as if she truly liked *him*.

# Chapter Thirteen

THANKS TO HENRI'S VERY WELCOME warning, Nicolette added Sébastien and Gaëtane to her list of people she needed to keep a very close eye on. The list was approaching an almost unmanageable length. In her time with *La Tapisserie,* she'd tackled remarkably complicated assignments. Her innate ability to sort through entanglements and navigate ever-changing situations had not only been useful in their efforts to help people in dire straits but had also helped bolster her faith in herself.

But that faith too often wavered, just as it did now.

Henri greeted her as she entered the drawing room that afternoon. It was easy to return his friendly welcome. They were pretending to be interested in one another, yes, and she still hadn't sorted out the mystery of what he'd so frantically hidden from her on that first day, but she found him an easy person to spend time with. And she could not entirely shake from her memory the feel of her heart fluttering whenever his hand brushed hers.

"Lucas has only just told me you never claimed the prize for our victory in his questing game," Henri said.

"I assumed *you* had claimed it," she said.

Lord Jonquil held his hands up in a show of innocence. "I cannot be held responsible for the fate of abandoned sweets."

"You ate them, didn't you?" Nicolette shook her head. "One final blow to your archenemies."

"Digby did it," Lord Jonquil said. "All his doing."

"Lucas, you traitorous coward!" Mr. Layton declared from not too far distant, echoing the apparently common and well-rehearsed declaration Lord Jonquil had made during the quest the previous afternoon.

These gentlemen were such a delight.

"It seems we ought to have chosen the peppermint sweets as our 'something fleeting,'" Henri said.

"Indeed." Her amusement faded as her gaze fell on Gaëtane watching her from a grouping of chairs where she sat with Lady Mowbary and Mme Fortier. Her sister-in-law looked displeased to see her in conversation with Henri. Sébastien had warned Henri not to interfere in their efforts to "put to rights" what had gone wrong with Pierre. The more Nicolette thought on that declaration, the more uneasy she grew.

She'd once believed society's lies about the suitability of a potential husband resting upon material considerations. She'd had a glimpse at what life would have been like with a so-called suitable spouse. Now she was determined to either marry someone she could love and respect or not marry at all. But as a lady, she had so little ability to support herself. Her wealth was not hers to control but was tied up in her dowry. Setting her sights, however hypothetically, on a penniless gentleman without a home was not just irresponsible, but it would also doom them both to a hopeless and endless struggle that might very well bring down on them the same degree of misery she had so narrowly escaped.

With a start, she realized Lady Jonquil and Mrs. Barrington were standing where she had wandered and were watching her expectantly.

"Forgive me," she said. "I fear my thoughts were far afield."

With a look every bit as mischievous as the one her husband often wore, Lady Jonquil asked, "Dare I ask *to whom* those thoughts have been wandering?"

To her shock, Nicolette felt herself blush. She very seldom did that. "No one in particular."

Lady Jonquil managed to keep her expression very neutral, but her eyes betrayed a very real amusement. Mrs. Barrington set a hand in front of her lips, no doubt hiding a smile. It seemed Nicolette and Henri were playing their roles well; even Nicolette's cheeks were joining in.

Across the way, Lord Jonquil laughed, pulling the ladies' attention in that direction. Henri stood beside him still, smiling broadly. He really did have a lovely smile. Her enjoyment of it didn't have to be feigned. Her enjoyment of his company didn't really either. And he seemed to genuinely enjoy the time he spent with her. She'd kept most people at arms' length since Pierre's defection; she'd almost forgotten how it felt to want someone's company, to be at ease with someone other than Céleste and the other senior members of *La Tapisserie*.

"For what it's worth," Lady Jonquil said, "I think 'no one in particular' is a rather wonderful person. And he watches you even more than you watch him."

"I am going to continue insisting that I haven't the first idea what you mean."

Mrs. Barrington hooked a dark eyebrow. "And we will set aside discussions of Monsieur No One in Particular in favor of suggesting a jaunt to Swarkestone for a spot of shopping and some time away from the too-often-exhausting Gents."

"I agree with alacrity," Nicolette said. "Provided we also give ourselves time away from a certain Frenchwoman's too-often-exhausting family."

Mrs. Barrington's forehead creased in confusion too exaggerated to be truly sincere. "I thought you were fond of Miss Fortier's family."

"One of them, in particular," Lady Jonquil added with a barely concealed laugh.

"You two are trouble." Nicolette shook her head, pleased as could be.

"Yes, we are," Lady Jonquil said proudly.

Mrs. Barrington hooked her arm through her friend's. Something in the movement, in the lay of her arm, was stiff and odd, but everything about her expression and posture spoke of very real fondness. Was there no one at this house party who was not a puzzle?

In the very next moment, the butler stepped into the drawing room and announced that Mr. and Mrs. Beaumont had arrived to call on Mr. *Henri* Fortier.

The room was immediately on their feet, mixtures of welcome and confusion on all faces. Nicolette forced herself to produce that same expression rather than the relief she actually felt. At last, she was going to make the acquaintance of the two people she'd been sent to meet with.

"They are here to call on *you*?" Lord Mowbary asked Henri, apparently unconcerned about speaking unkindly and accusatory to one of his guests.

"While conversing with the Beaumonts yesterday, I discovered that they had not yet been called upon by you," Henri said. "I further suspect they have not received any invitation to make the acquaintance of your guests. While I am not in a position to bridge that gap with the Marquess of Grenton and his family or the Haddingtons or Saunderses, I find myself honored to undertake the introduction of M. and Mme Beaumont to your guests."

Lord Mowbary ruffled up but didn't say a word. Lady Mowbary looked more confused than anything. Nicolette hadn't had an overly large number of interactions with the host and hostess of the gathering, but she knew them well enough to realize they were unlikely to be humbled for long by their very obvious error.

Henri crossed to the doorway, where the Beaumonts had only just arrived, and immediately began introductions around the room. Though he started with Lord and Lady Mowbary, he quickly moved on to the others present: the Gents, Céleste, his brother and sister-in-law, Sébastien and Gaëtane, Lady Jonquil and Mrs. Barrington, and finally Nicolette.

"M. and Mme Beaumont, may I make you known to Mlle Nicolette Beaulieu of Paris. Mlle Beaulieu, I am most pleased to present M. and Mme Beaumont, a delightful couple, who, like you and I, are French." He had offered, in the hearing of all present, an easy excuse for her to have conversations with this couple without sparking suspicions. It was not often her missions with *La Tapisserie* were accidentally aided by someone with no idea what she was attempting. Here was yet another reason to be grateful for Henri.

"It is an honor to make your acquaintance, Mlle Beaulieu." Mme Beaumont offered a deferential curtsy.

"The honor is mine," Nicolette said. "It is always a pleasure to meet a fellow Frenchwoman."

The new arrivals were soon situated in the room. M. Beaumont was pulled into conversation with the Gents, a group so friendly that Nicolette doubted anyone who interacted with them ever felt ignored. Mme Beaumont sat beside Nicolette, who was once more sitting with Lady Jonquil and Mrs. Barrington. Céleste, poor thing, was being held nearly hostage by her sister-in-law and brother, who were asking Lord and Lady Mowbary if it was true that they had neglected to see to it that the Marquess of Grenton and his family, which included a son of eligible age, had been called upon and invited to call in return. It seemed they were not as decided on a match specifically between Céleste and Lord Aldric as their behavior up until then had indicated.

Nicolette managed to catch Henri's eye. She nodded very briefly toward his sister, hoping to get the message to him that Céleste might appreciate a bit of a rescue. A quick but subtle nod was offered in return, and Nicolette found she could breathe more easily. How quickly she had gone from being terribly suspicious of him to trusting him. In all truthfulness, it was unlike her.

Mme Beaumont proved quiet and soft-spoken. She seemed a bit overawed by her company. It was not at all what Nicolette had expected, knowing the lady was already a member of the marquis's circle. But Nicolette ought to know better by now that there was more than one type of person who could be an asset in *La Tapisserie*'s efforts. There were some who were quiet, some who were gregarious. Some were very logical and leaned toward overthinking, while others acted more impulsively and with great passion.

*La Tapisserie* was not enormous, but it was varied.

The Beaumonts did not remain more than half an hour. Having called on a guest at the house party rather than the host and hostess, it behooved them to keep the visit short and cordial. They received the expected offer from Lady Mowbary to call again and a declaration of intent on *Lord* Mowbary's part to call on them at their estate.

"I hope that while I'm here, I can also call upon you at Eau Plate," Nicolette said, mentioning their estate nearby. "I would so love to speak of Paris and France and discover what places and people we might have in common."

Mme Beaumont nodded eagerly. "I would enjoy that. I have missed France these past years. I long to see Versailles again."

"I was there a few weeks ago," Nicolette said.

Mme Beaumont squeezed her hands. "We will have so very much to talk of. Please call on us at your earliest convenience."

Under any other circumstances, Nicolette would have happily suggested that Céleste call at Eau Plate with her, but she needed to undertake a private conversation with the couple.

No sooner had the Beaumonts departed than Lord Mowbary demanded his brother follow him to the book room. No doubt, Lord Aldric was about to be unfairly harangued for the embarrassment his brother had endured. Nicolette did not envy Lord Aldric the coming interview.

"The Beaumonts seem delightful people," Lady Jonquil said. "And I so enjoy speaking French with French speakers."

"Your grasp of the language is startling," Nicolette said. "Though he might not appreciate my saying so, I find your accent more authentic even than Lord Aldric's, and his is remarkable for one who does not hail from France."

"I am told Lord Aldric's mother was French, and he spent portions of his childhood in that country. That, no doubt, accounts for his proficiency."

"What accounts for yours?" Nicolette asked.

"Genius," Mrs. Barrington offered with an equal degree of teasing and sincerity.

Lady Jonquil shook her head. "Hardly. My nursemaid and governess were both French. I learned the language from them, and they taught me to speak well."

"Am I to assume, then, that your butler was from Spain, your lady's maid from Italy, and the gardener from . . . ancient Rome?" Mrs. Barrington asked with a laugh. "You speak the languages of those places with utter proficiency as well."

Lady Jonquil smiled. "I enjoy learning languages."

"As do I," Nicolette said. "Henri told me you and I have that in common."

Something in that simple sentence caught Lady Jonquil's attention. The tiniest lift of her eyebrow was all that changed in her expression, and yet Nicolette did not miss it. "Have I said something amiss?"

Lady Jonquil shook her head. "I have not before heard you call him Henri. Considering the two of you have spent an increasing amount of time together, I simply found myself pondering the change."

*Oh dear.* They were meant to give the impression of a *hint* of interest, not inspire gossip.

"Like Mme Beaumont, I deeply enjoy the company of my fellow Frenchmen. And I have found that M. Henri Fortier is very good company."

"You will hear no argument on that front from us," Mrs. Barrington said.

"Have you had the opportunity to know his sister better?" Nicolette asked. "Céleste is a dear and delightful person. I fear she is feeling a bit lonely during this house party. Avoiding the traps her oldest brother and sister-in-law lay has meant avoiding the other guests as well."

"I have noticed that," Lady Jonquil said. "Our shopping excursion should offer her a bit of a respite."

"Thank you for thinking to invite her as well, Lady Jonquil."

"Please, call me Julia." She made the request with sincerity.

Nicolette was not accustomed to the ease with which this group drew people into their friendship. There was danger in that. The closer people got, the more easily secrets could be discovered. But refusing Lady Jonquil's request would not save her from scrutiny; it would likely invoke *more*. "You are most welcome to call me Nicolette. Both of you."

"I am Violet," Mrs. Barrington said.

Other than Céleste, Nicolette hadn't any real friends. She hadn't even before Pierre's defection. Truth be told, she wasn't entirely sure what to do with the budding friendship she sensed in these ladies. She didn't know if she was more excited or nervous.

Into their conversation, Lord Jonquil bounced. It was the best way in which to describe the way he moved about a room. He plopped onto the chair Mme Beaumont had been using and faced his wife. "You will never guess what news I have heard from Collingham." He looked to Nicolette. "Collingham is the area where Julia and I grew up."

Nicolette nodded, now understanding the reference.

Lord Jonquil's attention was once more entirely on Julia. "Walter Sarvol is married."

"Someone married him?" Julia sounded genuinely shocked, an indication that her reaction was sincere rather than sneering.

Lord Jonquil nodded. "The only people in the neighborhood who haven't been entirely knocked down by the shock are Walter himself and his parents, who are convinced their son can do no wrong. *That* son, at least."

"Is his bride someone we know?" Julia asked.

Lord Jonquil shook his head. "She is Caroline Sangster. My mother says she hails from Surrey. Both of my parents say she seems a sweet-natured lady, which makes her current situation even more tragic."

"Her name alone endears her to me," Julia said.

Nicolette wasn't certain what was meant by that, but she didn't feel herself in a position to insert herself into the conversation.

"When we are next at Lampton Park, we should call at Sarvol House, perhaps offer the poor lady a bit of friendship to counter the no doubt wretched marriage she finds herself in."

Lord Jonquil managed to share this and his less-than-flattering evaluation of the gentleman central to it in a way that did not feel like vicious gossip or casually tossed-out insults. There was concern in his voice. And as he watched his wife, there was unmistakable joy in his eyes that Nicolette felt certain had nothing to do with the topic of discussion. His look of delight increased every time Julia spoke. When she met his gaze, his smile grew subtly broader and his posture grew more relaxed, as if every instance of attention he received from her set his world to rights once more.

"Did the letter include any word of your father's health?" Julia asked. "Your mother's last missive indicated he'd not been feeling entirely well of late."

Lord Jonquil nodded. "He is still a bit tired, a bit worn down. But Mother is confident he will recover if he doesn't overexert himself."

Julia reached over and took his hand. "I am certain he will."

He raised her hand to his lips and pressed a quick kiss there. He then kissed the tips of his fingers on his other hand and touched them to his wife's rounded stomach briefly, gently, and as naturally as breathing. Then he hopped to his feet once more and made his way back over to the Gents with his usual fluid energy.

Julia offered no explanation of the fingertip kiss, but Nicolette felt certain she understood what she'd seen. Julia and her husband were expecting another addition to their family, and he, devoted father he had shown himself to be, had offered a bit of instinctual love to the unborn child he already cherished as much as his sweet infant son.

Pierre would never have done such a thing. She didn't think he would have despised any children they'd have had, but she could not imagine him doting on her or on their offspring.

Thoughts of Pierre brought back to mind the conversation Henri had relayed to her. Sébastien intended to "put to rights" what had gone wrong when Nicolette's engagement to Pierre had been severed. She worried deeply about

what that meant. Perhaps it meant the efforts of distracting her family from
attempting a match between herself and Lord Aldric were not proving as fruitful
as she and Henri had hoped. Perhaps it meant they had someone in mind in Paris
with whom they hoped to broker a match, one she feared would be worryingly
like Pierre.

Lord Aldric returned to the drawing room, having apparently finished
receiving his set down from his brother. He looked as unshaken and unreadable
as ever. Nicolette didn't think it was because his brother's lecturing didn't bother
him. More likely than not, it was a calm that came from familiarity with the
experience.

Henri watched his friend while simultaneously attempting to keep his sister's spirits up. He looked torn. Nicolette *felt* torn. She wanted to help Céleste as
well, and she felt Aldric deserved support also, but she needed to avoid whispers
where that gentleman was concerned and keep clear of any schemes Sébastien
and Gaëtane had concocted in their efforts to "put things to rights."

More than anything, she wanted to go sit with Henri, to enjoy his company
and the sense of calm and reassurance she felt when she was with him. Kind
eyes, a heart-warming smile, and caring companionship . . . Heaven help her,
she didn't want to be wrong about him.

# Chapter Fourteen

THE NEXT DAY, AT A reasonable hour for making calls, Nicolette requested a carriage be prepared, and she was subsequently delivered to Eau Plate for what would seem from the outside to be an unexceptional visit between neighbors.

Upon arriving, she was ushered in by the butler to the drawing room, where M. and Mme Beaumont greeted her warmly. Fortune was smiling upon her; almost immediately, she was in the Beaumonts' exclusive company, with not even a servant hovering in the doorway.

Nicolette began immediately, choosing to speak in French. "You will forgive the haste with which I produce this topic, but the opportunity has arisen and I dare not squander it." She slipped from the pocket hidden in the folds of her dress a letter. "I have been charged with the responsibility of giving this to you."

M. Beaumont accepted the letter. He flipped it over and broke the wax seal. "This is the seal of *La Tapisserie*," he said in a whisper. Both he and his wife looked immediately at Nicolette.

She dipped her head in acknowledgment.

M. Beaumont rose and crossed to the door, closing it quietly but firmly.

Once he had rejoined them, Nicolette offered her explanation. "I am a senior member of *La Tapisserie* and am charged with discussing with you the Marquis de Lafayette's current request." She motioned to the letter. "But I implore you, read his words first."

The couple sat very near each other, both earnestly reading what he had written to them.

Nicolette was not overly nervous, but she was keenly aware of every expression flitting over the couples' faces, every sound of movement in the corridor. She'd never doubted the marquis's insistence that secrecy in this matter was of paramount importance. But the letter he'd written to her had solidified her determination to do all she could to protect that secrecy.

"Trust is one of the first casualties of war," Lafayette had written. "Its demise often begins before the first shot is fired."

Should violence take hold in France, as they feared, years might pass without knowing who could be trusted. Bloody revolutions were known to cause near-constant changes in authority, with each new regime seeking to stomp out anyone seen as a threat. That included those who now held sway, those who might for a time after the powder keg was lit, and those helping anyone with a newly acquired target on their back to escape the proverbial arrows. *La Tapisserie* would be far more successful and far safer if they weren't expending energy and resources attempting to keep track of who was in possession of information they ought not be.

After a moment, the Beaumonts returned their gaze to her. Their expressions had shifted from surprise to determination.

"We are told to look to you for details of what the marquis is asking of us."

Nicolette nodded. "I can tell you nothing until we can be certain that not even your servants will overhear."

The three of them were soon undertaking a leisurely walk on the pebbled path encompassing the expanse of the large back lawn. There would be no risk of a servant stumbling upon them or of a neighbor wandering nearby.

"The marquis fears there may soon be violent upheaval in France. The danger that would bring has led the marquis to make plans against the possibility." Nicolette spoke quickly. "It is his belief that should the whispers of revolution he is hearing come to be, there will be many amongst our countrymen seeking refuge away from France. England is a likely destination, as it is not terribly far away. He wishes to begin establishing a network of Frenchmen in this country who can be depended upon to provide refuge or passage for their countrymen. Not knowing the exact threats that might send these poor souls away from their homeland, he feels it best that this network be capable of managing this in utmost secrecy."

"We know a great many Frenchmen now living in England," Mme Beaumont said.

"While we do not have reason to believe that those fleeing this potential violence in France would be pursued after they've reached England's shores, we still must keep our arrangements here secret. Knowing who is participating on this side of the Channel will give clues as to who is taking part on the other side. And there *will* be danger there. Furthermore, we do not yet know who might need our protection nor from whom they would be fleeing. Should we prove careless in our communications now, we might very well find ourselves attempting to assist people who are fleeing from someone who knows everything we have put in place and can circumvent it all."

M. Beaumont walked beside his wife with his hands clasped behind his back and his eyes narrowed in thought. "Until we know for certain that these plans do not require secrecy, we would be wise to proceed on the assumption that they do."

"Precisely," Nicolette said. "A secret can always be revealed. But a secret, once revealed, can never be made a secret again."

"How long must we keep this secret?" Mme Beaumont asked.

"Potentially forever."

"And how many people would we need to find refuge for?" Mme Beaumont watched Nicolette as they slowly walked.

Nicolette shook her head. "There is no way to know yet."

M. Beaumont asked the next question. "And those whom we hope will provide that refuge cannot yet be told of these plans nor of *La Tapisserie?*"

"Most will never be told about *La Tapisserie*," Nicolette said. "Should the need for safe passage arise, the reason for it will undoubtedly be apparent. We needn't ever reveal information about the group making the arrangements."

"The marquis did not give us an easy assignment," Mme Beaumont said.

"He seldom does." Nicolette knew that all too well. "Before I depart for France, the marquis wishes me to receive a report from you on your proposed network. I suspect I will be the one to communicate with you over the coming months and years, though I will obviously do so in cipher."

"I daresay we will need a trusted contact in London," M. Beaumont said.

"Most certainly," Nicolette said. "And that someone will likely need to be a member of *La Tapisserie* already. Leave that to the marquis and the senior members of our organization."

"Are not *you* one of the senior members?" Mme Beaumont asked.

"I am." What little pride she felt at being able to say that was always undermined by the self-directed doubt she'd not been able to entirely shake these past two years.

She was stronger than she had been but almost no one saw it or valued it. To far too many, she was still the rejected fiancée, the Ice Lady, the Queen of Bears. She was unreachable and sharp-edged, fearsome when needed, intimidating.

And she was lonely. But sometimes being lonely was better than being hurt.

# *Chapter Fifteen*

WHILE NICOLETTE HAD BEEN CALLING on the Beaumonts, the Gents had called at Tafford, the home of the Marquess of Grenton. From what Nicolette was led to understand, they knew of him from their time in London but were not so well acquainted that he would have felt himself in a position to call at Norwood Manor, having not yet been invited to do so by Lord Mowbary.

The Gents, upon returning from the visit, had announced to the gathering that the Marquess and Marchioness of Grenton were so pleased to have such a gathering of the *ton* nearby that they intended to host a ball in a mere three days' time, and the entire party at Norwood was invited. Lord Mowbary hadn't seemed to know whether he ought to be pleased at the invitation or offended that it had been extended via someone other than himself.

Lady Mowbary had launched immediately into an all-consuming discussion of what ought to be worn, a topic which had held the unwavering attention of Céleste's sister-in-law and Gaëtane. Julia, Violet, Céleste, and Nicolette had taken what felt to be a far calmer and more logical approach: they made good on their previously vague plans to undertake a spot of shopping.

And thus it was, the day after Nicolette's visit with the Beaumonts, the four young ladies ventured to Swarkestone. They walked along the market cross, enjoying a delightful excursion away from the house and those who were making the house party less enjoyable than it would have otherwise been.

No one in the group could have a new gown made for the ball, both on account of how soon the event was occurring and how few options there were in Swarkestone for such things. Had they more time, they might have sought out a seamstress in Derby or Sheffield. But as it was, they visited the millinery shop in this village to seek out some lovely accessories and the haberdashery on the market cross for some very lovely ribbon the ladies could provide their lady's maids for creating adornments. In reality, all of the ladies knew the trip had been more an escape than a focused effort.

Having enjoyed their excursion, the ladies approached the spectacularly small inn where Lord Jonquil had arranged with his wife to meet at an appointed time, carriage primed and ready to make the return trip to Norwood. Through the large bow window, Nicolette spotted Lord Jonquil but also Mr. Layton, Mr. Greenberry, and Henri enjoying time in the inn's public room.

Lord Jonquil spotted them first. He smiled broadly, no doubt at Julia. She returned an expressive wave before turning back to the other ladies. "We'll offer them a moment to finish and reconcile with the proprietor. I suspected Lucas would not have the carriage ready upon our return. He tends to lose track of time."

"He does this often, then?" Nicolette asked.

Julia's expression was softly amused and undeniably besotted. "Quite often. But he is so lovely a person to lose track of time with that I can hardly hold it against him."

Nicolette turned to Violet. "Are they always this nauseatingly in love?"

The corners of Violet's mouth twitched. "Always." She adjusted the shawl pinned over one shoulder, its edges hanging low over her left arm. "And any couple with half a brain between them aspires to be as nauseating as Lord and Lady Jonquil."

Nicolette met Céleste's eye. They'd spoken over the years of what they imagined their future married lives would be. While they'd both hoped for contentment, and Nicolette had added to that hope actual happiness, neither had ever imagined being truly smitten and adored in return.

In the next moment, Henri emerged from the inn. He offered greetings to them all, including a quick brotherly kiss on the cheek to Céleste, but his attention was immediately on Nicolette. His smile was that of a person happily delighted with himself. "I have something for you."

Nicolette was intrigued. "Have you?"

He nodded.

Before Nicolette could say anything more, Violet did. She hooked her arms through one each of Céleste and Julia's, with the perpetually stiff one threaded through Julia's. "We shall wander through the gardens until the carriages are ready." She wiggled her dark eyebrows, the motion clearly meant to tease.

Nicolette was growing ever more accustomed to the way this group interacted. She liked it very much.

"No need to scamper off." Nicolette assumed an overly regal bearing, something that made them all smile more broadly. "M. Fortier and I will make a circuit of the gardens. I should hate for you all to miss out on an opportunity to look the quiz standing here in front of the inn, awaiting something or other."

They laughed at her pretended ostentatiousness. Henri smiled. Heavens, she grew more and more fond of that smile every time she saw it. How had she been so utterly unaware of it in Paris?

He offered her his arm. She slipped hers through it, and the two of them walked around the side of the inn where sat a plain but well-maintained garden. It was a very public location, and no one was likely to take exception to the two of them wandering there alone.

"I hadn't meant to end your time with the ladies early," Henri said. "And I fear you will have heightened expectations of my offering that will render it rather disappointing."

"Julia was being shockingly romantic in her discussions of her husband. I am quite pleased to have escaped more of that."

His chest shook with a silent laugh. "They are rather obviously in love. All the Gents had hoped to one day be at least not unhappy in their marriages. Seeing what Julia and Lucas have has led us all to set our sights a little higher."

She studied him. "Were you in search of such a match when I knew you in Paris?" She didn't remember him expressing those sentiments. "I don't recall you speaking of such things in any detail."

His movements grew a bit stiffer and noticeably more uncomfortable. "I—did a poor job of expressing my hopes. That was not—I have not always been adept at—My study of poetry did not teach me to adequately express my feelings aloud as I might have hoped."

She had embarrassed him. That had not at all been her aim. "Please forgive me, Henri. I didn't mean to make you think ill of yourself. While I don't remember that time in tremendous detail, I do remember that I enjoyed speaking with you and that I missed you when you left."

"You did?" His expression held both hope and doubt. *Doubt?*

"Of course I did. How could anyone not miss you when you were away?"

He set his hand atop hers, resting on his arm. "My father disliked that I lived away from home, but I can guarantee he did not actually miss me."

"You spoke of him a little in Paris, and Céleste has told me about him. I believe I can, with authority, declare that his opinion of anyone and anything ought not be trusted."

His thumb brushed lightly over her hand. Even through their gloves, the touch was tender and delicate, and it sent shivers of awareness through her just as his taking of her hand during their quest had done. Even during her earliest days in the whirl of society, the attention of a handsome gentleman hadn't fluttered her heart like this. There was something different about Henri Fortier, something delightful, something she feared she had, in fact, missed in Paris.

"You are saying very kind things about me," Henri said with a smile, "and I haven't even given you my offering yet."

Her heart flipped about, something it was doing with alarming frequency. "I'd forgotten you had something for me."

"We were rightly declared winners of one of the prizes in Lucas's hunt. And then he proceeded to eat the winnings."

"I don't suppose I will ever be able to forgive him for that," Nicolette said with a sigh.

Henri's smile didn't fade. "Knowing he obtained sweets from the confectionery shop here in the village, I went there myself when we first arrived this afternoon." He paused under the shade of a tree and pulled from his pocket a small paper-wrapped bundle. He slipped his arm free of hers and turned to face her directly. With a hint of a bow, he presented her with the bundle as if it were the greatest of treasures. "Your prize, mademoiselle."

She accepted it and peeled back the corners of the paper. Inside was a handful of assorted sweets. "These are for me?"

His eyes danced with the pleasing satisfaction that came from having imagined an idea and seen it through. "You said you have not ever had a peppermint or anise sweet, and I found myself wondering what others you haven't tried. So I chose several. You'll have to tell me which you like best, and I'll make certain to bring you more during this house party."

She held the small bundle in her hands, pressing it to her heart. "You would do that for me?"

"In a heartbeat."

Nicolette sighed, the tiniest bit of a laugh in the sound. "You say that as if everyone is simply clamoring to do kind things for me. I assure you that is not the case."

He brushed his hand lightly along her arm. "It ought to be the case, Nicolette. You ought to be the recipient of unending kindnesses."

Once more, his touch sent waves of delight crashing against her oft-guarded heart. His was not the practiced flattery she'd encountered in the past.

And the sincerity of his thoughtfulness stood in utter contrast to the treatment she'd had from Pierre.

She stepped a bit closer, near enough to lose herself for a moment in the depths of his brown eyes. She set her hand lightly against the side of his face. "*Merci, mon* Henri." She brushed a kiss to his other cheek, lingering for just a moment, all the while fighting her desire to simply set her arms around him and hope he would hold her. The strength of that desire both surprised and worried her. She turned and made her way quickly toward the front of the inn, forcing herself not to so much as look back at him.

If she weren't very, very careful, she could find herself falling truly in love with Henri Fortier.

# Chapter Sixteen

"SELFISHLY," STANLEY HAD SAID DURING their final year together at Cambridge, "I hope you eventually fall in love with an Englishwoman."

"Do you have a particular Englishwoman in mind?" Henri had answered, both amused and intrigued.

"Do *you?*" Stanley had replied.

"The Fortiers have standing in France, but I can't imagine any lady here would look twice at me."

"Nonsense." Stanley had assumed a theatrically arrogant mien. "You are a friend of the younger son of the Duke of Hartley, the heir to the Earl of Lampton, and the heir to the Baron Farland." He'd smugly straightened his cuffs at his mention of himself. "Also among your friends is the younger son of the Barrington family, who are inarguably good *ton*. The Greenberrys are also well thought of, and you have a close friendship with one of their number. And if nothing else, the ongoing, self-inflicted collapse of the Layton family makes everyone adjacent to them more interesting by association."

Stanley had never actually made light of any of their struggles, but he'd had a knack for helping them all find reasons to laugh when life was giving them ample reasons to never do so again.

"Other than interesting friends, I fear I haven't much to offer a lady." Henri had shrugged. "I'm rather pitiful, really."

The expression Stanley had worn most consistently was one of friendly amusement, but there'd always been a deep caring and compassion in his eyes. In that moment, his features had pulled in a formidable look the Gents had all learned to recognize as the precursor to his fierce defense of one of them. "Your father is wrong. He always has been. And any lady who cannot immediately spot the lie in what he has told you your whole life doesn't deserve to be part of that life."

"Easier said than done," Henri had replied.

"Fortune favors the bold, my friend. And you deserve good fortune more than almost anyone I know."

Nicolette had also insisted that the assessments Henri's father had made of his character ought to be ignored. She'd said she'd missed him after he'd left Paris. And in the garden at the inn, she'd called him *mon* Henri. *My* Henri. And she'd kissed him. On the cheek, yes. But a kiss. A lingering, soft, tender kiss.

Surely he was not seeing or hearing or feeling a connection that did not exist. He'd done that once before and was keen to avoid a repeat performance. It was not merely a matter of wishing to stave off embarrassment; he also did not wish to impose upon her. Gentlemen who relentlessly pursued ladies despite having received absolutely no encouragement or who had been openly *dis*couraged from doing so were not the sort of people Henri wished to emulate.

It was with this contradiction weighing on his mind that he crossed paths with Niles, who looked equally lost in his thoughts.

"Is something weighing on your mind?" Henri asked.

Niles smiled a little, the look fleeting and not terribly convincing. "I might ask you the same thing."

Niles was not generally one to start a conversation, but he also never seemed opposed to the idea of joining one. Giving it a bit of thought, Henri realized he had far fewer conversations with Niles than with any of the other Gents. That was a shame, really. Did Niles ever feel neglected or thought less of? Henri hoped not.

"Allow me to hypothesize what might be on your mind," Niles said. "Mlle Beaulieu is quite lovely, and she has shown herself to be witty and intelligent, and you very obviously enjoy her company."

Thoughts of Nicolette lifted his spirits. "She was very much that way in Paris as well. A person cannot help but enjoy her company."

"Talking of her now, you're smiling," Niles said, "but when I first crossed paths with you, you were not. Either you are terribly confused, or she was not the only thing you were thinking of." They were walking as they spoke, and their steps had taken them inside the billiards room on the north end of the house where Lucas and Digby were indulging in a game.

"Henri smiling while he is talking about someone?" Digby repeated, having apparently overheard the comment. "Must be Mlle Beaulieu."

"And frowning when Niles first saw him?" Lucas repeated that part. "I daresay Jean-François inspired that reaction."

Henri shook his head. "Pride goeth before the fall, my friends."

"In this case"—Digby pointed at him with his billiard cue—"pride goeth before the correct guess, I daresay."

Niles plopped himself on a chair in the room, watching the conversation with his usual grin. He was one of the happiest people of Henri's acquaintance, and yet there seemed to be an underlying dissatisfaction peeking out now and then.

"For your information," Henri said, "both my smile and my scowl have arisen from thoughts of the same person."

Lucas stepped back from the billiards table and pressed an open palm to his heart, then gave Henri a look of emotion-tinged delight. "I am that person, aren't I? You were thinking what a wonderful fellow I am and scowling because you could never live up to it."

"I don't imagine at any point in history an archbishop has felt he didn't compare favorably to a jester," Niles said with a laugh.

Henri assumed his pulled-brow expression of pious disapproval. "This is the ridiculousness that inevitably ensues when we have a discussion without Aldric and Kes present."

"Were we having a discussion?" Digby looked from one of them to the other. "I thought we were undertaking a guessing game. I refuse to participate if this is going to devolve into somber conversation."

Though Henri did often prefer to keep his troubles to himself, the confusion he felt outweighed his desire for privacy. "Niles was correct. I have been thinking of Nicolette."

"Even when you were scowling?" Lucas asked.

"Even then."

Digby narrowed his gaze on Henri. "You smile when you think of her. That smile turns to a scowl of uncertainty without your mind shifting topics." He nodded slowly as if a great many mysteries were suddenly being sorted. "You're falling in love."

Henri was quick to shake his head. "I would not go so far as all that."

"I would." Lucas cracked his cue against an ivory billiard ball, sending it rolling across the table. "Confusion is one of the primary symptoms, my friend."

"I will not deny that I am confused. I believe I have some reason to suspect she might be partial to me, and yet, there is ample reason for me to doubt it."

"What are the reasons?" Digby asked.

"I knew her in Paris during my last visit to that city, and I grew deeply fond of her."

In a voice as dry as dust, Lucas said, "Nothing turns a lady away from the idea of caring for a gentleman quite as swiftly as that gentleman *liking* her."

"Heaven forbid!" Digby declared dramatically. Then, in a voice pitched a bit higher than usual and with mannerisms clearly meant to represent a very fine lady of Society, he said, "I would think highly of you, sir, except that *you* think highly of *me*, and that casts such doubt on your intelligence."

Henri shook his head. "I suppose I can be grateful Stanley isn't here. This little performance of yours would have grown to ridiculous proportions if he were participating."

"It's no use changing the subject," Lucas warned. "Stanley was a performer, but I learned from his sister how to be shockingly stubborn."

"You were stubborn before Julia stole your heart," Niles said.

"But not *shockingly*," was the theatrically delivered rejoinder.

Digby did not seem the least distracted from their initial purpose. "What are the reasons you doubt Mlle Beaulieu has developed a fondness for you?"

"While in Paris, I was made painfully aware of her requirements for a potential suitor, and I fulfilled very few items on her list."

"It is possible her requirements have changed," Niles said from his comfortable position watching them all.

"I suspect some have," Henri acknowledged. "But no lady can be faulted for recognizing that a gentleman's financial and social situation must be taken into consideration, as they have such a direct impact on hers. I haven't sufficient income for securing my own comforts, let alone those of anyone else. I haven't even a home to claim as my own. And my social position is shaky."

"The Fortiers are a family of significant standing," Digby countered.

"In France, yes. But I don't live there. And I would be very much surprised if she didn't include 'lives in France' on her list of requirements in a suitor."

"So those are your reasons for suspecting she would *not* be interested in you as a suitor." Lucas gave Digby a look that clearly indicated he felt Henri was protesting too much before returning his attention to Henri once more. "What are your reasons for thinking she might be interested despite that?"

"She has seemed to enjoy spending time with me. She took my hand while we were hunting out items on Lucas's list of challenges. She smiled at me in such a way . . ." For a moment, he was lost. The memory of that smile. Only when he realized his friends were grinning at him, barely holding back laughs, did he recollect himself and pushed on. "And I'm all but certain she came within a whisper of truly kissing me yesterday."

Their smiles were replaced by wide-eyed looks of surprise.

"I do not imagine that Mlle Beaulieu is a young lady who goes about 'almost kissing' just anyone," Niles said. "That seems to me more than ample reason to think there's a possibility of attachment."

Henri began pacing. This was the debate that had been raging in his mind for a day now.

"Everyone at the house party has begun to wonder if perhaps you've caught her eye and she yours," Digby said. The game of billiards had been entirely abandoned. "You spend quite a lot of time in each other's company."

Henri's lungs deflated once more. "It is a ruse," he admitted with a sigh. "She was annoyed at her family for pushing her at Aldric. We were both frustrated with my family for doing the same to Céleste. So we concocted this scheme in which we would give the impression that perhaps there might be something resembling the first buds of interest between us."

Lucas nodded. "Now you don't know how much of the interest you are sensing is genuine and how much is part of this scheme you've tossed yourselves into."

"Quite a mess we've found ourselves in, isn't it?"

"For whose benefit did she 'almost kiss' you yesterday?" Niles asked, something in his expression indicating he thought Henri more foolish than he needed to be. "I suspect if this near kiss happened in full view of anyone from the house party, we would have heard about it."

Digby was nodding. Lucas seemed to be contemplating what Niles was explaining. Henri was still a bit lost.

"If I had to guess," Niles continued, "I would say this happened with no witnesses and under circumstances that would do absolutely nothing to further your bit of playacting."

"That's true." Henri tried to keep the hope he felt at bay. "We were entirely alone." He looked at each of his friends in turn. "It couldn't have been a ruse, as there was no reason to play our parts with only the two of us present."

Lucas dropped a hand on Henri's shoulder. "While it is not a guarantee—I am fully aware that ladies can be remarkably confusing—I do think that moment ought not be dismissed outright. I can't say the lady is top over tail in love with you, but I daresay the interest you are sensing isn't entirely imagined."

Oh, how he wanted to believe it. As much as he had insisted he was too wise for such a course, his heart was ready to love her fully and completely and even more than he had three years earlier. But he also knew how entirely his heart had broken the last time. He knew the pain of that still lingered, and he wasn't certain he could put himself through it again.

"Even if she is interested, and even if I am—which, I'll point out, I haven't said I am—"

Digby actually snorted, something uncouth enough that he seldom did it. Niles laughed. Lucas wore his trademark grin, one so similar to what Stanley had always worn that it never failed to put Henri in mind of the friend they all still grieved.

"Take it from someone who spent far too long denying that he was in love with the lady of his very dreams," Lucas said, "you are falling in love with her. Where that love will lead or how this story will play out, I don't know. But the first step is admitting that you hold affection for her."

"Admitting *to her*?" The very idea struck panic in his heart.

"Lands, no," Digby scoffed. "'There's a possibility she doesn't think me an imbecile' is hardly firm enough footing for confessing love."

"Where were you three years ago?" Henri muttered.

Three pairs of eyes pulled wide. The length of a breath passed, then they all burst out laughing.

"You *told her* three years ago that you were enamored of her?" Lucas asked through his continued laughter. "I would ask how poorly that went, but you not only returned from Paris unattached but have also never spoken of it."

"I made the most elegant and heartfelt confession I could manage, and she . . . was not interested."

"Oh, Henri." Digby shook his head. "You should have told us."

"So you could have commiserated?"

"So we could have mercilessly taunted you," Lucas countered. "And then commiserated." A look of understanding suddenly flashed across his features. "This is the piece of the puzzle Julia is searching out. She insisted from the moment we learned the Beaulieus were invited to this gathering that there was more to your acquaintance with Mlle Beaulieu than her friendship with your sister."

"Mlle Beaulieu has not seemed uncomfortable around you," Niles said.

"She doesn't . . ." He took a breath, forcing himself to complete the embarrassing admission. "She doesn't appear to remember that I was in love with her. Indeed, her recollections of our acquaintance are vague and relatively benign."

"Even your 'elegant and heartfelt' declaration of love?" Digby pressed.

What could Henri do except shrug?

"Are you certain she understood what you were saying?" Niles asked. "I can't imagine most ladies would simply forget being told they were the object of someone's undying affection."

Again, he could do nothing but shrug.

"Even by the usual Gents standard, this is quite a mess, Archbishop," Lucas said.

"What ought I to do?" Henri asked, though part of him dreaded the answer.

"Miss Georgie has plans to commandeer the seaside house of a family acquaintance in Hampshire," Lucas said. Miss Georgie was Violet's ten-year-old niece. "I'm certain she would allow you to explore the joys of self-imposed hermitry with her."

"As appealing as hermitry is," Henri said, "I do not think it is the best answer to my difficulties."

"Allow me to offer you the same thoughts I shared with Lucas and Kes when they were making a mull of their respective love lives," Digby said. "I shudder to think how often I will have to have this conversation with the rest of you." He made an overly dramatic show of being annoyed before pushing forward. "Love can sneak up on a person, can start without us even realizing. But once you know you feel something, it no longer makes the least sense to sit around and do nothing. You are beginning to love her. *Again*, apparently. If you think the possibility of being loved in return is worth reaching for, tiptoe into the water, allowing her response to guide you. If you think it utter foolishness and that pursuing those feelings would result in misery for either of you, keep your distance. But for goodness' sake, sitting about, twiddling your thumbs, bemoaning the complexity of it all, will accomplish absolutely nothing."

"I don't know that I could bear to have my heart broken again," he admitted in a quiet voice.

"Love is always a risk," Lucas said. "But for the right person, it is a risk worth taking."

"And if I might add a thought," Niles said. "It is entirely possible that nothing will come of this tentative connection, but not everyone is afforded the chance to choose the person with whom they spend the rest of their life. If there is even the possibility of making that decision for yourself, don't waste it."

There was both wisdom and heartache in those words. But it proved precisely the nudge Henri needed. He'd wallowed so long in the pain of heartbreak that he'd not stopped to acknowledge what a privilege it truly was to have any choice at all in the matter. He suspected Niles would give almost anything to have some hope of that himself.

It was with this determination and this newfound understanding that he left his friends behind and went in search of his brother.

As if fate wanted to make certain Henri didn't lose his courage, he found his brother alone in the book room. It was an opportunity he was unlikely to be afforded again. Similar discussions to the one he was contemplating had not gone well, and he'd little reason to believe that would change.

*Fortune favors the bold.*

*Stronger and braver.*

Henri stepped inside and screwed his courage to the sticking place, as the Bard would have said.

"Might I have a moment of your time?" Henri asked.

Jean-François looked up slowly from his book and nodded without any real degree of urgency.

"I have been meaning to discuss a matter with you in recent months." Henri sat on a chair near his brother's. "I would like to broach it now."

Jean-François set his book aside. "What is this topic?"

"I am aware of the terms of our father's will." Henri chose to strike straight to the heart of the matter. "I know what my income from his estate was designated to be."

Jean-François's posture stiffened almost imperceptibly. The change actually proved motivating. It was the first indication Henri had ever had that his brother recognized his actions in this matter were not entirely aboveboard.

"Father has been gone for nearly five years," Henri continued. "For the first while, my income matched what I was promised. It, however, has been reduced repeatedly since then. In the last six months, my promised income has been cut down to the point that I am receiving a tiny fraction of what I ought."

"Are you accusing me of not honoring our late father's wishes? Of being a poor steward of his estate?"

Although Henri was, in fact, accusing him of precisely that, he could sense it would not be best to say as much. "I simply want to understand. The amount was very clear. In fact, you even stated at the time how brief and precise my portion of the will was. Father included no flowery language, no words of hope for my future, or words of love for me. He *did* have kind things to say about his favorite dog."

Jean-François, for the first time in recent memory, looked a little sad on Henri's behalf.

"I want only to understand," Henri said, realizing, even if Jean-François did not, that they were speaking of more than his reduced income.

"That bit of father's will was very straightforward," Jean-François acknowledged. "The complications arose elsewhere in the inheritance."

"Such as?" Henri pressed. As much as he wanted to have the money to live on and a chance to settle somewhere, he found he wanted even more earnestly to have a connection with his brother again, to have a reason to think well of him once more.

The Gents teased him about his determination to avoid thinking ill of people even if they deserved it. The truth of the matter was that inclination didn't come from saintliness; it was the result of exhaustion. Bitterness was a heavy burden to carry.

"The Fortier holdings include a very small estate near Nantes," Jean-François said. "I was only vaguely aware of it before. We never traveled there, and Father never spoke of it. From what I have been able to ascertain, Chalet-sur-Loire was part of Mother's dowry."

The Hartley holdings in France had been part of Aldric's mother's dowry. Such a thing wasn't unusual.

"I discovered as I examined Father's papers that Chalet-sur-Loire had been set aside in our parents' marriage agreement as available for the use of a younger son, provided the older son inherited the Fortier lands at a young age and didn't have need of it himself and hadn't any children of an age to take up residence."

"I have been left an estate?" Henri had heard nothing of this. His mind could not make the least sense of it. He'd spent years attempting to find a place to live. Could it be possible he'd had one all along?

But Jean-François shook his head. "The estate is a Fortier holding, and it is not severable. But it was meant for your use."

"What has this to do with my income being reduced?" Henri had expected some surprises but nothing of this nature.

"Properties require upkeep and effort; Chalet-sur-Loire is no different. As it was meant to be your residence, your income is addressing the needs there."

It was reasonable on the surface, but below that veneer of correctness was rot. "Chalet-sur-Loire, as you pointed out, was not given to me, and I have no ownership of it. It is an inseverable Fortier holding, which makes it the responsibility of the Fortier estate. You haven't the right to withhold my income and spend it on something that is *your* responsibility."

Henri recognized his mistake on the instant. Jean-François's expression hardened, leaving him looking far too much like their father for Henri's peace of mind. "Do not lecture me about *responsibilities*, Henri. Our mother was desperate for you to return, and you didn't. Father made every attempt to bring you back to France, but you were too stubborn to think of anyone other than yourself. You gallivanted about *this* country and are now complaining that I haven't given you enough money. Playing the immigrant gentleman may have had its appeal when you were younger, but the time is long past for you to abandon this game and assume your *responsibilities* at home."

"It was never a game, Jean-François," he said. "This country is my home now."

"You have family in France. You have a house in France and, with it, would have ample income enough to live on. And you would be where you belong."

Jean-François likely had no idea the precision with which his darts were hitting home. He was offering all the things that felt out of Henri's reach, and yet they came with far too many entanglements.

"Here I have the Gents," Henri said. "Chance brought us together as friends, but we have chosen each other as family. Were any of them given charge over my income and my future, not one of them would cheat me of it as you have. Because they are family to me and they love me as family ought."

For just a moment, Jean-François looked hurt. For the length of a breath, he looked like the brother Henri had once known, the one who had cared what happened to him, the one who had wanted them to be close. But that moment passed in the blink of an eye, and Jean-François's expression hardened once more. "And what of Chalet-sur-Loire? I happen to know you don't have any place to call home. And what of an income? I happen to know that is insufficient."

"I didn't realize you were aware of my search for a home here."

"A gentleman of your age must wish for a roof over his head."

Henri didn't mean to press the matter of his income, lest his brother inadvertently guess that he had gone against the family wishes and was publishing poetry to supplement his insufficient funds.

"French law would be on my side in the matter of you withholding my funds and using them to cover expenses which legally are yours," Henri said. "Any judge who heard the matter would order you to return every livre of my income to me, possibly even to pay me for what you have withheld these past years."

Jean-François was unmoved. "In France, fortune and social standing hold tremendous sway with the law. *I* still have both."

There was far too much truth in that. The injustices of the law in both France and England would likely one day require a reconciliation, an undertaking that was more likely to be blood-soaked than peaceful. He suspected neither country would escape some degree of upheaval and turmoil in the decades and centuries to come.

"Am I to understand, then"—Henri kept his words calm—"that you have no intention of restoring the income our Father's final wishes promised me?" He hated that he already knew the answer.

"You have before you two choices, Henri," Jean-François said as he stood. "You can return to France, where you were always meant to be. You can make your home at Chalet-sur-Loire and have the income promised you and once more claim your standing in French society, securing for yourself a bright future. Or you can remain here, living off the charity of these gentlemen you think of as family, discovering just how far the pity of foreign friends can extend." Jean-François walked to the door, then turned back to look at him. "You never should have left France, Henri. The Fortiers belong there. We always have, and we always will."

# *Chapter Seventeen*

"I am very curious what the home of an English marquess is like," Sébastien said as their carriage rolled toward Tafford, where the ball was being held. "I have been to the homes of a few marquises in France, and they were decidedly elegant. One hopes we are not about to discover that an English marquess is something of a letdown."

Nicolette inwardly cringed. Sometimes her brother said things that gave the impression of significant arrogance. He was proud, and life in the French upper class tended to teach a person to value appearances and class divides, but at his heart, he was a good person. Yes, he was trying to "put to rights" her lack of an engagement, but he truly was a caring brother. Her wincing in that moment came from the reminder that she had once viewed the world in ways that aligned with the impression given by his rather unmeasured declaration.

"Lord Jonquil indicated that this ball isn't likely to be as much of a press as many such gatherings are," Nicolette warned them. "The ball was decided upon and held very quickly, without time for all the significant families within traveling distance to make the journey."

Gaëtane waved that off. "I am certain there will be enough enjoyable people in attendance to render the evening perfectly acceptable."

That her sister-in-law didn't acknowledge any prospect for disappointment was suspicious. When people did not behave as they usually did, especially when that change came quickly, one did well to pay very close attention.

Nicolette watched her brother and sister-in-law as the carriage drew to a stop in front of Tafford. They were studying the edifice of the grand country home.

"I daresay the evening will prove adequately interesting and beneficial," Sébastien said.

He and Gaëtane exchanged a knowing glance, the sort married couples often employed when discussing something both of them were privy to and did not need to speak aloud. But what could that something be? They might still have hopes where Lord Aldric was concerned. She suspected they also hoped this evening's gathering would afford them the opportunity to make the acquaintance of the marquess's unmarried heir.

She would be wise to know what she was facing, so she introduced the topic. "Do you suppose Lord Yesley will be present this evening? I'm not certain the school holidays have coincided with the ball." Referencing school was perhaps a bit of an exaggeration, but the future marquess *was* younger than she. As much as she had not enjoyed the way Pierre had paraded her about like a treasure to be gawked at, she did not relish the idea of a husband so young that she would feel more like a nursemaid than a wife.

There was no reaction to her question from either of her companions. That only raised her suspicions further.

They alighted from the carriage. Tafford was grand by all estimations, a conglomeration of many styles and eras, the fingerprints of generations. There was something so pleasing in the almost haphazard nature of it. It felt welcoming and warm even before one set foot inside.

Lord and Lady Grenton and their son stood in the entry hall, greeting guests. The host and hostess proved as congenial and welcoming as their home had promised, though there was more friendliness than sophistication in their approach. Lord Yesley, who could not have been more than twenty or twenty-one, seemed pleased to make the acquaintance of each person who passed by. He had the look of one who had once had red hair but the color had darkened and calmed over the years. He also had the look of one who was genuinely friendly and enjoyed people for their own sake rather than any benefit to himself.

The ballroom proved a perfect match for the resident family. It was tasteful and lovely and not the least ostentatious. Even before her time in *La Tapisserie*, Nicolette had been an observer of places and people. She'd found over the years that some homes, some buildings, some locations had an emotion to them, a lingering sense of things gone by. A person could feel instantly at ease or apprehensive, peaceful or on edge, buoyed or saddened simply by entering a space. Tafford immediately imbued a person with a feeling of welcome and calm.

Nicolette had given some thought to what she would like her eventual home to feel like, should she claim one. The time she had spent, appropriately chaperoned of course, at Pierre's house in Paris, had left her uneasy. She had initially dismissed the experience, assuming it was nervousness or the unfamiliarity of the space. The more she had come to know Pierre, the more she had realized his home felt the way it did because of his presence there.

What would Henri's home feel like if he had one?

She shook that from her thoughts quickly. Her mind wandered to Henri with alarming frequency of late, and those thoughts were pleasing and comforting and, in the short time since their interlude in the garden in Swarkestone, set her heart pounding a bit.

"I believe this will be a nice evening," Gaëtane said, glancing around the room. The guests who were present added a colorful brilliance to the space. "I have every hope it will be a particularly excellent evening for you." On the final word, she looked at Nicolette.

People who were plotting often gave themselves away with the tiniest widening of their eyes when hinting at the very thing they were so convinced they were keeping hidden. That exact expression flitted through Gaëtane's eyes, and Nicolette was instantly invested in what her sister-in-law might say next. But Gaëtane did not seem at all inclined to continue speaking.

Céleste arrived at Nicolette's side and, hooking an arm through hers, led her away without so much as a word of explanation or apology to Sébastien or Gaëtane. That was one benefit of having a friend of such long standing of whom her family approved. They had a freedom to interact with each other that existed in very few other relationships.

"You were so late in getting here that I was a little bit afraid you'd decided not to attend," Céleste said.

"You know my brother and sister-in-law adhere to the Paris timetable," Nicolette said. In Paris, tardiness was an art, and the Beaulieus were virtuosos. "As you have been here longer than I, offer me your thoughts on the gathering."

They had often taken this approach in Paris. The Fortiers, while generally not arriving overly early, didn't make their appearance at social events quite as fashionably late as the Beaulieus.

"There are a few families from a bit farther afield here tonight but not overly many. I would say the arrival of the crowd from Norwood has nearly doubled the number of people who would have been here otherwise."

A decidedly small gathering.

"Everyone seems perfectly amiable," Céleste continued. "There is variety, as expected. Some seem a bit pompous while others seem pleased simply to be included. Our host and hostess are remarkably friendly. I am hopeful that now that they have met Lord Yesley, my family will abandon any thoughts of a match there. He is a puppy."

"I thought Niles Greenwood was Puppy." Nicolette shifted her eyes to her friend, maintaining a very serious expression right up until Céleste's composure broke and they both laughed lightly.

"I confess, I did not know at all what to think of the Gents when I first met them," Nicolette said. "I find myself very much wishing you and I had friends like them in France. They have their oddities, yes, but they have good hearts, and they are kind and loyal. I cannot imagine any of them treating each other the way some in Paris do."

Céleste nodded solemnly, the expression not a theatrical one. There were those in Paris society who were merciless. Even before her time with Pierre had brought about a transformation in her, Nicolette had not liked that aspect of interactions with the *bon-ton*.

"Julia says that all of the Gents enjoy dancing," Céleste said. "Neither of us should want for partners tonight."

"I suspect they are well-mannered enough that our sisters-in-law will not want for partners either." She took a glance around the room. "Although, based on the imbalance in the numbers, I suspect no lady is going to spend much of the evening sitting about."

The gathering was quite heavy with gentlemen. She didn't know if the local populace had simply seen a tremendous number of sons in the current generation and the one preceding or if the local young ladies simply weren't in attendance. The result was the same regardless of the cause. Many gentlemen would be sitting out the dances.

Nicolette and Céleste had been walking together around the edge of the ballroom, and their steps brought them to the place where the Gents and Julia and Violet stood. All expressed delight at being together and offered happy observances of the gathering. This was another thing Nicolette liked about this group. Among them, sophistication wasn't proven through dissatisfaction. And they didn't demonstrate their discerning taste by belittling others.

"We had hoped to have a moment with the two of you free of your families' presence," Lucas said. "Henri excepting, of course."

"In discussions of my family, I always consider Céleste and myself to be the exceptions," Henri said, somehow managing to sound as though he were delivering holy writ rather than a jesting observation. Perhaps that was part of the reason they called him Archbishop.

"We know the two of you, as well as Aldric"—Lucas tipped his head in the direction of that gentleman—"are rather anxious to give your families the impression that none of the pairings they have in mind would be the least desirable."

"Most decidedly," Céleste said.

"Undesirable doesn't begin to describe the situation," Aldric added.

Nicolette chose only to smile.

"We haven't been able to decide whether it would be best if he never dances with either of you so as not to afford your families a chance to declare 'What a lovely couple!'" Lucas managed to deliver the declaration in a rather absurd French accent. "Or if we would do best to have him dance with you both as part of nothing more than a rotation of partners."

Nicolette was accustomed to needing to strategize, but this plotting was quite different from what she usually undertook. "I notice there are significantly more gentlemen present than ladies."

A few in the group nodded, apparently having noticed themselves.

"I suspect Céleste and I will not want for partners tonight. Thus, I believe if Lord Aldric does not dance with us, his doing so will not draw any undue attention. What it is more likely to convey is that he was not overly anxious to secure either of us as his partner rather than intentionally ignoring us."

Julia nodded. "I had similar thoughts myself. It would be best if at least a couple of the other Gents dance with each of you, lest we give the impression the entire group is somehow overlooking you both."

They all agreed.

Niles, however, added, "Should something odd happen and either of you is left without a partner, which I don't imagine will actually happen, and we have already all danced with you once, I do not think it would serve our purposes for Aldric not to do the gentlemanly thing." He was quieter than his friends, and she suspected a great many in Society were just as likely to ignore him as to take note of him, but Niles Greenberry had shown himself to be a good person. She hoped, for his sake, he someday met someone who saw in him the worth that far too many overlooked.

The musicians were striking up a minuet. Kes took Violet's hand and led her to the nearby chairs. It seemed they meant to spend the set together but did not intend to join in dancing. Perhaps Violet did not usually dance, likely on account of whatever injury had rendered her arm rather stiff and uncooperative. Nicolette had not yet sorted the mystery of that.

Lucas offered his wife a wonderfully and beautifully executed bow. "My lady," he said with equal parts theater and tenderness. "Would you do the honor of standing up with me for this set?"

"If I dance the minuet with you, does that mean you will not be dancing the allemande with me?"

When he looked at Julia, the love in his eyes took a person's breath away. They had the kind of connection poets wrote epochs to. "I will save all my allemandes for you, my darling Julia." He led his wife to the other dancers, the two of them making a tremendously handsome couple.

Digby claimed Céleste as his partner, another striking couple.

Nicolette knew Lord Aldric would not be asking her to dance with him. Far from offended, she thought it a good strategy. She didn't doubt the Gents would take it in turns to see to it she had a partner. As she thought on who might ask her now, her heart pounded out a rhythm that in her foolishness sounded a great deal like Henri's name.

He was still standing where the others had been. He turned to face her, then offered a bow. She returned it with a curtsy. He smiled, and her heart all but burst beneath her ribs.

"I'd be very honored, Mlle Beaulieu, if you would agree to dance with me." He made the request in French.

Nicolette set her hand in his outstretched one. Though they both wore gloves, there was a warmth there, just as there had been at the inn. It was reassuring and peaceful. Somehow, he managed to set her heart aflutter and calm her mind all at the same time. They were playing a part, yes, but she was absolutely certain his kindness and enjoyment of her company was sincere. Though she felt foolish, she realized she'd begun to hope that he cared for her beyond their efforts to help his friend and his sister.

The minuet began. Nicolette fluttered her arms in the graceful movements that marked the opening measures of the elegant dance. The overlapping circles the couples undertook in their group followed. Their steps brought Nicolette to Henri once more.

"You remain one of the most graceful dancers I have ever seen," he said.

"Did we dance in Paris?"

He dipped his head. "Once."

They were separated again, but she watched him, her cheeks heating upon realizing his eyes followed her as well. Had he done so during that one dance in Paris? How could she have forgotten? How could this feeling not have engraved itself permanently on her mind and heart?

Every time the steps of the dance brought them together, his smile turned tender. She mattered to him; that seemed clear. But what that meant in the end, she didn't yet know.

As the music ended, she bent into the deep curtsy as he struck the elegant bow that always closed the minuet. The gathering applauded the dancers. Henri led her with her hand in his, moving regally and with great dignity back among the other guests.

Sébastien and Gaëtane stood not far distant. Both looked very nearly thunderous, as close as they would have allowed themselves to become in company. Truth be told, they also seldom looked truly upset when *not* in company. She missed the teasing interactions she usually had with her brother. This feeling of being at odds with him was as unenjoyable as it was unfamiliar.

She understood Sébastien's disapproval, to an extent. Henri hadn't fortune or an estate. He was a Fortier, which placed him at the very apex of the most glittering circles. France would welcome him with open arms should he choose to return. But in England, though he had connections to some very fine families, he had no title or wealth or the degree of social cachet her brother and sister-in-law found necessary.

"I can whisk you away to Julia and Violet if you would prefer," Henri said quickly and quietly. He had, it seemed, noticed the direction of her gaze and the disapproval she anticipated having to confront.

But before Nicolette could accept his offer, Céleste, who stood not terribly far distant, gasped. She was so well-versed in social interactions that such a gaffe could not be caused by anything insignificant.

Nicolette looked at her, then followed her gaze to the doors of the ballroom. The blush that had stolen across Nicolette's cheeks at Henri's kind offer of escape turned instantly to ice as every drop of blood drained from her face. A gentleman had just arrived, one she had not expected to see ever again, certainly not in this tiny corner of England: Pierre Léandre.

# Chapter Eighteen

ALL NICOLETTE'S SELF-GUIDED TUTORING IN maintaining a neutral and unreadable expression failed her. All thoughts fled her mind.

Pierre had disappeared so entirely from Paris that she had wondered over the last two years if something horrid had happened to him. While she was relieved to see he was still living and appeared to be whole, the greater part of her had not and still did not want to see him again.

Yet, here he was.

She didn't think she had managed anything beyond the slightest expansion of her lungs from the moment of his arrival; however, Sébastien was undertaking introductions to the Gents, Lord and Lady Mowbary, and Julia and Violet.

"I have a guess as to the identity of this new arrival," Henri whispered, "and if I am correct, I suspect you might appreciate a hasty retreat."

"It *is* tempting." At last, her lungs allowed her to take a full breath. "But I suspect running away is not my best option."

"What would you like me to do?"

She glanced up at him. "Are you offering to fight my battle for me?"

"*With* you." He set his hand atop hers where it rested on his arm. "You lead the charge, *Capitaine* Beaulieu, and I will do whatever you ask of me."

"How skilled are you at enduring rampant awkwardness?" Nicolette asked with an inward smile.

"My time amongst the Gents has given me ample opportunity to develop that skill."

Oh, he was good for her heart. "Will you promise not to abandon me?"

"I will remain stalwartly at your side," he said. And she fully and immediately believed him.

Sébastien ushered Pierre to where she stood. She would not be granted so much as a moment to collect her thoughts or regain a sense of calm.

During her time among *La Tapisserie*, she had learned to quickly assess people's postures and behavior. Sébastien was a little uncomfortable and ill-at-ease. He was doing his utmost to hide the fact that he was not gaining near as much pleasure from the return of his would-be brother-in-law as most anyone would have guessed. Pierre wore an expression of relaxed gratification, as if his abrupt return were hardly noteworthy, but his smile, one often complimented for its symmetry, currently tipped higher on one side, a tiny, almost imperceptible smirk that made the almost hidden smugness in his eyes easier to spot.

That decided for her how to proceed. She would allow him to be "introduced" rather than acknowledge their connection without prompting. She didn't do so in order to insult him but to counter the upper hand he clearly already thought he had.

"Nicolette," Sébastien said. "See who I have found."

She kept her expression neutral as she looked to Pierre. "Monsieur."

"It is a pleasure to see you again, Nicolette." Pierre had always possessed impeccable manners, but they slipped in that moment. Even when they were engaged, they did not use each other's given names in such a public setting.

She turned a bit toward Henri. "Might I make introductions between yourself and this new arrival?" Nicolette didn't have to see Pierre's face to know he would find fault with this approach. To ask for Henri's acquiescence was an indication she felt him to be Pierre's social superior. The Fortiers were far more esteemed than the Léandres, but Pierre would not see things that way.

"Of course, Mlle Beaulieu," Henri answered as impeccably in his civility as Pierre but with actual sincerity.

"M. Léandre," Nicolette said, "may I introduce you to M. Henri Fortier, whose family, you likely know, resides at Fleur-de-la-Forêt." The Fortier's grand family home was known by all and envied by many. "M. Fortier, this is M. Léandre, who resides at . . ." She pulled her brows together in an expression of pondering. "It is not known these past years where he resides, but M. Léandre did at one time make his home in Paris."

Both gentlemen offered the other a bow of acknowledgment. Pierre's was a bit clipped, and Henri's was unexceptional.

"What brings you to Derbyshire, M. Léandre?" Henri asked the very question Nicolette wished to have answered.

"The kindness of lady fortune, it would seem." Pierre smiled at Nicolette. "And in another act of divine benevolence, I have arrived at your side just as the musicians are striking up another tune."

They were playing the opening strains of an allemande, in fact. She could not dance again with Henri so soon. Pleading with one of the Gents to whisk her away before Pierre could claim her for the dance would be both humiliating and contradictory to the impression of neutrality she was attempting to convey. But she was not ready to spend that much time with him yet. Her thoughts were too jumbled for any degree of equilibrium.

Without warning and without so much as a meeting of eyes, Lucas placed himself a little between her and Pierre. He sketched a gracefully executed bow. "Mlle Beaulieu, I do believe this is the dance you agreed to honor me with."

Utter relief washed over her. "Forgive me, Lord Jonquil, for having kept you waiting."

"Not at all." He offered his arm, and she accepted it.

They stepped away from the others, making a circuit of the room as partners sometimes did before joining the dancing.

"This is the allemande," Nicolette reminded him. "All your allemandes are promised to your wife."

"Julia would skin me alive if I were to leave a friend of hers to the company of a man who, even at first acquaintance, appears to be a person of questionable character."

Lucas had realized that in a matter of minutes. *She* hadn't recognized Pierre's true character for months. She sighed. "I cannot fathom why he is here."

"The Gents will act as your bulwark tonight, providing you with as much buffer as you wish. And I have every confidence Julia and Violet will find a means of hearing any whispers regarding his arrival that might shine a light on his unwanted presence."

"I do not wish to ruin the evening for any of you," she said.

His grin was subtle but mischievous. "There are few things the Gents and our ladies enjoy as much as thwarting a blackguard."

"You will think me ridiculous," she said, "but I don't know for certain if he is a blackguard. Unreliable, thoughtless, and cunning certainly. But I do not know if the pain those traits inflict is done intentionally."

He led her to a place among the other dancers. "Intentional or not," he said quietly, "the Gents will do all we can to prevent that pain."

"Thank you," she said.

"*Avec plaisir.*"

"There must be something we can do about M. Léandre," Niles said from his position near the windows of Henri's bedchamber. The Gents had gathered there early the next morning, all agreeing to take their morning meal on trays in that room.

"I don't know that there is much to be done," Henri said. "He is now here as Mowbary's guest." That invitation had been extended the night before.

"Mowbary has a knack for making life miserable," Aldric said with a sigh. "He ought to have realized Léandre was not wanted by most of the guests here."

"Nicolette looked at the newly arrived Frenchman with much the same expression I gave my tailor when he suggested I pair a burgundy waistcoat with scarlet pantaloons." Digby shook his head, his mouth pulling in a line of clear annoyance.

"Is that an undesirable combination?" Niles asked seemingly in innocence, but the Gents knew him well enough to see the teasing expression in his eyes.

"Burgundy and scarlet?" Digby managed to sound as if combining the words in a sentence, let alone on his person, was almost too much to bear. "Try it sometime, Puppy. All and sundry will declare you an utter quiz."

The Gents could lighten any discussion without making light of difficult situations.

"M. Léandre and Nicolette were once engaged," Henri said, hearing the sigh in his words.

That brought everyone's eyes to him once more.

"They were betrothed two years ago, sometime after I last saw her. She told me she was miserable and that he knew she was miserable but didn't care."

"Far too many men don't." Lucas pushed out a tense breath.

"She said her feeling at the end of their betrothal was that she had made a fortunate escape." He rubbed at the tension between his eyes. "At least her admittedly vague memories of me were not steeped in misery."

"I suspect her memories won't be vague this time," Niles said. "No one watching the two of you would ever believe you are entirely indifferent to each other."

The others offered their agreement.

"You're different when you're with her," Kes said. "You're more the Henri I met upon joining you all at Cambridge: focused and determined, yes, but also lighthearted and a grand addition to any lark."

"Instead of the pitifully dull Archbishop I am now?"

"There is *nothing* pitiful about our Archbishop," Aldric declared firmly.

Choruses of "Here, here," joined declarations of "Indeed," around the room.

"You're my friends." Henri shook his head. "You have to say things like that."

"We could just as easily call you a hulverhead," Lucas said. "Stanley would have if he'd heard you echoing your father's words and, worse still, believing them."

"He did tell me quite often to stop listening to my father's evaluations of me," Henri said.

"We've *all* told you that over the years," Lucas said. "I think it is time you listened."

# Chapter Nineteen

Though she had planned to call on the Beaumonts the day following the ball and had adequate reason to do so, Nicolette couldn't entirely argue that abandoning Norwood Manor and rushing to the neighboring estate hadn't felt more like an escape than her previous call there. She could work on behalf of *La Tapisserie* and not worry about Pierre lurking around every corner.

Navigating the very sensitive work she did on behalf of an organization that operated clandestinely and in potentially quite dangerous matters felt like being cocooned in tranquility and safety compared to even a moment in the drawing room with Pierre. If the marquis could see how quickly she'd scampered off after less than twenty-four hours of her one-time fiancé's taking up residence at Norwood Manor, he would likely lose all faith in her judgment.

She was seated at the table in a small sitting room at Eau Plate, M. Beaumont to her left and Mme Beaumont to her right. In front of them was a rough but adequately drawn map of Britain. On it were dots made in a very unique shade of purple ink. Beside each dot was a symbol. There was no key, nothing that would explain to anyone seeing the map what those dots and symbols indicated.

The three of them knew.

"This is the home of the Gilbert family," M. Beaumont said, continuing the conversation that had been ongoing for several minutes and pointing at a purple dot a bit above the last one they had discussed. "Though they are several generations removed from France, they are proud of their heritage. They are good hearted, reliable, and loyal."

"And generous," Mme Beaumont added. "Amandine Gilbert was one of my first friends in this country."

The description brought Henri to mind. He was not several generations removed from France, but he, too, felt a sense of pride in being French, and he was as kind and loyal and generous as anyone she knew, her first true friend in this country as well.

M. Beaumont indicated yet another dot. "This is the home of Lord and Lady Jonquil, who are at your house party. They do not have French connections, but even before we met them here, we heard of their good and kind hearts. I suspect if we find ourselves in need of someone nearly in Scotland, they could be counted on to offer refuge to our countrymen."

"I suspect the same is true of Mr. and Mrs. Barrington and Mr. Digby Layton. I do not think Lord Aldric or Mr. Greenberry have homes of their own that they could open to our cause."

"Does M. Henri Fortier?" Mme Beaumont asked.

"Unfortunately, no. Elsewise, I would have suggested him immediately."

"How all of this is arranged and organized will depend upon who it is who is seeking refuge," M. Beaumont said. "Will it be the bourgeoisie? The poorest? The laborers? The aristocracy?" He shrugged. "We are unlikely to know until the need is already upon us."

Nicolette did not for a moment think that those whom the Beaumonts were recommending would refuse to offer help to those who were comparatively lowly in status.

"Though it does not reflect well upon our homeland," Nicolette said, "should those in the most danger prove those of the least means, I suspect very few of them will have the ability to escape. I would hope some would. Perhaps that is one of the reasons the marquis is making these arrangements, to make it easier to assist those who could not otherwise seek refuge. But as I have pondered the efforts he has charged us with here, I can't help but suspect that he feels those who now enjoy the most comfort and safety are likely to be the ones fleeing here because they find themselves quite suddenly without either."

M. and Mme Beaumont met each other's eye. It was sadness and distress Nicolette saw there but not surprise. They, too, had surmised what the marquis had left unsaid.

"Thus far, only one person whom you have indicated on this map"—she tapped it with her finger—"is already part of our circle. He resides part of the year in London, which provides us a piece of this puzzle."

"A crucial piece," M. Beaumont said.

Crucial but insufficient. "We must have someone near a port on the southern coast. There are too many eyes in London. The risk of these efforts being discovered would be very high in that city."

"I am attempting to identify someone in Plymouth or Portsmouth," M. Beaumont said. "But I've not thought of anyone yet."

If they didn't know anyone, she certainly didn't. "I would prefer to return with that part of our plan firmly in place. None of the rest of this works without a point of arrival."

M. Beaumont rolled the map up and neatly tied it with a ribbon. He tucked it into a well-disguised compartment at the back of a drawer in a nearby lowboy. Even if someone found it, there would be no way for them to ascertain its purpose. With enough inspection and a great many questions, a person might sort out that the dots corresponded to French families of the Beaumonts' acquaintance. But even that could be very innocuously explained as M. Beaumont's efforts to help his wife understand the locations of their various friends throughout this country she was not terribly familiar with.

But Nicolette felt certain the excuse wouldn't be needed. This was a quiet household, one very few people entered. It was the perfect place for tucking away things of significance.

Then, as if fate meant to mock her further by disproving her declaration that this was a quiet and uneventful house, a quick knock at the drawing room door preceded the entry of the butler, though he only just tipped his head inside. "Someone has called," the man said, looking at his employers with that expression most butlers had perfected, one which was equal parts deference and staid propriety mixed with an almost eager excitement at the thought of being able to toss someone unceremoniously from the house.

"We are available to receive visitors," M. Beaumont said.

Nicolette did not need him to explain the reason for readily welcoming a visitor after having only just secreted away important documents. To refuse visitors when it was known that she was present would be odd enough to be noted. It wouldn't do to lay the groundwork of their secretive efforts under a cloud of suspicion.

In the next instant, the butler announced, "M. Pierre Léandre." And for the second time in as many days, the realization that he had arrived in a place where she had neither expected nor wanted him tied Nicolette's stomach in a knot.

She knew the end of her engagement had been a stroke of luck. She knew having him as a former fiancé rather than an unwanted husband was a fortunate thing. But his return had tossed her back into the turmoil she'd endured when he'd first left. All the doubts, all the wondering if there was something inherently wrong with her. Being faced with him moments after having to acknowledge the gaps in her *La Tapisserie* efforts was dealing her an unexpectedly potent blow.

He entered, looking as sure of himself as ever. When Nicolette had crossed paths with him in Paris years earlier, his confidence had seemed to her an indication that he claimed a firm and fitting place in society, as was expected of a person of his standing. She hadn't recognized it for the arrogance it was.

While the curtsies and bows were exchanged, Nicolette met Mme Beaumont's eye, offering an unspoken testimonial of her feelings. The minute nod she received in return told her as nothing else could that her wishes on the matter of Pierre had been quite easily and quickly understood.

"I heard that Norwood Manor boasted French neighbors," Pierre said. "I simply had to come meet you for myself."

It was a rather shocking breach of etiquette for a gentleman who prided himself on his social acumen. If he had heard about the Beaumonts, it would have been through someone in the party who had already been properly introduced to them. He ought to have enlisted someone to make the introduction.

His eyes darted to Nicolette. The tiniest pursing of his lips made clear what he was thinking: he had every expectation of her bridging the gap by making the introductions. He hadn't been this easy to interpret when they had been engaged. Her powers of observation had grown more keen, and she had gained a better understanding of people.

How tempting it was to simply stand in silence and let him fret. But though Pierre had never shown himself to be violent, she knew he could be vindictive. She had no desire to see him ruin the remainder of her time at the house party. It was far easier to simply appease him in this matter. "M. Léandre, this is M. and Mme Beaumont. Monsieur and Madame, this is M. Léandre."

"A rather graceless introduction," Pierre said with a confused glance in her direction.

"Would you rather I hadn't undertaken it at all? I did so only because you did not arrive accompanied by anyone able to do you that service."

In response, he skipped over his usual habit of pursing his lips and went straight to narrowing his eyes.

"Where is it that you make your home?" Mme Beaumont motioned Pierre to a gathering of chairs on the far side of the room. "If it is in England, I daresay my husband is familiar with it."

As Pierre reluctantly followed to where she indicated, M. Beaumont remained behind with Nicolette. "Please do not allow us to detain you any longer, Mlle

Beaulieu. You have been so lovely to give us so much of your time today. Thank you. And we do hope that you will call again."

Bless them, they were offering her an easy escape. Pierre would no doubt be upset, but other than her likely ill-conceived mishandling of introductions, there was little he could honestly criticize in her behavior. He would find something though. She felt certain he would.

In the meantime, she needed a moment to herself, time and peace enough to steady the ground beneath her feet. She didn't trust Pierre nor place much store by his opinion of her. But she was struggling with the reminder of how very wrong she'd been and the years of pain and humiliation he'd heaped on her by disappearing as he had.

She'd been enjoying the house party, making a little progress with her *La Tapisserie* efforts, and letting herself feel a growing connection to Henri. Pierre's arrival threatened to ruin it all.

# Chapter Twenty

"Nicolette!" Henri's voice carried across to her as she stepped out of the carriage in front of Norwood. He rushed toward her, apparently having been walking along the drive. "I only just heard that Pierre followed you to Eau Plate. I am sorry I wasn't able to offer you any warning."

She slipped her arm through his. "The Beaumonts offered me a means of leaving quickly. But I think I would have enjoyed seeing you rush to the rescue."

"I would have been excruciatingly heroic." He set his hand atop hers where it rested on his arm, something she liked more than she would have guessed the more he did it. "Pierre would likely have dissolved into a puddle of mortification, knowing how comparatively craven he is."

Behind them, the carriage was rolling its way toward the stables, and the footman who'd handed her down had stepped inside once more.

Nicolette leaned a bit against him. "You are decidedly heroic, Henri Fortier."

He shook his head. "You are the first person to ever say that to me, Nicolette Beaulieu."

"I predict I will not be the last."

He laughed, but was his laugh one of disbelief or amusement? Did he truly not think himself heroic? He had been in the process of rushing to Eau Plate in the hope of warning her about Pierre, and that after being unfailingly supportive and reassuring throughout the ball at Tafford.

"Lucas has another diversion planned," Henri said as they walked into the house. "I am not entirely certain *what* he means to propose, but I can assure you it will be ridiculous."

She grinned. "Excellent."

Finding the rest of the Norwood Manor guests was remarkably easy. They simply followed the sound of laughter to the drawing room.

Lucas spotted them immediately. "You have arrived just in time. We are about to begin one of our favorite games."

Nicolette ignored the weight of her brother's eyes on her from across the room. They did not always agree with each other, but until he had sided with Pierre and participated in the ambush she had endured at Tafford, she'd trusted him.

"The Gents seem to play a great many games." She looked at Henri. "Which one has earned the accolade of favorite?"

Before he could answer, Lord Mowbary did. "Grown gentlemen who regularly indulge in juvenile contests. It is the oddest thing."

"Simply because something is enjoyed by children does not make it beneath the enjoyment of adults," Niles said in his unruffled but firm way.

"There's a reason *children* spend their days in the nursery," Lord Mowbary countered, "and *adults* spend their days elsewhere."

"If there are no adults in the nursery, then who is tending the children?" Digby asked in a deceptively befuddled tone.

Lord Mowbary looked thoroughly annoyed but did not rise to the bait.

Lord Aldric, in the same neutral and disinterested voice he usually employed when speaking to his brother, said, "You needn't participate, Mowbary. It is not in the nature of anyone amongst the Gents or our ladies to force our will and dictates upon others nor to shame them into abandoning the innocent pursuits that bring them pleasure."

For just a moment, the two brothers looked at each other, both wearing expressions of annoyance but neither speaking out loud precisely what he was thinking.

Lord Mowbary glided from the room with a look of superiority so ridiculous it was almost humorous. His wife followed shortly behind. Jean-François and Marguerite did not quit the drawing room entirely, but there was no indication either meant to participate in the game to be proposed. Sébastien and Gaëtane were, no doubt, of the same mind.

Pierre would also likely disapprove if he were present. That would have been enough to prevent Nicolette's participation when they'd first been engaged. Even in the first few weeks and months after his disappearance, she'd been exceptionally careful about the impression she gave and the narrow line she walked. Now, with Pierre's return, she could feel herself growing unsure once more.

Perhaps an afternoon spent playing an unapologetically ridiculous game strictly because she wished to, without thought to the impression she was making, would prove just the reminder she needed of how strong she'd learned to be these past two years.

"Which game have you chosen?" Henri asked Lucas.

"Hide-and-seek," Lucas answered with a grin.

Chuckles rumbled through the group.

Was there more to the game than Nicolette realized? "The ones who are not seeking find a place in which to hide themselves and hope to not be found? Is that the approach taken here?"

Julia, who looked as excited about this game as her husband, explained, "It is, though we will not forbid individuals hiding in the same place. And a person can change his or her hiding location but must do so without being found."

"And what occurs when a person is found?" Nicolette asked.

"That person begins seeking as well. The last person to be found is the winner."

"Will the winner be promised sweets that are then eaten by other people?" She eyed Lucas out of the corner of her eye, and the dryness of her voice and expression earned her laughter all around.

"Such a thing would never happen." Lucas made a show of being deeply offended by her accusation. After the briefest of moments, he joined in the laughter around him and continued with his instructions. "Niles agreed to seek first. He'll stand at the window and gaze longingly out at the grounds while we rush about and find places to hide. We are limiting our scope to the public rooms on the ground floor."

Nicolette's excitement grew, a sure sign this odd activity was doing her good. These past two years, every decision, every movement, every word came with potentially dire consequences. She had been fighting for her autonomy and her survival. To claim both in this moment through means of a simple game was a lovely thing.

Niles wandered to the window and, as promised, set his gaze outside so he couldn't see what was happening behind him. The group began rushing about, all of them leaving the drawing room.

"Best hurry, Nicolette," Henri said, slipping away from where she stood.

"Best hide well, Henri."

He laughed as he left. She waited only a moment before leaving the drawing room as well. She'd only just set foot in the corridor when Sébastien and Gaëtane pulled her aside.

"You cannot truly intend to participate." Sébastien sounded almost appalled at the possibility.

"There's no harm in such an innocent game," Nicolette insisted, anxious to be on her way so she could find a place to hide.

"No harm?" Gaëtane repeated with a note of panic. "You must know Pierre would not look upon this undertaking with approval. Lord Mowbary has already expressed his displeasure, which he might very well whisper to his father. There are many of our countrymen who spend time enough in England to be swayed by the opinions of an English duke. Shocking both gentlemen might undo all the strides you have managed to make these past two years."

Gaëtane's explanation lessened some of Nicolette's annoyance. They wished to save Nicolette from misery and difficulty. She could hardly find fault with that. And better still, she could set their minds a bit at ease on the matter.

"As His Grace's younger son is participating, I cannot imagine he would be anxious to denounce the activity to all and sundry," Nicolette said. "I believe we needn't worry about the duke's disapproval."

"Even if *he* does not take exception, Pierre certainly will." Sébastien didn't sound the least bit assuaged.

She breathed through the hint of emerging trepidation that declaration inspired. During her engagement and in the months that had immediately followed, that hint would have quickly grown into panic. It didn't rise to that point now. She chose to see that as proof that she wasn't as shaken by Pierre's return as she had feared she was. "Though I risk shocking you," she said, "I no longer care what Pierre Léandre's opinion of me or my activities might be."

"Please, Nicolette. Take care before making such declarations." Sébastien's tone shifted abruptly. He was no longer offering a forceful admonition. He was making a plea.

In the next moment, Niles emerged from the drawing room. Though Nicolette was baffled by her brother's entreaty, she found she was more disappointed at being caught out by the seeker so quickly.

But Niles, dear man that he was, simply set his hand perpendicular to his temple, effectively acting as a blinder like those placed on horses and blocking her from his view as he passed. It was theatrically done, no doubt so she would realize that he recognized what was happening and did not mean to ruin her enjoyment of the game.

That small show of kindness and consideration firmed Nicolette's resolve further. She had once thought the shallow fickleness too often found at the height of society was the epitome of what she ought to aspire to. Her narrow escape from that gilded trap had forced her to decide for herself who she was and who she meant to become. She wished to be kind and compassionate. She wished to stand up for herself but not run roughshod over others. She wished to be thoughtful, loyal, and dependable. She wished to never become so high in the instep that a simple game was beneath her.

And she wished to never again connect herself to Pierre Léandre.

"I will leave you to decide whether or not you wish to inform M. Léandre of my participation in the afternoon's activities," she told her brother and sister-in-law. "He is currently away from Norwood Manor."

Sébastien looked as if he meant to continue arguing the point. She was out of patience and likely also out of time. Once Niles found someone and that person began seeking as well, she could not guarantee that remaining in the corridor wouldn't prove her undoing in the game. She stepped around her brother and hurried off, hoping to find a place to hide.

Sébastien and Gaëtane were not mean-spirited people. She did not even think *they* disapproved of the game nor wished to ruin her enjoyment of it. Neither of them had ever been controlling in that way. In the days, weeks, and months following Pierre's departure, her brother and sister-in-law had been everything a heartbroken and worried lady could hope for: supportive and reassuring. They had been pushing her toward making a match in the past six months or so, but she didn't think that anxiety arose from anything other than concern for her, which made their sudden acceptance of her feckless former fiancé even more disconcerting.

She was about to slip into the breakfast room, hoping to find a place where she might tuck herself, when little Lord Draycott and his nursemaid turned the corner of the corridor. The nursemaid offered a quick curtsy, and he executed a very well-made bow. Nicolette answered with a curtsy to the little lordling.

"Have you been for a walk?" she asked, seeing that he was dressed for the out of doors and his cheeks were pinked.

He nodded. "What are you doing?"

"We are playing a game of hide-and-seek," she said. "Do you know how to play?"

He shook his head. He was an only child, so it was possible he didn't get to play many games.

"It is a simple game," Nicolette said. "I could easily explain it to you if you would like to play."

Lord Draycott looked up at his nursemaid. She didn't seem particularly inclined to lean one way or the other.

Nicolette had only just reminded herself that she didn't wish to aspire to be pretentious, but acting the part could be useful at times. She met the eyes of

Lord Draycott's nursemaid and declared, "I will take charge of Lord Draycott. This game is entirely appropriate for children and is being undertaken entirely in the public rooms of the ground floor. You may return to your duties." She held out her hand to Lord Draycott, and he took it with a look in his eyes that spoke loudly of gratitude. She stepped with him into the breakfast room and had the pleasure of hearing the young boy's indifferent nursemaid continue on her way.

"The game really is simple," she told him. "We will find a place to hide ourselves, and we wait there, hoping that those who are going about seeking do not spy us. If they do, we will begin seeking as well until everyone has been found, and the game begins again."

Lord Draycott grinned. "I think I will be very good at this game."

"I am pleased to hear that, as we will be hiding together." She motioned to the room. "Where should we place ourselves?"

Lord Draycott gave it a moment's thought, then indicated the far side of the sideboard. "If we sit on the floor over there, someone might peek into this room and still not see us."

"Excellent," Nicolette said.

They made their way there and sat on the floor. She sat with her back to the side of the sideboard and he with his back to the wall, but near enough that his little legs leaned against hers.

"You sound like you are from France," he said, whispering, no doubt in an effort to not give away their hiding place.

"I am," she said.

His face brightened. "I know some French words. I have a tutor, and he is teaching me."

"What have you learned so far?"

He assumed a very serious expression. "*Un, deux, trois, quatre, cinq.*" He paused a moment, thinking. "*Bonjour. Merci.*" He looked up at her once more, earnest hopefulness in his eyes.

She took his hand in hers. It was still warm from his walk outside. Perhaps his nursemaid had not wanted to prolong the outing and had insisted it be undertaken at an overly fast clip. "Your French is coming along excellently."

"My grandmother was from France," Lord Draycott said. "Uncle Aldric said so. I asked my father once."

"Did he tell you about your grandmother?"

Lord Draycott shook his head. "He told me to stop bothering him. He was very busy with very important things. He is often very busy."

"My father was also often very busy," Nicolette said. "I do have an older brother, and when we were little children, he was a fun playmate."

Lord Draycott shrugged, the movement almost continental. That, she suspected, was the influence of his tutor. "No one in the nursery answers my questions."

"Does this happen on matters other than your grandmother?"

He nodded. "I once asked my father if I would have a brother or sister. He said he already had an heir and didn't need any more." The little boy shook his head. "I don't know what that means, but I think it means no."

Over the course of her life, Nicolette had known more than one type of parent who caused their children sorrow. There were those who were cruel and those who were indifferent. This poor boy seemed to have the second variety to such an extreme that in many ways, it had become the first.

"Though I did not know your grandmother," Nicolette said, "I do know France. Should you wish to know anything about the place she came from, I will tell you all about it."

"I know a great deal about France too."

She didn't even have to look up to know that the voice coming from behind her was Henri. Her heart pounded and raced and flipped about behind her ribs. That she had grown quite partial to him was growing increasingly apparent.

"Oh." Lord Draycott sounded disappointed. "Have we been found?"

Henri sat beside the boy. There was something so delightful about seeing a gentleman of his station, dressed fashionably and with great dignity, literally lowering himself to converse with a child. "I am still one of the hiders and am in search of a new place to secret myself."

The little boy, without warning, scrambled onto Nicolette's lap but turned to face Henri. "We have to sit very close, or we will be seen."

Henri shifted so he sat where the boy had been sitting, his leg now brushing against hers. Whereas the positioning had been a sweet, very childlike trust when assumed by the tiny lord, the exact same arrangement with Henri sent a shiver of nervous excitement through her.

"I know how to say some French words," Lord Draycott declared. Without waiting to be invited to do so, the little boy riffled off the same words he had said for her.

"*Très bien*," Henri said.

The boy leaned back against her. "I know what that means," he said. "My tutor says that when I say something correctly."

"Do you ever speak French with your uncle Aldric?" Henri asked.

He nodded. "Uncle Aldric speaks French with me, and we play cricket, and he tells me about my grandmother." His voice dropped ever lower. "I like when Uncle Aldric visits me, but my father doesn't."

Nicolette wrapped her arms around him. He still felt very warm. Enough time had passed since his walk about the grounds that he ought to not still be overheated.

"Did you know your uncle Aldric is one of my very best friends?" Henri said, keeping his voice to a whisper. "I like when he visits me."

"You could be my friend too," Lord Draycott said.

"I would like that, Lord Draycott."

"Could a friend call me Roderick?"

"If you would like," Henri said.

The boy nodded. "Can you call me Roderick, too, miss?" he asked her.

"If you would like."

She brushed her hand against his cheek and found it more than merely flushed; it was hot. His forehead was as well.

She turned him a little in her arm so she could look more closely at him. "Roderick, are you feeling unwell?"

He sighed, and his whole posture seemed to melt. "I didn't want to tell you, because you would make me stop playing the game. No one plays games with me."

She pressed a kiss to his forehead, something she remembered her nursemaid doing when she felt unwell. Unlike far too many children, she had been blessed with a nursemaid who had been wonderfully kind.

She met Henri's eyes. "He's feverish. I think we had best take him to the nursery."

"I want to keep playing," Roderick said, his tremulous voice breaking her heart.

"If you will rest for a day or two, you'll feel much better." She hoped she was not giving poor medical advice. "Then, I promise we will play games with you."

"Do you solemnly promise?" The weakness in his voice undermined the authoritative impression he was likely hoping to make.

"I solemnly promise," she said.

"As do I," Henri said.

That satisfied their little companion.

Henri wisely suggested he carry the boy. Though Roderick was young yet, he was certainly not an infant. Carrying him all the way up several flights of stairs and to the nursery would be tiring.

The boy curled against Henri, trusting him immediately. They walked quickly, Nicolette at Henri's side as he whispered reassurances to the boy.

They were fortunate enough to cross paths with Céleste. Nicolette quickly explained the situation and asked her friend to find someone who might send for the local doctor as well as the boy's parents.

They saw him settled into his own bed in the nursery wing, the staff attending to him, fetching water to sponge him and generally showing more concern than Nicolette had feared he would find there. His parents arrived, and she felt herself not quite as necessary.

She took a step back but didn't leave. She intended to remain until she knew how he was. Henri had not left either. He slipped his hand into hers and held it, silently and tenderly.

How could she possibly have believed that she could be happy with the shallow shows of insincere attachment she'd had from Pierre? Moments like this, when one was truly cared about and supported, when concern and compassion came as naturally as breathing . . . that was what she wanted most of all.

# Chapter Twenty-One

THE LOCAL MAN OF MEDICINE was quick to arrive at Norwood Manor. He was old enough to be a grandfather to the children he was looking after—*children* now being the appropriate description, as all three occupants of the nursery wing were feverish. A nursemaid had also fallen ill.

Henri had stepped out of the nursery with Nicolette to allow for more room inside. All the children's parents had gathered there, and it was there that Henri and Nicolette sat waiting on a bench not far from the nursery door. She kept her hand in his, something he was trying very hard not to read too much into. He'd been wrong before. When she leaned against him and closed her eyes he felt himself more than justified in seeing a degree of tenderness in the moment.

He had deeply liked Nicolette when he'd known her in Paris. Looking back, he realized the absurdity of his belief at that time that they had forged a bond deep enough to begin imagining a future together. Now, with the benefit of several years of life and perspective, he felt himself far more able to make a decision of such magnitude. This time he had been the recipient of inarguable affection from her, which gave him greater confidence moving forward. Even with that, he didn't intend to proceed hastily, having seen the disastrous results of impulsiveness in such matters.

So he sat with her hand in his, a hint of jasmine in the air around them, and let himself simply enjoy the moment while utterly refusing to acknowledge that she would soon enough be returning to France, a journey he could no longer afford to make. Avoiding undue haste likely also meant losing his second chance at happiness with her.

*With contradict'ry aim I stand,*
*Rent in twain between two lands.*

The lines emerged whole and formed in his mind, a silent iambic-tetrameter confession of what he felt and what he feared. England was his home. France, his homeland. The Gents were here. The life he dreamed of was here. His poetry, however quietly received, was published here in this land's language, the language of freedom for Henri. But the means of supporting himself and a house in which to live were promised him in France. In that land, he could claim time with Céleste and Adèle, acting as buffer between them and the misery his brother too often inflicted.

And Nicolette was there.

*Mon* Henri, she had called him. In his mind, she was swiftly becoming *ma chérie. My darling.* He'd called her that in Paris, but she'd clearly not seen much in the endearment. It certainly hadn't been returned, but neither had it been objected to.

Henri spied a familiar but unwelcome person just then reaching the top of the distant stairs. Pierre Léandre had a knack for arriving where and when he wasn't wanted.

"I believe you are soon to have a visitor," Henri whispered to Nicolette.

She sat fully upright once more. Henri pointed toward the approaching figure.

"*J'en ai marre,*" she muttered.

"What would you like me to do?"

"I will attempt to head off any problems he means to cause." She rose as she spoke. "When I return, no doubt in a miserable mood, have a quip or a joke ready. I suspect what I will want more than anything is to laugh."

"I will set my mind to thinking of something amusing."

She smiled at him before stepping away and meeting Pierre before he reached the nursery. They stood at a bit of a distance, but Henri could still hear.

"You abandoned me at Eau Plate, and now you are avoiding me here." Pierre did not, it seemed, feel the need to offer so much as a word of greeting.

"I had visited with the Beaumonts for as long as civility permitted, and I am in this wing of the house now because the children in the nursery are ill and I am concerned."

"They are not your children," Pierre's tone was conciliatory, but his posture was defiant. "I am certain their nursemaids and parents are providing sufficient attention." His eyes flicked to Henri before settling on Nicolette once more. "And you are receiving all the attention you need as well, Nicolette."

"Monsieur, you do not have leave to address me so informally."

Pierre laughed in much the way uncharitable people did when interacting with a person deemed slow or simple. Henri forced himself to remain seated and silent; Nicolette hadn't asked for his interference, and he was determined to let her preferences determine how he proceeded, just as Digby had suggested.

The doctor stepped out of the nursery and into the corridor, with Lucas beside him. Henri's attention shifted, though he kept an eye on Pierre and Nicolette, wanting to be of help where he could.

"I realize you are worried," the doctor said, "but I need you to take a moment to regain your equilibrium."

Poor Lucas looked frazzled. "I really am not usually one to panic," he insisted. "I lost my youngest brother to fever, the brother Philip is named for. I suppose my brain is dredging up that grief."

The doctor set his hand on Lucas's shoulder. "Allow me to settle your mind. All of the children are feverish, but none of them, including your son, is acting as if he or she feels truly awful. I do believe that is a good sign. Things can certainly change, but I also see no rash, no indications of inflammation of the lungs. All three children are still eating and drinking. Children have fevers sometimes, my lord. Not all of those fevers are dangerous."

Lucas nodded slowly, taking deep breaths.

In the other direction, Pierre was pleading with Nicolette, speaking entirely in French. "I have not had the opportunity for a single conversation with you since my arrival. Surely that is not so very much to ask."

"At this moment, it is far too much to ask. Until I know the state of the children's health, I will remain here."

"You don't think Philip is in tremendous danger?" Lucas asked the doctor.

"The child is young, and he must be watched closely. But I have been looking after ill children for a very long time, Lord Jonquil, and I am not at this moment concerned about *him*."

There was an odd emphasis on the word him. Henri turned more fully toward *that* conversation.

"Then who is it you *are* worried for?" Lucas pressed.

"The nursemaid who is feverish is faring worse than the children. She is miserably unwell. There are some fevers that are more concerning when contracted by adults than by children. And for most adults, even those are not dangerous."

*For most.*

"Why do I sense you are about to contradict that?" Lucas watched the doctor closely.

"Not a contradiction," the doctor said, "but a continuation of the explanation. Fevers that cause more noticeable and difficult illness in adults can be dangerous for women who are with child. We don't understand why, but being in that condition comes with added susceptibility."

"Julia's in danger?" Lucas asked in a whisper.

Henri was on his feet in a moment. He didn't wish to abandon Nicolette while Pierre was being a pest, but Lucas looked ready to drop.

"At the moment, she seems perfectly hale and hearty," the doctor said. "As all instances of this fever have occurred in the nursery, I can't help but think that its cause is in the nursery. I think it best that your wife avoid this wing of the house."

"But she is in there right now." The hint of panic that had been in Lucas's face when he'd first stepped into the corridor returned tenfold.

Henri stepped up beside him.

The doctor nodded. "I need you, while maintaining what calm you can, to convince your wife to leave the care of your son to others and to stay away from the nursery until these fevers have passed."

Lucas shook his head emphatically even as he pressed his thumb and middle finger to either side of his forehead, rubbing at the tension there. "She'll never agree."

"You need to try," the doctor said. "With how sick the nursemaid is already, should your wife contract this fever, I would be *very* worried for her and the child she carries."

Henri could hear every breath Lucas took. He set his hand on Lucas's shoulder, hoping to convey to him that he was not alone. That was what the Gents were for each other: family and unwavering support and the promise that none of them would ever be alone.

"There's still a chance Philip could grow quite ill," Lucas said, his voice quivering. "Julia and the baby could be laid low by fever as well." Henri could feel him shake. "I could lose my entire family." The whisper was strangled by emotion.

"Things are not so dire as that now," the doctor said. "Which is why now is the best time to take precautions. I have already sent for a doctor in a neighboring village, one I trust implicitly. Between him and me, the children and anyone else who grows ill will be very well cared for. I do believe this fever will run its course without tragedy. But we mustn't be neglectful."

Nicolette arrived at Lucas's other side. Pierre was nowhere to be seen. She spoke into the silence that pulled long among them all. "Thank you for your attentiveness and thoroughness, doctor. Please know you also have a house full of people who are eager and anxious to be of help."

"We'll do all we can." Henri added his promise.

The doctor returned to the nursery.

"What am I going to do, Henri?" Lucas sounded defeated already.

"Julia needs to be away from the nursery. We are going to see to it that she is."

"She will never agree to it," Lucas repeated. "She would lay waste to all of us if we stood between her and her child."

"Were the situation reversed," Nicolette asked, "and *you* needed to avoid the nursery for your own safety despite your son being there unwell, do you suppose Julia would fail to convince you?"

The tiniest, fleeting smile flitted over Lucas's face. "She would move mountains if need be."

"I've seen you *climb* literal mountains, Lucas," Henri said. "And I've seen you move figurative ones, especially for Our Julia."

"Time to do so again," Nicolette said. "Tell her little Philip has five honorary uncles in the Gents and three honorary aunts in Violet, Céleste, and myself who will make absolutely certain your little one will never want for tender familial affection. And you"—Nicolette held Lucas's gaze—"need to trust your friends enough to allow them to care for your child, your wife, the child who is yet to arrive, and yourself. I think they have more than earned the faith you ought to have in them."

Lucas looked more steady in his footing, far less likely to crumble. Nicolette's kind but firm words were helping.

Henri's mouthed "*merci*" earned him a quick smile from her.

"You likely both think me rather ridiculous," Lucas said, "standing out here in the corridor nearly in panic and tears while my family needs me to be strong."

Henri shook his head. "Compassion and concern for the people you love is not weakness, Lucas. That kind of loyalty created the Gents to begin with. That is the bond that holds us together, the bond of a chosen family."

"Family is who you choose," Lucas said.

Swallowing down a bit of emotion himself, Henri said, "Stanley taught us that every day he was with us. He chose us, and in doing so, he made a family. Your family is under the protective wings of the family he created. Do what is best for the well-being of Our Julia and Philip and the little one who will join us next."

Lucas breathed a little easier.

"While you do that," Henri added, "Nicolette and I will rally the troops."

"I suppose it is fitting for you to gather troops with the support of *Capitaine* Beaulieu."

With a smile that was just the right amount of understanding and humor, Nicolette said, "Does this mean we are setting aside our blood rivalry?"

"Nothing short of my Julia's welfare could convince me to do so. For her sake, I'll forgive you for stealing things in your determination to emerge victorious in your quest."

"And I will forgive you for eating all the peppermints," Nicolette said.

"I would never," Lucas insisted.

Henri turned his friend in the direction of the nursery. "Attend to your family, Lucas. We will see to the rest."

With shoulders set and a confident stride, Lucas returned to the nursery.

Henri held his hand out, and Nicolette set hers in it.

"*Merci beaucoup,* Nicolette." He pressed her hand to his heart, holding it there with his own. "Stanley was always better at lending his strength to whichever of us needed it than any of the rest of us were. I don't know what I would have done if Lucas had fallen completely apart just now."

"He wouldn't have," Nicolette said. "He was worried, and that shakes even the most stalwart of souls, but I've never known a man who loves his family the way Lucas does." Her voice broke. "Love that strong can't be sunk by the weight of worry. Love like that survives and grows and flourishes."

"Theirs is the kind of love everyone wants, really. It is what we all need. We simply don't always realize it."

She met his eyes. There was something hopeful but unsure in her gaze. "Do you think it's possible for everyone to find that? Or once we do, to actually keep it?"

He wanted to answer yes, to insist that once a person found love, fate would simply not be so cruel as to take it from them. But he already knew fate was standing in their way. His poverty collided with her family's control of her fortune. Her life was in Paris, and his was in England. Her family would never approve of him; *his* family would never approve of him. But at the very least, she ought not feel doomed to a life with the likes of Pierre Léandre.

"I am sorry I abandoned you during your confrontation with no one's favorite Frenchman," he said. "I'd intended to be available should he prove more noxious than usual. But—"

"Lucas needed you," Nicolette easily acknowledged. "That was where your attention needed to be."

"But it meant you were alone in having to deal with Pierre."

"A situation I had best grow accustomed to. I doubt I will be entirely free of him in Paris."

"You make me wish I were returning to Paris as well." The truth of that struck him. He had not missed Paris the past three years. He'd missed France only because he'd missed his sister and longed to know his niece better, but he found himself longing for Paris now.

Nicolette kept her hand in his as they walked the corridors of Norwood Manor, ready to rally the Gents to the cause of the Jonquil family. The feel of her touch and the joy of her company proved bittersweet. If only there were someone who could rally to the cause of Henri and Nicolette and the impossible dream he was beginning to suspect she might share with him.

# Chapter Twenty-Two

THE DOCTOR'S PREDICTIONS PROVED ALMOST shockingly accurate. Forty-eight hours had passed, and the children in the nursery were already almost entirely recovered. The first day had seen them a bit tired and worn, but none of them had been particularly ill. The bout of illness had been hardest on Philip, which was not surprising, considering his very tender age, yet even he was feeling better. Another of the nursemaids had also taken ill. She, like the first, felt far worse than any of the children had.

Everyone had taken it in turns to help look after the little ones. Julia had kept away from the nursery. Nicolette suspected doing so had required a Herculean effort. Thus far, Julia showed no signs of taking ill herself. The last time Nicolette had crossed paths with Lucas, he had seemed far less burdened than he had since the ordeal began.

There was something so lovely about serving a friend in this way. How ridiculous she now felt, having spent so many years of her life thinking that the pursuit of fashionable approval and the envy of society were worthwhile goals. She'd never necessarily thought it better than being a good person or helping others, nor had she viewed the two as mutually exclusive; she simply hadn't realized how utterly unsatisfying her first goals had actually been.

She was finishing up her turn as the one in the nursery looking after Philip. It was also affording her an opportunity to play games with little Roderick, as she'd promised she would. And Adèle was joining in, a show of bravery for her.

Nicolette had taken time to teach Roderick a French children's song. She'd realized quickly that Adèle already knew it, which had helped convince the girl to play along.

"*Je les ai vue taper les mains,*" Nicolette sang, bouncing Philip in her arms.

Adèle showed Roderick they were meant to clap their hands.

"*Je les ai vue taper les pieds,*" Nicolette sang.

Adèle began stomping her feet. Roderick mimicked. The two children clapped and stomped a circle around Nicolette as she continued. Philip giggled, watching the children play the musical game.

Nicolette smiled at her darling little Lord Draycott as he stomped past, and she received a delighted grin in return. How she hoped Lord Aldric found a way to spend more time with him. The boy came to life when he wasn't being ignored.

They reached the chorus of the song, which she'd taught Roderick to sing. Even Adèle sang along.

*"J'ai vu le loup, le renard et la belette.*
*J'ai vu le loup et le renard danser.*
*J'ai vu le loup, le renard et la belette.*
*J'ai vu le loup et le renard danser."*

Both children collapsed on the floor as the song ended. Tiny Philip looked at them, then at her, taking in every detail.

"You should sing that song for your French tutor," Nicolette said. "He will be so pleased."

"Do you think my grandmother knew that song?" Roderick asked, still lying on the floor.

"I suspect your *grand-mére* knew it and sang it with her own children."

He took a deep breath, letting the air out on a pleased sigh. "I like that song."

Philip leaned against her. He'd been a little bit fussy when she'd first arrived, but she'd discovered he was calmer when she was moving.

Was that a common thing with infants, or with *this* infant, who, like his father, didn't hold still? Whatever the reason, she was happy to oblige. She was doing a kindness for Julia, who had shown her such kindness from the very beginning of this house party. When Nicolette inevitably returned to France, she would miss the Gents and their mischievous camaraderie. She would miss Violet and her easy friendship, and Julia's wit and compassion. She refused to think about how much she would miss Henri.

Though she hadn't done much beyond singing and walking about with Philip, she was tired. She felt rather foolish admitting that even to herself. She knew that Niles and Digby had taken their turn, looking after Philip during the wee hours of the night and earliest morning. Those gentlemen had every reason to be exhausted. Perhaps it was simply the strain of having so very much on her mind.

She would appreciate lying down as soon as she was afforded the chance.

Violet arrived on the tails of that thought. "I'm here to take your place."

Roderick was on his feet once more, earnestly trying to convince Adèle to play *J'ai Vu le Loup* with him again.

Violet motioned to the little baby in Nicolette's arms. "How is he?"

"Enjoying watching his playmates with no indication of distress. He doesn't even feel feverish."

"That is a relief. He has a hoard of honorary family who will all be deeply relieved to hear that."

"There's something remarkable about these Gents," Nicolette said.

"I said much the same thing over and over again when I first met them," Violet said. "It does make me wish I could have met the one who brought them all together."

"Stanley?" Nicolette guessed.

Violet nodded. "He still has such an influence on them, in the good they do and in their mischievousness. That combination is a hallmark of who they are."

"I do not mean to be nosy," Nicolette said, "but I have noticed tremendous stiffness in your left arm and that you favor your right. I only mention it because I am unsure if I ought to transfer our sweet little bundle into your right arm, the one you use more often, or your left arm, the one that seems a little less agile and, thus, might be more suited to the unmoving task of holding him."

Far from offended, Violet laughed a little bit. "You and Julia are birds of a feather. She sorted out the matter of my arm faster than anyone else has before or since. I will let you in on a secret that's not entirely a secret. I wear gloves at all times, not because I'm ashamed of what they conceal but because people are sometimes . . . difficult when unexpectedly confronted with this reality."

That was an intriguing beginning.

"I lost my left arm to infection. It is noticeably stiff and not the one I use very often because it is a prosthesis."

That unexpected explanation made everything Nicolette had observed make perfect sense. "It must be a remarkable prosthesis to appear as natural as it does beneath your glove."

"It is the most remarkable prosthesis I could possibly imagine. My husband and I, with the help of an apothecary and his clockmaker father, have been improving upon it over the last year. This is the second iteration we have created."

On that declaration, Nicolette found another of her unacknowledged assumptions obliterated. So often those who had difficulties with their health or their abilities or their mobility were assumed to be quite miserable as a result of their circumstances, which was something to be universally pitied. But Violet had just declared that she loved her prosthesis. Perhaps those tools and devices that people utilized as part of their less-than-ideal circumstances came to be loved and appreciated rather than resented.

"So, to answer your question," Violet said, "when I have held Philip, I have done so in my right arm, as I am more sure of its ability to make any adjustments necessary when he grows wiggly or squirmy."

The transfer was quickly made, and Philip was snuggly held by another of the people who dearly loved him. With that duty discharged, Nicolette gave a hug to Adèle and Roderick, then slipped from the nursery. She truly was quite tired. She hadn't slept overly well the night before, her mind spinning on any number of things. Perhaps she would do well to lie down rather than join the gathering for the evening meal. No one would blame her. The entire house had been under a heavy cloud.

But first, she thought she might look for Julia and offer her reassurance that Philip was doing quite wonderfully. Not wishing to intrude upon Lucas and Julia's privacy, she opted to search for them in the sitting room and drawing room first. If she found them there, she would deliver her message. If not, she would do so after she'd had a moment's rest herself.

She'd not yet reached her first destination when Pierre appeared out of nowhere. With that practiced smile of his, he declared, "There you are, Nicolette, I seem to have such trouble claiming even a moment of your time."

She kept herself calm and composed. She would not allow him to undermine her once again. "I don't know if you have heard, but there is illness in the nursery, and most of us have been doing what we can to see to the children's comfort."

As usual, Pierre did not appear the least concerned by the veiled criticism.

"There is something of great importance I need to talk to you about," he said.

"I have just spent hours looking after an infant and two children who have been ill for two days," she said. "I wish at the moment to reassure the baby's parents, then go rest for a time. Can we please discuss whatever it is that is pressing on your thoughts *after* I've had a chance to rest?"

"You have made ample time for everyone in this house these past days except for me," Pierre said, his placating demeanor setting her teeth on edge.

"You say that as though you have claim on my time." She had intended to avoid this interaction by simply dismissing his request and going on her way, but he was beginning to upset her.

"I assure you, Nicolette, I do."

"M. Léandre, I have not given you leave to use my given name."

"Again, I would remind you that I very much have claim."

She kept her annoyance as tucked away as she could manage and attempted to step around him.

He took hold of her arm. His grip was tight though not painful. There was something worryingly possessive in it. "We need to talk."

"I have nothing to say to you," she said.

"That is just as well. Your role in this is to listen." He turned her a bit, enough to be looking at the door of the book room. Sébastien stood there, watching her. Though he didn't look angry or upset, he didn't seem shocked that Pierre was holding her hostage, and neither did he appear ready to object to Pierre's demands on her time and attention.

"You do need to listen to what he has to say," Sébastien said.

So great was her surprise at his declaration that she found herself escorted into the book room before a single word of objection could rise to her lips. She recollected herself in time to reject the seat Pierre had chosen for her, one on a settee beside himself, and opted instead for a single chair facing the spot he had selected.

She made absolutely certain not to give any indication that she was the least put out by this very frustrating situation. She had learned from *La Tapisserie* that obvious discomfort could put one at a disadvantage.

"I'm sure you must realize that I am concerned." Pierre spoke without any degree of sincerity.

"What are you concerned about?" Perhaps if she allowed him to grumble a bit, he would make his point, and she could be on her way.

"You have been very short with me, denying me even a moment of your time."

"I have no obligation to you."

Rather than his usual look of superiority or patronizing patience, Pierre's eyes took on a gleam of triumph. Very few things truly shook Nicolette any longer. But in that moment, she was truly upended.

"Is not a lady under some obligation to listen to what her fiancé has to say?"

"We are not engaged."

He reached across and patted her hand. She swatted him away.

There was a laugh in his expression. "Oh, sweet Nicolette. You always did look at the world through such a simple lens. Our engagement never truly ended."

"Only a simpleton would argue that the would-be groom running off and disappearing for more than two years wasn't an indication that an engagement was, in fact, over."

"Perceptions and opinions mean very little." Pierre made the declaration so casually and easily. Yet she knew that to this man, perception was everything. He had always carefully planned every aspect of his appearance, everything he said, every place he went. And he had insisted on doing the same for her . . . *to* her during their engagement. Being perceived in the way he wished had been paramount.

Too confused almost to even answer, she looked at Sébastien.

"The marriage contracts were signed," he said. "They are binding. And he is correct: you are still engaged."

"He can make whatever claim he wishes," Nicolette said. "Our engagement ended when he left. I do not consider myself engaged to him now, nor will I ever again."

That same hint of pleading that had been in Sébastien's eyes the day of the hide-and-seek game returned. "He means to bring suit if you insist on breaking the engagement."

Bring suit? She was too shocked to respond.

"Your standing in society is good," Sébastien continued, "but this would be gossip fodder on a scale we've not endured before. It would be tremendously difficult to weather."

She pushed aside the surge of trepidation. Perhaps she could call Pierre's bluff. "Everyone said the same thing about returning to society after my then-fiancé fled into oblivion. I weathered that and emerged in better standing than before."

Pierre's expression lost its hint of mockery, but it did so in a way that upended her even more. His eyes hardened, and the faint lines on his face pulled in anger. "Should you choose not to honor the marriage agreement, I will press in the court my claim to your dowry, which I *am* legally entitled to, and I will insist on compensation for my lost expectations and the difficulties and injuries you've caused me in refusing to honor your legal obligation to me."

"You could take my entire dowry and compensatory moneys, and you know it would not bankrupt this family. One of the reasons you were so eager to enter into an engagement is that our family had a great many things you don't." And that wasn't even her strongest argument. "Emerging victorious in the suit is hardly a guarantee. The fact that you fled and I did not is ample evidence that it was you who brought our one-time engagement to an end, not me."

Sébastien didn't look reassured by that logic. Pierre didn't look concerned.

"There's one thing you must have learned about me," Pierre said. "I know how to make myself heard. How easy it would be to explain in tremendous detail to whichever authority heard our case how very hard I tried to keep you in line and convince you to be the sort of proper and acceptable young lady a gentleman would be proud to make his wife but that you proved so difficult a person, so determined not to honor any of the commitments you had made, that there was little for me to do but retreat to a place of peace and quiet to determine how best to move forward. There is a monk at Ligugé Abbey who has agreed to testify that I spent a good deal of time there these past two years in prayer and contemplation." His smile was as smug as could be. "What a tragic figure I will make. All of society will begin to see you quite differently. And all you have claimed to have suffered will suddenly be cast into doubt."

Only the training she had received kept her outwardly calm and collected. Her mind was spinning, and her heart was pounding. "It is your intention to ruin me if I do not agree to move forward with this?"

"It would ruin us all," Sébastien said.

"This is why you invited him here? Because he threatened you?"

"I didn't invite him," Sébastien said.

Pierre rose, looking down at her. "I certainly hope you do not choose to make this difficult for everyone." On that declaration, he left, his posture that of a man quite secure in his belief that all he wished for would soon be his.

"I'm sorry, Nicolette," Sébastien said. He sounded sincerely apologetic. "I didn't know what to do."

There was plenty her brother could have done. At the very least, he could have told her of Pierre's threats before Pierre himself did. But Sébastien looked so miserable and she *felt* so miserable that it hardly seemed the time for reproaches.

"We'll sort something out," she said.

"I hope so." He rose and left, his posture that of a man defeated.

She alone remained behind in the book room. The weariness she had been feeling upon leaving the nursery had turned to complete and total exhaustion.

She hadn't the first idea how to move forward, how to fix this, how to escape the web that had been spun for her. The one thing she knew was that somehow, she would avoid the trap Pierre had laid.

She was too overwhelmed to think entirely clearly. To her horror, she found herself tearing up. That was another thing that had changed about her in England. Despite all that had happened, she hadn't cried in two years.

She lowered her head and simply let the tears fill her eyes.

It was in this posture of vulnerability that the only person she trusted enough to see her in such a state entered the room.

"*Ma chérie*, what's happened?"

At the sound of Henri's voice, she rose as quickly as her tired body would allow her and threw her arms around him. He held her, and she leaned against him, feeling unequal to standing on her own much longer. But he wouldn't abandon her; she knew he wouldn't.

Henri brushed a strand of uncooperative hair away from her eyes but stopped halfway through the gesture. She felt him grow a little tense. He pressed the back of his hand to her forehead and then her cheek.

"Nicolette," he whispered. "You are burning up."

# Chapter Twenty-Three

QUITE A FEW PEOPLE AT Norwood Manor had taken ill. Henri was grateful to still be well. The doctor had declared that the infectious fever was likely throughout the house rather than isolated to the nursery wing at this point. He suggested that Julia be removed to the inn to avoid the illness, something they accomplished quickly. Anyone watching could tell Julia was not best pleased with the situation. And in the almost twenty-four hours since that had occurred, Lucas had made the journey to and from more than once, dividing his time between his son and his wife.

Aldric was unwell, as was Digby, though neither was worryingly so. Marguerite had taken ill. Several members of the staff were unwell, as was the housekeeper. Mowbary had a slight fever but seemed to feel better than the rest. The doctor's observation that the illness was striking adults with more intensity than the children was mostly holding true, but no one seemed to be in actual danger.

Roderick and Adèle already both felt well enough to be quite energetic, keeping those nursemaids who were still feeling well on their toes, with even the English nursemaids learning French children's songs and games. Philip was his usual giggly self once more.

It was these reassurances that Henri brought to Nicolette. Visiting her in the sick room wouldn't be frowned on, provided the door was left ajar.

He sat beside her bed as the doctor applied a light bandaging to the crook of her arm where he'd administered the bit of bloodletting generally used to treat a fever. Henri understood the doctor was doing all he could for Nicolette, but it ached his heart to see her ill enough to need such treatments. He was also grateful this doctor wasn't the sort to undertake copious bloodletting, as some did. Henri had too often seen people actually grow weaker under the care of an overly enthusiastic doctor.

Nicolette wasn't asleep nor incoherent. She winced as the doctor tied off the bandaging over the medicinal wound. Henri held her other hand, hoping to offer some comfort.

The doctor rose and smiled down at his patient. "I do believe we will not need to do that again," he said. "I am sorry it was necessary."

"As am I." Her voice was not so weak as to be worrisome. "I vow to be a very good patient."

The doctor's manner was reassuring and competent. "I suspect you will soon feel quite well indeed." He looked to Henri. "I will express no objections to you remaining if you promise to be a restful sort of companion."

"I vow that I will be," he said.

"I cannot imagine anyone being as calming and peaceful as Henri," Nicolette said. Perhaps she was a bit more incoherent than she appeared. Using a gentleman's given name in front of others was a significant breach of etiquette.

"Rest, as you promised," the doctor said. "I will check on you in a few hours." He left the door a bit ajar when he left.

"Is it true that half the household is ill?" Nicolette asked.

"I'm afraid so. The next few days of this house party will be very sedate, I fear." Henri kept her hand in his. "How are you feeling, truly?"

"Sick enough to be quite uncomfortable, but not so ill that I am horribly miserable. I simply long to be well again."

Henri knew the feeling. He suspected most everyone did. It was suffering without fearfulness but unenjoyable just the same.

"What can I do to be most helpful just now?" he asked. "I can sit quietly until you fall asleep, or I can talk with you if you prefer distraction."

"You were carrying a book in your hands when you came inside," she said.

He allowed himself to laugh a little. "I am beginning to suspect, Nicolette, that there is very little that you do not notice."

She squeezed his hand ever so lightly. He knew perfectly well that she was not in any danger, but it still reassured him that she had strength enough to grip his hand.

"I brought a volume of poetry with me so that if you fell asleep, I would have something to read." He had also brought it to study. It was his own, and he hoped that by studying what had been deemed publishable before, he might finally manage to complete the third and final work for his next collection.

"Would you read to me?" she asked. "I do like poetry, and it seems it would be a very restful sort of activity. I did make a promise to the doctor, after all."

Nervousness tiptoed over him. He'd never read his poetry to anyone. He knew people read his work—the book had sold enough copies for the publisher to be interested in another volume—but he'd never actually witnessed anyone's response to what he'd written. Yet, that nervousness did not prove enough to convince him to avoid the undertaking.

He was curious what she would think and if she would approve. With a quick breath of reassurance, he opened the cover and turned to the page on which his first poem began.

"Where cliffs of chalk stand proud 'gainst crashing waves,
The daily batt'ring on its side engraves
A tale of ages past, and battles lost,
Of vict'ries claimed, of fickle fame, of love star-crossed."

As he continued on with the poem, he could see the tension easing from her, tension he hadn't even realized was there until it had begun to disappear. She was finding his words soothing. That proved a tremendous compliment.

Upon finishing the first poem in the collection, he lowered the book to his lap and met her eye, nervous about what she might say.

"Oh, Henri. That was lovely."

"Truly?"

She nodded, but the movement was very small, no doubt owing to her illness.

"It wasn't long enough to fill the entire volume," she said.

"There are two more poems, one of approximately equal length at the end, and the one in the middle is quite a bit longer." He had taken that same pattern with his next book. The poem he was attempting to complete now would be a shorter one, which, in theory, ought to have made it easier. Yet, he was struggling mightily.

"You said you studied English poetry at Cambridge," Nicolette said. "You must understand it very well."

"I can say with great confidence that I understand this particular poem exceptionally well."

"Are you an avid reader of this poet?" Her brow pulled a bit. "You might have told me who it was, but I know little of English poets."

"No one knows who this poet is," he said. "The author is identified as 'a gentleman.'"

"Must a gentleman hide the fact that he writes poetry?"

"Not necessarily. The Earl of Carlisle published his poetry under his own name and was praised for it. The same is, unfortunately, not true of ladies. While poetry is more acceptable than writing novels, it still is a bit frowned upon when undertaken by ladies."

She seemed to be pondering. "If gentlemen are permitted to admit to the writing of poetry, why do you suppose *this* gentleman does not identify himself?"

He had been teasing her about not missing any details, but that was proving uncomfortably accurate. "Perhaps there are those within his circle who disapprove, and he must, therefore, hide his identity."

"True friends would not object to such a thing," she insisted.

*True friends.* He had the truest friends in all the world but hadn't managed confidence enough to tell them of this accomplishment. "One would hope a person's family would not condemn him for it either," he added.

Her hand shifted a little, her fingers weaving through his. In a soft voice, one rendered tender rather than weak, she said, "Do you ever intend to tell them?"

She knew. His most closely guarded secret, and she'd discovered it. *Une catastrophe! Un désastre total!*

She squeezed his fingers. "I knew you studied poetry and did so in English. I've seen you hastily tucking away papers you did not wish me to see, and I've wondered what that was. You said just now that a gentleman poet might wish to hide his identity from his disapproving family, and heaven knows your family disapproves of a lot of things. All of the pieces were there; I simply needed to put them together."

"It has to be kept a secret. That is crucial."

"I won't tell anyone," she promised.

"But you sorted it; Jean-François might also. He can't know. The consequences—" He took a shaking breath.

"He would disapprove?" She asked the question the way one did when one already knew the answer.

"He would punish me." He pushed out a tense breath. "My father leveled very effective threats when he was still alive. My brother would follow through on them."

"What would he do?"

"Cut me off from Céleste." Just speaking the words aloud struck fear in his heart. "He would refuse me entrance at the family estate while she was there, whisk her from Paris should I arrive in that city. He would intercept her letters and mine." Anticipated grief broke his voice. "I would lose my sister."

"Your poetry is important to you, but so is your sister." Her eyes were a bit hazy with lingering illness, yet she watched him closely.

"The two are not of *equal* importance to me, I assure you. Céleste means the world to me."

"I would not have assumed otherwise."

He'd kept this secret for so long. Nicolette's discovering it had brought immediate panic, but that distress was quickly easing. She hadn't condemned him nor laughed at him. To at last have someone to talk with about it was proving a relief.

"I have harbored some hope that my publishing efforts would provide enough income to supplement my inheritance, especially since my brother is refusing to give me what I was promised."

"He's cheating you?" Nicolette attempted to sit up a bit, apparently riled up by the revelation.

"You have sworn not to exert yourself," he reminded her. "If the doctor finds out I am the reason you broke that vow, he will likely wring my neck."

She leaned back on her pillow once more.

"There was apparently a provision in my father's will that I was to be permitted the use of a small family estate near Nantes. My brother neglected to tell me that he has been using portions of my inheritance for the upkeep of that house and land, despite the fact that the estate belongs to the Fortier family and is meant to be funded as such."

"He is cheating you but in a way that he can attempt to justify."

Henri nodded. "And he's using it to extort me."

She looked concerned. "Extort you to what end?"

"My family was never happy that I left France. He's attempting to force me to return. I don't think he actually wants me there but rather wants to claim the triumph of managing something our father never did."

She watched him, clearly attempting to sort things, likely debating which questions she ought to ask him and which ought to be left unsaid.

"In France, I would have a place to live, something I haven't claimed here, and money to live on without the risks inherent in an income derived from the publication of poetry. And I could likely arrange for Céleste to live with me there." Speaking aloud the list of positive outcomes of returning to his homeland surprised him. There were more benefits than he'd realized. "But in France, I wouldn't have the Gents or the feeling of home I have known in this country."

"In addition to losing your friends' company, you would lose part of yourself," she said. "I realize you haven't asked me for advice, and you are welcome to entirely ignore it, but I think you should tell the Gents. Tell them of the house in France, the reasons you would be wise to return and the reasons you don't wish to. They might not have a solution, but you wouldn't feel so alone. And I think you should tell them about your poetry. Achievements are made more satisfying and troubles are lessened when they are shared."

He didn't know if it was weakness brought on by her illness or something more worrisome still, but in that very wise and hopeful declaration, he heard a tremendous amount of resignation. He inched his chair closer, his knees wedged between it and the side of her bed. He bent over, leaning near to her in the hope of helping her feel even more able to trust him. "What trouble do you need lessened, Nicolette?"

"I have discovered why Pierre has returned. Marriage contracts were signed before his disappearance two years ago, and he has decided to use that to his advantage."

"He would force you to marry him?"

"I cannot decide if his purpose is to force an actual marriage, or he simply is hoping to bolster his fortunes by seeking monetary damages. Neither one is a particularly desirable outcome."

"What amount is he demanding from your family?"

"The entirety of my dowry and likely a good bit more than that. I don't think the monetary burden would sink Sébastien. But Pierre has said that if I make this difficult for him, he will take the opportunity to destroy my reputation, my standing, and my family's good name by dragging it all through the muck in pursuit of what it is that he wants."

"Nicolette, I'm sorry."

"He made his threat moments before you entered the book room the day I fell ill."

Ah. That was why she'd been crying. She was a warrior, one who did not cry easily. That Pierre had brought her to that point did not improve the man's already low standing in Henri's eyes.

"If I might quote to you a bit of advice I very recently received," Henri said, "you really ought to trust your friends with this. They might not have a solution, but you wouldn't feel so alone."

Her smile was tiny, but it did grand things to his heart. "Do you suppose the Gents and their ladies would offer me support?"

"Unflinchingly," he vowed. "And whatever help they can. They are as good and loyal a group as you will ever find."

"In the end, there might be nothing that can be done."

"Never fear," he said. "That is the point at which the Gents would commandeer the Duke of Hartley's yacht and aid in your escape."

"From Portsmouth or Plymouth, perhaps?" She smiled a little. "I've heard those are convenient port cities."

"We are far too sneaky for that. We would set sail from a private dock so as not to be caught out and make all possible haste toward some undiscovered cove where Pierre will never think to look."

"As tempting as that is, I suspect there is not actually a good solution to my difficulties."

"I feel the same way," he said. "But having support in a hopeless situation is an improvement over the alternative."

Her eyes were growing heavy. He could see that she was ready and needing to rest. "Sleep well, *ma chérie*. I will see you when you wake."

"Will you read me more of your poetry?" she asked in a whisper.

"If you'd like."

"I very much would." Her eyes remained closed.

If he'd been asked an hour ago how he would feel knowing his most closely guarded secret had been discovered, he would have assumed he'd be consumed with hopelessness. But Nicolette knew. She knew, and he wasn't worried. He was relieved and grateful. A remarkable turn of events. A remarkable lady.

He stood and leaned over to press a kiss to her cheek, which was still a bit flushed with fever. Eyes still closed, she smiled softly, and his heart simply melted.

There was no point denying it any longer: he had allowed himself to fall in love with her again.

# Chapter Twenty-Four

A PRIVATE YACHT SAILING TO and from private docks. Nicolette had not been able to clear that idea from her mind since Henri had made the suggestion in jest. It was precisely what *La Tapisserie* needed to complete the marquis' preparations. The Beaumonts were attempting to identify possible participants in Plymouth or Portsmouth. But when Nicolette had mentioned those two port cities to Henri, he had turned her thoughts in a much better direction, away from a city altogether.

Knowing where the escapees made port would make it easier for anyone pursuing them to discover their place of departure from France. Those fleeing would be intercepted. Those assisting would be uncovered. If the situation were even half as dire as the marquis feared it would become, such an enormous failing would have catastrophic consequences.

She'd already realized they needed to avoid bringing refugees to larger port cities, but there was significant benefit to avoiding even small villages. Taking that approach on both sides of the Channel would protect all involved.

The day after her fever broke, she sent Henri to Eau Plate with a note for the Beaumonts relaying the need to find a property on the southern coast with its own private dock or inlet. She had no idea how easy or even possible that request might prove, but she knew it was their best chance for success. She sat on a bench at the tree-lined edge of Norwood's back lawn and waited for Henri to return.

Being out of the house for the first time since taking ill was proving a welcome change, though she couldn't entirely shake the feeling of disappointment and anxiety that her time in England was growing so short. Only five more days.

"Mlle Beaulieu!" Little Roderick called out to her as he rushed back to where she sat. His nursemaid had brought him outside for his daily bit of fresh air, and he'd been showing Nicolette every wildflower he could manage to pluck. "What are these?" He set a handful of white blooms on her lap.

"These are"—she refrained from saying *were*— "daisies."

"Are there daisies in France?" Roderick asked her a great many questions about France, though he had abandoned his attempts to do so in French.

"*Oui*. We call them *les pâquerettes*."

"Are they an important flower in France?" he pressed.

"They are very abundant in France," she said.

Roderick leaned against her legs, his face pulled in an expression of deep thought. "Is there a very important flower in France?"

"The *fleur-de-lis*," she said, allowing her voice to turn a little dramatic. "The shape of that flower is found all over France. Even the king himself considers it very important."

"Are those flowers here?" Roderick looked around, eyes wide with anticipation.

"I have not seen any," she admitted.

"I will find you one," he said. "Uncle Aldric would help me. And Mr. Henri would help me."

"Mr. Henri knows this flower very well," Nicolette said. "If anyone could find it, he could."

"And he would find it for you." Roderick spoke with absolute surety. "My uncle Aldric said that Mr. Henri likes you even more than poems. I think that means he likes you a lot."

She bit back a smile. "I would be very honored to know he liked me more than poems."

"That would mean you were important to him," Roderick said, "like the flower that is important in France."

"It is very nice to be important to people, isn't it?"

He nodded.

From a bit of a distance, the nursemaid called out, "Lord Draycott, we need to continue on our walk."

The boy pouted. "She likes to walk."

"I will visit you in the nursery later," Nicolette promised.

He made his way back to his nursemaid, looking none too pleased to be abandoning his adventure with flowers. His departure did, however, leave Nicolette with more quiet in which to think and watch.

She'd told Henri she would be waiting in this spot, explaining that the fresh air and change of scenery would do her good. It was also ideal for far more practical reasons. The spot was visible from the windows of the house, lending propriety to her meeting with Henri. And she could see in all directions, preventing anyone from sneaking up on her and discovering things they weren't meant to know.

It was an odd thing, being so careful about messages being delivered when the danger associated with those messages being overheard would not arise for years, if at all. Anticipatory caution likely always felt a bit ridiculous until the time one was desperately grateful to have made the effort.

Soon after Roderick rejoined his nurse, Nicolette spotted Pierre making his way directly toward her. Unless he had done so while she was sleeping or a bit incoherent with fever, he'd not looked in on her during her convalescence. That had been one benefit of being miserably ill. The other, a delightful benefit, had been Henri's frequent visits and listening to his poetry. He'd even read her two that were yet to be published. Why could not *he* have been the one approaching in that moment?

Pierre offered a bow as he reached the bench where she sat. It was very properly executed and even the most uncharitable evaluation had to acknowledge that it was graceful and elegant. It was also insincere.

"A pleasure to see you, Nicolette." He sat beside her without being invited to do so. "You must be grateful to be feeling better."

"I *was*, M. Léandre."

"Your brother has assured me the house party will continue only one more week, though that is longer than had originally been planned."

She'd not heard that Sébastien had chosen to extend their stay. Was it on account of the illness that had gripped the household, or was he also not overly eager to return to France and the legal spiderweb Pierre had spun for them? Whatever the reason, she had two additional days in the place where she was happy, two additional days with Henri.

"One more week," he repeated, "then we can all return to Paris."

"What is your aim once we are there, monsieur?" Nicolette asked. "Are you intending to force me to marry you, or would you rather line your pockets with money you hope to be granted by the court?"

Pierre shrugged. "I'd settle for either."

"How flattering."

"You found my attention flattering two years ago."

Nicolette mimicked his shrug. "We have all been foolish at some point in life."

"And here you are, being foolish again." Pierre shook his head. "One must wonder if you are entirely in control of your faculties. A husband needs to know these things about his wife."

"You are not my husband. I am not your wife. And I am in full possession of my mind and faculties."

Pierre pressed a hand to his heart, a posture obviously meant to convey innocence or concern, but it was ruined by the smirk he couldn't entirely hide. "You do not need to convince me, *mon cœur*. Others might have concerns though. How will I convince them?"

"It is not your place to convince anyone of anything where I am concerned."

He leaned closer and lowered his voice to an almost sinister whisper. "But that is precisely what I intend to do, Nicolette: convince anyone and everyone of whatever serves me best. And you know I can be extremely persuasive."

He absolutely could be; she'd seen it herself. But she would not let him see so much as a flinch at the well-aimed threat. "I know you can be extremely dishonest, and I fully expect you to be in this matter."

"Which leaves you with a decision to make, Nicolette: cooperate, or see yourself and your family destroyed."

He would make good on his threat. She knew him too well to believe otherwise.

"How do you define cooperation?" she asked.

He sat upright once more, his posture relaxed and casual. "I have not yet decided."

She refused to let him see that he was upending her. "I cannot imagine you actually wish to marry me, not when you could have the money you want and marry elsewhere."

"Marriage is a far simpler way to obtain that money—the courts are notoriously laborious. And when one's wife seems a bit mad—making shocking accusations, driving a man to flee, being ungrateful for her husband's many kindnesses—well, that is easy to address as well."

That was his plan, then. Obtain the money he wanted and dispose of her either through rumors started in court and the drawing rooms of Paris or by declaring that she was mad and having her locked away somewhere. Perhaps that was what he'd intended from the beginning, and the last two years had been a respite rather than a true escape.

"My brother will never permit you to do such a deplorable thing." She hoped that proved true.

Pierre looked entirely unimpressed. "I had no difficulty convincing him not to cause me grief when I informed him of my intention to visit you here. A few reminders of my position and the havoc I am in a position to wreak was plenty."

"You invited yourself, then?" She'd known Sébastien hadn't brought Pierre to Derbyshire, but she hadn't been certain who had.

"I go where I wish to go." Pierre's attention shifted, his eyes focusing on the pebbled path leading to where they sat. She followed his gaze and spotted Henri being pulled toward them by Roderick, who had, it seemed, escaped his nursemaid.

Pierre rose. "I look forward to your *cooperation*, Nicolette." With the tiniest of disconcerting chuckles, he walked away.

As his steps took him past Henri, the two men eyed each other but didn't appear to exchange any words. Roderick didn't allow Henri to slow his steps even a little, and Pierre continued on toward the house. Henri and his tiny guide moved to the bench where Nicolette sat exhausted and concerned.

"Who was that man?" Roderick said.

"The man who was just here?" Nicolette asked.

The boy nodded. "He looks angry when he talks to you. I told Mr. Henri he needed to make that man go away."

Nicolette looked up at the dear gentleman who'd been called to her aid. "You came to rescue me?"

Henri smiled and laughed a little.

"You're his floor of lee," Roderick said earnestly. "He wouldn't want you to be sad."

"Floor of lee?" Henri's confusion only added to the amusement in his expression.

"The flower," Roderick said. "It's important for people in France."

"*Fleur-de-lis*," Nicolette explained. "Roderick thinks I am as important to you as the *fleur-de-lis* is to France."

Henri turned to his guide and, in a conspiratorial voice, said, "Mlle Beaulieu is *very* important to me."

Roderick offered a firm nod of acknowledgment. "Then, don't let that man make her sad."

Henri sat on the bench beside Nicolette and took hold of her hand. "I won't."

That seemed to satisfy the little lord. He scampered off to where his nursemaid impatiently waited for him.

Henri turned his attention fully to Nicolette once more. He held her gaze, studying her with obvious concern. "If that blackguard has made you cry again, *ma chérie*, I will have something to say to him, though not everything I 'say' will involve words." Somehow, even when offering to inflict violence on a known snake, Henri's presence was inherently peaceful.

"He has made me angry and, I'll admit, more than a little distressed, but I am shedding no tears over him at the moment."

Henri took her hand, which he seemed to do without even thinking. It had become a common thing between them. "Did M. Léandre make new threats, or was this a repetition of the already established ones?"

Her worries diminished at the reassurance of his touch. "He heavily implied that should he decide that marriage suits his purposes more than destroying me through the courts, he will, after we are wed, declare me mad and have me locked away."

"It seems, then, enduring his destruction of your reputation and likely giving him all the money he intends to claim is your better option, horrible as it is."

She rested her head against his shoulder. "When I am feeling a little more myself, I'll attempt to sort this out."

"Do you need to return to the house?" he asked gently.

"It is nice to be outside," she said. "And here we can have a little privacy, which we wouldn't be afforded inside."

"Which brings us to the matter of the missive I was charged with delivering and the one I have been given in return."

He set a sealed letter on her lap. As much as she wanted to simply sit and enjoy a few quiet minutes in his company, she needed to know what the Beaumonts had said in return.

"I find myself intrigued by the fact that both letters were sealed," Henri said. "I hadn't intended to read either one, but taking that extra precaution makes me think the messages were particularly . . . sensitive. Either that or I am not as trustworthy as I'd like to think I am."

She looked up at him, dismayed to realize she'd given such an impression. "It is not a reflection on you, I swear to it."

"Which means the missives are not casual communications." He offered a quick nod. "I give you my word that I will keep my eyes on the shrubbery while you read your letter."

Darling, wonderful Henri.

She quickly broke the wax seal and unfolded the parchment.

*Mlle Beaulieu,*

*The seaside is quiet this time of year. An excursion to the coast would do wonders for the health of anyone adjusting to this climate, though few make their home there.*

*M. Beaumont*

They didn't know of anyone with a home on the coast that fit their needs. No private inlet or dock. That was particularly frustrating given how little time she had left to finalize these arrangements. Communicating with the Beaumonts from France would be far more difficult and slow.

She folded the letter once more, attempting to decide what to do next.

"You look worried," Henri said. "Whatever topic you are communicating with each other about, it is clearly personal and of great importance to you."

"It is both."

He set his arm around her. "I told you about my poetry, and you've told me about Pierre. If this is something you are ready to share, I hope you know that you can."

As one of the more senior members of *La Tapisserie*, she was permitted to share what she felt necessary with those she found trustworthy enough. Henri certainly met the latter requirement. And as she pondered it more, she realized that telling him some of what they'd been doing would enhance their efforts. He knew a great many people throughout this kingdom. His participation would expand their net.

"If I share this," she said by way of warning, "you would have to keep it *entirely* secret, even from the Gents. That is not something I would propose lightly."

"Is this secret matter something I would be ashamed for them to know of?" Henri asked.

"No."

He had a way of watching her that left her feeling well and truly *seen*, as if the person she was and the burdens she carried mattered to him. She had never known anyone quite like him.

"And would my knowing of this secret-but-not-shameful matter help you?"

She couldn't help the earnestness that entered her voice when she answered, "Yes."

Henri took her free hand in his and raised it to his lips and gently kissed her fingers. He then rested their entwined hands against his heart. "I hope you know that I would do anything I could for you, *ma chérie*. That carrying a secret, if doing so lightens your burdens, would be a welcome load to bear. That you are, after all, my floor of lee."

How easily he brought a smile to her lips and a flip of delight to her heart! "Were you this wonderful in Paris? Did I miss this somehow?"

His soft smile contained just enough sorrow to tell her she had missed a great deal.

"What was missed in Paris three years ago can be blamed on youth and inexperience," he said.

"We weren't exactly infants," she said.

"I believe in some ways, we were." He rested her hand on her lap once more but turned to face her more directly. "Tell me what you can of these worries and what I can do to help you with the burden you are carrying."

Nicolette took a breath to steady herself. After one more quick glance around to make absolutely certain no one was nearby, she began. "I cannot tell you who, but there is someone in Paris, someone trustworthy and intelligent and experienced enough to be depended on in such things who has ample reason to believe that France, should her trajectory not change, is on the path to revolution."

Henri's expression grew immediately somber.

"So strong are these suspicions that a group of people are secretly endeavoring to organize a means of helping our countrymen flee France should the need arise." She was speaking quietly and softly. No one could overhear, yet she felt it best to say what needed saying in as efficient a manner as possible. "As it is our belief that those needing to flee the country will do so under threat, we are making our plans in secret so that those we might one day help reach refuge can do so without being found out."

"*Vraiment?*" His disbelief emerged as a whisper.

"There is the possibility this won't be needed after all, but the possibility that it will is too great to ignore. And we suspect those who participate in the earliest stages of these refugees' flights will be in the most danger. Those recruited in France will be taking the biggest risk. In England, those receiving escapees as they make port somewhere on the southern coast will be taking the bigger risk."

Henri nodded even as he released a tense breath. "The Beaumonts are assisting in these arrangements?"

She nodded. "But they do not know of anyone trustworthy and likely to be sympathetic to the cause should the need arise who lives on the southern coast, away from any cities or villages, whose house has a dock or some other means of receiving people who have arrived by boat."

"That is a very specific requirement."

She sighed. "But our efforts will fail without that need being met. I cannot tell you details of other things being done or that have been done in the past; they are not my exclusive secrets. But I need help finding someone on the southern coast of this country willing to court potentially significant danger. Without that, we cannot hope to save the lives we very much fear will need saving should revolution erupt in our homeland."

"And you think it likely the predictions of upheaval will prove true?"

"The one who issued the warning has experience enough to know the early indications."

Henri's brow pulled. "Are our families in danger?"

"Possibly." She'd not admitted that out loud even to herself until now. "I don't know that they would be *specifically* targeted or in greater peril than others, but violent upheaval is, by nature, chaotic and unpredictable."

"This network you are creating here would help them make safe passage if the need arose?"

She swallowed. The possibility that her own family or her dear friend might need to take advantage of the arrangements she was making had hovered in her mind just beyond her active thoughts. There was no avoiding the topic now. "That is the hope, yes. Whoever needs it and is able to take advantage would be able to. The extensiveness of our arrangements will determine how many we can help. The extensiveness of the revolt would determine how many needed to."

Henri's eyes were pointed ahead, but his gaze seemed unfocused. "My father considered me too incompetent to undertake *anything*. My brother considers me an embarrassment to the family. Céleste thinks highly of me, but I can't help but suspect that part of her is disappointed in me for not being more a part of her life. I would very much like to help your efforts, but I feel I need to warn you that I might, in the end, simply disappoint you as well."

He was a person of integrity. He was trustworthy and cared for people. He was intelligent and resolute. That his family had managed, inadvertently in Céleste's case, to make him feel so inept and unwanted boiled Nicolette's blood a bit. Everyone ought to see his worth, ought to recognize how remarkable he was.

"I have no doubt as to your competence," she said, "and I trust you implicitly, which I assure you is a rare thing for me."

A hint of color touched his cheeks. "It is a real shame you don't need someone living in a small estate in Nantes," Henri said, "because I have a brother who would be delighted to see me settle myself there."

She knew he was jesting, but she had a sincere question. "Do you think you could be happy returning to France and an estate so closely tied to your father and your brother?"

"I can make the best of almost any situation," he said. "I would find a way to do so in this matter as well."

"But you hope it doesn't come to that?"

"I confess I do."

Her heart dropped a bit. She'd not realized how much she'd begun to hope that he would do precisely that. France was her home. If England remained his, what hope did she have of seeing him again, of having his company, of perhaps discovering something more between them?

But he was too dear to her for her to wish him to do something that would make him unhappy.

And even if he were to abandon his dreams of making a home for himself here in his adopted homeland, she had Pierre to contend with in France. The end result of his reappearance had yet to be determined, but it would certainly be unpleasant. Perhaps it was for the best that Henri would not be pulled into that impending disaster.

"A person ought to be able to build a life where he will be most happy," she said.

"And where would *you* be most happy, Nicolette?" His arm around her tucked her a bit closer. "You ought to be permitted to claim that happiness as well."

"Paris is the only home I have ever known," she said. "But Pierre will be there now. I cannot say I will continue to like the city as well as I have."

"Have you given more thought to asking the Gents to ponder ways of thwarting him?" Henri asked. "I do think they would do all they could to assist you."

"Even if they offer me only hope, I would be grateful."

"I, for one, mean to hold out for a miracle," he said.

She closed her eyes and forced herself to breathe slowly and calmly. "We could use a great many miracles, Henri."

She felt him press a kiss to her temple. She didn't know whether to simply melt against him or let flow the tears she held back. They really did need a tremendous bit of good fortune in so many areas of their lives. Though she had regained her strength and equilibrium and determination over the past two years, in so many ways, she had lost her ability to believe in miracles.

# Chapter Twenty-Five

"ONLY LUCAS WOULD CHOOSE so odd a location for the day's business," Henri said as he walked between Aldric and Niles toward the banks of the river Trent later that afternoon.

He'd told his friends he needed help addressing a particularly cumbersome situation, and rather than gathering together in the book room or the drawing room or any place an ordinary group of people would, Lucas had immediately declared that they would convene at the riverbank. Lucas never did things by halves, and he certainly never did things in an ordinary way.

"Stanley would have wholeheartedly approved," Niles said.

"He might have suggested that we hold our discussion on the roof of Norwood," Aldric said with a light laugh. He was much improved from the illness that had tiptoed around the household.

"I will never forget the day we managed to get a chaise-cart on the roof of the library at Trinity Hall." Niles grinned from ear to ear.

Henri assumed his most Archbishop-esque demeanor. "As the group's resident saint, I must express my disapproval of such a disruptive and irresponsible lark." He allowed the tiniest twitch of his lips. "But as Henri Fortier, Gent, that was brilliant." That one moment of triumph was among the Gents' greatest undertakings.

"Stanley lived a lot of life in his twenty-five years," Aldric said.

Speaking of Stanley had been incredibly difficult in the first couple of years after his death. It was a little easier now. They didn't miss him any less, but perhaps they'd simply grown more familiar with the grief of his absence.

The three were the last to arrive at the river.

Julia held little Philip in her arms, he having fully recovered from his fever and the doctor feeling it safe for Julia to return to the house. They sat beside Violet and Nicolette, all the ladies utilizing cushions atop blankets spread over the grass on the bank of the river. Lucas and Digby were skipping rocks. Digby, as always, looked regal; Henri didn't imagine there was anything their King did without panache. Most in the *ton* didn't know there was more to Digby than his appearance. Henri sometimes wondered if *Digby* saw more in himself than that. Kes stood with his back against a tree trunk, jotting something in a notebook. He was forever doing that, hurriedly recording his ideas for inventions.

Henri spent a tremendous amount of time working on his passion for poetry, but he had always done so clandestinely. That he'd come here to reveal that secret made him a little nervous. It wasn't that he didn't trust the Gents; there was simply so much riding on his admission.

When it had been suggested that the ladies join them at this gathering, turning it into something of a picnic rather than a simple meeting, Henri had asked that Céleste not be present. He felt guilty about that, but should word of what Henri revealed somehow reach Jean-François, he wanted to make certain Céleste could not be accused of keeping their older brother in the dark.

"You've arrived," Violet said, waving them over.

Her greeting turned the others' attention toward them. With an alacrity very common to him, Lucas abandoned his rock skipping and bounded over. It was little wonder he and Stanley had led the Gents on so many merry adventures. The two of them together had been like a roaring river: ever moving, ever pushing onward, filled with an abundance of energy and endless possibilities.

"We found ourselves a spot where we can have some privacy without drawing the suspicions of those whom we would rather not look on us with suspicion," Lucas said. "And in an entertaining twist, we are about to receive a confession from Archbishop."

Henri shook his head at the absurdly ridiculous description Lucas had provided. Those who didn't know him well might think he didn't take seriously issues that deserved earnestness. Those who *did* know him knew the opposite was, in fact, true. Lucas plopped onto the blanket beside Julia, offering his finger to Philip to grab hold of. Niles took a seat on a nearby rock. Aldric stood with his back to Norwood and his full attention on Henri.

"It is no secret that my brother has been withholding from me an increasing portion of my income from my father's estate. I confronted him about this and have been made to realize that his aim is to render my economic state so dire that remaining in England will no longer be feasible. He is attempting to accomplish what my father could not and force me back to France."

The uproar that followed did his battered soul a great deal of good. Other than Céleste, his family had wanted him in France only to prove that they were right and not because they actually liked having him there. He found himself doubting whether or not his insistence on remaining in England was simply stubbornness as well. But these Gents, his brothers by choice, put paid to that argument. He wanted to remain because they made this home to him.

"I've been attempting to find an estate I could let but have struggled on account of my diminishing funds. I have a very small income independent from my brother, but it is so meager that I am unlikely to find anything within my means large enough to accommodate any Gents gatherings, so I won't see all of you very often."

"Henri, do you have a second given name?" Julia asked, the question entirely unexpected.

"Yves."

She nodded. In the next instant, her bearing transformed into one of a mother reprimanding with kindness and firmness a child who had gone a bit astray. "Henri Yves Fortier, you absolute hulverhead." Somewhere in that scolding mother was such a heavy dose of loving humor that for reasons he couldn't identify made Henri emotional. "Do you for even a moment think that the size of your eventual home or the extent of your income would determine whether we continue to seek you out and include you in our lives?"

"One grows weary of always needing charity." He heard in his own voice the misery he tried so hard to keep hidden.

"There is no charity involved," Kes said. "We chose long ago to be family to each other. Family looks after one another."

"Tell that to Jean-François," Henri said.

"And Mowbary," Aldric added.

"And a great many others who are best left unmentioned," Digby drawled.

They had all known Digby since he was young, Lucas from the time they had both first arrived at Eton. None of them had ever heard Digby speak about his family beyond references as vague as the one he'd just made. They knew bits and pieces from Society's whispers, but Digby steadfastly refused to discuss any member of his family.

"What is the source of this additional but meager income you mentioned?" Kes asked.

He'd not admitted this to anyone beyond Nicolette. He looked to her now as he felt his courage dwindling. She nodded, encouraging him with the small, silent movement.

"My other income has not and likely will not make me wealthy, but it might keep me from poverty should my brother cut me off."

"Have you taken up the trade of grave robbing?" Lucas asked.

"Highway robbery?" Niles guessed.

"Common thievery?" Even Aldric joined in the jesting.

"*Un*common thievery?" Digby adjusted.

Henri pulled from his pocket the volume of his poetry. "This is the book that I produced as part of our questing game early in the house party."

A few nods confirmed that the group remembered.

"It contains poetry written by 'a gentleman.' I studied poetry extensively at Cambridge, quite to my father's disgust. His disapproval was made sharper by my insistence on studying works written in English."

In near-perfect synchrony, looks of understanding pulled at Julia and Kes's expressions. They were often the first to solve puzzles.

"I told my father once that it was my intention to someday write poetry," Henri continued. "He was livid. I honestly thought he would simply disown me. But that likely wasn't punishment enough in his view of things. Instead, he found an ultimatum I could not ignore."

They were all quiet and still, which was an odd thing for this group. They were boisterous, adventurous, and at times a bundle of chaos, but when one of them was struggling, they were focused and determined.

"My father told me that if I pursued the path I had intended, he would cut me off from my sister. I would not have been permitted to see her again. I couldn't bear that. Even then, I had the goal of bringing her to England to live with me, away from our father." He'd disappointed her in that as well. "Jean-François heard my father's threats at that time and did not take exception to them, though he was not yet the churl he is now. He would inflict the punishment Father promised should I defy his wishes in this. I know he would."

Aldric stood, feet shoulder width apart, arms folded across his chest: the posture they all knew as his General's pose. He was sorting things through, determining what had happened, what might happen, and what the situation truly was. "Are you this 'a gentleman' bloke, publishing under the umbrella of anonymity?" He motioned his head toward the book in Henri's hand.

Henri nodded. "And heaven help me if my brother ever sorts that out."

"None of us is going to say anything," Kes assured him.

"Why didn't you tell us?" Lucas asked.

"For the same reason I asked Céleste not to be here today. Asking people to carry a secret often requires them to lie about it and, should it be discovered, be blamed or mistreated for having kept the secret in the first place."

"You are our Archbishop, and as such, pay close attention to those dozen or so commandments we hear so much about in chapels," Digby said.

"Ten," Henri said. "There are ten of them, and I am well aware of the 'Thou shalt not lie' one. I am rather pitiful in other areas of my life, but I do my best to abide by that very basic rule."

Digby ran a finger down the length of his lace cuffs, straightening nonexistent wrinkles. "I would wager you are unaware of the footnote: 'If thou art a Gent and another Gent has been burdened with a particularly difficult situation and a bit of misdirection or minor falsehoods on his behalf would actually be the more charitable and compassionate path, then thou shalt absolutely lie and do so with fervor and enthusiasm.'"

Henri turned his head a little away to hide his grin, doing his utmost to hold back a laugh.

"Do not think you are fooling us," Lucas said. "We know our Archbishop is laughing at that bit of blatant blasphemy. Shocking!"

"You said you anticipate this continuing to be a source of income for you," Julia said. "That must mean you have some expectation of publishing another volume."

It was a tremendous benefit having friends who were both enthusiastic and remarkably intelligent.

"The publisher of this first volume intends to publish a second, provided I can complete the final poem they are expecting. I'd hoped to work on it during this house party, but I . . . found myself . . ."

With an unrepentant grin, Lucas said, "Distracted?" His eyes darted toward Nicolette.

All the Gents burst out laughing.

"I propose," Violet said, "that for the remainder of this house party, each of us dedicates ourselves to making certain Henri is given time to himself every morning before the activities begin, standing guard at the door of whatever room he is writing in if need be. And if that means telling his brother and sister-in-law a Banbury tale about Henri jaunting about somewhere entirely free of poetry, so be it."

Henri very much liked the idea but cringed at the doing of it. "Thou shalt not lie," he repeated halfheartedly.

"Footnote," Digby tossed back without hesitation.

For the first time in all this, Nicolette spoke. "You are a good person, Henri, and you try very hard to always do the right thing. Though that makes you hesitate in this, you don't need to. Now that you have finally allowed your friends to know of this pursuit, further allow them to help you in the best way they can. Finish this poem, and you'll finish your volume. Publish that, and you'll have some income. Publish another, and you'll have more still. In time, you'll have that house you wish for and, I am quite confident, will soon enough be able to see your sister free of any constraints placed there by Jean-François."

"Let me offer a bit of hard-earned wisdom," Lucas said. "When a remarkably intelligent woman offers you a bit of very intelligent advice, you would do well to take it."

Henri set his shoulders. "I do think with a couple of hours every morning over the week that remains of this gathering, I could have my final poem ready to send to my publisher." Even as he made the declaration, he felt assured it was not overly optimistic. A sense of relief he'd not felt in ages rushed over him. Here there was hope.

"Now," Julia said, "it's time we address whatever Nicolette's problem is."

All eyes shifted to Nicolette.

"Whatever do you mean?" she asked.

"Though you have not said as much," Julia said, "the annoyance you initially felt at the arrival of M. Léandre has clearly shifted into something far more like panic. As you have seen, this group excels at helping each other. And now we extend that to you."

Nicolette looked to Henri. "You did say I ought to share this with them."

He nodded as he sat beside her and took one of her hands in his, feeling his own burdens lightened.

She addressed the others. "Pierre and I were once engaged." She quickly explained the same history she had shared with Henri, and everyone listened with as much concern as they had offered Henri. "I thought perhaps Pierre had returned because my brother had foolishly offered him encouragement."

"That was not the case?" Aldric clearly doubted his hypothesis.

"My brother seems as displeased with his arrival as I am. Pierre contacted him and said he would be here during this house party and that Sébastien would do best not to object."

"You didn't tell me that," Henri said.

"Pierre only just told me in the moments before you and I spoke this morning." The tiredness in her face was more than just lingering illness. It was bone-deep exhaustion. "I suspect Pierre has squandered what fortune he had and is looking to shore up his assets. Unfortunately, he defected *after* the marriage contracts were signed two years ago. He has realized that gives him some hope of recourse in the law."

Understanding was beginning to pop up on the faces around them.

"He means to either force me into a marriage, then, he heavily hinted, see me committed to an institution or locked away in an isolated country estate so he needn't be bothered with me, or he means to bring a breach-of-contract suit against my family, in which he intends to not only take possession of my dowry and a healthy sum from the Beaulieu family coffers but will also drag my name and my family through the mud while he does so. Either way, he means to destroy us all, and I haven't the first idea how to stop him."

Silence followed the heavy recounting. Nicolette looked at them all, brows drawn, clearly concerned that she had managed to present them with a problem they had little desire to address.

Henri leaned closer to her and in a whisper said, "I would wager this silence will last another five seconds." He threaded his fingers through hers. "*Cinq. Quatre. Trois.*" The Gents were all looking at each other. "*Deux. Un.*"

Almost on cue, multiple conversations erupted simultaneously.

"How did you do that?" Nicolette whispered back.

"They have been the most significant people in my life for thirteen years. I know them well."

"Yet, you only just told them of your poetry," she pointed out.

"Unfortunately, my father's words have planted themselves too firmly in my heart. Even people I know I can trust and people I know care about me are approached with caution."

"You seem to trust me," she said.

He kissed her hand, as he'd found of late he very much liked to do. "And you seem to trust me."

"We wanted a miracle." Nicolette smiled at him. "Perhaps this ought to count."

"Do you know if M. Léandre has any holdings in England?" Aldric asked from the midst of the flying conversations.

"None that I know of," Nicolette said.

Aldric gave a quick nod and then returned to his discussion with Kes.

Nicolette looked to Henri. "Do you suppose they have an idea already?"

"It seems they've a thread they are chasing. I promise they will not give up."

She reached up a hand and gently touched his face. "Are you going to give up?"

"It is not in my nature to do so." He turned his head enough to brush the briefest of kisses against the palm of her hand. "I'll not give up on my poetry or on finding a home. And I refuse to give up hope."

"Hope of what?" she whispered.

"Hope for a future that includes you." Where he found the courage to very nearly repeat the confession of affection he'd made to her years earlier, he didn't know. Then, she had smiled and waxed philosophical on the requirements in a potential match and the future that would bring. This time, she smiled and leaned against him. He put an arm around her and held her while all around them, their dearest friends were doing all they could to keep hope alive.

# Chapter Twenty-Six

THEY WERE A JOVIAL GROUP making their way back to the house from the riverbank. Henri had Nicolette on his arm, surrounded by his dearest friends. Except for the absence of Céleste, Henri could hardly imagine a more perfect arrangement.

Lucas turned about, walking backward and facing Henri and Nicolette. "Have you considered writing a poetic work in which the first letter of each line spells out the name of your favorite Gent?" He motioned to himself.

"This is not a collection of acrostics," Henri said.

"A shame." Lucas turned back around, snaking his arm around Julia, who held Philip still.

"They are a very happy little family," Nicolette said.

"Yes, they are."

A footman and several maids rushed to the front door as the group stepped into the entryway, accepting their now-empty baskets, cushions, and blankets they had used at the riverside, and aiding them in divesting themselves of their outerwear.

All appeared as it should be, but Aldric seemed to sense something different. "Did something happen while we were away?" he asked the footman nearby. "You all seem a little on edge."

"His Grace has arrived," the footman answered in a tense and quiet voice.

All the Gents' eyes shifted immediately to Aldric. It was no secret he and his father had an increasingly difficult and tense relationship. While Aldric and Mowbary would often snap at each other, Aldric had taken the tactic with his father of simply being very, very quiet and, as much as possible, very, very absent. They'd found a means of enjoying this house party, even with Mowbary there to make it miserable.

Having the duke present as well would change that.

"It seems we need to change tactics," Nicolette said quietly. She claimed the attention of a maid in the entryway. "Is Mlle Fortier in the drawing room?"

The maid shook her head. "I think she is still in her bedchamber, Miss Beaulieu."

Nicolette nodded and tugged Henri by the hand toward the stairs. Normally, they would have moved immediately to the drawing room to offer their greetings to the new arrival. Henri knew Nicolette was well aware of social expectations; she would not be violating them without reason.

She knocked at the door of Céleste's room, which was opened the tiniest bit, enough for Céleste herself to glance out. Upon seeing them on the other side, she opened the door fully and motioned them inside. "You have heard, then?"

Nicolette nodded. "We've come to formulate a plan."

Henri was a bit lost, but he trusted these two and was willing to help with whatever was currently making them so frantic.

"We've kept Jean-François and Marguerite a bit at bay these past weeks," Céleste said, "but a simple word to His Grace, especially with me there in proximity with his son, and my family's suggestions might become a ducal demand."

Henri's heart dropped; she wasn't wrong. "I warned Aldric about that very thing, worried Mowbary would write to his Grace and Aldric would likely be in receipt of matrimonial orders from his father."

Céleste dropped onto the bench at the foot of her bed. "What am I to do? I'm certain your friend is a decent gentleman, but if I find myself forced to marry him, I will commandeer whatever vehicle is at my disposal and take myself to the nearest convent, steadfastly refusing to leave for the remainder of my life."

Henri felt it unwise to say as much, but he was relatively certain Aldric was equally opposed to the idea. It was a shame this gathering had led to his friend and his sister being at odds. They'd met very briefly many years earlier and had managed a friendly indifference. That would likely never be the case again.

"I am absolutely certain," Nicolette said, "that the Beaumonts would be pleased as anything to have you visit for a day or two. They love people but would likely give you as much privacy as you preferred. They being French, it would be easy to explain your visit as you having struck up a friendship with your fellow countrymen and wishing to a spend little time with them before the house party ends."

"I'm to be banished?" Céleste asked with frustration. "I do like the Beaumonts, and I'm certain I would enjoy their company, but it will be so lonely there with all of you here."

"As lonely as a nunnery?" Nicolette asked dryly.

Understanding and something like resignation entered Céleste's expression.

Henri sat on the bench beside her. "The Beaumonts are so nearby that we can all come to visit you every single day. And you could meet us on the riverbank or in the village. You likely would need to do so for only a couple of days while we see if Jean-François or Lord Mowbary means to make trouble. And we can spend that time redirecting attention."

"What am I to do in the evenings?" She asked. "If I come here and spend time with everyone, then we risk putting the duke on the scent. But if I remain at Eau Plate, I'll miss everything."

Henri put an arm around her shoulders and tucked her against him, squeezing her affectionately. "I know it's not ideal, and I will be miserable without you here, but would it be worth the risk of drawing the duke's attention?"

"You mean worth risking being forced to marry Lord Aldric?" Céleste said. "Again, I don't mean to insult your friend, but I would endure a great deal to avoid that."

"Then, I do think this is our best approach."

"Provided we take the tactic of not allowing it to be discussed with your brother or seeking his approval," Nicolette said. "I believe you should pack a few things and go directly there. As I have no doubt M. and Mme Beaumont will be delighted at your company, any objections made by Jean-François and Marguerite would seem remarkably unfeeling and rude."

Henri nodded only to realize Céleste was doing so in perfect synchrony with him. They both knew that appearing ill-mannered, at least to those outside of their family, was something their brother and sister-in-law would avoid by nearly all means possible.

"I know you don't like being at home, Henri," Céleste said, "but you must promise me you will visit France soon. Coming to visit you here hasn't worked out in quite the way I'd hoped it would."

He kept her in his brotherly embrace. "I will do everything in my power to make certain I see you far sooner than recent history would suggest."

"If you are willing to join us in Paris instead of only visiting when we are at Fleur-de-la-Forêt, we might see you more often."

"Returning to Paris isn't—It hasn't been—" How could he explain, especially with Nicolette in the room? He'd avoided Paris because he'd known she would be there, and his embarrassment coupled with his broken heart had made the very idea of crossing paths with her too painful to even contemplate.

"Wherever you choose to make your journey, we can be grateful Father is no longer making everything drastically worse," Céleste said.

Somehow, Henri needed to make certain he saw his sister more often than he had. If he had any hope of his brother restoring his income or his poetry proving more lucrative than he had any right to hope, he would have already begun formulating a means of having Céleste live with him in England. They would both be happier. However, he would never see Adèle if that plan worked out. The very possibility of losing his connection with her sent a wave of disappointment crashing against his heart.

Céleste's lady's maid slipped inside a moment later, Nicolette having apparently rung the summoning bell. Nicolette offered very quick and brief instructions.

The maid nodded emphatically. "I had wondered what could be done." She spoke in French, there being little reason to speak anything else. "I do not wish to see my mistress entangled in an arrangement she does not care for."

"None of us wants to see that happen," Henri said. "Please help her prepare to depart as soon as possible." He turned to Céleste. "Nicolette and I will arrange for a carriage to take you both to Eau Plate. Meet us along the east side of the house."

While there *was* a sense of relief as Nicolette and Henri stepped from Céleste's room with a plan for helping her avoid the fate neither she nor Aldric deserved, there was also sadness. His days with his sister in England were numbered, and she was required to depart for the sake of her own future.

"I know it is terribly unfair," Nicolette said, clearly having understood the emotions she'd seen in his face. "We will visit her quite regularly over the coming days. And the Beaumonts can be trusted."

"They would not be part of your whispered arrangements otherwise," Henri said, his voice as quiet as he could make it. They were entirely alone as they made their way toward the stairs, but he still felt caution was necessary.

They had a carriage called and ready by the time Céleste and her lady's maid arrived at the meeting place. Nicolette assured them that she and her own maid would see to the remainder of Céleste's things. Getting her out of the house swiftly was of greater importance at the moment.

As the carriage rolled away, Henri released his bated breath. Now that he didn't have to present a resolute facade for Céleste's sake, his disappointment was surfacing.

Nicolette turned to face him. "Why did you not wish to return to Paris?"

The question was asked in a tone of curiosity rather than accusation, but he still felt a little on the defensive. "Visiting the family's country home was easier to arrange."

"But likely more uncomfortable." Nicolette threaded her arm through his. "Paris would offer more opportunities to be away from Jean-François."

"Visiting the family home was not simple, by any means, but it was still less complicated than Paris."

She studied him but didn't press. He'd come to know her well enough to suspect he would not be permitted to avoid the subject indefinitely. Explaining would require laying bare what she'd misunderstood and what he'd regretted for so long. He would feel ridiculous and inept and pitiful and all the many things his father had insisted he was. For Nicolette to see that side of him was not an exciting prospect.

"We'd likely do best not to give the impression that we've been alone together since returning to the house," Nicolette said. "I'll wait a bit after you have entered the drawing room to enter myself."

He nodded his agreement, then stepped inside the house and into the drawing room. The duke was deep in conversation with the French guests, leaving Henri to move unnoticed to where Aldric stood.

"Where did you disappear to?" Aldric was tense, as he so often was when faced unexpectedly with his father.

Across the room, Mowbary looked absolutely smug, while Lady Mowbary looked ready to faint. She was likely nervous about her abilities as a hostess being evaluated and found lacking by her domineering father-in-law.

"I was not here because I was saving your hide," Henri said.

Beside them, Niles chimed in. "Are archbishops allowed to reference a person's hide?"

That brought a touch of a smile to Aldric's face, which was good to see under the circumstances.

"Nicolette and I have just seen Céleste off to Eau Plate," he said quietly and quickly. "She is going to visit the Beaumonts for a couple of days to reduce the chances that the duke will begin pondering the possibility of his younger son making a very beneficial French connection."

The annoyance grew one-hundred fold in Aldric's eyes. "Sometimes I suspect my father enjoys making me miserable."

"*My* father certainly did," Henri said.

Niles nodded with acknowledgment but didn't offer any observations of his own. His grandfather was a little imperious. They'd all been a bit shocked when the older gentleman had shown his grandson a small mercy and allowed the arranged marriage required of Niles to be delayed until he was thirty years old. He'd been granted a few fleeting years to live his life as he chose. But Niles was nearly thirty-one. The Greenberry family patriarch would summon him home at any moment to pay the proverbial piper.

Nicolette stepped inside next. She held herself in exactly the way she had in the Paris salons and balls where Henri had first made her acquaintance. She was graceful and friendly, put people immediately at ease. She was the *crème* of Paris . . . and he was pitiful.

Henri pushed his father's words from his mind and replaced them with Stanley's. *Stronger and braver.*

A complication quite suddenly occurred to Henri. What if the duke got it in his mind that *Nicolette* would make a good match for his son? That was a possibility that needed to be nipped in the bud.

Henri moved in her direction, managing to come even with her just as she arrived beside her brother and sister-in-law, who were in conversation with the duke himself. Henri offered her his arm, which she accepted readily.

"Nicolette, there you are." Sébastien seemed genuinely pleased to see his sister. "Your Grace, might I make you acquainted with Mlle Nicolette Beaulieu, my sister. Nicolette, this is His Grace, the Duke of Hartley."

The duke executed a perfectly mannerly bow. Nicolette's curtsy was everything graceful and proper.

The duke looked to Henri and offered a more brief but still correct bow. "Mr. Fortier, a pleasure to see you again."

"And it is a great honor to see you again, Your Grace," Henri replied.

"How delightful. The two of you are already acquainted," Gaëtane said. "We have only just had the privilege of meeting the duke."

Henri remained there, Nicolette's arm woven through his. The duke would not have been his first choice for company, and Henri was thoroughly annoyed that the man had arrived, but knowing his efforts were saving Aldric from having to interact with his father and was gaining Céleste time to make good her escape, he felt rather heroic. Having Nicolette at his side, he felt as strong and brave as Stanley had believed he was.

# Chapter Twenty-Seven

NICOLETTE'S MIND WAS SPINNING ON yet another matter. That afternoon when she had first been introduced to the Duke of Hartley, Gaëtane had indicated that they had not ever met him before. That, on its own, would be unexceptional; the Beaulieus had no real connections in England, and as far she knew, despite his wife's having been French, the Duke of Hartley had not set foot in France in a great many years.

The Beaulieus' status in France had no bearing on the duke's status in England. He did not seem at all interested in establishing any new French connections. He treated her brother with the appropriate civility but had given no indication he was anxious to forge a lasting connection. And her brother had seemed pleased to meet His Grace but in a way that would be expected when meeting a person one was unlikely to encounter again.

Why, then, had His Grace invited her family to attend this house party?

The ladies had retired to the drawing room after dinner. Nicolette didn't know what reason Henri had given his brother and sister-in-law to explain Céleste's absence, but it seemed to have been accepted, and other than the Gents, Julia, and Violet expressing their sincere regret, her departure was not overly talked about.

Jean-François and Marguerite were likely afraid of embarrassment were the topic belabored in front of the duke. That worked to Céleste's advantage. Though she was a woman grown, her oldest brother still had a great deal of control over her comings and goings. But she'd managed this relocation without earning a lecture or punishment or being forcibly retrieved by Jean-François. Nicolette suspected her friend would take greater delight in the situation if her temporary change of residence had been undertaken out of pleasure.

With the gentleman still at their port in the dining room, Nicolette took the opportunity to speak with her sister-in-law. "His Grace seems quite a regal gentleman."

Gaëtane nodded. "And one of undeniable significance in England."

"Sébastien must have been thrilled to receive his invitation to this house party." She had no idea how her brother would have actually reacted, but she was hoping Gaëtane revealed a little bit about her brother's shock or lack thereof.

"Once he discovered from Jean-François who the Duke of Hartley was, Sébastien was quite pleased."

She'd been correct, then, that her brother had no connection to His Grace that would explain any of this. "I wonder what inspired the duke to extend such an invitation? We are well-known in Paris but not in London."

Gaëtane tipped her shoulders back the tiniest bit, an indication that she had, to a small extent, taken Nicolette's musings as something of an insult. "To be well thought of in Paris is not an insignificant thing."

"I had not intended to imply that it was," Nicolette was quick to say. "I simply find myself delightfully curious as to who it was that suggested he invite us." She managed to keep her tone that of a gossip in pursuit of a few exciting whispers.

"I read the letter from His Grace," Gaëtane said, dropping her voice. "It said that we had been well spoken of by an acquaintance of his, and he wished for his family to know us better." Her brow pulled almost immediately. "I almost wish we had not accepted. Perhaps M. Léandre would not have decided to bother us had we not been near to him."

*Near to him?* "Were we not nearer to him when we were in France?"

"We had been here a couple of days when a note arrived for Sébastien from M. Léandre, declaring that he knew we were at Norwood, and as your fiancé, he felt it rather unfair of us not to have informed him. He said he would see us in only a couple of days—too quickly for him to have been in France."

For two years, all of Paris had wondered where Pierre had gone. He hadn't any property in the countryside of France, but none of his acquaintances or friends had indicated he'd been spending time at their homes.

In this brief conversation, one she'd not even known she'd needed to have with her sister-in-law, she had pieced together two very odd but telling events. Pierre had, it seemed, been in England for at least a portion of his disappearance. And the Duke of Hartley had invited them on the suggestion of someone he knew in England. Other than Henri, whom she didn't for a moment think was the acquaintance spoken of, she could think of no one in England who might have whispered their name in the duke's ear except for Pierre.

If that suspicion was true, it left her with a pressing and difficult-to-answer question: Why?

# Chapter Twenty-Eight

THE VERY NEXT MORNING, THE Gents made good on their promise to help Henri complete his poem in time for publication. Were Stanley still with them, he would have offered Henri a hardy, "I told you so." Early on in Henri's days among them, he'd been skeptical of their friendship and loyalty. A person who had been told by his own father his entire life that he offered very little and was deeply unwanted was unlikely to believe without an excessive amount of evidence that he was, in fact, valued and wanted.

Following a jovial breakfast, Lucas and Julia whisked him away to the book room and installed him there with all he needed to do his work. Julia remained in the room, sitting in a chair beside the nearly closed door. Her role for the morning was to send away anyone who came with the intent to interrupt him. Violet often did precisely that for Kes and would, no doubt, be part of the rotation.

Henri was making tremendous progress and felt himself a breath away from his goal, but sometimes, the mind was both willing and unable. He rose from his chair and slowly paced the room.

From her position near the door, Julia looked up from her book, likely a scholarly text of some sort.

"Sometimes, I rise and walk," he explained. "It helps my brain find energy enough to continue working."

She nodded with a look of absolute understanding. "I think Lucas fears the floor of our book room at Brier Hill will be worn to slivers from my pacing in there while I'm studying. I simply point out to him that we will have to invite Mr. Simpkin back to relay the stones in Lucas's garden. That is where he does his walking and thinking."

At a quick knock on the door, Henri moved in that direction, intending to open it, a decision he made more out of habit than anything else. Julia firmly motioned him back toward his desk.

He'd not entirely sat on his chair once more when the now fully open door revealed Nicolette on the other side. Henri stood again.

"I've come to undertake the changing of the guards," she said.

Julia grinned. "I think that would defeat the purpose. You see, the guard is meant to prevent distractions, not create them."

Nicolette was undeterred but not angry. "If I promise to only have the briefest of conversations before insisting he returned to his poetry, will you allow it?"

From his spot a bit removed from the ladies, Henri asked, "Does anyone care to ask me what I think?"

"This is a military matter, M. Fortier," Julia said firmly. "*Capitaine* Beaulieu is requesting a change of post, and I am considering it."

"You outrank a captain, do you?" Henri asked.

"If you asked my husband, he would insist I rank somewhere near a general."

Henri laughed lightly as he lowered himself into his chair. How good for his soul were his friends. Again, he took a moment to thank the heavens for bringing Stanley to the cricket field outside Cambridge all those years ago. He counted that moment as a turning point in his life.

"I can secure you a few minutes' privacy," Julia said. "But after about five minutes, I will need to open the door again. The last thing either of you needs is a scandal."

"*Merci*," Henri said.

Julia slipped out, closing the door behind her until it was only slightly ajar.

Nicolette leaned against the edge of the desk, facing him. He took one of her hands in his. For a fraction of a moment, he let his imagination picture them just that way in years to come, together and happy in a home of their own.

"Gaëtane told me last night that when the invitation arrived at our home in Paris for us to join in this house party, it was the first time my brother had ever heard from or of the Duke of Hartley. They were not acquainted before, not even in passing."

That seemed a little odd.

"And while my family has very good standing in Paris and throughout France, we do not have significant enough connections in England to bring our family to the attention of the duke. And though he issued the invitation and did so because he said someone had spoken highly of us, he does not seem overly anxious to build a connection."

Henri leaned his elbow on the desk and rested his chin against his upturned fist as he listened.

"I also learned that Pierre was already in England when we arrived and knew we would be here, and I am beginning to suspect that Pierre was the one to convince the duke to invite us, likely specifically so he could ambush us here."

"Pierre would have had to be here for some time to have made such inroads with His Grace," Henri said.

She reached out and brushed a bit of hair back from his forehead, sending his heart pounding. "Pierre has been unaccounted for these past two years. It's possible he's been in this country all along."

Her hand nearest him still rested on the desktop. Henri slipped his free hand closer to it, their fingers a breath from touching. "If Pierre has been in England, he's not made much of a splash in social circles. I've been in London for the Season these past two years, and I've made note of my fellow Frenchmen there. I don't remember seeing him or hearing him spoken of."

"How did Pierre become so well acquainted with the Duke of Hartley that he could suggest this invitation be extended?" Nicolette's hand slipped a bit closer to his. "The duke doesn't strike me as someone who is easily persuaded."

"He's not." Henri slid his smallest finger over hers. Such a simple touch, yet it sent an echo of awareness through him. He forced himself to keep to the topic at hand despite the growing temptation to pull her into his arms and thoroughly distract them both. "The duke forms and maintains connections based on what benefit he personally derives from the relationship, even when it comes to his own sons." Aldric, as a spare, was not afforded a great deal of importance, respect, or attention from his father.

Nicolette passed her hand lightly over the back of his, bending her fingers around the side, a gentle and tender and breath-catching connection. Focusing on their discussion was growing more difficult. *For him*, at least.

"Pierre must provide some benefit to His Grace," Nicolette said, "though I cannot sort out what it could possibly be. Pierre has good standing in Paris, but his fortune has been squandered."

Henri ran his thumb along her fingers. "The duke may be looking to get a footing in France. With the tensions between our two nations of late, that is both a difficult and potentially lucrative prospect."

"The financial situation in France is growing quite tenuous. The Assembly of Notables was unable to reach any kind of consensus, and the inequities of the recent trade agreements with this country are only heightening that difference. Anyone able and willing to utilize it to their benefit at both ends of trade would find themselves in underhandedly obtained fine clover."

"Pierre certainly seems capable of underhandedness." Henri shifted his hand enough to be palm-to-palm with her before threading their fingers together. "And most of the aristocracy of England makes money through investments. The Duke of Hartley may have some investments in France that Pierre helped arrange, investments that took advantage of the issues the Eden Agreement was meant to address."

"'Questionably legal' arrangements, you mean." Nicolette fussed with the same errant bit of hair she'd brushed from his face a moment earlier. "I wouldn't put it beyond him. And if those 'investments' are now less lucrative, that would explain his sudden intention to enrich himself at my expense."

Henri lifted their entwined hands to his lips and kissed each finger in turn. "We will find a way of thwarting him, *ma chérie.*"

Her fingertips drifted from his hair to his jaw, lightly brushing, lingering. "I was so thickheaded three years ago, Henri. You were kind and clever and one of the only people I knew with whom I didn't feel the need to act a part. How did I not realize what a rare and remarkable thing that was?" Her eyes darted for a fraction of a moment to his mouth. "I was sad when you left. Did I tell you that?"

He shook his head, the impact of Nicolette Beaulieu studying his lips having rendered him temporarily unable to speak. He did, however, have the presence of mind to rise from his chair and set his hands on the desk on either side of her, leaning enough to look into her vividly blue eyes.

"I was so foolish, Henri. I was told so often what I ought to value and embrace that I believed it. I believed it, and it was all lies." She set her hand against his chest, just above his heart. "And now those lies are going to ruin everything."

He leaned ever closer. "Everything's not ruined, Nicolette. We're here together, and there is still hope."

She tilted her head, her jasmine perfume tickling his senses. "I'm trying very hard to hold on to that hope, Henri," she whispered.

"Perhaps I can help."

Her hands softly cupped his face. "Please try, *mon cher.*"

For years, he'd imagined kissing her and how her lips would feel against his. The reality of it was even better. *Soft. Warm.* But her hands holding his face, keeping him close as she joined in this first kiss, undid him. Every thought fled but her.

He broke the kiss only long enough to whisper, "*Ma fleur-de-lis.*"

She whispered back, "*Mon* Henri."

He lifted his hands from the desktop and wrapped his arms around her. She hooked her arms around his neck as he pulled her flush to him and lifted her from the desk. *Soft. Warm. Perfect.* Her kiss. Her embrace. Her.

A knock at the door broke through the moment. From the other side, Julia called out, "That is five minutes. No more distractions, *Capitaine.*"

Nicolette smiled at him. She pressed the briefest of kisses to his lips. "You need to finish your poem, Henri," she said quietly.

"I'd rather keep kissing you," he admitted.

She brushed a single fingertip over his lower lip. "Poetry first. So much depends on it."

Only after she had slipped from his embrace and sat in the chair near the open door did Henri return to his abandoned parchment on the desk. Though he made an effort at *appearing* to write, his mind refused to think of anything but Nicolette and the utter perfection of kissing her.

# Chapter Twenty-Nine

The most effective spy is the one no one suspects. Lafayette taught Nicolette that, and it had served her well in her work for *La Tapisserie*. She intended to implement that strategy once again.

Of all the people present at this house party, there was one the Duke of Hartley was least likely to suspect was digging for information: Niles. He was quieter than the other Gents, had an air of innocence, and held himself in a small way that made people forget he was present. And when they did remember, they would never for a moment evaluate him in terms of a threat. But Nicolette had seen for herself that he was observant and clever.

"How you work your way around to *the question* is up to you," she explained to her accomplice while Henri kept an eye on the duke. "Simply don't raise his suspicions."

"I think I know how to introduce a topic that will make the question seem natural," Niles said.

"Perfect." Nicolette glanced at Henri and nodded.

She walked at Niles's side, the two of them arriving casually at a card table. Several had been placed around the drawing room, cards being the evening's chosen pastime.

Niles took up the deck sitting on the table. "A shame we don't have four players."

"M. Henri," Nicolette called lightly, "would you join us for a game of *quarante de rois?*"

"*Je serais ravi.*"

"We are in need of a fourth," Niles said.

On cue, Henri turned toward the duke, standing not far off. "Do you play *quarante de rois*, Your Grace?"

With a proud tilt to his chin, the duke said, "I most certainly do."

"We would be honored and humbled if you would deign to join our table," Henri said, motioning to Nicolette and Niles. A brilliant approach. The duke was deeply invested in the deference he felt he deserved.

They formed teams, with Niles being the duke's partner for the game. That would help, as the duke would be less inclined to distrust him. His Grace shuffled the cards, giving them the perfect opportunity to begin; his attention would be divided.

"I received a letter from my mother today," Niles said. "She was quite pleased to report she'd had a visit from Sir Milford Argall. Imagine how overwhelmed with delight she will be to hear I have been partnered with the Duke of Hartley in a game of *quarante de rois*."

Nicolette wasn't entirely certain how Niles meant to shift this into the topic they needed to broach, but she was choosing to trust him.

"If you tell her that, all of England will know of it by week's end, I dare-say." Henri offered a smile that had likely helped earn him the sobriquet of Archbishop—it was innocence and compassion and a natural friendliness.

"Is the post so swift in England?" Nicolette asked. "I have only just received a letter from an acquaintance in France that was sent to me mere days after I left." Establishing in the duke's mind that she had the ability to communicate things to and receive information from France was essential. "Do you often send correspondence abroad, Your Grace?"

"On occasion." He fanned out the cards, so they could all choose one and, thus, determine who would deal first. "There are often delays in messages between countries."

Nicolette nodded and smiled, hoping to convey a shared experience and the feeling of connectedness that came with it. They needed his defenses to remain low.

Niles drew the high card and took up the deck to deal the first hand.

"Did your mother have any other bits of gossip to share?" Henri asked Niles. "You know how Digby enjoys a good tale."

Niles assumed a contemplative expression. Heavens, he was proving remark-ably good at this. He looked across the table at his partner in cards. "Your Grace, is there any reason people might be speculating about a connection between you and M. Léandre?"

It was the precise question Nicolette had asked Niles to pose.

She had learned the efficacy of that question: "Is there any reason people might be saying . . ." It placed into the recipient's mind the possibility that people were indeed saying what she'd implied they were. And if there was any degree of truth underlying the thing purportedly being spoken of and that thing was at all shameful or underhanded or secret, the recipient of the question would almost always begin framing the "accusation" in a more favorable light or attempt to denounce the unidentified informants.

"I made his acquaintance in London a couple of years ago." The duke's response was offered casually as he played a card, but there was tension in his posture that hadn't been present before. "I am, I suppose, seen with him now and then."

The duke took the first trick, though his expression did not return entirely to one of pleasure. The next trick was dealt quite as if nothing of note was happening. In the silence, the duke did precisely what Nicolette hoped he would: he kept answering.

"I suppose there might be some who think M. Léandre and I are more connected than we actually are. People are forever wishing to discover someone is a close associate with a duke."

Nicolette offered him a look of compassionate understanding. "That has happened to a few people in France. Close association with M. Léandre is something not many people wish to be accused of."

The comment hit its mark. Anyone watching would know the duke did, in fact, have a closer association with Pierre than he would wish *anyone* to know of.

"I would not ever associate with anyone who was met with such universal disapproval," the duke insisted. His card playing was sloppier than it had been. "Indeed, *I* was among the first in London to question if his business dealings were entirely acceptable."

"Very discerning of you, Your Grace." Henri managed to offer the remark with a believable mixture of approval and lack of concern.

"Should any conjecture reach my ears," Niles said, "I will make certain to defend you quite vehemently, Your Grace."

Oh, that was brilliant. A quick reminder that Niles had a gossip-hungry mother with whom he regularly corresponded but done in a way that wouldn't feel like an *intentional* threat. Brilliant.

The duke and Niles lost every remaining trick, no doubt the result of His Grace's spinning thoughts. An inelegant and quickly offered word of excuse preceded the duke's hasty departure.

Once they were alone, Niles and Henri looked to Nicolette.

"We let him fret," she said quietly. "The longer he wonders and worries about what is being whispered in Society and amongst men of business"—that revelation from His Grace had been very telling—"the more likely he is to convince himself that he is in a bind."

"Do you think it likely the connection between the duke and our resident villain is a financial one?"

"I know of people in France who are enriching themselves by circumventing the current trade agreement between our countries." It had, after all, been the discovery she'd made during her previous assignment with *La Tapisserie*. "I cannot ignore the possibility that something of that nature is occurring here as well."

Henri gathered up the cards, the game—both the one they were literally playing and the one they'd pursued clandestinely—now ended. Pierre, of all people, began moving in their direction. Would Nicolette ever reach the point where his presence didn't send her folding into herself? She disliked that he made her feel small, but she took pride in knowing that she recovered from the experience faster every time it happened.

His Grace intercepted Pierre and pulled him to a different group of guests. That was one benefit she hadn't anticipated: the Duke of Hartley would be very careful not to give Pierre the opportunity to contradict the explanation he'd offered them.

To Niles, Henri said quietly, "Saying that you'd received a letter from your mother was a bit of genius, Puppy."

"An easily conjured one, seeing as I *did* receive a letter from her today."

Henri grew a bit still, watching his friend with concern. "Was it simply a gossipy report from home?"

Niles released a breath. "No. I'm being summoned to Cornwall at my grandfather's insistence."

"The time has come, then," Henri said softly.

"It seems so." Niles rose. "As I will be leaving in the morning, I had best make this an early evening."

Little else was said before Niles left. Henri watched him go, grief in his eyes.

"Is his grandfather ill?" Nicolette asked.

"No. This is not a summons to a deathbed; it is a demand of fealty." Henri met her eyes across the table. "The Greenberry family has plans for Niles, ones he cannot avoid any longer."

# Chapter Thirty

HIS GRACE LEFT THE NEXT morning to call on the local families with Mowbary. With both of them gone, the tone of the house party was greatly improved. And with the source of her difficulty temporarily away and quite possibly on his way to call at Eau Plate, Céleste jaunted back over to Norwood to rejoin the house party for the day.

It did Henri's heart good to see how eagerly the Gents, Violet, and Julia welcomed her back. Even Aldric, though not overflowing with expressions of delight, greeted her cordially.

"I do wish I could return for these last few days," Céleste said, standing beside Henri near the tall drawing room windows. "The Beaumonts are lovely people, and I am enjoying their company, but heaven knows when I will see you again after I return to France."

Henri tucked her into one of the hugs he'd given her since she was little. He was more grateful than he could say that she hadn't yet outgrown it. "If I can think of a way to prevent His Grace from running roughshod over everyone, I will ride to Eau Plate myself, no matter the hour, and bring you back with all possible haste."

"I told Nicolette you were the very best of brothers. I'm pleased to have been so very correct in that."

"And I am pleased that Nicolette shares your good opinion of me. When last I knew her, she wasn't quite so sure."

"I know she didn't think poorly of you then," Céleste said. "She spoke of you a few times after your visit and always had very complimentary things to say."

*I was sad when you left.* She'd said that in the moments before he'd kissed her . . . and *she'd* kissed *him*. He was being careful not to misread her feelings again. He didn't think he was mistaken in what that kiss had meant. And yet, hard-learned lessons were difficult to forget.

"Does she say complimentary things to you about me now?" he asked.

Céleste laughed lightly. "She has a great many things to say about you now, all of which make me, as your sister, a little bit sick to my stomach. I cannot fault her taste; you are a wonderful person."

"For the record, my dear sister, I think you are a rather wonderful person yourself. And I will miss you terribly when you return to France."

Céleste's eyes darted a bit away. "Speaking of France." She motioned with her head toward Pierre Léandre slithering his way around the room toward them. "He will be there when we return. You don't truly think Nicolette will be forced to marry him, do you? I have to believe he'll be thwarted, but far too many horrible people before him have managed to get what they want but didn't at all deserve."

"While I can make no guarantees," Henri said, "I will tell you that we have all been working to find a means of undermining him."

The aspect of their plan that was still missing at the moment was an understanding of exactly what it was the man had been doing in England that had the duke so concerned. Though the duke had clearly tried to hide it, he'd been shaken by the suggestion that people might manage to sort out the connection between them. Henri was leaning toward Nicolette's suspicion that the two men were involved in underhanded business dealings.

"Monsieur. Mademoiselle." Pierre offered a quickly sketched bow to each of them.

"Monsieur." They answered in near unison, returning his gesture with as little enthusiasm as he had initially offered it.

"How unusual to see you not in the company of my fiancée," Pierre said.

"Fiancée?" Henri asked innocently. "Have I met her?"

Pierre's jaw tightened a bit. "You have spent far too much time in this country, Mr. Fortier. You have grown uncouth."

As innocently as Henri had spoken, Céleste said, "I didn't realize you were acquainted with gentility."

Pierre's pretense of friendliness was quickly dropped. Henri preferred it that way. It was more familiar. His father had never wrapped his anger and disapproval in lambs' wool.

"I cannot imagine you are unaware of the situation," Pierre said. "Neither do I believe you are actually foolish enough to believe any future you might have in mind with Nicolette could possibly come to be."

Henri made a show of pondering that deeply. "It was my understanding *you* were the one with deep concerns about your future where Mlle Beaulieu is concerned."

"A gentleman does what he must to navigate hostile waters."

"It seems you and I are sailing on different seas," Henri said. "I've not found the water hostile."

His voice pitched low and his eyes cold and calculating, Pierre said, "You will discover very quickly that you don't belong amongst the Beaulieus, no matter your family's standing. Her brother is well aware that you are penniless, no roof over your head, a hanger-on in England, little more than a stranger in France. Your friendship with a handful of acceptable gentlemen will not be enough to overcome those shortcomings. Everyone knows that you have no future and no prospects. Nicolette might enjoy playing the rebel for a time, amusing herself with the idea of thwarting her family's expectations, but she knows as well as you do, as well as *I* do, that you have nothing to offer her, that connecting herself to you will leave her as penniless, homeless, and hopeless as you are."

"I won't deny my circumstances are not ideal," Henri said, "but I can also say that I never had to take a lady to court and beg a judge to force her to acknowledge my existence. Say what you will about the state of my affairs, but *yours*, monsieur, is pitiful indeed."

Céleste, without a word of explanation, slipped away. Had hearing all her brother's shortcomings and struggles listed so plainly embarrassed her? Was she ashamed to have discovered how very pitiful he actually was?

"Odd that your sister has never married." Pierre sneered. "One must wonder if the gentlemen worth considering are reluctant to connect themselves to a family who cannot seem to address the issue of their failure of a brother. She seems a decent sort of girl; it's a very real shame she is suffering because of this."

"I am certain, monsieur, you realize that a gentleman of manners and civility does not speak condescendingly about a lady," Henri said.

"And *I* am certain," Pierre shot back, "you realize that keeping her hidden while the duke is in residence does not improve anyone's opinion of her."

How Nicolette ever thought this man could make a good husband in any way, Henri would never know. But such was the strength of lies told over and over again.

"One hears the strangest rumors about your connection with the duke," Henri said.

Pierre shrugged. The possibility of whispers clearly did not concern him as much it had the duke the day before. "We've undertaken some business together. I have shown myself quite useful in enriching his coffers."

*Business.* Just as they had suspected. "Not many businessmen spend time in high society."

"I don't consider myself a businessman," Pierre said. "I simply know a good opportunity when I see one."

"If you have managed to turn a profit in recent years, having only connections to France and this country, then that is a remarkable accomplishment."

Apparently forgetting he was supposed to be at odds with Henri, Pierre preened a bit, clearly pleased with the compliment. "Those who could not make the past few years profitable haven't the imagination to deserve it."

That proud declaration was more revealing than Pierre likely realized. It was a confirmation that gave Henri very tempting bait for a much larger fish.

He dipped a little bow. "I wish you the greatest of luck in your future imaginative opportunities." On that declaration, he stepped away.

Pierre looked momentarily disappointed. Perhaps he had hoped to continue the pointless verbal sparring. There was tremendous satisfaction in disappointing a scoundrel.

Henri intended to find Nicolette and reveal this latest bit of information to her, but he was intercepted first by Céleste dragging their brother behind her with a look of fierceness on her face that made Henri take a step backward.

She placed Jean-François directly opposite Henri, facing him, and turned herself so she could look at them both. "Explain it to me," she demanded.

"Explain what?" Jean-François asked.

"M. Léandre said that everyone is aware that Henri has no home and is absolutely penniless. I have read our father's will. Henri should have ample to live on, perhaps not in luxury, but certainly not in penniless poverty. Explain it to me."

Jean-François looked to Henri, an expression on his face that was clearly meant to ask for assistance in making the explanation.

Henri held up his hands. "You created the mess, Jean-François. I think you had best do the explaining."

"The income our father set aside for Henri is being used for the upkeep of Chalet-sur-Loire."

She shook her head. "That is a Fortier holding. Its upkeep is your responsibility. Explain why he doesn't have income."

Henri was too confused not to comment. "You know about Chalet-sur-Loire?"

"Jean-François leaves papers all about, and I have looked over a few of them. Through those perusals, I learned of Chalet-sur-Loire, but our brother must be very careful in the way he accounts for his stealing of your inheritance, as I've not yet come across any record of that."

"*Stealing?*" Jean-François's temper was quickly heating.

"What else can I possibly call it?" Céleste demanded. "He was left an income, promised it in our late father's will. Chalet-sur-Loire is a Fortier holding, but you have taken *his* inheritance to meet obligations that are yours? That is stealing. There are no two ways about it. So explain to me why you have done this and why I shouldn't be boiling with anger about it."

Her impassioned defense of Henri, while likely futile, was touching.

"The house was meant to be his," Jean-François said. "His to live in, his to oversee. It is time he stops refusing to return home. Should he choose to do so, I will gladly meet the expense of its upkeep with the Fortier coffers. By not living there, he is burdening me, and I am choosing to acknowledge that burden."

"By stealing from him?"

"You keep using that word," their brother said through tight teeth.

"Because it is the correct word," Céleste insisted. She looked at Henri. "You have a home in France?"

"So it seems. I was told of it for the first time during this house party when I confronted Jean-François about my missing income."

Céleste nodded. "You have been gone a very long time; I can understand why you would not have heard of any of this." There was no accusation in her words, but Henri felt it just the same. She had been navigating a difficult home life while he had been away, too far from her to ease the burden of home. To Jean-François, she said, "And do you mean to stop this horrific criminal undertaking of yours?"

"*Criminal* is overly harsh," Jean-François said. "He is welcome to ask the opinion of the courts if he chooses, but he won't because I do not think he actually disapproves as much as he says he does."

"With my income being taken from me," Henri said, "I have not the means to return to France to litigate this."

A sharp frown tugged at Céleste's features. "Jean-François's stealing your income is the reason you have not been back to France as often as I would like?"

"I can't afford the journey at regular intervals," he said. "Each visit requires months and months of scrimping and saving."

Céleste's ponderous expression shifted in the moment to a quiet, calm resolution. "You should have told me," she said softly. Then she turned to look at Jean-François once more. "I've missed my brother all these years, and I didn't have to. I've worried that he didn't wish to see me, but that was not at all the case. *You* were preventing him from visiting, and you knew it."

"If spending time with him is so important to you, explain to me why you are spending the last few days of this house party at a neighboring estate rather than here with him." It was the first undeniable indication Henri had seen that Jean-François was genuinely upset about that. Their brother had maintained a neutral facade on the matter, no doubt to keep up appearances among the other guests.

"I am certain Henri gave you a reason for my being at Eau Plate, but know that *you* are the reason I am missing this all-too-fleeting time with him."

Jean-François's gaze narrowed on her. "How is your removal my fault?"

"I am beginning to suspect every bit of unhappiness this family has experienced since Father's death is your fault."

The defiance in Céleste's posture and the tightness of Jean-François's mouth bore an air of familiarity for them both. It seemed they were often at odds with each other like this.

"If Henri would take up residence where he is meant to be," Jean-François said through his clenched jaw, "you would see him all the time. He would be living in France. He would have a home. He would have income. He would be where he is supposed to be."

Though Henri immediately recoiled at the insistence that France was where he was supposed to be and that he ought to simply bow to his brother's demands, a different thought crept into his mind. Jean-François was actually correct in one respect: if Henri took up residence at Chalet-sur-Loire, he would have a home and income. Those were the very things that stood in the way of him building a life with Nicolette. Those were the only objections her brother had expressed.

Céleste's gaze narrowed on Jean-François. "How do you think Paris would react to hearing you have been stealing money from your own brother? That you have been perpetrating a crime against a member of your own family, a family who is well thought of in our circles? When we are next invited to Versailles, how do you suppose Their Majesties would feel to hear that you, who they have welcomed somewhat regularly to the palace, have knowingly dishonored the wishes of your late father?"

Jean-François looked confused and a little concerned. "Why our private matters should reach their ears, I cannot say."

"Because I want my brother back," Céleste said firmly. "And if I have to drag my other brother through the mud to accomplish it, so be it."

"Céleste," Henri said, "you do not have to do this."

"I mean to fix what he has broken."

"You do this and you will destroy Adèle as well," Jean-François warned.

"Do not think me so lacking in social refinement as that. One does not frequent the circles we occupy and not learn how to apply finesse to even the worst of situations. Believe me, brother, I am more than capable of spinning this tale in a way that you alone will emerge muddied by it. Decide how you want the next few years to play out. It is entirely in your hands." She held her chin at a defiant angle and watched him, almost daring him not to bow to her demands.

Though his pride never slipped, he offered a little dip of his head. "I will take this into consideration." His eyes met Henri's for a brief moment, and what Henri saw there was not truly apology or resignation; Jean-François was contemplating his options. "An estate that is not lived in is very difficult to maintain. I do not think our mother would be happy knowing her dowry is being neglected."

The barb hit its mark. Mother had suffered a lot in her marriage. Chalet-sur-Loire had come to the Fortier family when she did, and it was sitting abandoned.

As Jean-François walked away, Céleste said, "I do not know if he will relent in the end. He has become even more hard-headed in the years since you last visited." The fire remained in her voice, but there was doubt there as well. "If your income is restored, would you finally be able to secure a home for yourself?"

"Possibly," Henri said. "There is always Chalet-sur-Loire. I could live there."

But Céleste shook her head. "You wouldn't be happy living in France. But I hope you will visit more often if you are given more of your income."

He pulled her into a full hug, a show of affection not usually displayed in such a public setting. But after what she had just done for him, he could think of nothing that could more adequately express his gratitude. "I will come to see you as often as I can. And I've not abandoned hope of having you come here to England. If I can find myself a home, would you consider living with me?"

"Even with your income fully restored, you would hardly be wealthy. I want you to have enough to marry, Henri, not support a spinster sister."

"You are hardly a spinster."

"I am knocking on that door," she said without any hint of self-directed pity. "Secure your happiness, Henri. Someone in this family deserves it."

He held her ever tighter. "Given the choice, my dear sister, I would want that someone to be you."

He felt her laugh a little. "It is no wonder they call you Archbishop. You are forever thinking of and doing good for others."

"I decided long ago I wanted to be the very opposite of our father, and I can think of no better way to manage it."

She leaned back a bit, enough to look into his eyes. "Choose to be the opposite of him in *this* way: marry a lady you love, who loves you in return, and build a happy life together. I know coming to this country, studying in the language our father despised, creating a life that he could not dictate or control, was your initial act of rebellion. It is time to stage the greatest rebellion you have ever imagined. He would have loved nothing more than for you to be alone and unhappy, drowning in regrets. Claim the life he would have never wanted you to have."

# Chapter Thirty-One

HENRI KNEW THE DUKE TOOK a walk around the garden every day at mid-morning. It was not a stroll undertaken for pleasure but one taken at a quick clip with a look of determination. He looked like a brigadier preparing to storm a fortified castle.

Henri's own father had often worn a thundercloud expression, especially when upset with his children. Seeing something so similar on the face of the gentleman he had stepped outside to confront ought to have sent him into retreat. He had so often embraced retreat or appeasement to keep himself safe from his father's cruelty.

But he didn't even hesitate now. What he was doing would help people he cared about. That, he had learned, was where he found his courage. Stanley had set that example for them all and had lived with that kind of compassion. Henri had found strength in doing the same.

He came up even with the duke. They were of a very similar height and stride, so Henri didn't struggle to keep pace. "Might I have a private word with you here where there are not many people present?" he asked.

"If you've come to beg for money, I will tell you now I don't extend financial charity to people simply because they are friends of my younger son."

Henri didn't let even that snide remark deter him. "What I wish to discuss is not a favor but rather an observation."

The duke looked a little confused. But to Henri's delight, he also looked intrigued.

"As you know," Henri pushed on, "I am originally from France. I still have family and friends and a great many connections there with whom I am in regular contact." The Gents would have teased their Archbishop mercilessly over that decided exaggeration. "I feel it would be uncharitable of me if I did not drop a bit of a warning in your ear."

"A warning about what?" His Grace asked in clipped tones.

"You noted during our card game that you have a connection, however minor, with M. Léandre. You also stated you have ample reason to believe that people who are aware of that connection or who study the time the two of you spend together might come to the conclusion that your 'minor' connection is not so minor after all."

"People might think that." A tendril of worry wrapped loosely around the admission.

"M. Léandre is known to have attempted to recoup a lost fortune in the last couple of years by undertaking trade activities. It is suspected that neither his country's government nor the government of this kingdom would look upon his methods with approval. And despite the recent passage of the Eden Agreement, which ought to have stopped some of these activities, there is little reason for anyone to believe a man of his stamp would suddenly abandon such tactics. What, after all, do laws matter to one who has learned how lucrative violating those laws can be?"

The duke's lips pressed thin. He watched Henri as they walked, a searching and uncertain glance, one generally employed when a person was trying to decide what it was the other person was thinking. After a moment too long to possibly have gone unnoticed by the least observant people, he said, "And what has M. Léandre's poor character to do with me?"

"What do you think it has to do with you?" Henri borrowed a tactic from Nicolette and left the question dangling between them, allowing the duke to convince himself to answer.

"I think you are accusing me of undertaking illegal trade practices." His Grace spoke through a tight jaw.

Henri shook his head slightly. "I've made no accusations, Your Grace. But I don't believe I am the one whose evaluation of the situation is most crucial in this matter. Others, I fear, might have their own conjectures."

"People do sense a connection between us," the duke admitted once more, "but I think they overstate it."

"Do they know your connection is entirely concerned with matters of trade?" Henri asked, keeping his voice calm and light.

The duke didn't answer. He didn't truly have to.

"This is the warning I've come to deliver," Henri said. "I do not intend to drop any whispers in any interested ears. I simply wish for you to know that there is a very high likelihood those whispers will begin anyway. Your rank and status would likely protect you from the worst consequences of anything that

might seem underhanded in your business with M. Léandre." Henri ignored the
unease that flashed in the man's eyes. Speaking of all this in terms of things that
*might* happen would keep the duke from retaliating against him in the moment.
"But I have experienced Lord Mowbary's clumsiness when hosting gatherings
and interacting with people. It likely will come as no surprise to you that he
scolded guests during this house party for undertaking perfectly unexceptional
activities without first seeking and receiving his approval. He made no effort to
call on the significant families hereabout, and if not for the efforts of Lord Aldric,
your eldest son would likely have offended the entire neighborhood."

The worry in the duke's eyes was supplanted momentarily by annoyance. "I
have tried to teach him, but he is so arrogant —" The duke seemed to suddenly
realize he was speaking ill of his heir and the future holder of his title. He stopped
and pressed his mouth tightly closed as they continued their walk.

"Your acumen and your established place in Society would help you weather
any conjecture where M. Léandre is concerned," Henri continued. "But Lord
Mowbary is already disliked and thought poorly of. He would never recover. By
the time Lord Draycott was made Duke of Hartley, the scandal still might not
have passed. This could be the undoing of generations of the Benick family."

"And you mean to blackmail me over this?" His Grace snapped. "Don't
think I am unaware of your financial situation."

"I would not call this blackmail, Your Grace, but simply recounting a situation and the impact it would have on your family."

The duke's eyes darted to Henri. "You have come to plead on behalf of
my family?"

"Your younger son is one of the best people I've ever known. Other than
yourself and Lord Mowbary, most everyone agrees with me. But with the
potential of this scandal eventually being known, coupled with the way in
which he is treated, which I fear most of the *ton* would see as further confirmation that the Benicks are not the pattern cards of propriety they ought to be,
you have placed him in an untenable situation."

"What is it you are suggesting I do?"

"To begin with, cut ties with M. Léandre in matters of business *and* social
interactions. To take advice from him on the matter of whom to invite to your
family's house parties will only confirm suspicions, not undermine them."

Guilt inched into the lines of the duke's face. He hadn't, it seemed, a knack
for hiding such things. Should the matter of his likely illegal investments come
to light, anyone watching him even casually would know in an instant that he
had indeed taken part.

"And," Henri continued, "I would advise that should you hear others are considering investing with him, you warn them that you do not believe M. Léandre's character is entirely honest and that they ought to proceed with caution. But I would advise you to do so very subtly so they do not begin thinking too hard on how much time *you* spent with M. Léandre before beginning to acknowledge the kind of person he is."

"He can be very convincing." The duke's voice emerged more quietly.

"As many people have discovered, to their cost," Henri said. "Even those who benefit from association with him for a time eventually discover he has no loyalties to anyone but himself and his own enrichment."

The duke nodded, the movement resigned. "If I do this, you will not participate in nor confirm any of the rumors you are hearing?"

"Even disassociating yourself with M. Léandre will only do so much to take the teeth out of those rumors. With this dark cloud hanging over your family, Society will look at your disparate treatment of your sons and find they still have questions about your judgment."

The duke actually stopped, rooted to the spot and turned a concerned look on Henri.

"Lord Aldric is the son of a duke, and not merely any duke: the Duke of Hartley." Henri held the duke's gaze. "Yet he is homeless, treated by you more like a servant than a member of a respectable family. If you think the *ton* has not noticed, then you have not been paying attention. It is tarnishing your family name and the respectability of the title so attached to it."

"You're telling me that if I don't treat my youngest son with kid gloves, these rumors will begin in earnest?" The duke had picked up what Henri hadn't said: that he had information enough to make life very difficult for him and his oldest son.

"Not kid gloves but with the respect that the son of a duke ought to be shown. Give the gossip-hungry no reason to wonder why the Hartley title is of so little importance that Lord Aldric's connection to it warrants him no deference. And because the younger son of a duke being without so much as a roof over his head when his father has multiple estates at his disposal would fuel the whispers you are eager to avoid, I would . . . *suggest* . . . that you grant him the use of Norwood Manor to be his home for as long as he has need of it along with the income needed to run it properly."

"Mowbary will most certainly argue against his brother being granted this consideration."

"Maybe bear that in mind when you are tempted to treat your eldest son like an angel and your younger son like a parasite."

"I will agree to what you ask," the duke snapped, "but that doesn't mean I will endure insults."

Henri dipped his head. "I will await word that the use of Norwood has been transferred to Lord Aldric and will watch to see if your treatment of him adjusts accordingly."

"Will you keep to yourself what it is you have learned until then?" the duke pressed.

"Should all you have agreed to occur, I am perfectly capable of keeping my discoveries to myself."

"And that is all you mean to ask? No demands for yourself? No fortune to make up for what you don't have? This is a rare opportunity for you to line your pockets."

Heaven knew he needed funds and a house every bit as much as Aldric—more so even—but that was not his aim here. "This was never about me, Your Grace."

Henri might have been mistaken, but he thought he saw a momentary flash of respect on the duke's face. In the end, whether it was respect, contempt, annoyance, or resignation, it didn't matter. Aldric would have a home and a future. When in public, his father would treat him better, and he suspected the duke would make certain Mowbary did as well. It wouldn't change the difficulties in that family, nor erase the years of misery Aldric had endured, but some of his suffering and worries for his future would be lightened.

The duke continued with his forceful morning walk. Henri turned back toward the house and simply breathed. His life had, at times, felt like a series of failures, but he had just accomplished something inarguably impressive.

Pierre's English support and investors would soon dry up. If Sébastien could gather evidence of the man's illegal activities in France, that would undermine the legal action Pierre meant to take. Perhaps Nicolette's dowry would not be snatched away by her former fiancé's cruelty. That would offer her some freedom and some options. Henri felt he had ample reason to believe that she wished for a future with him as much as he wished for one with her. Nicolette still having access to her dowry would mean, should they decide to build that future together, they would have something to live on while Henri's poetical efforts slowly grew into something sustainable and Jean-François continued to "take into consideration" the matter of Henri's commandeered inheritance.

But if not, Henri had the estate held for him in France to fall back on. He and Nicolette could build a life there. They would be together. Returning to his family's homeland would not be his first choice, but Nicolette would *always* be.

# Chapter Thirty-Two

NICOLETTE HAD NOT SEEN HENRI all day. She missed him. She missed him more deeply than she would have imagined after the passage of only one day. She'd always loved Paris, longing to return after even brief excursions elsewhere, but the thought of returning now, without Henri, not seeing him every day as she had this past month, made her reluctant to leave.

No, it was more than reluctance. She was sad, grieving. Paris would be horribly lonely without him. She suspected it always would. But Pierre's suit could tie up the family finances and her freedom of movement for years. Though she would never willingly acquiesce to his alternate demand that they marry as they had once intended to, she knew far too many ladies had been forced into unwanted marriages. That might very well be the fate that awaited her. She had mere days left of Henri's beloved company, and she feared she would be spending a horrifying amount of that time plagued by these worries and uncertainties.

What she wanted for these remaining days was to be held by him, whispered to, kissed. She wanted to be loved as much as she loved him in return, but free of the cloud of uncertainty hanging over them.

Everyone gathered in the drawing room in anticipation of dinner that evening, but the gentleman she most wanted to see was not among them.

She spoke to Julia in a low voice. "Have you any idea where Henri has gone? I've not seen him all day."

"He was away from the house this morning and then rode over to Eau Plate this afternoon to visit Céleste."

Nicolette ought to have guessed he'd gone to see his sister. In addition to being a good man with a good heart, he was a good brother.

"It has been so lovely coming to know you these past weeks," Julia said. "I do hope you will write after you return home. We will miss you terribly."

"And I will miss all of you. I wish everyone lived closer."

Julia rested her hand against her rounded middle, something Nicolette imagined most expectant mothers did without even thinking. "The Gents have long teased Henri that if they allow him to wander too close to the southern coast, he might not be able to resist the lure of France."

"His love for his sister and his niece is great enough that they pull his heart there, even when he knows he will be mistreated by his brother," Nicolette said. "We likely ought not suggest swimming the Channel; he might actually attempt it."

With a smile that was both friendly and teasing, Julia said, "Especially knowing *you* are in France."

It was an exaggeration, yes, but Nicolette felt the underlying truth of it. The idea of attempting an entirely doomed swim across unforgiving waters felt less ill thought out if it meant seeing Henri again. "If you happen to know a little piece of property available near the southern coast, do let him know of it. Should his brother do the honorable thing and restore Henri's income, I would be quite pleased to hear he'd secured a home within swimming distance of where I am."

As if speaking of him conjured the gentleman himself, Henri stepped into the drawing room in that very moment. Nicolette's heart soared. And then, upon realizing Céleste was with him, it swelled near to bursting.

Céleste was welcomed with embraces from Violet and Julia, who had swiftly made her way there, and warm expressions of pleasure from the Gents.

Nicolette had every intention of weaving her way through the crowd and offering her own delighted expressions of welcome to her dearest friend. But as he so often did, Pierre ruined everything.

"It seems we are to have an addition to our numbers this evening," he said.

"We?" Nicolette repeated that one word. "I did not realize you were one of the hosts of this gathering."

"There's no need to become snippy," Pierre said. "It would behoove you to remember that is not a very pleasant character trait in a wife. A husband is likely to grow very weary of it."

"Then, for your sake, I hope you find a lady willing to marry you who is not snippy."

"I know you think that you are terribly clever, but I will warn you, making a nuisance of yourself is not going to improve things."

"You know this from experience, I assume?"

His veneer of civility slipped, revealing the calculatingly arrogant man underneath. Nicolette had seen it now and then toward the end of their engagement, and it had unnerved her every time. It did so again now.

Into the tense moment came Sébastien. Nicolette braced herself. Though she knew her brother didn't approve of Pierre and didn't particularly wish to bend to his demands, she also knew Pierre had placed her brother in an impossible situation. Sometimes appeasing a villain was the best way to avoid being further harmed by him.

"Your sister is behaving in a most unfortunate manner," Pierre said. "She's speaking to her fiancé rather disrespectfully."

"Truly?" Sébastien looked at Nicolette. "I wasn't aware you had become engaged. Who is the fortunate gentlemen?"

For the length of a moment, Nicolette's mind did not comprehend the full meaning of her brother's words. But then the truth dawned. Sébastien didn't intend to leave her to fight this battle alone, neither did he seem inclined any longer to simply bow to Pierre's demands.

"I assure you, Sébastien," Nicolette said, "should I deem a gentleman worthy of such consideration, I will make certain you know."

Pierre was undeterred. "You can play this game if you wish, but you know the rules, and you know the outcome."

"The one thing I do know with certainty," Sébastien said, "is that the outcome will not be what you expect. I know what it is you are demanding of us and the way you expect us to respond. I think you will be very unpleasantly surprised, which will be exceptionally enjoyable for the rest of us."

The two men watched each other through narrowed gazes, both sets of shoulders squared, both assuming a posture of anticipatory combat.

Nicolette slipped her arm through her brother's. "Let us go greet Céleste. I've missed her these past days."

Without a word of farewell or departure, they left Pierre standing where he was. She didn't think for a moment he had truly been cowed by their allied front. And she knew Pierre might prove successful in some of his aims. But it felt good to know they hadn't bowed to him.

"How was it any of us ever thought well of him?" Nicolette wondered aloud.

"I ought to have looked out for you better. I ought to have realized what he was."

"He fooled us all, though I cannot excuse myself. I met Henri Fortier before I ever laid eyes on Pierre. I had seen for myself what a good and kind and honorable man truly was. To have known him and not realized how far short of that mark Pierre came was, I think, one of my greatest failures of judgment."

Sébastien patted her hand where it rested on his arm. "I hope you know that my concerns regarding M. Henri Fortier are not at all about his character. I gave him a bit of a dressing down before Pierre's arrival. I had just learned Pierre intended to join us here and cause precisely the trouble he eventually did. I was in a panic, I'm embarrassed to say."

"I panicked more than a little when I first saw him at the ball," Nicolette admitted.

"My concerns about Henri went beyond that though. His struggles would become yours as well should you marry. No home and no income, a brother he is at odds with. I also know he doesn't return to France often, and that would mean you wouldn't either. I could not, in good conscience, encourage a match that might very well render you homeless and very far away."

They had only just reached Céleste and Henri when the duke himself entered the drawing room, and everything stopped. That would have been the case with the arrival of any duke, but this particular one had been in a rather thunderous mood that day.

His Grace received the expected bows and curtsies. His eyes fell on Céleste, then darted between her and Henri. To Nicolette's shock, and she would wager everyone else's as well, he made his way directly for the two of them.

"Your Grace," Henri said, "it is my great privilege to make you known to my sister, Mlle Céleste Fortier of Fleur-de-la-Forêt in France. She has been enjoying a visit with the Beaumonts in this neighborhood and is now able to rejoin us. Céleste, this is His Grace, the Duke of Hartley, father of our host, Lord Mowbary, and our friend Lord Aldric."

Céleste executed a curtsy that was utterly precise in its depth and grace and deference. Nicolette had always admired that about her friend. She seemed to know almost by instinct how to navigate any social situations. For Nicolette, it had always required study and effort.

"It is a pleasure to have you at Norwood Manor, Mlle Fortier," the duke said.

"I'm very pleased to be here," Céleste said. "It is always a joy to spend time with my brother, and to do so in such a lovely home to which your younger son has warmly welcomed his friends is a further delight."

It was another brilliantly executed move. She gave a reason for her presence that could not be misconstrued as one in pursuit of a match. She elevated Aldric's guests in a way that Mowbary would never have done, and she had offered compliments to His Grace that would help secure his good opinion of her.

The butler opened the large doors of the drawing room that led to a very short corridor, on the other side of which was the dining room. He dipped his head to the duke, a signal that dinner was ready to be eaten.

Nicolette was seated nearer Pierre than she would have preferred, but she felt more equal to it than she had in years. And Henri was not very far away. Conversation was light and relatively general, and as Nicolette was on the same end of the table as His Grace, she found herself occasionally part of his discussions. That he was arrogant and gratingly proud was readily apparent. But she also found he was intelligent and seemed to have a genuine interest in learning of people and places.

"I have been so pleased to be a guest here at Norwood Manor," Pierre said to the duke as the fish course was removed. "It has afforded me an opportunity to spend time with my fiancée, which I have not been granted in some time."

Nicolette stiffened and bit back the rather sarcastic retort that rose to her lips. She had very nearly convinced herself they would have a pleasant enough meal before Pierre, had yet again, made trouble.

Henri, who sat directly across from her, was not so reticent as she. "You will forgive me for inserting myself into the commentary." He addressed the duke. "I feel it my duty to warn Your Grace that this is a declaration you should treat as significantly suspect. M. Léandre and Mlle Beaulieu are not, in fact, engaged. You can ask the lady herself, and she will confirm it. Some gentlemen—I must again make certain Your Grace realizes this is not a common failing amongst Frenchmen in general—feel it perfectly acceptable to insist that the lady they demand be required to marry them also be treated as suspect in matters of the truth and intellect and understanding. Mlle Beaulieu has, even before M. Léandre's unexpected arrival, been very forthright about the status of her heart and hand, and M. Léandre has been forthright about very little."

The entire room descended into silent shock. Everyone knew this about Pierre, but to hear Henri, who was generally very soft-spoken and avoided speaking ill of people in company when he could, make so blunt an assessment of Pierre's character was startling.

"It sounds to me as though this is an attempt at fraud," the duke said.

"Unfortunately," Henri said, "that does seem to be the case."

"I should call you out for that," Pierre said, his temper flaring.

"If you dare make a scene at my table, *I* will call *you* out." The duke spoke slowly and firmly.

Never before had Nicolette seen Pierre silenced so immediately.

"While I have everyone's attention," the duke said, "I wish to make an announcement. This does not generally happen at the dinner table, but I daresay it will make for a more pleasant discussion than the one I might otherwise be required to participate in."

Nicolette had no idea if he was referencing Pierre's displeasure, the conversation at the table in general, or if the statement was simply more evidence of his acerbic personality. Quite frankly, she didn't overly care. If it meant Pierre would be quiet for the remainder of the meal, she would accept any insult His Grace meant to offer.

With everyone watching him, the duke continued on. "Norwood Manor is a lovely home, as Mlle Fortier pointed out and as I have been reminded in my short return visit these past days. It is not used often, and I have decided that is a shame. I am determined to see a Benick in residence. Thus, beginning this very moment, I am giving the use of this estate to my younger son, Lord Aldric. It is entailed and will remain part of the ducal holdings, but it is time and past someone lived here."

All around the room, shock registered on the faces of those present, most especially Lord Mowbary and Aldric himself. Apparently, neither of the duke's sons had been informed of this decision. When Nicolette looked at Henri, she didn't see surprise but rather a smile of quiet satisfaction. He'd known even before the announcement had been made. Had this been his doing?

"Thank you, Your Grace," Lord Aldric said, apparently having found his voice once more.

"Do not make me regret this," the duke muttered.

Nicolette wasn't entirely sure, but she felt certain she heard Henri clear his throat.

The duke's eyes darted in that direction, then he amended his comment. "I'm certain you will be a good steward of the responsibilities you have been given."

And that seemed to shock the duke's younger son every bit as much as suddenly being given a place to live.

Emotion tiptoed over Nicolette's heart. Henri *had* done this. He had somehow secured a home for his friend, even when he didn't have one himself. And he had wrangled from the duke a willingness to treat his second son with some degree of kindness.

She had told Henri not many days past that they were in need of a miracle, and he had just produced one.

# Chapter Thirty-Three

THE GENTLEMEN DID NOT LINGER over their port. In fact, the ladies had hardly had time to settle into the drawing room when the gentlemen joined them. All of them, that is, except for the duke and Pierre. Nicolette thought that both an oddity and a very telling exclusion.

Nicolette caught Henri's eye, and he crossed directly to her.

"There is quite a glaring absence," she said quietly.

"The duke has very recently been made aware that some of what M. Léandre has undertaken the last two years is more . . . *provable* than he would have guessed. He has been made to realize that it would be in his best interest to cut that connection and drop a few warnings to others who might benefit from a better understanding of who M. Léandre really is."

"Did that warning come from you?" she asked.

She would never not love the deeply French way he shrugged.

"If Pierre loses all his English business dealings, he might grow worryingly desperate," she said.

Henri took her hand and held it softly, gently. "I suspect a snake as slippery as he will not be easily routed. This will make life very difficult for him and will likely send him away from England altogether."

"But he will, without a doubt, retreat to France. I won't be able to escape him there."

"I mentioned to your brother in the brief moment the gentlemen remained in the dining room after the ladies' departure that His Grace had reason to believe Pierre was involved in illegal trade involving France and that was the reason Pierre was being looked on with such obvious disapproval. I think Sébastien can use that to build a case against your would-be fiancé."

Nicolette lowered her voice. "The group of people I secretly work with are aware of others involved in illegal trade dealings. With that additional information, we might even be able to *prove* Pierre had his fingers in a putrid pie."

"That would help," Henri said.

Nicolette breathed an inward sigh of relief. *La Tapisserie* would provide her with the information she needed. She could counter the damage Pierre meant to do, but that wouldn't prevent the pain he would cause.

"Are you also the reason His Grace has given the use of Norwood Manor to Lord Aldric?" she asked.

Henri didn't quite manage to hide his smile. "Let us simply say my sister is not the only Fortier who knows how to utilize a bit of extortion for good."

"Whom is she extorting?"

"Our brother. I don't know that anything will come of it in the end, but she's attempting to right a wrong."

In the matter of Henri's income, Nicolette was certain of it.

"Do you ever feel as though you are so close to fixing seemingly impossible problems, but the impossibility of it all keeps rearing its head?" Nicolette asked.

Henri raised her hand to his lips and kissed her fingers. Her hand would feel empty when she returned to Paris. Everything would feel empty.

"I wish I had the answers," he said. "But I'm doing my best to hope for the best."

They stood a moment in companionable silence. Was Henri's heart heavy with thoughts of being apart? Hers certainly was. Yet what could they do?

Standing not far distant, Lucas motioned for Henri and Nicolette to join him, Kes, and Digby. Aldric was in discussion with his brother, a conversation that didn't appear to be entirely friendly. No doubt Mowbary was not pleased with his father's announcement at dinner.

"We have had a thought," Lucas said. "The more we've discussed it, the more it makes sense. This suit Pierre has threatened you with has all its legal teeth in France. We cannot prevent that from moving forward. But Digby is entirely certain that French law can exact no punishment or enforce any ruling on your person if you are not residing in France."

Nicolette looked to Digby, uncertain why the King would feel so sure of this when, as far as she knew, he had no background or education in the law, certainly not in *French* law.

"Though it is not something of which I ever speak, nor will I do so now, I assure you, mademoiselle, I understand the reach of international law better than I wish I did."

Nicolette could sense both his sincerity and his displeasure at the topic, and she vowed she would never press the matter.

"We know that one of your great concerns," Lucas continued, "is that you will somehow be forced by law or by ruling or by Pierre himself to marry against your wishes. But we can say with certainty that that cannot happen if you are not in France. Kes is awaiting a response from his brother-in-law, who is an expert in the laws of this land, which would provide some clarification and a little more detail, but French authorities cannot enforce punishments against a person in England. They can insist on moneys connected to estates and holdings in France, provided that money resides there, but they cannot force you to marry."

There was both relief and concern in that realization. "If I stay in this country rather than return home with my family, I would escape a forced marriage. All of my finances will still be tied up though. Everything of mine can only be accessed through my brother's estate, which will be entangled in Pierre's suit."

"We don't know how to make the logistics of it work," Kester confessed. "We realize it is an extremely complicated thing for you to remain behind when your family departs, but even if you could stay only temporarily, a year or two while this is dragged through the French courts, you would have a chance of emerging on the other side free."

"Penniless, homeless, yes. But free," Lucas added with his usual dry but compassionate humor.

"I suppose I might find a family looking for a French governess," Nicolette suggested. "Julia told me her governess was French."

Lucas nodded. "Many are. I realize it is a tremendous comedown for you, but it might see you through the next couple of years."

"I will ponder it," she told them.

Henri, still holding her hand, walked with her around the edge of the room, his silence, no doubt, an effort to allow her space in which to think. She had a great deal to think about, and time was not on her side. They would be leaving this house party in only a couple more days to begin the long journey back to France. She needed to decide whether she was making that journey with her family.

"Though I do not relish adding a complication to the already complex matter you are pondering," Henri said after a while, "I feel I need to tell you that I've given a similar matter some thought."

She watched him, intrigued and curious and already a bit overwhelmed.

"My family's estate in Nantes is mine to use anytime I choose. I would have no expenses connected to the running of the estate. I would have a roof over my head and Jean-François would restore my income. If you decide to return to France, if you resume your life there, I mean to do the same. My home would not be in Paris, but I could come and see you there. And you and Céleste could visit me at Chalet-sur-Loire. I am hopeful Céleste might even come live there, free of our brother's tyranny."

She looked up at him. "I know what this country has meant to you, Henri. You fought for so long to build a life here. Returning to France would mean losing your dream."

"That dream would be utterly empty without you."

"And being together in a place where you never wanted to be would hardly be a dream for either of us. I couldn't be happy knowing you had lost your happiness."

He pressed her hand to his heart. "You are my happiness, Nicolette. I've been here in England these past three years embracing the dream I had built for myself, and though it will likely both shock and amuse you, I have missed you almost every minute of the last three years. I've missed you to the very depths of my heart, despite the fact that you don't even remember me being in Paris."

"I most certainly remember," she said fiercely. "I'm embarrassed to admit to the many holes in my memories of that time, but I didn't forget you. I never did. I never could."

He offered her one of his soft smiles, the one she'd come to love so much, the one that both warmed and reassured her. "I loved you then, you know. I even told you I loved you."

"I would have remembered that." But she could tell by his expression that he had done just as he said, and she didn't, in fact, remember. "You said, 'I love you'?" she pressed.

He guided her toward the tall windows. "I believe I was a bit more poetic than that, but I confessed my feelings."

"And what did I say?" She was almost afraid to hear the answer.

"That a gentleman without the means of supporting a wife and family ought not be shocked when that prospective wife does not share his enthusiasm."

She shook her head. "I would not have answered so coldly. I held embarrassingly wrong views on what made for a good marriage, but I know I would have at least acknowledged your feelings. I know I would have."

Henri began to look unsure. "I have repeated the conversation as nearly verbatim as I can, and yet I, too, find myself wondering at that discrepancy.

You were not, and still *are* not, an unfeeling person. I do believe you would have kindly acknowledged my expression of affection, and yet, you didn't."

Heaviness pulled her heart lower in her chest, weighing her down further. "Yet another seemingly impossible puzzle." She sighed. "I do not know that I can bear many more." With a humorless laugh, she added in a whisper, "A fine bit of resignation for one charged with undertaking highly sensitive and complicated missions."

"There is an answer to all of this, Nicolette. I know there is. And we'll find it together."

This time, she raised his hand to her lips and gently kissed his fingers. "Together," she repeated.

# Chapter Thirty-Four

THE NEXT MORNING SAW HENRI installed once more in the book room, working on the poem his publisher was waiting for. He was achingly close to being finished. He'd spent his time since breakfast analyzing every word and every syllable, counting out the meter of each line, testing the rhythm in his mind.

Nicolette was there as well with the door a bit ajar for propriety. She'd spent the morning pacing with a look of uneasy contemplation. Her mind was heavy, and he wanted to help.

When her steps took her past his desk yet again, he reached out and took hold of her hand.

She turned an apologetic gaze on him. "I'm keeping you from finishing your 'letter,' aren't I?" The group had taken to referring to his poem as his "letter" as a means of preventing Jean-François from learning of it.

He shook his head. "I'm actually very nearly done."

"Truly?" Her face lit. "Will it reach London in time?"

"I have every hope that it will." He rose, taking her other hand in his. "I am far more concerned by the weight I see in your expression."

"My family leaves for France tomorrow, and I still don't know what I mean to do." She took in, then released a deep breath. "I do think becoming a governess would be my only option for remaining here whilst my money is tied up in France. But taking employment would mean not being able to travel as I wish or spend time with the people I most want to be with."

"You mean Lord Mowbary?" Henri asked the question with the feigned earnestness that Stanley had so perfected when teasing the Gents about any number of things.

The approach worked the same magic in that moment that it had so many years earlier. The heaviness in Nicolette's eyes lightened a bit. She even smiled.

"I will miss him most of all," she said.

"As will we all."

Her mouth turned down once more, and her forehead creased in thought. "If I return to France, I'll not have to seek employment and I would be able to continue my efforts with my contacts there, but I would be within reach of the courts. Even with our knowledge of Pierre's underhanded dealings, his suit against me and my family does hold some merit. I cannot say with any certainty what that would mean for my future if I were to return home."

"What else is weighing on you?" he asked.

"Is this all not enough?"

"It is plenty," he said. "But there is more. I can see it in your eyes."

She slipped her hands from his and began pacing once more. "The Beaumonts have not been able to find what we have been looking for."

The southern coastal property with a private dock or inlet. He'd been putting his thoughts to the matter as well and had come up empty-handed.

"The LeCheminant family lives near Dover, but they are too far inland for our purposes." She turned, facing him once more. "This might very well be the last task I am given by . . ." She glanced at the slightly ajar door and didn't finish, though no one was there. No doubt she didn't care to risk speaking more specifically. "I am beginning to think it will all end in failure."

"I thought the same about my 'letter' until very recently," he said. "And I've believed for three years there was no hope of securing your affections. And I didn't believe that anything could be done to help Aldric's situation or convince my brother to consider the possibility of not making my life a misery."

"You are suggesting I allow myself to hope for the best?"

"I think it is worth doing," he answered.

She took another deep breath, then set her shoulders. "I will sit in the chair by the door as I'm meant to be doing, and I will ponder on all the reasons I have to be hopeful rather than all the questions I cannot yet answer."

"Wise," he said.

"And you, *mon* Henri, should sit at your desk again and finally finish your letter."

"Also wise." Though it was tempting to cross to her and pull her into his arms, perhaps even kiss her again, he did need to finalize his poem. It was an important step toward the possibility of independence and a life with this woman he loved so much.

He retook his seat and read over what he'd written. The poem was not overly long, nor did he think it the most polished poetry ever written, but it was well composed, and it spoke from his heart. The best poetry arose from the soul.

The door opened fully, and Lucas stepped inside.

Nicolette gave him a theatrical look of warning. "If you've come to interrupt him, I will be forced to slaughter you. He is almost finished with his letter."

Lucas set his hand on his heart. "I would not dream of interrupting an archbishop, *Capitaine* Beaulieu. I have arrived in the role of messenger." He held out a sealed letter. "This arrived for you, and I convinced the footman to allow me to deliver it. Couldn't risk having him earn the wrath of our vengeful *capitaine*."

She took the missive and eyed it closely. "It's from the Beaumonts." Nicolette would want some privacy since the topic was likely to be a sensitive one.

"Please, feel free to go find a place to read your letter," he said.

"I won't abandon you when I'm meant to be keeping watch."

"I won't consider myself abandoned," Henri assured her.

"I'll take my turn being guard," Lucas said. "And I vow only to offer distractions that match those Nicolette offers when she is in here."

Henri snorted, something he didn't do often. "No, thank you," he managed to say.

Lucas shrugged. "Pity."

Nicolette was distracted enough by her letter that she slipped from the room without acknowledging the teasing and closed the door behind her.

"Are you really almost done?" Lucas asked. "With your poem, I mean."

"Not 'almost.' I am on the verge of declaring this ready to be sent to London."

Lucas crossed to the desk, genuine excitement in his expression. "Congratulations, Henri."

"It's not an accomplishment most of Society would herald, but I'm pleased."

"To the devil with 'most of Society,'" Lucas declared. "You should be proud."

"Do you think if Stanley had realized all those years ago that he was inviting a future poet into the Gents rather than a champion cricket player that he would have changed his mind?"

"The cricket was an excuse, Henri." All hint of teasing had left Lucas's voice. "He watched you during our first term at Cambridge but didn't feel his French was good enough to be anything but a nuisance."

"He was never a nuisance," Henri insisted.

"I knew him from infancy. He was sometimes an enormous nuisance." Lucas chuckled. "Stanley spent the Christmas term break practicing his French. Did he ever tell you that?"

Henri shook his head.

"Aldric called him all sorts of a fool to have delayed making your acquaintance over a lack of French when Aldric was as fluent as any native speaker. But Stanley—" Lucas swallowed. "Stanley said he could tell you felt unwanted and that he'd seen, to his anger, that too many of our fellow students weren't willing to make even a small effort."

"His French was rough for quite some time after I first became a Gent."

Lucas smiled as he nodded. "But he worked really hard at it, more so than he did his actual studies at Cambridge."

And all because he wanted Henri to feel wanted and welcome. "He was a remarkable person."

"Yes, he was." Lucas slapped a hand on Henri's shoulder. "So, to answer your question: no. He would not have changed his mind about you being part of this chosen family. And he would have celebrated you finishing this poem in the loudest and most boisterous way he could think of, because he would be bursting with pride."

Stanley would have cheered him on through it all, that much was certain.

"Sounds to me like I need to ask the new head of this gathering to allow for a boisterous celebration tonight," Henri said. "If Stanley would have celebrated, then we should too."

That next evening, the Gents and their ladies, along with Nicolette and Céleste, were afforded a rare opportunity to spend time exclusively with each other. Aldric had quickly and fully embraced his role as host of the party being held at the estate that had been deemed his. He'd managed, without giving offense, to divide the gathering into two groups: his father, brother, and sister-in-law, as well as Jean-François, Marguerite, Sébastien, and Gaëtane, were granted use of the drawing room for a sedate evening of likely uncomfortable silence. Pierre was still in residence but had, apparently under orders from His Grace, been effectively banished to his chambers.

Aldric's chosen guests were gathering in the book room to celebrate, just as Henri had requested. Yet, their mood was more somber than likely any of them would have preferred.

"I do wish Niles were still here," Julia said. "And not only because it would mean his family had not finally begun the efforts he'd hoped so much to avoid."

There'd not been time enough for Niles to reach Cornwall, let alone for a letter to be sent back. But none of them doubted the summons Niles had received would result in his being betrothed and wed to an unknown lady of his family's choosing. And they were all worried for him.

Everyone would be going their separate ways in another day or two. Lucas and Julia were bound for Nottinghamshire to see their families and await the arrival of their second born. Aldric would likely remain at Norwood, assuming the reins and finding his place here. Kes and Violet would return to their home in Cumberland. Digby would go home to Yorkshire. Henri would make his way to London. He would have to give up the rented rooms he usually kept there. They were not within his means any longer, but he knew there were some less expensive lodgings in less desired corners of the capital where he could place himself until an invitation arrived to spend time at the home of one of his friends. He suspected it would come from Lucas and Julia upon their return to Brier Hill in a few months' time. Céleste would be returning to France, and heaven only knew when he would see her again.

No one knew what Nicolette meant to do, and that weighed heaviest on his heart. If she returned to France, he would forgo his search for new lodgings in London and return to France as well. Though she worried it was a sacrifice he would resent, it didn't feel like a sacrifice.

Yes, he would miss England. He would miss seeing the Gents as often as he did. And yes, in some ways, it would feel like his brother had won. But to have a home and the means of traveling to Paris to see Nicolette, to the family home to see Céleste, and to England now and then to see his friends would be a welcome change in circumstances. And he felt certain obtaining an estate and income would answer all of the concerns Sébastien had about him.

Henri could court his beloved Nicolette in earnest. And this time, he felt certain his affection was returned. They would be together. Whether in France or England or the antipodes, it wouldn't matter so long as they had each other.

"We're meant to be celebrating the letter you'll be sending to London in the morning," Lucas said.

"I have told Céleste the truth of it," Henri said to the group as a whole. "After hearing her very expertly deal with our brother a few days ago, I decided it was rather ridiculous of me to think she would be frustrated at having to navigate the oddity of keeping this truth from him."

"In other words," Céleste said dryly, "he was reminded that I am no longer a child."

There was some truth in that. The group smiled and laughed and generally gave him a difficult time over that. Céleste had been welcomed among them, and he loved his friends all the more for it. If only she didn't live so far away.

"Do you mean to leave us in suspense?" Julia asked. "All this time, we watched you toil over the work and yet haven't the least idea what you composed."

"We demand a recitation," Digby declared in his royal King voice.

"One does not ignore an edict from a king," Henri said with a little bit of a laugh. The only person he'd ever read his poetry aloud to was Nicolette while she was recovering from her fever. But this latest one had not been read aloud to anyone. He didn't truly need to *read* it. The words were committed to memory.

He rose and turned to face them all. "It hasn't a title. No doubt they will assign one, likely the first line of the poem itself. That is often the approach that is taken."

"It is no use stalling," Lucas called out. "You know we are not overly patient."

Lucas liked to tease, but there did seem to be anticipation in everyone's eyes, and Henri suspected they might not care to be left waiting much longer.

He looked at Nicolette, feeling more than a little nervous. His beloved Nicolette, his fleur-de-lis, gave a little nod of encouragement.

He took a breath and closed his eyes a moment. His courage restored, he began.

"With contradict'ry aim I stand,
Rent in twain between two lands.
One is lit with flowers bright,
The other by sublime starlight.

"A searing fire is one way felt.
The sting of ice that does not melt
Upon the other path is found.
To both I am forever bound.

"My mind is called to what I've known,
And mem'ries of what once was home.
Yet calls the road that leads to where
I breathe now more familiar air.

"In her is found the now and then,
The song of hope, the sighed amen,
Both fire and ice, both flow'rs and stars,
The future, past, the near and far.

"Where e'er the path that guides her feet,
In what far clime her heart doth beat,
Howe'er oft I depart or bide,
Home is where my love resides."

Henri swallowed and looked at his darling once more. A sheen of tears clung to her lashes. She sat with her hand pressed to her heart. As if reciting the poem he'd struggled with for so long had drained him of all the words remaining to him, he simply watched her in silence. She rose and walked slowly to where he stood in utterly painful uncertainty. She didn't speak as she pressed her hand to his cheek, looking deeply into his eyes.

He'd tried so hard to be flowery and poetic three years earlier. He'd wanted his declaration of affection to be impressive and romantic. But she hadn't even realized what he'd been confessing, what he'd been feeling. For years, what he'd felt as a soul-crushing rejection had, in reality, been a failure of words. *His* words. He didn't want to risk that happening again, no matter that he felt his poem expressed his sentiments clearly. "Home is where you are, Nicolette," he whispered. "Wherever you are."

She slid her hand to his chest. "And what if 'where I am' is Derbyshire?"

"What do you mean?"

"The letter I received today from the Beaumonts was an offer to stay with them when my family leaves for France. They knew of my predicament and didn't wish to see me forced to choose between poverty, becoming a governess, or placing myself at the mercy of the French courts. I can remain there for as long as I need."

"And do . . . do you mean to accept their offer?"

A little smile pulled at the corners of her mouth. "I think it might just be another of those miracles we have been hoping for."

Henri set his hand over hers, holding them both to his heart. "London is not an overly easy distance from here, but it is certainly easier than France. I don't know how frequently I could make the journey, but I will do so as often as I possibly can."

"Or"—Digby's voice broke into the moment—"you could kindly ask the newly installed resident gentleman at Norwood Manor if you can stay here instead of hying yourself to Town. This pile of stones is a *very* easy distance from Eau Plate."

Henri nearly held his breath as he turned to look at Aldric.

"You are a brother to me, Henri. Any home of mine will always be open to you."

A few days earlier, Aldric hadn't had a home to offer. And Henri had been certain he would soon be separated from Nicolette.

She spoke, pulling his attention to her once more. "If your brother does not relent on the matter of your income, it might be years before we can be anything other than guests at neighboring estates. We'd not be in a place to build a home of our own."

He lifted her hand to his lips and kissed her palm. "A home with you is worth waiting a lifetime for."

"I think you like me, Henri Fortier."

Though he felt certain she was teasing with the understatement, he refused to risk repeating his failure in Paris. "I *love* you, Nicolette Beaulieu. I have loved you almost from the moment I met you. And I will love you for the rest of my life."

There, despite a book room full of witnesses, despite the expectations of "proper" behavior, Nicolette kissed him. Henri needed no further encouragement. He pulled her into his embrace and kissed her with all the hope, all the passion, all the dreams he'd kept tucked into the quiet recesses of his heart for far too long.

She was indeed his now and then, his song of hope, his past, and, in every way, with every breath, the future he could finally let himself dream of.

# Chapter Thirty-Five

THE HOUSE PARTY HAD REACHED its conclusion. Nicolette would be staying with the Beaumonts. She could continue working on the *La Tapisserie* network of homes. And remaining in England, she was not in personal peril from Pierre's machinations. She might lose her dowry in the end, and Sébastien would still have to endure a legal battle, but they had limited the damage Pierre could do.

She had bid farewell to little Roderick earlier that day, he and his parents having made their departure. And she had given her brother and sister-in-law a final hug for the foreseeable future shortly thereafter. She would miss France. She hoped one day she could return, even if only to visit. And she would miss her family terribly, though she suspected Henri's heart was breaking even more on that score.

Nicolette stood in the entryway of Norwood Manor, watching as Henri and Céleste made their farewells. As far as Nicolette knew, their older brother had not yet relented on the matter of Henri's income. That would lengthen the time between reunions.

"I do wish you were returning to France with us," Céleste said to Henri. "But I'm also glad you aren't. That seems an odd thing to say."

He shook his head. "I understand the sentiment perfectly. I'll do what I can to come visit as soon as I'm able, but unfortunately a lot of that depends upon Jean-François."

Céleste looked to Nicolette. "And though I understand why you are remaining, both your legal reasons and your more romantic ones, I am going to miss you terribly."

Nicolette gave her friend a hug, knowing this would be a lonely and difficult journey for her.

Into the tender and heartrending moment came Jean-François himself, walking beside Marguerite, who was holding Adèle.

"A moment, Henri," Jean-François said without any of the brotherly affection that ought to have been present in their final conversation before the family was separated for who knew how long.

"*Tonton* Henri!" Adèle reached for her uncle.

Henri reached back and was soon holding his niece in his arms. "*Ma petite sauterelle*," he said, kissing her cheek. The dear girl leaned against him, clearly quite pleased with the arrangement.

"Has Céleste told you what has been decided?" Jean-François asked.

Henri shook his head, his eyes darting between his siblings.

Standing quite straight, his chin jutting proudly, Jean-François said, "I can, for the time being, see to it that three-quarters of the income you were expecting to have will be at your disposal once more. I will need a little bit of time to separate the finances of Chalet-sur-Loire from the Fortier expenses. If that proves possible, then the rest of it can be returned, but I make no promises on that score."

Three-quarters of his income returned? Jean-François's continued cheating of his brother was frustrating. But Nicolette felt relief that Henri was to at last have some of the income he was entitled to.

"You do realize that I do not intend to move to France?" Henri pressed. "I will begin looking anew for a home here once my income—however much of it I receive—is restored."

Jean-François dipped his head. "Céleste was certain that would be your choice."

"This is my home," he reminded his brother, "and it always will be."

Jean-François showed neither surprise nor pleasure at that. "I think Father always knew you wouldn't come back. It is time I accepted that as well."

"I should very much like to return and visit sometime," Henri said, enough hesitation in the declaration to make it almost a question.

Nicolette stepped beside him and set an arm around him, lending her support and reassurance. Little Adèle smiled at her, which did her heart good.

Marguerite filled in the silence. "You are always welcome, Henri." She sounded as though she meant it. "*Viens à maman*," she said to Adèle.

Before returning her to her mother, Henri hugged his niece tightly. "*Adieu, Sauterelle*."

Nicolette set a hand on his arm, hoping to offer a bit of compassion for the grief he would feel, knowing he might not see the little girl again for a long time, and she likely would not remember him when he did.

As Jean-François, Marguerite, and their daughter stepped outside to climb into the traveling carriage, Henri held Céleste back. "With my income restored,

I believe I could find a humble house somewhere in England. We wouldn't be living in high style or fashion, but you could live here with me, *Abeille*. You needn't go back. I can't imagine Jean-François will be at all pleasant about any of this."

Céleste threw her arms around her brother. "I would love that, but I cannot. I have to return to France. But I want you to write to me and tell me about your home when you find one." She looked to Nicolette, though her arms were still around her brother. "I want you to write to me as well and tell me everything: all the people you meet, the friends you make." There was emotion in the request, almost desperation.

Something was wrong.

"Céleste?" Nicolette lowered her voice. "What has you so upset?"

But Céleste shook her head. "I do have to go."

"You could stay," Henri said. "Stay at the Beaumonts' with Nicolette until I find a home of my own—"

"He finally relented," Céleste said. "But at a price."

And suddenly, Nicolette understood. And based on the sorrow and the shock on Henri's face, he too had just pieced it together. Jean-François had agreed to return most of Henri's income and allow him the freedom to remain in England, but only if his sister were shackled to France.

Henri hugged her fiercely. "We'll find a way around this, too, I'm certain we will."

"If nothing else," Céleste said, "you should be able to come visit me more often. Find a home on the southern coast, it'll be easier for you to make the journey."

"I'll see you soon," Henri said, "I swear I will."

"Be happy, Henri." Céleste hugged her brother once more. "Be shockingly, wonderfully happy."

She turned and moved swiftly from the house, climbing into the family carriage. Nicolette swallowed against the thickness in her throat.

"Céleste is going to be miserable." Emotion choked Henri's words.

"If I thought for a moment either of us would rest knowing the position she is in, I would never forgive us," Nicolette said. "We will find a way. We'll visit. We'll cajole. We'll do what we must to have her back again."

Henri nodded but seemed too heartbroken to speak.

They slowly wandered back into the house, which was very quiet. Digby had left, as had Kes and Violet. Of the Gents, only Aldric, Lucas, Julia, and Philip remained, and the young Jonquil family was about to depart as well.

They entered the drawing room as the two remaining Gents and Julia made their farewells. Philip was given extra attention from his "Uncle Aldric."

"We will be in the next county over," Julia told Nicolette. "And we anticipate being there for a couple of months. You can get word to us quickly should you need anything. And even if you don't, I hope you will write to me. I will miss you."

"Will you miss *me*?" Henri asked with a whisper of a laugh in his voice. He would continue to worry about his sister, but Nicolette was grateful to hear him sound a little less weighed down.

"I always miss you," Julia said. "I miss all the Gents when we're apart. You are family to me." Julia didn't often grow emotional, but she did then. This was a lady with a backbone of steel and a heart as soft as velvet.

Henri hugged her, much the same way he'd hugged Céleste. "*Notre* Julia. You will always be family to us. You and Lucas and your little ones. Always."

Julia next hugged Nicolette. "You are part of this family now, too, you realize."

"I know. And I am so very grateful."

"And we are all grateful that fate gave the two of you a second chance. No one could deserve it more."

"We still have a few obstacles to overcome," Henri said.

From a few steps away, Lucas said, "One of those 'obstacles' has just arrived in the doorway."

Everyone's attention shifted. Pierre hovered just outside the drawing room, glaring at Henri and Nicolette. Before either of them could take a single step in that direction, Aldric handed Philip to his mother and moved past them all with a look of fierce determination even the duke likely would struggle to match.

"There is a carriage waiting for you." Aldric blocked any potential path into the room. "It is time you began your journey to wherever you mean to toss yourself."

"Is this how you speak to a guest in your father's home?" Pierre drawled.

"This is *my* home, and you were never my guest." Aldric motioned him away. "France awaits, monsieur."

Pierre looked over Aldric's shoulder and directly at Nicolette. "Do not think you can hide from this. One way or another, there will be a reckoning."

"I am not afraid of you," she said, pleased to realize how true that was.

"Lucas," Aldric tossed over his shoulder, "care to help me rid us of a pest?"

"With pleasure."

"This is not over," Pierre hissed at Nicolette and Henri as he was "escorted" out.

"I do not think that is an empty threat," Julia said, bouncing her son but keeping her eyes on the now-empty doorway.

"I don't think so either," Nicolette admitted. "But his return to France will offer us a much-needed respite."

Henri held his hand out to her, offering the comfort of his touch and attention. "Céleste wishes me to find a home on the south coast. Is it wrong that I hope Pierre finds himself a home atop some far-off mountain?"

Nicolette leaned against him. "Perhaps an island in the middle of the ocean."

"Excellent suggestion." Henri pressed a kiss to her temple.

"Do you truly wish to live along the Channel?" Julia asked, watching them closely.

"I *would* like that," Henri said.

"Violet hails from Portsmouth," Julia said. "Her family knows a great many people in the area. I would not doubt someone among them might have a seaside property they are looking to sell or lease for a time. Write to her parents, Henri. Fate may yet offer you another miracle."

Henri set his arms around Nicolette, holding her ever closer. "Another miracle, *ma chérie*. Dare we hope for such a thing?"

"We're together, *mon* Henri. I cannot imagine a better miracle than that."

# Chapter Thirty-Six

*The Sussex coast, three months later*

THE SEA WAS QUIET, LAPPING serenely against the shore at a distance from the humble house Henri and Nicolette now called home. They had lived there one day and had been married only one week. Henri could not imagine being happier.

He sat on a humble rattan chair in the small garden that looked out over the Channel. Beyond the horizon was France. Out of sight but never out of mind. He hoped Céleste was happy. He hoped Adèle would retain some memory of him. Jean-François had honored his promise to return Henri's income to three-quarters of what it ought to be. The most recent had been enough to pay rent on this home Violet Barrington had brought to their attention.

In time, he hoped he and Nicolette could find a place of their own, one large enough for a family, for gatherings, for the life they meant to build together.

"Henri!"

He turned at the sound of his beloved's voice. She was moving quickly toward him from the house with what looked to be letters in her hands.

"*Voyez ce qui est venu!*"

So many times over the past week, he'd been rendered speechless by an overwhelming sense of shock and gratitude that Nicolette—the very Nicolette he'd loved and lost three years earlier—was here with him, loving him as he loved her, building a future with him. Was ever a man so fortunate as he?

She reached the bench he now stood beside. "We've both received letters." She placed one in his hand. "Our very first post at our new home."

He motioned for her to sit, then took the spot directly beside her, near enough to enjoy the now-familiar scent of jasmine that hung about her, near enough to press a kiss to her neck.

"No distractions," she said in mock rebuke. "We have letters to read."

"But distractions are so much more fun," he insisted, kissing her again.

"Henri. You are supposed to be the well-behaved Gent."

He laughed. "Have you not realized yet, *ma chérie*? None of us is actually well-behaved."

She pointed to his unopened letter. "That is from one of your ill-behaved friends, and he would be very put out if you did not open it immediately."

A quick glance revealed it had arrived from Lampton Park, Lucas's family estate. He and Julia had been unable to attend Henri and Nicolette's wedding on account of Julia's confinement being so close upon her. This letter, Henri sincerely hoped, brought news of a new baby and a mother doing well.

He broke the wax seal and read aloud as Nicolette eagerly listened.

> *Henri,*
>
> *I am pleased to inform you that we have welcomed a beautiful, delightful little boy into our family. That is not my biased description, mind you, as both of my parents have declared him utterly perfect, and no one questions their taste in babies. Though he wakes often, wishing for all the things newly born babies do, during the in-between times, he sleeps as much as his grandfather—who has become a connoisseur of napping—and the baby is as heartbreakingly handsome as his father—who tries not to be devastatingly good looking but cannot help himself. Clearly, this child has chosen to pattern himself after two paragons.*
>
> *Julia is recovering well and swiftly. She sends her love to you both and is, at this very moment, insisting I stop being ridiculous and attempt some semblance of a serious letter. Though she protests, I happen to know she is quite fond of my letters, ridiculous or otherwise.*
>
> *Philip already adores his little brother, though he clearly does not know what to make of him. I predict they will be the most mischievous of playmates and the very best of friends. Someday, long after they're grown, they will be neighbors, as our little Layton Henri Jonquil will inherit the Farland title and Farland Meadows, his estate bordering the one Philip will one day inherit.*

Layton Henri. For a moment, he could not keep reading. *Henri.* The first given name was clearly in honor of Digby. But the second . . . He didn't think he was wrong in believing that was chosen in recognition of *him*. Nicolette squeezed his hand, smiling broadly.

He returned his gaze to the letter and continued reading, despite his emotion.

> *Please promise you will both come meet him soon. Julia has vowed to teach him French. I have vowed to teach him to play cricket, though I leave the instruction in pitching to you. It was that skill, after all, that gave Stanley the excuse he'd been looking for to ask you to be one of us—a moment we all look back on with unspeakable gratitude.*
>
> *All our love to the both of you and our deepest joy that you have a home and, most of all, each other.*
>
> *Yours, etc.,*
> *Lucas*

"Layton Henri," Nicolette repeated. "How wonderful."

"Henry is Lucas's second given name," Henri said. "It is likely as much an acknowledgment of that as it is of me."

Nicolette shook her head. "They would not have made it French if you weren't meant to be a prominent namesake, *mon amour*."

A namesake. He would never have imagined such a thing when he had made his flight of rebellion to Cambridge thirteen years earlier. Stanley Cummings had changed everything. Literally everything.

"And what is your letter?" he asked Nicolette.

"It is from the Marquis de Lafayette."

She had been granted permission by the other senior members of *La Tapisserie* to inform Henri of the extent of their network and all they undertook. He was to become part of it, to aid where he could and support Nicolette in all she was given to do.

> *Mme Fortier,*
>
> *As you are away from Paris, allow me to offer a report on a matter here that concerns you. M. Léandre means to move forward with his breach-of-contract suit and has every expectation of being heard by the court, though the outcome is less certain. He has begun in earnest his campaign of discrediting you and your family.*

Nicolette paused for just a moment, worry flashing through her eyes. "He warned us he would continue to cause us grief."

Henri set his arm around her. "He will certainly try."

> *He is being laughed to scorn. You are known, liked, and respected. You are also being staunchly defended by many. There is, in fact, a certain marquis who has not hesitated to remind all who hear M. Léandre's deleterious declarations that he is disliked by everyone. While your family may yet be made to pay the scoundrel, the courts being often unreliable and much in this country being unpredictable at the moment, I do not believe there is any real worry of him causing any damage to the Beaulieus' standing or the respect your family rightly receives.*

Henri breathed a heavy sigh of relief and heard Nicolette do the same. Pierre would deal damage, Henri didn't doubt. And he might continue wreaking havoc even after the case had wound its way through the French courts. But Nicolette's brother and sister-in-law, who had proven reliable defenders of Nicolette and had welcomed Henri to the family with open arms had some hope of escaping too much pain at Pierre's hands.

"I suspect you and I haven't heard the last from Pierre Léandre," Nicolette said with a sigh. "At least we are currently enjoying a respite."

"One I hope lasts a long time," Henri said.

She continued reading.

> *As you are married now and living in England, I hope to ask your thoughts on a purchase I am considering. I have a lovely tapestry depicting a seaside dwelling, and I find myself longing to spend time in such a bucolic spot. If you know of one, perhaps one that is currently occupied by tenants with an owner who does not wish to be in residence, do pass that along to me. I have a great many friends in England I would enjoy sharing the experience with.*
>
> *Yours, etc.*
> *Lafayette*

Nicolette turned wide eyes on Henri. He would wager that last bit of the letter was a code, but he was not yet acquainted enough with their form of communication to make sense of it.

"He wishes for the *La Tapisserie* to purchase this house. No doubt he intends it to be a more permanent part of the proposed network here, which he is giving his approval of."

"What does that mean for us?" Henri asked.

"I would wager we would still live here, facilitating the efforts and work of the organization. But we would not need to pay rent."

"Truly?" He could hardly countenance such a thing.

"Truly. We could set aside what income we have, and years from now, even if all my dowry and inheritance is lost to Pierre, we could still find a home of our own. And in the meantime, we could travel. We could see your sister. Eventually, your income from Jean-François would not be needed, and we could fetch Céleste, as he would no longer have anything to tie her there with."

"More miracles." He repeated the phrase they had often used when unexpected solutions arose to the difficulties they struggled to address.

"It's impossible to say how long all that would take," she acknowledged. "And if revolution does come to France, that will complicate everything. But, *mon* Henri, this is hopeful. This is promising."

"A miracle."

In the distance, the waves continued lapping against the shore. A light breeze stirred the bushes in the garden, where they had vowed to plant every flower they could find that bore even a passing resemblance to the *fleur-de-lis*.

Hope. And promise. They had both.

And most wonderful of all, they had love.

# About the Author

SARAH M. EDEN IS A *USA Today* best-selling author of witty and charming historical romances, including 2020's *Foreword Reviews* INDIE Awards Gold winner for romance, *Forget Me Not*, 2019's *Foreword Reviews* INDIE Awards Gold winner for romance, *The Lady and the Highwayman*, and 2020 Holt Medallion finalist, *Healing Hearts*. She is a two-time Best of State Gold Medal winner for fiction and a three-time Whitney Award winner. Combining her obsession with history and her affinity for tender love stories, Sarah loves crafting deep characters and heartfelt romances set against rich historical backdrops. She holds a bachelor's degree in research and happily spends hours perusing the reference shelves of her local library.

www.SarahMEden.com